Also in the Dreamland Series

Titles by Dale Brown

DALE BROWN

AND
JIM DeFELICE

BLACK WOLF

A DREAMLAND THRILLER

HARPER

An Imprint of HarperCollinsPublishers

HARPER

An Imprint of HarperCollins*Publishers*
10 East 53rd Street
New York, New York 10022-5299

First Harper premium printing: December 2010

Printed in the United States of America

Visit Harper paperbacks on the World Wide Web at
www.harpercollins.com

10 9 8 7 6 5 4 3 2 1

Whiplash: Duty Roster

Lieutenant General (Ret.) Harold Magnus

Magnus once supervised Dreamland from afar. With Colonel Tecumseh "Dog" Bastian as its on-the-scene commander, the organization succeeded beyond his wildest dreams. Now as deputy secretary of defense, Magnus hopes to repeat those successes with Whiplash. His handpicked commander: Bastian's daughter, Breanna Stockard.

Breanna Stockard

After retiring from the U.S. Air Force to raise her daughter and help her husband's political career, Breanna found herself bored with home life. She was lured back to a job supervising the development of high-tech wizardry under a combined CIA and Pentagon program. But will she be happy behind a desk when her agents are in trouble?

Jonathon Reid

Reid's official title is Special Assistant to the Deputy Director Operations, CIA. Unofficially, he's the go-to-guy for all black projects, the dirtier the better. He knows how to get around Agency politics. More importantly, he knows where all the Agency's bodies are buried—he buried half of them himself.

Colonel Danny Freah

Fifteen years ago Danny Freah won the Medal of Honor for service far beyond the call of duty. Thrust back into action as the head of a reconstituted and reshaped Whiplash team, he wonders if he still has what it takes to lead men and women into battle.

Nuri Abaajmed Lupo

Top CIA operative Nuri Lupo is used to working on his own. Now the young CIA officer has to adjust to working with a quasimilitary team—at least half of whom he can't stand.

Chief Master Sergeant Ben "Boston" Rockland

Boston finds himself shepherding a group of young CIA officers and special operations warriors across three continents. To do it successfully, he has to be part crusty old dog and part father figure.

Hera Scokas

Despite her ability with languages and the black arts of special operations, Hera Scokas hasn't been able to climb the CIA career ladder as quickly as she wished. Now that she's been given her greatest opportunity, she faces her greatest challenge: taming her personality to get the job done.

Captain Turk Mako

An Air Force pilot on special assignment to the Pentagon, Turk Mako thinks of himself as the last of a breed. Real live fighter jocks are being rapidly replaced by "back home boys"—pilots who control unmanned aircraft from hangars in the States. Mako is out to prove neither he nor his profession is—obsolete.

Al "Greasy Hands" Parsons

Once responsible for the teams that kept Dreamland's top aircraft in shape, the former chief master sergeant is now Breanna Stockard's right-hand graybeard and fixer.

FLASHBACK: REVOLUTION

January 1998

———

1

Moldova, east central Europe
1998

MARK STONER RAN FOR THE AEROSPATIALE HELI-
copter, trailing the rest of the commando team as
it headed for the last of the four helos.

We made it, he thought. We're OK. We're
good.

Good, good, good.

The CIA officer jumped into the helicopter just
as it started to lift off the ground. He lost his balance, spinning toward the floor as the helo shud-
dered against a sudden buffet of wind. One of the
Romanian commandos he was with grabbed him,
easing his fall.

Stoner looked back toward the door just in time
to see the chopper clear a row of trees by bare
inches, the angled tops of the evergreens like
sharp black spikes in the night. As the helicopter
banked around the woods to set a course west-
ward, a large slash appeared in the sky, a sword
that seemed to swing up from the ground

But this was an optical illusion. The black shape
was the spire of the church they had struck, the

haven for rebel guerrillas who had nearly succeeded in destroying Romania's gas pipeline network. Aided by Russia, the rebels had come perilously close to plunging Western Europe into a very cold winter. That wasn't going to happen now.

But Stoner hadn't come just to prevent that. The CIA agent had been after evidence proving Russia had helped the guerrillas as part of a bid to raise its prices for natural gas, and to keep Eastern Europe under its thumb. Stoner had grabbed a computer and disks from the church basement that proved just that. The colonel who had led the men was already transmitting some of the files back to his headquarters via a data link Stoner provided, courtesy of the Dreamland Whiplash deployment team.

No matter what happened now, the operation had been a success. A big success—one more win in a résumé filled with wins.

But to Mark Stoner, the mission was a loss—a deep pit of blackness that drilled into his chest. To get the information for the raid, he had tracked down one of the guerrillas' key leaders, a woman named Sorina Viorica. He'd gone behind the lines, met her, and helped her escape when other rebels turned against her.

Along the way, he fell in love with her.

It didn't change their arrangement: she gave him the information he needed for the raid, he helped her escape Romania.

Yet it changed it profoundly. He could count on one hand the times he'd been in love, and not use half the fingers.

"Great mission!" shouted Colonel Brasov, the Romanian commander.

"Yeah," said Stoner.

Brasov began thanking him for saving his men from an ambush.

"You are hero for us," the colonel told him in his unsteady English. "Real hero."

He added something in Romanian. His men nodded, adding their own words of praise.

Stoner shrugged them off. What was a hero?

The soldiers looked at him as if he was super-human, as if he was part of a different race. But he wasn't. He was just like them—he was flesh and blood, creaky bones and cramped muscles. There were moments when he hesitated, sec-onds ticking away under fire, times when he felt fear.

Fear in his gut. Paralysis that filled him like a damp wind collecting over a bog.

People didn't understand how much it really took. The bosses back home didn't know the price of each mission, of each instance where someone looking from the distance could say, "Good job. Good mission. Way to go."

Another star in the folder, eh, Mark?

He died a little bit every moment on those mis-sions. He felt dead now—heart pumping, lungs filling, but just as certainly dead inside.

Stoner's sat phone began to ring. He pulled it out but had trouble hearing.

"Stoner, this is Dog."

It was Colonel Tecumseh "Dog" Bastian, the leader of Dreamland himself, miles away, over the border, circling in an EB–52 Megafortress to provide radar coverage.

"This is Stoner!" Stoner yelled into the sat phone, trying to make himself heard over the helo's turbines.

"Stoner, tell your pilot and Colonel Brasov there are four MiGs headed in your direction," said Colonel Bastian. "They're about ten minutes away from the helicopters."

"Four what?"

"Four MiGs. Russian fighters. Get the hell out of there. Get over the border."

"We're working on it, Colonel."

Stoner turned to Colonel Brasov and tugged on his arm.

"There are fighter jets headed in our direction," he said. "They're about ten minutes away."

Brasov's face blanched—he'd said on takeoff that it would take the helicopters roughly thirty minutes to reach the border—then went forward to the cockpit to tell the pilots.

There were thirty soldiers in the rear of the helicopter, along with two of the prisoners, a dozen boxes from the church, and the two footlockers. There were also several bodies stacked at the back. The Aerospatiale was designed to hold about twenty-five men, counting the crew; the extra weight slowed it down dramatically.

Brasov returned, a frown on his face.

"We will stay very low to the ground," he said, shouting in Stoner's ear. "They may not see us on their radar. But it will be tight."

The helicopter suddenly veered hard to the left.

Stoner had trouble staying on his feet. The chopper ran a tight zigzag across the fields, the pilot trying to get as close as possible to the trees and buildings so the Aerospatiale would blend into their radar returns and be lost to the MiGs. It was a time-honored solution to the problem of escaping more powerful aircraft.

The problem was, the aircraft they were trying to dodge had look-down radar specifically designed to counter that tactic. And the French-made helicopter wasn't the most maneuverable chopper in the air.

Stoner realized they were going to be caught. They had to do something desperate—sacrifice themselves maybe, to save the others.

"We're not going to make it," he told Brasov finally. "We can't outrun them."

The colonel nodded grimly.

"A mother bird when its nest is being attacked pretends to be wounded, drawing the predators away," Stoner continued. "You could do the same—have one of the helicopters peel off, get the MiGs interested, then land. Everyone runs for it—the MiGs come down and investigate. The other choppers get away. We make our way home by foot."

Instead of answering, Brasov went forward to the cockpit. Stoner glanced around the cabin. The troops were quiet now, aware they were being pursued.

"You are full of good ideas, Mr. Stoner," said Brasov, returning. Then he added, "The Russian aircraft are almost on us."

"How far is the border?"

The colonel just shook his head.

"I would not ask my men to make a sacrifice I was unwilling to make myself," he said.

"Neither would I," said Stoner. He glanced around the cabin as Brasov spoke to the pilots. It was one thing to risk his own death, another to risk those of the men around him. He'd just saved a bunch of them. Undoubtedly they were thinking about their families, about getting home, and now he was dooming them.

Colonel Bastian was under orders not to interfere. Bastian wasn't exactly known for following orders, but in this case he might not have any choice. He was too far away to intercept the MiGs.

Still, Stoner found himself wishing he would.

The helicopter popped up suddenly. Stoner fell back against the bulkhead, then slipped and fell on the deck. Two of the Romanian commandos helped him to his feet.

One of them said something in Romanian. Stoner thought he was telling him not to lose hope. He nodded.

Never lose hope. There's always something.

Something.

He grabbed the spar as the helicopter whirled hard into the turn. The pilot had spotted a small clearing on the hillside ahead. He launched flares in hopes of decoying the Russian missiles, then pushed the nose of the helicopter down, aiming for the hill.

The helicopter blades, buffeted by the force of the turn, made a loud *whomp-whomp-whomp* sound, as if they were going to tear themselves off.

Everyone inside the helicopter was silent, knowing what was going on outside but not really knowing, ready but not ready.

"When we get out, run!" Brasov yelled. "Run from the helicopter. As soon as you can, make your best way over the border. It is seven miles southwest. Seven miles! A few hours' walk."

The men closest to him nodded, grim-faced.

The helicopter pitched hard to the left.

"You are a brave man, braver than I gave you credit for when we met," Colonel Brasov told Stoner as the force of the turn threw the two men together.

"You, too," said Stoner.

"Until we meet again."

Brasov held out his hand.

As Stoner reached for it he thought of Sorina Viorica, the way she'd looked on the street in Bucharest. He thought of the mission he'd had in China a year before, where he came close to being killed. He thought of Breanna Stockard, who'd parachuted with him into the water. They spent the night together in the rain, without any hope of rescue. Now he saw her smiling face in the aircraft just after they were picked up.

He thought of his first day at the Agency, his graduation from high school, a morning in the very distant past, being driven by his mom to church with the rain pouring and the car warm and safe.

There was a flash above him, and a loud clap like thunder.

And then there was nothing, no memory, no thought, no pain or regret.

NEEDS

The present: May 2012

—

2

Berlin, Germany
2012

YOU ARE INVINCIBLE.

The man they called Black Wolf heard the voice in his head, the words playing on an endless loop. He tried to block them out but could not. They were always there, part of an inner voice he could not control.

But there were many things he could not control.

You are invincible.

He was not invincible at all, nor was he a demigod, though some treated him as one. On the contrary, he knew very well the limits of his abilities, and had constant reminders of his mortality.

But he didn't care much for what other people thought of him. He didn't care much for other people at all.

The Black Wolf had obligations which he could not escape. He had duties and assignments. But he considered himself separate from them, separate from everything. They called him Black Wolf. He called himself . . . nothing.

The man they called the Black Wolf moved up the stairs to the balcony of the Konzerthaus Berlin, the famous orchestra house in eastern Berlin. A large crowd had come to hear a young Czech prodigy play a selection of Mozart, Vivaldi, and Bach with the Konzerthausorchester Berlin. Barely fifteen, the pianist was already famous and celebrated; it was said his music would move stones to tears. But a good part of his fame—or was it notoriety?—came from theatrical touches.

He dressed as a pseudogoth. His head was shaved, and while he wore black tie to the concert, he could generally be counted on to pull off his jacket and shirt at the end of the show and toss it to the crowd. Sometimes he would throw his trademark black T-shirt as well, and take his final bows bare-chested.

Witnessing such a spectacle, a reviewer for *Le Monde* had recently counted five tattoos in various spots on the pianist's upper body. The prodigy had responded in a Facebook posting that he would gladly show her the rest at a private concert.

This wasn't particularly adventurous stuff in other genres, but it was a revolution in classical music. The young man's shows were always sold out, and generally attracted a much wider ranging audience than the typical symphony concert.

Wolf found his seat in the balcony just as the lights dimmed. He listened impassively as the program started. A Mozart selection warmed up the audience. The notes darted back and forth in an intricate web, echoing themes, underlining them, then taking them apart. If many had come for the show, it was the music that transported them. The young man with the shaved head and tattoos played as artfully as anyone who had graced the stage since it was built. In his hands, the music became immortal.

The Black Wolf wasn't interested in transcendence. He scanned the audience, looking for Helmut Dalitz. For Dalitz was scheduled to have his own reckoning with mortality before the program ended.

Helmut Dalitz was a wealthy international businessman. Once a banker, he now made his money by buying distressed properties across the world, fixing them or otherwise making them viable, and then selling them. He did this most often with apartment buildings, though he also did it on occasion with commercial properties.

It was one of the commercial properties that had brought Wolf here. For Helmut Dalitz, through a company that he owned, had bought a large, nondescript building in Rome, Italy, the previous year. The building, on Via Nazionale not far from the Termini train station, was a nondescript twelve story structure badly in need of maintenance.

There were many ways that maintenance could be done; since there were a number of vacant stores and offices, workers could have started with the vacant spaces, then gradually moved on, shuffling the existing tenants in and out of the different units like a game of musical chairs. Doing things piecemeal like that was common in Italy, where work tended to progress at a very leisurely pace, and disrupting old traditions for the sake of some new paint and a few daubs of plaster was antithetical to the national psyche.

But Helmut Dalitz was not Italian. More importantly, he disliked disorder, and the idea of slowly renovating his building did not sit well with him. It smacked of chaos and conflicted with his timetable for turning a profit. And so he had the building closed entirely, kicking out all of the existing tenants, something he was allowed to do by the terms of the sale and the tenants' leases, even if these terms conflicted with the spirit by which most of the tenants had held their property.

Among the tenants he had kicked out was Giuseppe DeFrancisco, an eighty-year-old man who ran a small tobacco shop on the side street. The shop had not turned a profit in several years, and in fact the rent was paid now entirely by the man's grandson. Unfortunately, the grandson had been concentrating on his business affairs in southern Italy when the first notice of the pending eviction came. By the time he realized his grandfather was going to be kicked out, it was too late to stop it—not that Helmut Dalitz or his minions would have listened to reason.

The thugs his minions hired were deaf as well. They hadn't listened to the old man's pleas, who begged them right up to the moment they placed him on the curb. They didn't listen to his complaints, or even to his cry for help a few moments later, when he began suffering from a heart attack. A passerby called an ambulance when he found the old man on the ground a few minutes later; by the time the ambulance fought its way through the morning traffic, Giuseppe DeFrancisco was dead.

The men who had put him out wouldn't be listening to anyone now. Wolf had taken care of them two weeks before on a trip to Rome. Now it was their employer's turn.

Wolf cared little for the justifications of the murder, though they had been important to the old man's grandson. While he could have used his own organization to extract revenge, the grandson considered this a matter of the heart rather than business, and deemed it wiser to keep the two separate. And besides, the Wolf and his employers were said to be even more efficient than the mafia.

Helmut Dalitz was sitting in the third box on the right of the stage. He was seated very close to the rail, listening intently to the music. Behind him sat two bodyguards, dressed as impeccably as he was; they were a sharp contrast to his daughter, who though not slovenly, could easily have afforded something more stylish than the plain black polyester pants and print silk shirt she wore.

She was alone. The Black Wolf had expected her boyfriend to be with her. This was not necessarily a problem for him—one less potential obstruction, perhaps—but he noted it nonetheless.

The night's performance was grouped into three sections. As the first came to an end, Helmut Dalitz rose with the rest of the audience and applauded. And then, being a man of habit, he kissed his daughter on the cheek and told her he was going home.

Even with his superior hearing, the Black Wolf couldn't hear the conversation. But he saw the girl shaking her head, and guessed what her father was saying. Helmut Dalitz habitually left the concert hall before the last intermission, and obviously he had decided to leave now.

Habits were a bad thing, especially when someone was aiming to kill you.

The girl would be pleading with him not to leave her alone. And he would suggest that she come with him.

She was torn. What would she decide?

To stay. She turned away abruptly.

Easier for him.

The Black Wolf waited to make sure that Helmut Dalitz was actually leaving, then turned and walked swiftly to the exit. He slipped easily between the people making their way down to the restroom and the large hall at the front of the orchestra house to stretch their legs. He moved quickly, almost lithely, despite the bulk of his legs and shoulders. His body had the fluidity of a much lighter and, it had to be admitted, younger man. While Wolf thought of himself as barely into his early twenties, he was in fact over fifty.

Not that anyone seeing him would have guessed that. On the contrary, he looked exactly as if he were in his twenties, just reaching his physical peak, with a bright future yet to come.

The Black Wolf reached the marble hallway at the front of the building, pausing near one of the elaborate columns. Helmut Dalitz would approach from the right, accompanied by his bodyguards; a third man would be waiting just outside, alerted by radio.

Taking him in the concert hall was tempting—there were so many people present that he could sidle right up to Dalitz and shoot him with the silenced gun. But getting away would be problematic. He wasn't so much worried about witnesses as simply being able to slip quickly through the crowd. Outside would be easier.

A surge of people blocked his vision, and he lost Dalitz momentarily. The Black Wolf took a step in the direction he knew Dalitz would take, then stopped. He scanned the faces, looking.

One of the bodyguards was walking at the far end of the hall. Wolfe realized Dalitz must be in front of the man, though he couldn't see him.

Why was he that far away? Had he changed his mind—was he going back to his daughter?

No. His escorts were simply trying to avoid the worst of the crowd.

It was too late to cut him off. Wolf took a step back, sliding toward the door on his left.

The worst thing to do was to rush. He had to move slowly and deliberately. If he did not kill Helmut Dalitz now, he would kill him later, or tomorrow, or the next day. Success was the only thing that mattered in this assignment, not timing.

The crisp Berlin air invigorated Wolf as he came through the doors. The square in front of the theater was yellow, lit by clusters of old-fashioned lamps at each of the corners. He paused, getting his bearings. Dalitz turned right, toward the Gendarmenmarkt. If he followed his usual practice—and being a man of habit, he surely would—he would walk up Markgrafenstrausse toward Französische.

Wolf started down the steps. The light in the square was dim, but he could see as well in the dark as most people could see during the day. He quickened his pace, turning parallel to his quarry.

Dalitz's two bodyguards moved closer. Did they sense the danger?

No. They were just doing their job, closing up ranks, anxious to get to the next waypoint.

The Black Wolf put his hand into the pocket of his overcoat, gripping his pistol. The gun and its bullets were made completely of carbon composites. They wouldn't trip the most finicky metal detector, yet the bullets were as fatal as Magnums at a hundred yards. The long, boxy barrel had a noise suppresser; the bullet sounded like a metal slug dropping through a vending machine, and was only a little louder.

The Black Wolf picked up his pace, moving closer.

He liked to be close, not just to ensure that he hit the target, but to viscerally feel the kill. It touched something inside, some primitive emotion. Nothing else he felt came close to that feeling. It was the feeling of life, as paradoxical as it seemed: only in someone else's death could he actually live.

Helmut Dalitz turned the corner. Wolf notched up his pace even higher, careful not to break into a run.

The white Mercedes was waiting just ahead.

The two bodyguards were spaced three and a half meters apart, trailing their client by a half pace each.

Wolf was ten meters behind them.

Seven.

Five.

He pulled the gun from his pocket. The man on the right started to turn.

A single shot took him down. Wolf swiveled, his left hand grabbing his forearm to steady the gun. He caught the second bodyguard in the temple.

And then it was Helmut Dalitz's turn.

The businessman turned, his face an expression of utter surprise.

The Black Wolf grinned, and squeezed the trigger.

3

Room 4, CIA Headquarters Campus (Langley)
McLean, Virginia

"GOOD MORNING, COLONEL FREAH. HOW WOULD YOU like your coffee?"

Danny Freah turned to the ceiling as the elevator car plunged down toward its destination. "How do you know I want coffee?" he asked.

"You always want coffee," responded the voice.

"I can't break the pattern?"

"Breaking the pattern would be unexpected."

The elevator stopped and the door opened.

"Colonel Freah, you did not answer my question," said the voice.

"Surprise me," said Danny, stepping out into the wide hall in front of the elevator. The space looked like the bottom level of a mall parking garage. A spider work of girders, beams, and pipes ran through it.

They weren't for show, exactly, but the overall look was definitely intentional. The insides of the nondescript building—known only as Room 4— had an ambiance that mixed high-tech functional and blow-your-mind weirdness.

Case in point was the gray wall facing Danny at the far end of the room. He walked toward it, then straight through it.

Danny Freah was still so new to Room 4 and the high-tech gizmos associated with it that it felt eerily cool to do that. But he was too professional to admit it—or give in to the temptation to do it a few more times for fun.

The wall was not an optical illusion, exactly. It could keep someone out if the security system didn't want them in. The barrier was a physical manifestation of an energy array—a kind of force field in layman's terms, though the man responsible for inventing it, Dr. Ray Rubeo, hated the term force field.

Absolutely hated it.

Danny knew, however, that Rubeo did have a sense of humor, which apparently he'd programmed into the automated assistant that had questioned him about coffee in the elevator. Sitting in the beverage center at the left of the desk as he entered was a steaming cup of cinnamon herbal tea.

Pretty much the last thing Danny would ever drink.

"Very funny," he told the computer. "Coffee. The usual."

"The system still has some kinks to be worked out," said Danny's boss, Breanna Stockard, who was standing over a nearby desk.

"No—it's my fault," said Danny. "I should have known better than to try to outsmart something Rubeo rigged up."

The coffee, very strong and hot, spurted through the dispenser into a fresh cup. While the automated assistant and the beverage center were a brand new addition to Room 4, their presence in the high-tech control area wasn't a surprise. Back at Dreamland, one of the technology section's proudest achievements was a zero-gravity coffeemaker, which could keep the crews aboard Megafortresses and other large aircraft pleasantly caffeinated no matter what the combat conditions were.

"I'll meet you inside," said Breanna, waving a hand to dismiss the computer screen that had been floating in front of her. "Everyone else is here."

"Gotcha."

Danny waited for the last drops of coffee to settle into the cup, then raised it slowly to his lips, cooling it with a gentle breath. He'd only been working for Whiplash—the *new* Whiplash—for two months, and things still felt a bit . . . different.

A full-bird colonel, Freah had recently been assigned to the Office of Technology, a special direct-report agency that answered to the Joint Chiefs of Staff. On paper, he looked like just another pencil-pushing staff officer, paid for his advice and experience. In reality, he headed Whiplash, one of the most exciting commands in the military.

A joint venture with the CIA, Whiplash aimed to combine up-to-the nanosecond intelligence capabilities with a covert action team. It was modeled on the Air Force's Dreamland program that had so much success a decade and a half earlier, under Breanna's father, Lt. Colonel Tecumseh "Dog" Bastian. Breanna had recruited Danny specifically to head the military end of the program.

They'd had one success so far, on a mission that had stretched from Africa to Iran. For Danny, it felt good to be back in the mix again; most of his assignments since Dreamland had been administrative and supervisory. This post got him back on the front lines with gusto. But it was also a lot of work. He'd spent the weeks since returning home recruiting people and trying to smooth out differences between the two halves of the team—military and active CIA. He was still working on the training routines they needed and filling in his command structure. He was inventing, improvising, and even stealing as the need arose.

He'd tapped another old Dreamland Whiplash hand—Ben "Boston" Rockland, now a chief master sergeant—as his main personnel guy, dealing with young bucks and their egos.

Bucks and does; it was a coed force.

Boston was in Florida at the moment, putting their recruits through their paces. They had twenty-four newbie "shooters" or Whiplash troopers, drawn mostly from active military commands, each with different specialties and strengths. Eventually Danny planned to have some forty-eight troopers to form the core of a covert strike force. They could be deployed as a group, or work in very small teams, depending on the assignment. Whiplash technology would increase their effectiveness exponentially.

Danny took a sip of the coffee—it was perfect, naturally—then walked down the hall to the conference room.

"Colonel, good morning," said Jonathon Reid. Reid was the CIA director's liaison to the project, Breanna's equivalent in authority. As the lines of responsibility went, Reid was in charge of operations for the specific missions, while Breanna's ultimate say was over strategic and funding issues. But as a practical matter, their responsibilities were shared. Reid had the immediate access to intelligence as well as the people who commissioned the ops. Breanna, as a member of the Pentagon, held sway over most of the personnel, and thus the means for completing the mission. Though in many respects they were opposites, they worked together remarkably well.

Danny took a seat at the conference table across from Nuri Abaajmed Lupo, nodding at him as he sat down. Nuri was a CIA officer who'd preceded him into the program—the first and for a short time only member of Whiplash. He was young but extremely capable, as he'd shown in Africa and Iran. Nuri did, however, have some difficulty dealing with the fact that Danny was the one in charge. He was also used to working alone.

"Now that we're all here, we can begin," said Reid. "Screen."

A screen appeared above the center of the table. It was another projection.

"The man on the ground in a pool of blood is the deputy defense minister of Poland," said Reid. His voice was dry and raspy. "You may remember seeing something about it in the daily intel briefings. That's the ministry behind him. Yes, this murder was carried out in broad daylight, inside a secure facility."

Danny studied the images as the screen changed, showing first the surroundings, then the autopsy photos. Finally he had to look away— something about seeing death treated that clinically turned his stomach.

"You'll note that the deputy minister was shot in the forehead," continued Reid. "That wasn't a sniper shot. It was at close range, with a very distinctive bullet. Something like this."

Reid reached down to his briefcase and removed a manila envelope. Holding it upside down, he shook out what looked to Danny like a model of a bullet, with a rounded top and in an unusual shade of brown.

"This is a bullet?" said Nuri, picking it up.

"Carbon composite," said Danny. "Right?"

"Yes, Colonel," said Reid. "There's no metal. We imagine that it was fired from a weapon that also had no metal, as whoever fired it had to get past a metal detector."

Nuri passed the bullet over to Danny.

"This killed him?"

"That's not the actual bullet, no," said Reid. "That's something one of our labs was working on. The actual bullet is in Poland. This is another murder, more recent," Reid went on, changing the slide. "Yesterday as a matter of fact."

A new image appeared on the screen. A man lay on a sidewalk, blood around his face and mouth. This time Danny couldn't see the bullet wound. The picture had been taken at night, and the flash glinted off an unseen window just to the right of the image area. Two other bodies lay on the ground nearby.

"The dead man is named Helmut Dalitz," continued Reid. "MY-PID, please display Herr Dalitz's professional dossier."

The computer complied. MY-PID stood for Massively Parallel Integrated Decision Complex, and referred to the network of interconnected computers and data interfaces that were at the heart of the Whiplash project. Not only did the network of computers provide an integrated database and security system for Room 4, but it also could be used by field ops, who connected via a tiny interface device that looked like an MP3 player.

"This one is a businessman," said Nuri. "And he's German. What's the connection?"

"The only hard connection is the bullet," said Reid.

"So they were murdered by the same man," said Danny. "I mean, person."

"Maybe not the same person," said Reid, as Breanna slipped into the room and sat down. "But it's a good bet that the organization is the same. This image was captured by a surveillance camera near the Polish base. We think it's the killer, or one of the people working with him."

Danny looked at the photo. It wasn't exactly much—a figure, estimated by the computer to be six feet one inch tall, approximately 220 pounds—stood sideways in the grainy distance. His face was covered by shadow.

"I don't even see how you can tell if that's a man rather than a woman," said Nuri.

"Wait," said Reid.

The computer began peeling away the layers, modeling what it thought the man looked like based on the shadow it had seen. It was a generic image, something like the computer-generated models used on online clothing sites when you wanted to buy semitailored clothes.

"So who is this guy?" asked Danny. "Or guys?"

"They're called the Wolves," said Breanna. "They're murderers for hire, and they operate in Europe. The murder in Berlin was an anomaly. It was ordered by a mafia chieftain in Italy. His compatriots wouldn't authorize the killing, and so rather than cause trouble with them, he reached out to friends in Russia. They have a business arrangement selling stolen vehicles there—he exports them, they sell them."

Reid picked up the thread again, explaining that the Italian state police had the mafia member under surveillance; their phone taps recorded a conversation with one of his Russian mafiya partners asking for the hit. The price was unusually expensive, but success was guaranteed—three million euros to take down the businessman, and another two million to kill some of his associates.

"Not so coincidentally, the sum coincided with money the Russian owed the mafioso," added Reid. "He didn't even try to haggle. He was very angry—in his mind, the businessman had caused his father's death, and the reluctance of his associates to authorize revenge added insult to injury."

The Russian had then contacted someone outside of Russia with details. Unfortunately, information had been sent in at least three different messages, all via e-mail. Only one had been recovered—and that was by accident, part of an NSA program aimed at Russian intelligence. But it was enough to connect the murder definitively to the Wolves, even if the bullet hadn't been recovered.

The Russian contact was subsequently placed under electronic surveillance.

"Unfortunately, he is no longer with us," continued Reid. "The Italian was not the only person to whom he owed money."

"So we're going after criminals now?" asked Nuri.

"The assignment is a little more complicated than that," said Breanna. "The Russians seem to be hoping to disrupt the NATO meeting in Kiev set for ten days from now. The ministers are supposed to vote on Ukraine's membership, and the thinking is that this group has been hired to kill some of the ministers supporting the addition."

"Or members of the Ukrainian government who

support membership," added Reid. "It's not clear. They have been used for some political assassinations before. Most notably, Deng Pu's death."

Deng was a Chinese foreign minister who had opposed a new trade agreement with Russia. After his death—an assignation at his country house outside of Berlin—the treaty was signed.

"We're still working through the intelligence," admitted Reid after turning the projection image off. "Simply disrupting the meeting may be the Russians' primarily goal. And it's possible they're not after the entire NATO board. They may just want the possible Ukrainian representatives to it."

"What do the Ukrainians say?" asked Nuri.

Reid shook his head. "I haven't a clue whether they've been told. I suspect not."

"Apprehending the Wolves would be beneficial for a lot of reasons independent of NATO," said Breanna. "They're pretty dangerous assassins. Think about whom they've killed—a Chinese minister, a Polish defense official, a banker. And those are the murders we know about."

"So where do we start?" asked Danny.

"Berlin," said Reid. "Find out what information they have on the shooter and see if it can be added to our data. Anything is potentially of use, but a DNA sample would be useful."

"How unique is the bullet?" asked Nuri. "Carbon fiber has been around for a while."

"It's a carbon-based composite, not a fiber," said Reid. "It appears to be unique. The design is reminiscent of experiments the Soviets were doing roughly twenty years ago."

Reid clicked up a fresh slide of the bullets, showing close-ups of the bullets. He then proceeded to a series of cross sections, and finally comparisons with different types. Danny found himself starting to tune out due to information overload. The amount of data the CIA could gather on things dazzled him sometimes, but it was also frustrating—they knew all this, yet what they didn't know loomed much larger.

"One guess is that the bullets were left over from this old project," said Reid, his voice increasingly professorial. "That would fit with the theory that the Wolves are a group headed or sponsored by former Russian KGB or military, now on their own. But there's no hard evidence about that. And some of the murders we think they participated in didn't have these weapons. The choice would be made to evade metal detectors," he added. "They're a versatile group."

THEY SPENT THE NEXT HALF HOUR DISCUSSING LOGISTICS. Intelligence gathering wasn't Danny's forte, so he had no problem letting Nuri take the lead in handling Berlin. Danny would work from the other end, concentrating on Kiev and the upcoming NATO meeting.

For him, the key question was how closely to work with the security apparatus in Kiev. Close cooperation—under the cover of being a State Department security team—would mean immediate access to whatever intelligence NATO and the Ukrainian intelligence forces developed. But they would also put themselves in a position where they could compromise their own operation.

There was also a subtle conflict between the goal of protecting the NATO delegation and capturing the Wolves. As Nuri pointed out, it would be easier to identify the Wolves once they made an attempt on the NATO ministers. Ideally, once an assassin was identified, they could follow him and gather intelligence on the rest of the group. That meant letting him survive and even escape—or at least think he had. Anyone charged with protecting the NATO ministers wasn't likely to let that happen.

"Neither should you," said Reid. "Liaison with the security forces at the appropriate time. We'll establish you as members of the State Department security team, assigned to guard the American delegates."

"What's our prime responsibility then?" asked Danny. "Protect the delegates or catch these guys? Which do you want us to do?"

"Both," said Breanna. "We know it's a hard job. That's why you have it."

"If these guys are so good, why don't we just hire them over to our side and be done with it?" asked Nuri.

"As usual, Mr. Lupo, you have the logical solution," said Reid. "Perhaps when you meet them, you will be in a position to propose it."

4

Swamp Hill, Georgia

WITH NURI HEADING TO BERLIN, DANNY NEEDED SOMEone on the team with experience in Europe— preferably the Ukraine. Hera Scokas, a CIA covert officer who'd worked with him in Africa and Iran, had been in Kiev a few times, but couldn't speak the language fluently and didn't have a deep knowledge of the city.

Had this been a standard CIA operation, an officer or two or three could have been siphoned off from the station, temporarily assigned to help. But Whiplash was isolated structurally from the "regular" CIA, and Reid wanted to keep the partition in place. So he suggested they use an operative who was currently on leave from the Agency, but whom he felt might be talked back into active service for the job.

"Her name is Sally McEwen, and she knows Kiev very well," said Reid. "She was stationed there for years. She speaks the language like a native, and I suspect she'll be more than willing to come back to work for you. But you don't have to decide until you meet her."

"Can I get her personnel file?" Danny asked.

"I'd rather you drew your own conclusions once you meet her. She's the sort of officer you really have to meet in person. She is the right choice, Danny. I'm positive. But of course it's up to you."

"All right," he said. "How do I get in touch with her?"

"Ah, that is the problem," said Reid. "At the moment, she's not reachable by phone. And obviously we're not going to trust an e-mail or anything that's not encrypted. I'm afraid you'll have to contact her in person. She shouldn't be hard to find. I'll give you her address."

SALLY MCEWEN LIVED IN A SMALL HAMLET JUST OUT-side the Okefenokee National Wildlife Refuge in southern Georgia. The hamlet consisted of a few houses, a church, a restaurant that served only breakfast, and a small shop that proclaimed itself a Notions Store. All but the last were located on the old county highway, which had been by-passed in favor of a straighter route some eighty years before. From the size of its potholes, Danny wouldn't have been surprised if that was the last time it had been paved as well.

The Notions Shop sat on the hamlet's lone side street, a narrow, muddy street that dead-ended in a thicket of punk weeds and a murky pond after twenty yards. There were no numbers on the building, but since it was the only building on James Road, Danny guessed it had to be 19—McEwen's address. Except for the large sign along the roof that read NOTIONS in five-foot letters, it looked like a small ranch house. There was no driveway, or lawn for that matter—judging from the tracks, cars pulled into the muck between the road and house.

"What do you think happened to one through eighteen?" asked Hera, who'd come down with him.

"Probably sank into the swamp," said Danny.

Danny maneuvered the car into a three-point turn and slid the car into the most solid spot he could find.

"Cripes, Colonel—are you sure the car's not going to sink? All I see here is mud," said Hera, opening the door.

"Get out on my side if you want," said Danny. "Bag the colonel stuff for now, all right?"

"Aye aye, skipper."

A dog began barking as Danny got out of the car. A small patch of bricks marked a stoop at the front door. He went to the door, then rang the bell.

"It's a store—you can go right in," said Hera behind him.

"It's polite to ring the bell."

"It's a store," she said, reaching for the screen door.

The barking increased in intensity, then suddenly changed to a howling cry.

"Hush now, Brat. Hush now," yelled a woman in her early seventies as she opened the door.

She was short—perhaps five-two—and wore an oversized cotton sweater over a simple black skirt. Her shoulder-length hair was pulled back into a knot behind her head. She had the look of a slightly genteel lady who had fallen on more difficult times and had to support herself by muscle and ingenuity.

"Come on in, come on in, don't mind the dog," she said. "He gets lonely sometimes and wants to play."

Danny stepped inside. The front room was crowded with tables featuring an assortment of items. Everything from handmade tobacco pipes to an old mechanics tool set was on sale, crowded next to each other in a mishmash. Most had small tags with handwritten figures. A few had two or three, each price different.

The room extended to the left, then to the back of the house in an el shape. The leg of the el contained an assortment of different paintings, watercolors and acrylic landscapes. Directly ahead of them was a small kitchen.

"Are you looking for anything particular?" asked the woman, her voice sweet with the old South. "We have many fine items for sale."

"I wasn't actually looking to buy anything," said Danny.

"Well I'm sorry, suh, but the kitchen is closed today," said the woman. A slight edge crept into her voice. "If you're lookin' for any liquid refreshment, I'm afraid you'll have to move on."

"I'm looking for a Sally McEwen."

"Is that so?" answered the woman.

"You know her?"

"I might. Don't touch any of those paintings, girl," added the woman sharply. "Unless you're fixin' to buy one of 'em."

"Sor-ry," said Hera sarcastically.

"If you could tell me where to find Ms. McEwen, I'd be much obliged," said Danny, borrowing one of his uncle's South Carolina mannerisms and his accent.

"And if I did, who would be going to call on her?" asked the woman.

"Well, that would be me."

"And you're with what government agency?" the woman demanded.

"Well, uh, the Air Force."

"The Air Force? Air Force? Not the Treasury?"

"Treasury?"

"I told you not to touch," said the old woman, darting past Danny to Hera.

She was quick for an old bat, thought Danny. He followed her around the room to Hera, who was standing in front of a painting of a city.

"This is a very nice painting," said Hera, who was holding the painting in her hands.

"Flattery ain't gonna warm the skillet today, hon," said the old woman. "You're interested in buying, then you can put your paws on it. Otherwise, put it back."

"How much?"

"For you?" The woman looked at Danny and then back at Hera. "Not for sale. I wouldn't take money off a group of liars like yourselves. Pretending to be from the Air Force."

"I'm not with the Air Force," said Hera.

"Well, at least one of you values the truth." She took the painting. "But I'm still not selling you the painting."

"I was told that Ms. McEwen lived here," said Danny. "I'd like to talk to her."

"Well, you can't. Who told you she lived here anyway?"

"Friend of hers named Jonathon Reid."

The woman frowned, then put the painting back on its easel. She walked back to the front of the room, looking over the display of items.

"Did you hear me?" said Danny.

"Damn straight I heard you. Who the hell are you? Really?"

"I'm Danny Freah. I want to talk to Ms. McEwen."

"Why?"

"I'm afraid I can't tell you. It's kind of a personal thing. About a job."

"A job?" The woman laughed.

"You're her mother, right?" said Hera. "Or grandmother?"

"Whose mother, darlin'?" said the woman, laying her accent on thick.

"Listen, I'm sorry to bother you," said Danny. He reached into his pocket and took out a business card. It had his name and rank, along with a generic Washington-area phone number that could not be traced. He took a pen out and wrote down his personal cell number. "If you could tell Ms. McEwen to give me a call, I'd appreciate it. Either number. My cell's quicker. She could call or text me."

"She don't put much store in texting," said the woman, taking the card. "And she don't phone."

"Whatever," said Danny.

He reached for the door. The dog, which was somewhere downstairs, started barking again.

"I told you shut your trap, Brat," yelled the woman.

She reached over and closed the door.

"I'm Sally McEwen, Colonel Freah."

"No offense, but I'm afraid there must be a misunderstanding somewhere," said Danny. "I, uh—I'm looking for somebody—"

"A lot younger," said Hera.

"If Jonathon Reid sent you here, you're looking for me," she said. "He just neglected to give you all the details. Which is pretty much par for the course."

SALLY MCEWEN HAD WORKED IN VARIOUS JOBS FOR the State Department and CIA for more than forty years before being eased out by the past administration.

Eased as in pushed, and none too gently. But she had *not* retired. She damn well was *not* going to retire, and in fact went to great lengths to keep her classified clearance in order. She was officially on leave.

The Agency allowed its officers to take leaves of absence for up to five years while they pursued interests in the private sector. The supervisors who had signed off on McEwen's leave looked at it as a pleasant fiction for a field agent who was well past the freshness date but wanted to save face.

"I can have my bags packed in ten minutes," she told Danny, who was still having trouble believing the woman was, in fact, the CIA op he'd come for. "We must be going to the Ukraine. It's about the NATO thing, right?"

Hera whistled. "Good guess."

"More than a guess, sweetie. Russia must be plotting to keep them out, right? Of course."

"She's sharp," said Hera.

It didn't sound quite like a compliment.

"I, um—I have to talk to Reid," said Danny.

"I don't have a phone," said McEwen.

"That's all right." Danny took his sat phone out. "I'm going to just make the call outside."

The dog started barking again.

"Don't worry about him," McEwen told Danny. "His bark is worse than his bite."

Outside, Danny went over and leaned against the car before dialing.

"This is Reid."

"Jonathon, this is Danny Freah. I found Ms. McEwen."

"Is she willing to help?"

"She's more than willing. But she's—old."

Reid didn't answer for a moment. He wasn't exactly a spring chicken himself. If anything, he was several years—maybe even a whole decade— older than McEwen.

"Let me ask you a question, Colonel. Why do you want Sally on the mission?"

"I don't want her, not her per se," answered Danny. "I need someone who knows Kiev, who can talk the language like a native, and who can help make arrangements."

"And you think she's too old for that?"

"Yeah. And she's a moonshiner."

Reid laughed. "I don't think that disqualifiers her. Assuming, of course, it's true."

"Seriously—"

"Who you choose is up to you, Colonel. You know that. But I wouldn't have recommended Sally if I didn't think she could handle the job. You're not asking her to jump out of planes, correct?"

"No."

"She could probably do that." Reid laughed. "I

know she'll pass whatever physical the Agency offers."

"Yeah, but—"

"Your call."

Reid hung up.

Danny put the sat phone back in his pocket. He thought of himself as pretty old. In fact, he'd questioned himself several times during the last mission, wondering if he was still up to the rigors of an operation.

But McEwen—she was at *least* seventy.

He walked back into the house, not quite decided what to do.

Hera and McEwen were back by the paintings. Laughing.

Hera, laughing? That was a first.

Danny found McEwen pointing to a building in one of the paintings. He hadn't looked at it very carefully before; now he realized it was a street in Kiev.

"They had rented the flat out to a prostitute," said McEwen, continuing her story for Hera. "The prostitute got evicted, and we got it. Of course, we didn't know about the previous occupant. So here we are, trying to set up a safe house, and men knocking at all hours of the night, asking for Olga. *Ulll-ga*."

"Olga," repeated Hera, laughing hysterically.

She must be pretty good with people, thought Danny, to get Hera on her side so quickly. He'd had a lot of trouble winning her over.

"So what did Johnny say?" asked McEwen.

Danny had never heard Reid called Johnny

by anyone. Reid didn't seem like a Johnny. He seemed like a . . . Mr. Reid.

"He said that you know Kiev better than I know the back of my hand," Danny told her. "And that you can help me make some arrangements there."

"Damn straight. Let me get my bag."

"What about your store?" asked Danny.

"Ah, I don't get but two customers a year, except for the ones what want some old-fashioned."

She disappeared down the hall.

"That's the local White Lightning," said Hera.

"No shit," said Danny.

"She just sells it for her father's cousin. He lives out in the woods."

"She told you that?"

"We bonded."

"You think she can do the job?"

"What? Rent hotel rooms, find us rental cars? Hell yeah. God, she's perfect—who'd expect her? Little old lady a spy? No way."

McEwen returned with her bag.

"I'm gonna have to stop at the hardware store on the way out," she said. " 'Cause I gotta leave a message for Cuz, but he don't read."

"You're not going to tell him where you're going, are you?" asked Danny.

"Colonel—I've been in this business since before you were in diapers. Credit me with a little common sense."

"Cuz won't worry that you're gone?" asked Hera.

"He'll be a little sorry that he'll have to go back to cookin' on his own, instead of coming around and mooching off me every night," said McEwen. "But he'll be glad that he won't have to go splits on the profits. And that no one's yellin' at him to get his teeth fixed. Don't worry about him. He's not a bad cook when he puts his mind to it. Especially if you like barbecue on Christmas."

"It shouldn't be more than two weeks," said Danny.

"I hope we're going for a long time," said McEwen. "Much as I love this place, I'm done with it for a spell."

"I got a question," said Hera as McEwen put the Closed sign in place on the front door. "What does it mean that this is a notions shop?"

"It means I sell anything I have a notion to," said McEwen, closing the door behind her.

5

The Pentagon

BREANNA STOCKARD WAS JUST ABOUT TO LEAVE HER office at the Pentagon when she got an urgent alert on her encrypted messaging system asking her to call Jonathon Reid. She reached for the phone and dialed, knowing that the meeting she was headed to was unlikely to break up much before seven, and she had promised her daughter she'd be home soon after.

Reid picked up on the first ring, his raspy voice practically croaking in the receiver.

"That was fast," he told her.

"I have a meeting upstairs," she said. "What's up?"

"More data on the Wolves."

"And?"

"There's a Moldova link," said Reid. "It may just be a coincidence, but I thought I'd better tell you."

"What's the connection?"

"Transactions. I've forwarded the report to your secure queue," said Reid.

Breanna clicked the file open and waited while it was unencrypted. The system used a set of temporary, real-time keys, and occasionally the process of turning it from unreadable hieroglyphics to clear text could take several seconds.

The file opened. It was a listing of plane tickets that showed transit in and out of Moldova, a small landlocked country between Romania and Russia.

"Those accounts will be backtracked," said Reid. "They'll look for patterns, connections to other accounts. We may have more of a profile in a few days."

"Moldova may simply have been chosen because of its banking system," said Breanna. "The banking system is notoriously opaque to outsiders. Even insiders. And there are plenty of suspect mafia connections."

"Always a possibility."

Breanna looked at the data. None of the transactions were recent.

"These are all connected to the Wolves?" she asked.

"They're connected to accounts that were associated with the Berlin activity," answered Reid. "As I say, the Moldova connection is still tenuous."

Activity. An interesting way to describe murder.

"Everything is tenuous," said Breanna.

"Not everything," said Reid. "As for the identity—"

"The DNA is suggestive, not conclusive," she said.

Reid didn't answer. It was his way of reproaching her—worse, she thought, than if he had argued or even called her a name.

Not that Reid would do either.

"At some point we will have to address this with Colonel Freah," said Reid finally.

"We'll keep it where it is for now," said Breanna. "Until we have more information, I don't see any point in going down this road with Danny. It's still . . . far-fetched."

"Admittedly."

Breanna looked at her watch. "I'm sorry, I have a meeting."

"I'll keep you up to date."

"Thanks."

THE MEETING BREANNA WAS RUSHING TO COULDN'T start until she arrived, which meant that a dozen generals and three admirals stared at her as she came in the door. While her civilian position as head of the Office of Technology put her on a higher administrative level than most of the people in the room, she was still a colonel in the Air Force

Reserve, and not a few of the people in the room thought of her that way.

Sometimes she did, too.

"Sorry I'm late," she said, rushing in.

"Well, you're here now," said General Timothy "Tiger" Wallace. "Let's get moving."

Wallace gave her a tight grin, but the expression gave nothing away. He was the Air Force's chief of staff—the top boss—and a difficult man for her to gauge. He'd served with her father, and claimed to be a great admirer of Dreamland and everything associated with it. He and Zen occasionally had lunch together during his visits to Capitol Hill. On the other hand, he frequently butted heads with Breanna's boss, Deputy Defense Secretary Harold Magnus. The two had clashed when Magnus was in the Air Force some years before, and while they didn't openly feud—Magnus wasn't the type, and there was no percentage in it for Wallace—Wallace's animosity was often subtly displayed, especially toward Magnus's pet projects.

One of which Breanna had come to discuss.

"Thank you, General," she said, sliding her laptop onto the table. "Everyone is aware of the Sabre UAV program and its present status."

She nodded toward Steph Garvey, the two-star Air Force general in charge of the Sabre program. Garvey gave her a smile—genuine and easy to read.

"We have made good progress with the UM/F program in general," continued Breanna. "Including the Navy variant."

"That's a matter of opinion," grumbled Admiral David Chafetz. There was no mistaking Chafetz's attitude—he didn't like anything even remotely connected to the Air Force, and was a skeptic of unmanned aircraft as well. That was two big strikes against the Sabre program.

Officially designated UM/F–9s, the unmanned aircraft had been developed as replacements for the Flighthawks, the robot aircraft that helped revolutionize aerial combat in the late 1990s and early 2000s.

Though greatly improved over the years, the Flighthawks had a number of limitations, including range and speed. More importantly, their airframes were now well past their design age. Materials fatigue—both their metal skeleton and carbon-fiber skins—was starting to hamper their effectiveness. Internal fasteners had to be inspected before each flight on some of the high-hour aircraft—an onerous procedure that added several hours to the maintainers' routine chores. It was time for a new generation of remote fighters to take over.

The Sabres were that fighter.

Nicknamed after the fighter that had dominated the skies over North Korea during the 1950s, the UM/F–9 was the first UAV capable of sustained Mach speeds. (Though technically the Flighthawks could fly faster than the speed of sound, they could not operate reliably in Mach-plus regimes for several reasons unrelated to their airfoil.) Long and sleek, the aircraft used a hybrid ramjet pulse engine to fly; an array of maneuvering nozzles and high-strength carbon-based alloys made twelve g-plus turns routine. Tests showed that it was more than a match for even the improved F–22C Block–150s that had recently joined the Air Force's top interceptor squadrons.

But high speeds and maneuverability meant nothing if the aircraft could not be controlled. And this control system—called Medusa—represented the real breakthrough.

Like the Flighthawk, the Sabre was capable of "autonomous combat." In other words, it could figure out on its own how to take down an enemy, then do so. Unlike Flighthawks, Sabres could work together against an enemy, employing section tactics without human intervention. Data from one aircraft was immediately shared with all of the aircraft in the same flight. Spotting a group of four enemy planes, for example, the flight could decide to break into two elements and attack from two different directions.

While the Flighthawks had small onboard flight computers to handle many of the basic tasks of flight, they relied heavily on a centralized computer and a human controlling them, generally from an EB–52 or modified B–1.

Medusa did not exist separately from the Sabres. It was, as the man who invented it liked to say with his droll puns, a true "cloud computer." The interconnection of the units working together created the real intelligence.

But there had to be a human in the process *somewhere*. And that was what today's meeting was about.

Actually, the man who invented Medusa didn't agree that there should be any human anywhere in the process. It wasn't that Ray Rubeo had no use for his fellow man or thought that human intelligence was an oxymoron, though charges along those lines had often been leveled at him. Rubeo simply saw no need for a human "to muck things up."

"You don't steer a Sidewinder to its target," he had told Breanna on several occasions. "It's fire and forget. Same with this."

But the military was not ready to think about a squadron of aircraft as "fire and forget" weapons. And though Rubeo worked, as a contractor, for her, Breanna wasn't ready to think that way either.

So where did the Medusa "control" unit go?

At a secure base far from harm, like those generally used for the Predator and Global Hawk? Or a plane, like the Flighthawk system?

A satellite control system with a ground base could be used, but there were problems with bandwidth, and the cost was considerable—much more than Medusa, let alone the Sabres.

Medusa's range was roughly two hundred miles, a considerable improvement over the Flighthawks. Still, that was close enough that a savvy enemy could seek to locate and isolate the control aircraft. Simply making the plane run away would mean a cheap victory, as the Sabres would have to follow or lose their connection. That wasn't much of an issue for a system like the Flighthawks, originally designed to protect a bombing package: their job was to stay close to the mother ship in the first place. But it would be disastrous for interceptors.

The Air Force was pushing for a new version of the F–35 to act as the Sabres' controller. This would be a stretched, two-seat version of the stealthy lightweight fighter. There were considerable problems with such an approach, starting with the fact that the stretched F–35 couldn't carry enough fuel to stay in a combat area for more than an hour, far less than the Sabre. There was also a matter of cost, which would be considerable for a plane not even off the drawing board yet.

The Navy had gone along with the plan, grudgingly, because it would allow the Sabres to operate from carriers for the first time. But as Chafetz's demeanor made clear, their support was less than enthusiastic.

Breanna had come today to offer a different solution entirely.

"I should start by giving you all a bit of good news about the intelligent command system that flies the planes," she said, flipping open her laptop. "We call it Medusa. It's—"

"A Greek monster," quipped Chafetz.

Breanna smiled indulgently. Her solution would actually help the Navy, but she didn't expect to be thanked for it.

"The admiral knows his myths," she said. "Medusa is six months ahead of schedule. In fact, as you'll see at the demonstration next week— those of you who are going out to Dreamland— it's completely operational. Or would be, if we had more Sabres."

"We will have a dozen by the end of the year," said General Garvey.

"And that program is on schedule and on budget," Breanna offered quickly, not wanting to seem as if she was criticizing Garvey. "Along the way, we've made some improvements to Medusa's human input unit. It's now as compact as the units in Sabres. Which gave us an idea."

While talking, she had booted up her laptop. The computer found the secure local network, signing itself on automatically. Breanna glanced down and double-clicked on a PowerPoint icon. A pair of video screens began to rise from the center of the conference room tables.

"We'd like to propose a new aircraft as part of the control solution. Some of you will be familiar with it."

A jet came on the screen. It looked like a cousin of the F–22, perhaps by way of the YF–23 and a Bird of Prey. Black, with an oval double wing at the tail and stubby fins at its side, it was two-thirds the size of a Raptor, as the next slide demonstrated.

"The Tigershark?" asked Chafetz. "A Navy plane?"

Wallace cleared his throat.

"Actually, that began as an Air Force project," he said. "But it's dead. The company's bankrupt. No more aircraft can be built."

"At the moment, we have all we need," said Breanna. "There are three aircraft. They could all be given over to the program. That's one more than you need, at least for the next two years."

Three Tigersharks had been built and tested three years before. The aircraft was seen first as a replacement for the F–22, and as a possible fifth generation fighter for the Navy.

One had even appeared at a pair of air shows, as its maker—a small company formed by former Boeing and Lockheed engineers—tried to convince the military and Congress to award a contract for its development. Unfortunately, the wheels of government moved very slowly. While everyone agreed the plane was a winner, it couldn't win funding for production in the tight budget. While Congress promised to consider it the next fiscal year, the debt-ridden company had folded. Its assets were put up for sale to pay creditors.

At that point the Office of Technology had stepped in, purchasing the aircraft, some spare parts, and all of the design work. The Tigershark now belonged to the Office of Technology.

"How the hell do you see in that thing?" asked one of the admirals.

"Screens," said Garvey. "They provide a better view than your eyes would."

Breanna pressed the button on her pointer. A close-up of the body appeared, revealing lines for the cockpit access panel. The next slide showed a breakaway of the body, revealing the cockpit itself. The pilot's seat was pitched as if it were a recliner.

"We needed a high-performance aircraft to help us test Medusa," explained Breanna. "The Sabres weren't ready, and of course there are always questions about unmanned airplanes in test regimes.

In any event, one of the aircraft had been disassembled for some tests, and adding Medusa to the rebuild was not very difficult. We decided we would use it. The results have been so spectacular that it makes sense to show you what we have. You're scheduled to view the system tests with us in Dreamland next week—this is just an added bonus."

"Hmph," said Chafetz. Although he sounded unconvinced, he also seemed to be calculating the benefits.

"Why not just put the unit in an F–22?" asked Wallace. "If I might play devil's advocate."

"That's doable," said Breanna. "Though we would have to completely gut and rebuild the plane." She shrugged. "The Office of Technology doesn't own any of those, and the subcontractor wasn't in a position to commandeer one."

That drew a few laughs.

"This looks like just a backdoor way of getting the Tigershark into the budget," said Admiral Chafetz.

"It is one argument for it," admitted Breanna. "No one has ruled out the plane. They just weren't ready to fund it."

"I'd like to see it make headway in *this* Congress," said Wallace with disgust. Then he glanced at Breanna. "Present company and their relatives excepted."

"I haven't spoken to Senator Stockard at all about this," said Breanna hastily.

"Well you should," said Admiral Garvey. "Because it's a hell of an idea. When is the demonstration again?"

6

Berlin

DURING HIS RELATIVELY SHORT CAREER WITH THE CIA, Nuri Lupo had worked with a variety of foreign agencies, sometimes officially, sometimes unofficially. He'd had varying degrees of success and cooperation, but by far his worst experiences had come when working with the FBI, which he'd had to do three times.

The Berlin assignment made four. The Bureau could not be bypassed for a number of reasons, all of them political.

Actually the most important wasn't political at all: Reid had told him to work with the Bureau. Period.

"To the extent possible," said Reid. "Which means you will, at a minimum, make contact. Before you arrive. If not sooner."

FBI agents were, in Nuri's experience, among the most uncooperative species on the planet, at least when it came to dealing with the CIA. The two agencies were natural rivals, partly because of their overlapping missions in national security and espionage. But sibling rivalry wasn't the only cause of conflict. G-men—and -women—regarded "spy" as an occupation somewhere lower than journalist and politician. From the Bureau's perspective, the CIA sullied every American by its mere existence.

It was also no doubt galling that Agency field officers had expense accounts several times larger than FBI agents.

Nuri tried to use the expense account to his advantage, but had to use all of his persuasive skills merely to get the FBI agent, a middle-aged woman whose gray pantsuit matched her demeanor, to have breakfast with him as soon as he arrived in the city.

"I've already had breakfast," insisted Elise Gregor as they sat down in the small café a short distance from the airport. "And I don't want any more coffee."

"Have a decaf," said Nuri, trying his best to be affable.

"Just tell me what you want."

"I just need background," said Nuri. He stopped speaking as the waiter came over, switching to German to order.

"Eggs with toast, American style," said the waiter in English far superior to Nuri's German.

"That's it," said Nuri.

The putdown was regarded as some sort of triumph by Gregor, who practically beamed as she told the waiter in German that she would have a small orange juice. Nuri considered whether he ought just to leave, but the FBI might be of some use at some point in the investigation, and closing the door now didn't make sense.

Well, maybe it did. How much help could they possibly be?

"German's not one of your languages, is it?" Gregor asked as the waiter left.

"I can speak a little."

"Very little."

I'd like to see you handle Arabic, thought Nuri. Or Farsi. Or maybe a subdialect of Swahili.

"So what do you want?" said Gregor. "Why are you here?"

"I want to talk to the investigator on the Helmut Dalitz murder case."

"Dalitz? The banker?"

"Businessman. Do you have any information?"

She made a face. "That's too local for us to get involved in."

"You have nothing?" asked Nuri, surprised. The FBI had been briefed, to some degree at least, on the Wolves and the suspected connection to the murder. Was Gregor out of the loop? Or playing coy?

Coy. The word evoked images of sex kittens . . . a nauseating concept when connected with the woman sitting across from him.

"Why is the Agency interested?" Gregor asked.

"They don't tell me everything," said Nuri, deciding he could be just as hard to deal with as Gregor. "They sent me here to see what was going on."

"They didn't tell you why?"

"I think it has to do with money laundering," said Nuri.

"That's an FBI area of interest." Gregor's eyes narrowed. "Nothing like that has come up."

"So you *are* following the case?"

"From a distance," she said. "We're somewhat interested—not involved."

The orange juice and coffee arrived. Nuri took a sip of the coffee. It was surprisingly weak.

"I don't see where he could have been laundering money," said Gregor. "He was a respected businessman."

"Yeah, it's probably a total waste of time. That's the sort of crap they send me on these days," said Nuri.

Gregor frowned. "This is because of the connection to the Wolves, right?"

"Well, I—"

"All right. Let's go," she said, rising.

"But—"

"I have other things to do today," she told him. "If you're coming, come. And you better leave the waiter a good tip. They really like me here."

THE BERLIN DETECTIVE HEADING THE INVESTIGATION INTO Dalitz's murder was a thirty-something woman who spoke English with a pronounced British accent. She was also among the most beautiful women Nuri had ever met.

She was so pretty, in fact, that if she and Gregor were combined and averaged out, the result would still be among the top ten or so models in the world. Nuri felt his head flush just meeting her; her handshake—firm, not too eager but not unfriendly—weakened his knees.

"I will be very happy to tell you what we know," Frau Gerste said, leading them to her office in the upstairs of the municipal building. She worked for the national police even though her office was in the local police station; Nuri couldn't quite grasp the relationship between the local, state, and national police agencies but decided it was irrelevant for now.

"I am afraid that it is not much," Gerste continued, taking a seat behind her desk. This was unfortunate; it removed half of her body from view. "What we have does not seem to lead to much that is usable."

Frau Gerste recounted the details of the crime, which had happened in a relatively popular part of Berlin, in an area that had been under communist control before the Wall came down. There had been few people on the street at the time, however, and apparently the assassin and any assistants had gotten away without being seen.

"We would believe he was waiting somewhere outside," said Frau Gerste. "There are video cameras, but several blind spots. So he must have studied the area."

"It was a professional job," said Nuri.

"Very. The bullet was significant—undetectable by metal detectors," said Gerste. "We imagine this was because the killer was in the music hall with him, or thought he might be. There were detectors at the door. His weapon, I assume, would have been undetectable as well. Very unusual."

"Yes."

"From what I understand," she said, "the bullet is similar to one used in another murder, this one political. Do you have details on that?"

Nuri shook his head, trying not to make it too obvious that he was lying. It was terrible to lie to beautiful women.

"I have heard that there was an organization responsible for the political murder." Frau Gerste smiled—it was as if the sun had come out after a winter's worth of cloudy days. "Interpol's information is very limited. A code name, the Wolves. That is why your interest, perhaps?"

"Perhaps," said Nuri.

"Of course a professional committed the crime," said Frau Gerste. "But why? Helmut Dalitz did have some enemies, but hiring someone to murder him?"

"You don't buy the mafia connection?" said Nuri.

She made a face. "Revenge for a heart attack? Would you commit murder for a heart attack?"

"Well, I wouldn't commit murder," said Nuri.

"If you were the mafia, would you hire another killer?"

"If they owed me money or a favor," said Nuri.

She shrugged. "It doesn't make sense."

Frau Gerste preferred a more local motive—a jilted lover, perhaps, though the investigation had not produced one. There were rumors that the victim saw prostitutes and had a gay lover.

Gregor nodded vigorously as Frau Gerste proffered the theories—none of which had any firm evidence to back them up. But they would be more acceptable to a German, thought Nuri; they were signs of personal disorder, which would explain the external disorder of murder.

"Could the murderer have been working with someone on the inside?" asked Gregor.

"The inside?"

"Someone who was part of his business. Who would know where the video cameras were and the security arrangements. His daughter? I heard he was with his daughter and her boyfriend."

"The daughter was there. The boyfriend is no longer a boyfriend. We did check that possibility," said Frau Gerste, nodding approvingly. "That is something we continue to explore. Jealousy from the boyfriend. Perhaps he wanted a fortune."

The look in Frau Gerste's eyes—approval—would have melted Nuri on the spot had it been directed at him. It had a distinctly sexual tinge to it.

Aimed at Gregor, it seemed almost immoral, even sacrilegious. Nuri felt his stomach turning, just a little.

"Of course, with a little bit of planning, then it would be possible to compute the lines of sight at the square," said Frau Gerste. "No sources would be necessary."

"Maybe he is on the tape from a few days before," suggested Nuri, finally finding his tongue.

"We have thought of that. The tapes are kept for only forty-eight hours. There was nothing overly suspicious in that time."

Nuri found himself staring at Frau Gerste's profile. She wore her blond hair in a bob. Ordinarily not a perfect choice, he thought, though in this case she pulled it off.

And her breasts. . .

She turned suddenly to him.

"So why are two Bureau of Investigations agents interested?" asked Frau Gerste.

She gave him the look. It wasn't really approval. It was . . . something more basic. Nuri, blood thumping in his temples, was temporarily tongue-tied.

"He's not with the Bureau," said Gregor.

"No?"

"I'm a liaison with State," said Nuri, preferring not to use the words Central Intelligence Agency if at all possible. "We—there may be a national security connection."

"National security? Because of the Wolves? Ah. So you believe that?"

He had Frau Gerste's interest. Maybe he should admit to being with the CIA. Some women liked the excitement it implied.

"These things have to be checked," said Nuri apologetically. "But we do have a lot of resources. Perhaps they can be of help."

"What sort of resources?"

"DNA sampling. If you have something from the scene—"

"Nothing. We have our own labs. But we found nothing."

"Well, if we had access to billing done in the area, we might be able to find a pattern," offered Nuri.

"Billing?"

"Credit card payments, that sort of thing. Restaurants. See if the place was under surveillance. The person or persons might have bought something in the area. It'd be a long shot."

"German law makes that difficult to obtain," said Frau Gerste. Indeed it did, which was why he had to ask; the credit card companies would not simply part with the information, even to their American counterparts. "And that would be a needle in the haystack, I think you say."

God, she was beautiful, even when she was skeptical. What is it exactly, he wondered. Her blue eyes? They were set perfectly apart. Her nose—not too big, not too small. The lips were a little full, but that only sealed the deal.

Her face was unblemished and, surprisingly given her job, unwrinkled. And her breasts—not large, actually, but high and seemingly firm under her very proper blouse.

"Thank you for your time," said Gregor, starting to rise.

"You said that someone may have checked the video cameras," said Nuri. "I'd like to look at them myself. And the funeral. Was there anything unusual about the funeral?"

"Only the flowers."

"Flowers?"

"The dead roses. It is not clear whether they were deliberate or not."

"Would you happen to know the shop that sent them?" he asked.

A DOZEN BLACK, WITHERED ROSES HAD BEEN SENT TO the funeral. The state of the roses wasn't a matter of poor service—they'd been ordered that way.

Nuri talked Frau Gerste into taking him to the shop to see the owner. He was hoping Gregor would beg off because of her allegedly heavy schedule, but no such luck—she not only came, but insisted on driving. That left him in the back, slowly getting intoxicated on the scent of Frau Gerste's perfume.

The scent was hard to describe. A kind of exotic lilac thing. Spicy, yet sweet.

Like her, no doubt. He wondered what kind of lingerie she preferred.

"It's not the strangest order he's ever had, especially for a funeral," Frau Gerste translated as they interviewed the owner of the small shop. "One time he had to make a delivery with several mice's heads. He doesn't like to do it, but for the extra fee . . ."

"Can I get a copy of the invoice, or order, or whatever?" asked Nuri.

"I can't order him to give it," said Gerste.

"But he could give it to us voluntarily, right?" he asked.

"The laws regarded evidence in court—"

"But they apply to you," said Nuri. "Not me. And if I then made a copy available to you . . ."

"I don't know . . ."

"If the information came from the FBI," suggested Gregor, "then it would be usable."

"Hmmmmph," said Frau Gerste.

The order had come through an e-mail system. The owner printed it out. Nuri took it, then asked if there was a small office where he could use the phone. He wanted privacy, not the line—he pulled the headset for the MY-PID out and connected to the computer network.

"Good morning, Nuri," said the computer.

"Working on the personality modules again?" asked Nuri.

"Please repeat request."

"I need this order tracked." Nuri read in the particulars. The computer took several seconds before telling him that the order had come from a shop in Naples.

"Any known mafia connection?" asked Nuri.

It was another few seconds before the computer answered. The shop's owners had been named in two different indictments related to La Costra Nostra.

When Nuri came out of the office, Frau Gerste and Gregor were nodding solemnly as the owner of the shop told them, in German, about the fine points of caring for freshly cut flowers. It was all in the water, he said, and in the angle of the cut.

Nuri would have been content to let the conversation continue—it gave him a good chance to watch Frau Gerste surreptitiously—but Gregor noticed him gawking and abruptly asked him if he'd discovered anything.

"Definitely a mafia connection with the flowers," he said. "It reinforces the revenge theory."

"Perhaps," said Frau Gerste, sighing just a little.

7

Washington, D.C.

"Senator, I hate to say this, but you're going to be late for the White House. Again. I know you're only going in Senator Tompkins's place, but—"

"I'm on my way, Clarissa." Senator Jeffrey "Zen" Stockard smiled at his appointments secretary, Clarissa Tomey. "But I have a reputation to maintain."

"For being late?"

"You got it."

"They blame me, you know," said the secretary. "I'm sure they hate me."

"Broad shoulders," said Zen, wheeling himself past her desk. "Jason? Where the hell are you?" he said in mock anger. "You're late. Late again."

"Uh, Senator, I'm right here, sir," said Jason Black, who was standing at the door. "I've been, uh, waiting."

"No alibis, Jay. We all know it's your fault."

"Um, yes sir."

Zen laughed. He loved teasing his staff, especially Black, who was only a year removed from college.

"Can I trust you at the White House?" Zen asked as he rolled his wheelchair down the hall. "Coming in with me?"

"Um, uh, yes, Senator. I, uh—my tie's clean."

"You like seeing the President, don't you? Or at least that cute intern they have from the NSC that's always winking at you when we go over there."

Zen glanced up at Black, who was turning beet red.

"Hey, Zen," said Senator Dirks, approaching down the hall. "Got a minute?"

"Damned if I don't, but take it anyway," said Zen. Dirks was from the other party, but the two got along personally and even on occasion voted the same way. In fact, Dirks had been one of the early supporters of Zen's bill to establish a scholarship program reimbursing college graduates who joined the service as officers after graduation. The bill had just passed the Senate that morning.

"Have you heard what happened to Senator Osten?" asked Dirks.

"No," said Zen. Al Osten was the ranking senator on the Foreign Relations Committee. "I'm on my way to the White House. He's going to be there."

"No," said Dirks. "They just took him in an ambulance. I was right there. They think he was having a heart attack."

"Wow."

"The paramedics were here right away. Still, you don't know at his age."

"That's terrible."

Both men frowned. Even though Dirks and Osten were from different parties, as senators they were fellow members of the most exclusive club in the world.

"I was hoping we could grab lunch at some point," said Dirks. "I wanted to talk about the Air Force appropriations for their new jets. Maybe sometime this week?"

"Sure. Have your staff set it up with Clarissa," said Zen. "Better yet—the Nationals are in town. What do you say about a game?"

"Now we're talking," said Dirks. "I'll check the calendar."

"Don't check too hard," said Zen. "Thanks for your vote today, by the way."

"It's a good bill. Now all you need is House support. And your President."

"I'm working on it," said Zen. The President

was anything but *his* President. Even though they were from the same party, Christine Mary Todd and Zen often found themselves at loggerheads.

Which made him a little suspicious an hour later, when she seemed overly profuse as he entered the Oval Office with Jason Black in tow.

"Here is Senator Stockard," she said, without a trace of sarcasm. "Fresh from his victory on the floor."

"Congratulations, Zen," said Secretary of Defense Charles Lovel. "It's a good bill."

"Thank you," said Zen. "Thank you, Ms. President."

Zen nodded at Secretary of State Alistair Newhaven and National Security Advisor Michael Blitz, who were seated in a semicircle in front of the President's desk. Zen wheeled himself next to Newhaven, while Black joined the aides near the side of the room.

"Have you heard anything about Senator Osten?" asked the President. "His staff told us he was taken to the hospital as a precaution."

"That's more information than I have," said Zen. "I only just heard that he had a heart attack."

Todd nodded grimly. Before she could say anything else, her phone buzzed.

"That should be General Danker," said the President. "I'll put him on speaker."

Danker was the American representative to NATO. He was currently in Germany, touring facilities there. Zen had met the Army general when he was an aide to the Joint Chiefs of Staff a decade and a half before. Danker was more a politician than a tactician, which made him perfect for the NATO post.

Zen watched the others as they exchanged small talk with the general. Each had a different style and personality. Blitz leaned forward in his chair, eyes squinting slightly, a very serious look on his face even as he asked the general how his wife was. Newhaven fidgeted—he always fidgeted. Lovel was his usual easygoing self, making a joke about German beer.

President Todd, meanwhile, seemed impatient—also completely in character.

"So—the NATO meeting in Kiev," she said, bringing the brief how-are-ya session to an end. "Can we have an update on it?"

"The Russians oppose it, of course," said Newhaven, launching into a brief recap of the political situation.

Russia had long opposed Ukraine's addition to NATO. They were not politically in a position to do much about it—with the drop in energy prices, the Russian economy had slumped to its lowest state since the collapse of the Soviet Union. But they certainly weren't happy about it.

"There's intelligence that they might attempt to disrupt the sessions," said Newhaven. "Very good intelligence."

"I would say that physical threats to the participants cannot be ruled out," said Blitz. "They should be expected."

"I concur," said General Danker over the speakerphone.

They discussed the threats briefly. Such intelligence reports and warnings were much more common than people thought, but the fact that this had been connected to a legitimate government made it unusual. Still, there was no chance that NATO would call off the meeting, or that any of the members, including the U.S., would decline to attend. Terrorist-type threats had become an unfortunate fact of life in the post–9/11 era.

President Todd moved the discussion back to the importance of having Ukraine join NATO. She saw Russia's objections as a sign that the policy was a good one, though not everyone in Congress agreed. That was an important issue, since the new NATO membership would be part of a revision to the NATO charter and subject to Senate ratification.

"Senator Osten's illness could be a major problem for us," she said. "He was scheduled to be at the conference. If he's had a heart attack, I'm afraid that will complicate matters."

"Someone from the committee will go," said Zen. "It may even be me."

Todd pressed her lips together. "Senator?"

"I'm next in line. And I'm the only other one who supports the measure on the committee. In our party, anyway."

"It would be helpful if you attended, and then were able to persuade your colleagues upon your return," said the President.

"I don't think I've ever been to Kiev," said Zen.

"There will be impeccable security," said Danker over the phone.

"I'm not worried," said Zen.

8

Rome, Italy

NURI FELT THE WEIGHT OF FRAU GERSTE'S SIGH ALL THE way to Rome.

He also felt the weight of Gregor's shoulder, as they sat next to each other on a Euro C Flight direct from Berlin.

The C, Nuri was sure, stood for "cheap." The seats were so narrow a mouse would have felt crowded.

Gregor had insisted on coming, following a call from her supervisor. Apparently the Bureau was now worried that the CIA would crack the case and they wouldn't get any credit. On the bright side, she managed to get an appointment with a member of the Office of Special Magistrate, the antimafia police, that afternoon. Hence the flight.

She was uncharacteristically quiet for much of the flight, and Nuri tolerated her presence, if not her bad breath, until just before they were landing, when she began talking about Frau Gerste.

Why, she wondered, had Nuri found her attractive?

"Who says I found her attractive?" he asked.

"You were practically leering. 'Frau' means she's married, you know."

"I'm sure."

"She had a wedding ring."

"Really? I hadn't noticed."

"Because you were too busy staring at her boobs.

I hate it when men do that. Treating women like sex objects. It's disgusting."

You have nothing to worry about, Nuri thought to himself, but he kept his mouth shut, concentrating instead on the dossier MY-PID had provided on the man who apparently ordered the murder in Berlin.

The Italian newspapers had played up the tobacco shop owner's death, calling Giuseppe De-Francisco one of the "grand old men of Rome," an appellation that not even his most faithful customers could ever remember hearing during his lifetime. Established in 1956, his small shop had been a dusty holdover from an era that had passed as surely as the Caesars and chariot races. But his untimely death transformed it into a symbol of all Italy, which was being overtaken by the rapacious thieves of international finance, who cared not a wit for the ability of an Italian to buy a good cigar and catch up on the latest gossip of the neighborhood, be that neighborhood in an obscure Abruzzi town or Rome itself.

Giuseppe's connection to his mafia grandson was not mentioned in any of these feature stories. The obituary contained only the broadest hint: Giuseppe had only two surviving grandchildren, one in the U.S. and the other in Naples. Neither was named.

The grandson was Alfredo Moreno, a mafia chief well-known enough in Interpol circles to have a nickname—the Car Thief. He had not lived in Naples for more than a decade, preferring to spend most of his time at his hilltop estate thirty miles away in a town named Fuggire. So small it didn't show up on most maps, the town consisted of three buildings at an intersection of two rugged roads, an abandoned monastery building, and Moreno's hilltop property.

The estate had once belonged to a religious order, willed to them by a wealthy cardinal who had established the monastery. It had passed back into private hands somewhere in the sixteenth or eighteenth century. Sometime after that it had become the family home for the Morenos, and was passed down on Alfredo's father's side of the family for at least eight generations.

Its connections with the mafia were well-known and documented in the media. Alfredo had, of course, made all of the pretenses of going "straight," supposedly denouncing his mobster roots and becoming in the Italian phrase, *uno mano moderno*—a modern hand.

Alfredo was indeed modern, but then so was crime. Where his forebears had depended on handshakes and backroom conversations, he preferred encrypted BlackBerries and pay-as-you go cell phones.

He made a great deal of money importing and exporting—he brought in olive oil and other goods from Turkey, Syria, and Libya, and exported cars to northern Africa and occasionally the Middle East. The cars were stolen; the oil and food were generally mislabeled and occasionally transported in defiance of various international sanctions, such as those requiring inspections and others forbidding trade with places like Iran, which Libya was particularly good in circumventing.

Alfredo also supplemented his income by importing heroin from Afghanistan; it was a small amount of his overall business, but it did pay for the annual Christmas and Easter parties he threw in the town at the foot of his hilltop. It went without saying that he did not pay much in the way of taxes, though in Italy this was merely a sign of his smart business sense.

Nuri realized that while many Italian magistrates would have loved the headlines that would come from arresting a mafioso, they could not stomach the obituaries that would inevitably follow. But he wasn't counting on an arrest. He was hoping he could interest the Italian antimafia police in a visit to Alfredo's estate, at which time he might talk to Alfredo about the Wolves—a conversation he assumed would go nowhere—but also borrow whatever home computers he had in his house. For the intercepts that had yielded the conversations led to other conversations indicating he was making financial transfers via the Internet; one of them was surely going to the Wolves' account. With the murder so recent, there were likely to be traces of the payoff somewhere in the computer.

With Western countries under pressure from the U.S. and the UN to do something about the Afghan heroin trade, which had thrived despite the apparent demise of the Taliban, Nuri decided to use that as his opening. He focused on the evidence connecting Alfredo to the trade and skipping any mention of the murder in Berlin, which he guessed the Italians weren't too likely to care about.

A tall, thin man in his mid-thirties met them at the ministry. He introduced himself as Pascal La Rota, the magistrate who specialized in the Naples-area mafia. He had a military air—close-cropped hair, wide chest, and a nose that seemed to have been broken when he was a young man. He offered the two Americans *caffè*—in Italy, this meant espresso—then began looking at the evidence Nuri had brought along.

In the Italian justice system, a magistrate was closer to an American district attorney than a judge. They had a wide range of investigative powers and could be extremely unpleasant when crossed. Those who worked in the antimafia commission were reputed to be among the toughest in the nation—or the craziest.

La Rota impressed Nuri as neither. His manner was mild, almost studious. He put on a pair of glasses and began reading the information Nuri had brought, while Gregor spooned sugar into her coffee.

MY-PID had collected ships' manifests and various information on different shipments connected to Alfredo's empire. It showed that a middle-level heroin dealer in Florence who supplied a British network received yearly deposits into an Austrian bank account from one of Alfredo's companies. It connected a truck stopped at the French border with a hundred kilos of heroin to another of Alfredo's firms. And best of all, it included the transcripts of three phone calls between Alfredo and two contacts in Iran referring to shipments of flowers, which circumstantial evidence indicated was a code word for heroin.

The transcripts were clearly the smoking gun, a direct link between the mobster and the drugs. They had been recorded nearly eighteen months before, as part of an NSA program collecting raw intelligence from Iran. But they weren't of sufficient priority for even a computer transcription, let alone to trigger a human review. MY-PID had found them listed along with three thousand other files that it judged *might* have a connection to the heroin trade and Italy, and had done the brute translation work itself.

As valuable as they were, they proved a sticking point for La Rota.

"Interesting," he said, leafing through the papers. His English was good enough that he could read the summary sheet in the original without referring to the translation that had been prepared for him. "But, as far as this is concerned for evidence—I must tell you, Italian laws are very strict about wiretaps."

"When they want to be," said Gregor.

Nuri shot her a glare he hoped would laser a hole through the side of her head. He'd told her to say absolutely nothing.

A smile flickered in La Rota's long, pale face, and the hairs in his thin goatee rustled. But his tone was almost scolding.

"Whatever you and I may think of the law," he said, focusing on Nuri, "we must observe it."

"True," said Nuri. "Which is why the Libyan

government filed its own indictments. The conversations were recorded in its jurisdiction."

He unfolded a letter from the Libyan justice ministry indicating not only interest in the case, but promising that an arrest warrant would be issued by the appropriate authorities by the end of the day.

In Libyan time, "end of the day" meant within the next three months, a fact La Rota was clearly aware of.

"I have dealt with the Libyans before," he told Nuri. "On several occasions."

La Rota took off his glasses and began cleaning them.

"Still, this is very persuasive," he told Nuri. "I believe I will be able to get my superiors to consider action on its basis."

"I thought you were in charge," said Nuri.

"Oh I am, of course."

"Then can't you authorize a raid?"

The magistrate blanched. "A raid?"

"A visit, I mean," said Nuri. "An interview. To speak to Mr. Moreno?"

"You don't understand the situation, I'm afraid. One does not simply speak to Mr. Moreno."

"Arrest him, then."

"Perhaps we will be able to do that," said La Rota. "Once the commission reviews the evidence."

"How long will this review last?" asked Gregor.

Nuri glared at Gregor again, even though he would have asked the question himself had she not interrupted.

"A while," said La Rota indulgently.

"That's how long?"

"It is very difficult to predict."

"By the end of the day?" said Nuri, as suggestively as he could.

"A day? For something like this?" La Rota laughed.

"Not next week," said Nuri hopefully.

"Oh no, not next week. Something like this—a case has to be made. The way must be prepared."

"You're talking months," said Gregor.

La Rota held out his hands in a gesture that meant *if that*.

"Is there any way to speed up the process?" Nuri asked.

"Usually not."

"What if he murdered someone?" asked Gregor.

"Oh, I'm sure a man like Alfredo Moreno has been responsible for murdering many people," answered La Rota. "You would be surprised. These men are animals. They murder for pleasure, for business, for many reasons."

"If it was an important murder, in a prominent case?" said Nuri, grasping at straws.

"In that case, perhaps by July."

"I TOLD YOU THE ITALIANS WERE IMPOSSIBLE TO DEAL with," said Gregor as they walked out of the building. "It's a complete waste of time."

The FBI agent had said no such thing—just the opposite in fact: she'd expressed optimism that they would be inside Moreno's compound by nightfall. But Nuri was in no mood to argue.

"We can interview him ourselves," she continued. "I can get someone from the local office to act as a translator—"

"We're not interviewing him," said Nuri sharply.

"You're just going to drop it?"

"It's not my call," said Nuri noncommittally.

He nodded at the Italian policeman at the foot of the steps of the justice building, then walked in the direction of their car. One thing he had to say for the Italians—they didn't skimp when it came to police stations. The ministry was a veritable palace, with an exterior as grand as anything Nuri had ever seen in the States.

"We can arrest him on an American warrant," said Gregor. "I can arrange—"

"You and what army?" said Nuri.

Gregor had made quite a lot of progress in less than eight hours—first she was a wet blanket, now she was Wyatt Earp.

Nuri had rented a small Fiat, which put him uncomfortably close to the FBI agent once they got inside the car. She smelled as if she'd had salami for lunch.

"I'll drop you off at the airport," he said, programming the GPS. "You want Euro C, right?"

"Let's drive there," said Gregor. "It will only take us a few hours. We can scout it out."

"No, I have to get back to Berlin," said Nuri. "There are a few more things to check out up there."

"Drop me off at a rental place, then," said Gregor.

Had she guessed what he was up to and called his bluff? Or was she really intending on going there herself?

Either way, he couldn't take the chance of her interfering.

"I don't think it's a good idea to just drive around the estate," said Nuri. "Don't you have to clear your activities with your Rome office?"

"Not on this. My boss gave me carte blanche."

Nuri wracked his brain for ways to keep her at bay. He drew a blank.

"I'll tell you what," said Gregor. "I'll go with you to the airport and rent the car there. You have to turn this one in, right?"

"What would you do?"

"I give them a credit card—"

"What would you do with Moreno?" snapped Nuri.

"I'll just talk to him," she said.

"No one will ever see you again," said Nuri.

"I've dealt with these types of cases before," said Gregor. "And with people like Moreno. They're so full of themselves that they're easy pickings. They think the law doesn't apply to them, so they ignore the most basic precautions."

"I'd figure a guy like this would have his guards shoot first and ask questions later," said Nuri.

"They're not going to shoot a lost tourist."

"Maybe I will go," he said, finally giving up. "Just to see what the hell his place looks like."

"I thought you had a lot to do," said Gregor with mock innocence. It wasn't bad enough that she won—she had to rub it in.

"Yeah," said Nuri. "See if you can program the address into the GPS so we can at least find out what highway to take."

9

Kiev, Ukraine

"PURPOSE OF VISIT?"

"Tourism."

"How long are you staying?"

"A week."

The Ukrainian customs official inspected Danny's passport, flipping it back and forth in his hand to make sure the holographic symbols were displayed. Danny and the others were traveling with standard passports rather than using diplomatic cover, trying to maintain as low a profile as possible.

Sally McEwen had warned him that their entry at Boryspil Airport, about eighteen miles east of Kiev, would almost surely be recorded by the Ukrainian secret service, which was still run like an offshoot of the KGB. A video camera above the passport control desk was undoubtedly taping him, while the clerk's computer was running a check against his name. The Ukrainian technology was relatively old, however, and even if Danny was flagged as a suspicious American, it would take weeks for a file to be prepared with his photo. By then the operation would be over.

It was possible they would tell the Ukrainians that they were here. But for the moment the Ukrainians weren't to be trusted. No one was. It was the old CIA prejudice—we don't exist, and if we do exist, which we don't, you never heard of us.

Danny's own prejudice was the opposite: be

honest and tell people what was going on. It was a military mind-set.

"Enjoy Ukraine," said the customs clerk, handing his passport back.

Danny saw McEwen and Hera waiting a short distance beyond the stations.

"How'd you guys get through so fast?" he asked.

"You have to pick the right line," said McEwen. "But it helps to look like a little old lady."

"The secret to your success," said Hera.

"Don't be jealous, dear."

There were two rentals waiting for them at Hertz, so-called mid-sized Fords, which would have been considered subcompacts back in the States. Hera rode with McEwen, while Danny followed. McEwen might have been old, but she drove with a lead foot—he lost her before they'd gone two miles, and had to use MY-PID's GPS to find the hotel. By the time he got there, the two women had already checked in.

"Ready for a tour?" McEwen asked as Danny finished registering.

"Love to," he said. "Give me a minute."

The hotel was in an old building in the business district. While the facade was boring and plain, the interior had been renovated recently and the place still smelled of paint. The design mixed old-style plaster details with occasional chrome and sleek marble. It wasn't retro and it wasn't modern, but it somehow caught Kiev's spirit, at least as espoused by the chamber of commerce: "The future building on the past, moving ahead with expediency."

More than three million people lived in Kiev, making it one of Europe's largest cities. Besides being the capital of Ukraine, it was looked on as the center of opposition to the Russian bear, both politically and culturally, the counter to Moscow's notoriously heavy hand. That had both good and bad aspects—while it helped draw a vibrant class of artists and entrepreneurs, it also made it the focus of Russian resentments. There was a sizable Russian spy network in the city, McEwen warned; they should always proceed under the theory that they were being watched or about to be watched.

The city was slightly cooler than Washington had been, though not unpleasantly so; the average high for May was just under 70 Fahrenheit, and though it was still only mid-morning, the temperature had just topped 72. Danny could have gone around in shirtsleeves, but took his light leather jacket, where it was easier to keep his MY-PID.

The NATO meeting was to be held in the Kiev Fortress, a historic complex near the center of the city. A good portion of the fortress had been turned into a museum, open to the public; the rest consisted of government buildings. McEwen started there, taking them on a quick tour of the general area, driving Lesi Ukrainky Boulevard, a thick artery that paralleled the Dnieper River on the city's western half.

The road had just been paved, and unlike most of the city's streets, was smooth and pothole free. It was tree-lined, with an island through much of the middle; driving down it, Danny got the impression of an area that was sophisticated but slightly sleepy, as if it still belonged to the early nineteenth century. This was in contrast to the rest of the city, which over the past two or three years had undergone rapid growth. New buildings were everywhere along the river.

McEwen was surprised by the amount of change that had occurred in the past twelve or thirteen months; she kept marveling at the different buildings she said had sprung up since she last visited.

"We can take a tour of the fort tomorrow," the CIA officer recommended. "It'll be better to see the general layout of the city first, and set up some of the logistics. We need a place to operate out of."

"What's wrong with the hotel we just checked into?" asked Danny.

"What's the expression, Colonel?" said McEwen. "You don't shit where you live."

Hera laughed. "Do you kiss your grandkids with that mouth?"

"I don't have any grandkids. Or children, for that matter. We're going to want a place convenient to the museum where you can have people coming and going," added McEwen. "Someplace where a half-dozen Americans wouldn't seem odd."

"Minnesota would be perfect," said Hera.

"That might be a little far," said Danny. He hadn't remembered Hera being so jovial on their last mission, and she was downright taciturn at home. But she'd clearly taken a liking to McEwen.

"I know someone who owns a restaurant in that row of buildings there," McEwen told him, pointing to a row of one-story storefronts. "It's not a very popular place, which is a positive for us. We could probably use their back room. For a price, of course."

"You trust them?" asked Danny.

"To an extent. Never trust anyone, Colonel. Not with your life."

McEwen took them over, parking along the street about a block away. Danny saw instantly why she liked the area—it had a view of the museum's entrance, but seemed somehow invisible to it, or at least to the tourists who were mostly arriving by bus. There were four other storefronts; two were empty, and the other belonged to a tailor whom McEwen said only worked on Tuesdays and Thursdays.

It was just about dinnertime, but the restaurant had only two customers—a young man and woman with backpacks—who sat at a table next to the large plate-glass window in the front. They were staring at the menu as Danny and the others passed outside, talking in whispered tones as they came in.

If the place had ever had a heyday, this wasn't it. The tables and chairs were made of wood and looked to be about thirty or forty years old, their finish worn down by use, though the thick legs looked and felt sturdy enough. The walls were painted a yellow that had probably been bright when fresh but was now a kind of dull backdrop to the assorted paintings of Kiev that hung across them in a straight line, almost frame-to-frame, on both sides of the room. The paintings were in a variety of styles, by different artists, but were all the same size. They showed different landmarks in the city, along with a few from the countryside.

A waitress came out of the back. Dressed in a light blue skirt with a checkered blue and white blouse, she was twelve or thirteen, just at the age between child and young woman. About five-two, a little chubby, and nearsighted, she squinted when she saw them, pushing her head forward on her neck as if she were a gopher coming out of her hole.

Then she squealed.

"*Sal!*" she said, rushing toward them. "How are you?"

McEwen folded her arms around the girl. She said something in Ukrainian. The girl replied, then stepping back, said in English that she must only speak English.

"My English has became bad since I haven't saw you," said the girl. "I have to practice."

"Of course we'll practice," said McEwen. "These are my friends," she added, gesturing toward Danny and Hera. "Can we get something to eat?"

"Of course. Wait—mama is in the back."

"Sit," McEwen told Danny and Hera. She pulled out a chair, but instead of sitting, went over to the young couple in the front of the room. Danny watched as she asked them, in English, if they were having trouble with the menu, which was in Ukrainian. By the time the cook emerged from the back, she had made several recommendations and told them how to pronounce what they wanted.

The cook was a slightly larger version of the waitress. Her large red cheeks were puffed with a smile. She had flour on her forearms and just a daub of it in her hair. Her white apron, which was pulled so tight against her body it looked as if it would burst, was spotless.

"Sal, Sal, so long we've not seen you!" she said.

They embraced.

McEwen introduced them. The cook was the owner; her name sounded like "Nezalehno" to Danny. She promised to fix them a nice dinner, then disappeared with the waitress into the back.

"You're everybody's friend," said Danny.

"That's my job," answered McEwen. "Or it was."

"Can we trust them?"

"I keep telling you—we don't trust anyone. Not completely. But yes, to the extent we trust anyone." She lowered her voice. "Her husband died shortly after Kira was born. Kira's our waitress. She's the youngest of eight children."

"Eight?"

"They all worked here, at one time or another," said McEwen before continuing her explanation. "The father was killed in an auto accident with a man who turned out to be a Russian army major in the city on unofficial business. He seems to have been drunk at the time. It wasn't clear exactly what he was doing, but the end result was that he went back to Russia, and no compensation was paid to the widow. There was no trial, of course. So, Nexi and her family don't particularly like Russians."

"And they need money," said Danny.

"You're catching on, Colonel. But they're nice people besides. If I could pick someone to help, and who could help me—Nez would be a perfect fit."

"Are some of those yours?" Hera asked, pointing to the paintings.

"The one all the way to the right, over there," said McEwen, beaming.

"You had a lot of time to paint when you were here?" asked Danny.

"It was part of the job," said McEwen. "A way to meet different people, to circulate. It makes you uncomfortable, doesn't it, Colonel?"

"Painting?"

"It doesn't fit with your stereotype of what a spy does. And I don't look like one. That's what you're thinking," she said, her voice just loud enough for Danny to hear. "People get certain notions in their head, and they operate on them without really examining them. They feel a certain way about something before they even have a chance to experience it or see it. And that preconception colors everything. So you don't think that an old lady who paints—*paints!*—could possibly be gathering intelligence, persuading people to betray their country, or at least help another one. Right?"

"I guess."

"Who better to be a spy?"

AFTER THEY ATE, DANNY HAD MCEWEN TAKE THEM around to different hotels where she thought the Wolves might stay if they needed to rent rooms. The hotels were third and fourth tier establishments, places Ukrainians on a budget or small businessmen paying their own way might stay. The staffs, while friendly, spoke limited English. Asking about a concierge would have made them laugh. There were dozens of such places in the city, and keeping them under complete surveillance would have been impossible, even with MY-PID's help.

"We could plant a video bug near each entrance," suggested Hera. "That would give us at least some idea of who's going in and out."

"That might work," said Danny.

"If you don't mind my saying, Colonel, I'm not sure video surveillance would be anything more than a shot in the dark," said McEwen. "And it could even work against us."

"Against us how?"

"We can't possibly cover every place. They could stay outside of the city just as easily as in. Putting the video bugs in might give us a false sense of security—we'd focus on those sights."

"Good point," said Danny.

"I'm not suggesting we ignore them entirely, but if we have limited resources . . ."

"Where would we put the bugs?"

"The airport for starters. Train station. Obviously the area around the fort. If we have bugs left over, then we can think about the hotels. If I was planning some sort of action here," McEwen continued, "then I would be casing the area. That's the person we should look for. The team that would do the assassination wouldn't be here yet."

"When would they come?"

"Not until the day before. Maybe not even until that day. Unless there was a reason for it."

Danny nodded. He wasn't comfortable with the espionage aspects of the mission. Covert action tended to be relatively straightforward, even when extremely difficult—here's the target, hit it.

This was considerably more nebulous—find assassins whom no one knows, stop them from killing anyone, and then apprehend them.

This wasn't a classic Whiplash mission, he thought.

Then again, what was the classic Whiplash mission? He was thinking about the old days, when everything seemed more straightforward. This was the *new* Whiplash, in a much more complicated world. Alliances shifted every day, technology improved seemingly by the second.

Maybe he was just a little too old to keep up.

But age seemed like a ludicrous idea with McEwen around. She was as enthusiastic and energetic as Hera.

They continued on their tour of the city, driving by the U.S. embassy and Ukrainian government buildings, walking through Maidan Nzalezhnosti, the square and monument in the city center, and getting more of a feel for the place. McEwen was just about to take them on the metro when Danny's sat phone rang.

It was Nuri.

"I ran into a roadblock with the Italians," Nuri told him. "They say it'll be months before we can get in to talk to this mafia guy, Moreno. By that time, any data will be off his computer."

"How much did you tell them?"

"Enough to put him away for life."

"And they still won't move?"

"They'll move. They may even arrest him. But it'll be at Italian pace. Next year or so. I have another idea."

"Shoot."

"I want to go into the estate and steal the computer."

"What happens if you're caught?"

"Bad things," replied Nuri. "I'll just have to make sure I don't get caught."

"You need backup?"

"I can handle it. I talked to Reid and we'll have real-time infrared surveillance, so I'll know where everybody is."

Danny checked his watch.

"Flash is flying in from the States with a layover in Frankfurt," he told Nuri. "If I can get ahold of him, we might be able to change his plans and get him down to Naples tonight."

"All right. I like Flash."

Flash was John "Flash" Gordon, a former Special Forces soldier who'd teamed with Nuri during their first mission. He tended to be quiet and efficient—a rare but winning combination.

"Hera and I can come out as well," Danny added. He glanced at his watch. "We may not be able to get there until tomorrow, though."

"It's OK. It's not a hard job. I checked the place out. There are only two guards around the perimeter. The guy lives like a prince," added Nuri. "But he's way overconfident. Everyone's so scared of him nobody even tries to get up there. I'm sure the house is wired, but it shouldn't be too hard to get inside. There's only one slight complication."

"How slight?"

"The FBI is helping me."

Just from Nuri's tone, Danny understood that wasn't a good thing.

"Is that going to be a problem?"

"Only if I kill her. But it may be worth it."

10

Outside of Naples, Italy

As a CIA officer, Nuri was generally in the habit of getting other people to do his dirty work. Things like breaking into a mafia chieftain's home, bugging his office and his computers, were considerably safer when done by someone other than himself. But such arrangements took time, and in this case might very well be impossible. Besides, Nuri liked going places where he wasn't supposed to be. And this place didn't look nearly as well protected as it could have been.

He had done a few similar jobs before. As long as he didn't get caught—admittedly a singular caveat—they were relatively straightforward. He'd sneak in, sprinkle a few bugs in strategic places, kick on the computer and load a virus that would dump all of its information to a Room 4 server the next time it accessed the Internet. Bypassing the computer's security protocols was child's play, and if there was a local area network, it was easy to scoop everything up from a single computer.

To get to the computer he had to get into the estate, but that wouldn't be difficult either. A Reaper drone would provide real-time imaging through MY-PID, telling Nuri where the two outside guards were with the help of a synthetic imaging radar. The radar could penetrate the earth to roughly one hundred feet; it would have no trouble seeing into the house. The aircraft also had a small cesium magnetometer and an electronic field sensor aboard; the devices were sensitive enough to detect burglar alarms and computers, even when off—in effect telling Nuri not only what to avoid, but where to go.

Vineyards and olive groves surrounded the estate on three sides. A small booth near the top of the driveway about two hundred feet from the house looked to be the only permanent guard post. The two men who watched the place came out of the hut every thirty to forty minutes. Though their schedule was unpredictable, their route wasn't: one walked around the house to the west, one went east. They met at the back veranda, continuing onward back to the hut.

Approaching through the eastern olive grove would be the easiest; hedges blocked most of the view from the post, and a pair of farm buildings near the house would make for a natural jumping off point.

The house was an old stone structure, at least six or seven hundred years old. It had three stories aboveground and one below. A portico ran along the east and north of the building, a kind of two-story porch flanking the kitchen and main living area. A pool was located on the northwestern side. Nuri wouldn't know where the office was until the Reaper made its first overflight, but he suspected it was somewhere on the second floor, very possibly near the mafioso's bedroom.

Or in it.

Given that possibility, he decided he wasn't going to let insomnia jeopardize his mission: he armed himself with several syringes of an etomidate derivative, a powerful anesthetic that would put Moreno into a deep slumber almost instantaneously.

He was tempted to use one to get rid of Gregor. She clung to him like glue when he went to Naples International Airport, Ugo Niutta, to pick up Flash and the gear he needed, which had been flown in from the States via the Aviano air base.

In one breath she would say she didn't want to do anything illegal, in the next she would ask how they were getting onto the estate. Nuri kept the details to himself. He didn't need her, now that Flash was with him. The question was how to ease her from the picture.

A cliff would have done nicely.

Flash was flying on a diplomatic passport, and brought in a "pouch" of weapons and backup com gear. "Pouch" was a diplomatic misnomer—it was actually a small metal crate, securely locked. To carry it, they had to each take a handle at the side and walk out to the car.

"You could open the trunk for us," Nuri grunted to Gregor as they approached the rented Fiat.

"You didn't give me the keys," she said.

True, but somehow it felt like it was her fault. They packed up the car, then went off for something to eat.

Flash had been in the Army for just over ten years before deciding to work with a private security contractor. That gig, three months in an African hellhole, hadn't worked out the way he had hoped. He told Nuri in Iran that he'd spent his time guarding the brother of an African "president"—aka dictator for life. The man had a thing for guns, and liked to fire them at all hours of the night, and not always in appropriate places or directions. This wouldn't have been so bad if Flash had been paid as promised. In the end he had to take matters into his own hands, bartering for his pay—diamonds for his employer's life.

This might have complicated Flash's future, except for the fact that the president was overthrown a week after Flash left the country. He and his brother were executed by the new government. Flash held a private memorial service at a bar he liked in Oklahoma. He was the only attendee.

Nuri found a small restaurant on the outskirts of the city, far enough away from the crowded, medieval streets at the center of town where he could park the car without having to watch it. He was fluent in Italian—he'd spent some of his childhood here—and took charge of the ordering, sticking to basic spaghetti so heartburn wouldn't be a factor later on.

"So what's our plan?" asked Gregor after the waiter left.

"Eat," said Nuri.

"I mean later."

"The plan is, you go into the city, find a nice hotel with a good bar, and wait for us."

"That's it?"

"That's it."

The waiter returned with water and bread. The inside of the bread looked almost gray in the restaurant's dim light.

"I'm not going to a hotel," said Gregor.

"You don't want to do anything illegal, right?"

"You don't need backup?"

Flash stayed quiet, slowly sipping the water.

"What happens if something goes wrong when you break in?" asked Gregor. "Who's going to rescue you?"

"You're not coming in with me," Nuri told her. "Flash isn't either. This is a one-man gig."

"Your radio tells you what to do?" said Gregor. She was apparently referring to the MY-PID control device.

"No," said Nuri, a little louder than he wanted. He recalibrated his voice as he continued. "No one is telling me what to do. Flash is going to liaison between the Reaper and me. He'll be near the estate, down the hill."

"Who's going to watch his back while he's watching yours?"

"Here comes the spaghetti," said Flash, glancing at the waiter.

Nuri considered what to do while the waiter put down the platter of pasta and served family style. Gregor might be helpful; in any event, it was safer to keep her with them than have her in the city if he couldn't trust where she'd end up. Most likely she wouldn't screw him up, but there was always that distant chance that might come back to bite him.

"If you do exactly what Flash says," Nuri told her once the waiter retreated to the kitchen, "you can watch his back."

He thought he saw a look of pain pass over Flash's face, but maybe it was just a reaction to the spaghetti.

"It won't be illegal, right?" asked Gregor.

"If it is," deadpanned Flash between bites, "we're blaming it on you."

NURI'S MOTHER'S SIDE OF THE FAMILY CAME FROM Sicily, and counted a number of relatives with low-level associations with the Men of Respect, as the mafia was generally known there. The Sicilians and the Neapolitans got along only rarely, but they were alike enough as a general species for Nuri to form a sound dossier on what Moreno would be like: brutal in his dealings with the outside world, but completely complacent and lazy within the confines of what he considered his safe and untouchable haven. Calling him full of himself wouldn't begin to describe him. It was very likely that the two men watching his estate were related to him, drawing the assignment as a kind of family work program.

The Reaper was due to come on station precisely at midnight. Nuri wanted to be ready to get into the house by then; that would give him plenty of time to get in and out before dawn. If things went well, in fact, he should be out before the last bars closed.

The first sign of a complication came when he drove up the town road to familiarize Flash with the area. It was a little past eleven, and the few people who lived in the hamlet had long since retired; there were no lights on in any of the buildings. But as he drove toward the turnoff for Moreno's estate, he saw a dark Mercedes E class sedan parked in the center of the road. Nuri slowed down but didn't stop.

"Two guys inside," said Flash, who was sitting in the passenger seat. "Didn't look too friendly."

"They weren't there earlier," said Gregor.

"Is there another way up?" asked Flash.

"That's the only road. But we can get up there through the vineyards down around the bend here. Just a longer walk, that's all."

Nuri drove down the road, showing Flash how the road cut into the side of the hill. The old monastery was to their right, just below the vineyards. They could stash the car near the ruins.

"You two wait here," Nuri told Flash after pulling down the dirt driveway that led to the ruins. "I want to see if I can figure out what's going on. I'll sneak back behind the car and see if I can pick up anything from their conversations."

"You sure you don't want backup?" asked Flash.

"It won't be a problem. One is quieter than two. Test your radio and make sure we have a good signal."

Nuri got out of the car. He put on his Gen 4

night glasses, fixing the strap at the back of his head. While the glasses were slightly more powerful than the generation 3 glasses that were standard issue in the military, their real value was in their size—they were only a little thicker than swimming goggles, and weighed barely a pound.

Nuri rolled down the thin wire that ran from the right side of the goggles and plugged it into the MY-PID control unit, allowing the computer system to see what he was seeing. He checked his pistol—a Beretta fitted with a laser-dot pointer and a silencer—then did a quick check of the rest of his gear in the fanny pack he had around his waist. He'd taken a small can of mace and two of the hyperemic needles, but in truth he knew if he needed either, he might just as well use the gun.

He walked a few yards farther up the hill, moving through the trees as he approached the intersection where the guards were.

He was about fifty feet away when the dome light inside the Mercedes came on. He held his breath and went down to one knee as a Fiat approached from the main road. Reaching into his pocket, he took out a small microphone that was tuned to gather sounds from a distance. His fingers fumbled as he connected it to the radio headset.

The guard who'd been sitting in the passenger seat of the Mercedes got out and walked to the Fiat as it stopped. Nuri tuned his mike, but the Fiat's muffler was broken and the car drowned out whatever they were saying.

The guard straightened and waved. Nuri froze, sure that the man was waving at him. But he was only signaling his companion in the Mercedes, who backed out of the way to let the Fiat pass.

He strained to see into the car as it passed but couldn't see through the bushes.

"Computer, identify the occupants of the car."

"Query: which vehicle?"

"The Fiat."

"Unknown. One occupant. Driver. Unidentified female."

"Female?"

"Affirmative."

The Mercedes resumed its position blocking the road. The man who'd gotten out walked back over to the passenger side and got in.

"Can you identify the man who just got into the Mercedes?" Nuri asked the computer.

"Negative. Subject is approximately thirty years old. European extraction. Six feet three inches tall. Appears armed with a handgun in a holster beneath his jacket."

Nuri angled to his right, trying to get a better line of sight on the intersection when they stopped another car. He settled into another clump of brush about twenty feet from the road and waited.

Ten minutes later a second car came up the road. This one was a Ford. He had a clear view into the windshield, despite the headlights. There were two women in the front seat; the back seemed empty.

The driver rolled down the window as the guard approached. The two women were laughing, giggling.

"The party," she said in Italian.

The guard waved the Mercedes out of the way, and the car passed. Nuri retreated back to the old ruins.

BY THE TIME THE REAPER WAS ON STATION, THERE WERE a dozen people at the estate. Most were by the pool, though there were two in front of the house, near the cars. Nuri assumed they were guards and that the others were revelers.

"We'll wait for them to get good and loaded," he told Flash.

"How long is that?" asked Flash.

"Couple of hours."

"You're gonna wait that long?" asked Gregor.

"I can wait as long as I have to."

AT TWO-FIFTEEN NURI DECIDED HE'D WAITED LONG enough. "All right, we'll go up together," he told the others. "We'll go up to that hedge line near the house. You guys wait for me there while I go in. *Capisce?*"

"We got it," said Flash.

"Anything you say," said Gregor.

"No questions," added Nuri.

"No questions," she said.

They got out and started up the hill, moving easily through the vineyards.

"Nice goggles," said Gregor. "They're starlight goggles, right? Cat's eyes."

"You weren't going to ask any questions," said Nuri sharply.

"Oh come on. That was harmless."

"I could strangle you here and no one would ever know," snapped Nuri.

Just as they were approaching the barns, MY-PID warned that a woman was coming down in their direction from the house. Nuri stopped at the edge of the vineyard, waiting to see where she was going. A minute or so later one of the guards slipped from the guard house, a good ten minutes earlier than the normal schedule dictated. He walked in her direction; they met in a small garden about thirty yards from the house, whispering before finding each other in the moonlit shadows.

"They'll be busy for a while," Nuri told Flash. "I'm going to circle around. Watch what's going on with the MY-PID screen and let me know."

"Got it."

A few minutes later Nuri felt short of breath as he pulled himself onto the portico at the eastern end of the house. He knelt near one of the columns, catching his breath. Using the data from the Reaper, MY-PID had analyzed the circuitry inside the house and deduced that there were no alarm systems. It had also located the office on the western side of the house. He moved around the back, working his way toward the office.

Large French windows lined the exterior rooms on the first floor. He passed a large dining room and a living room before coming to the edge of the house.

Music was playing in the back; it was an Italian version of hip-hop, an odd blend of rhythms. Nuri slipped down to the bottom of the wall and peeked around. There were two or three girls in the pool, splashing each other and drinking out of champagne glasses. A man, presumably Moreno, was floating on a raft, his back to Nuri.

Let's go, Nuri told himself. *Get it on.*

He moved back to the French door and tried pulling it open. It was locked. A thin shiv took care of the simple latch, and it gave way easily. He slipped in behind the light curtains, walking into the mafioso's lair.

He got three feet when he heard the dog coming.

"Son of a bitch," he muttered. "Nobody told me about dogs."

11

Chisinau, Moldova

THE THIRST WAS OVERWHELMING. HIS WHOLE BODY ached. His hands shook. He curled his fingers into a fist and put them under his legs. He tightened his stare at the woman at the desk across from his chair near the door to the examining rooms and offices inside.

The drugs. He needed the drugs.

The clinic waiting room was nearly full. He willed the other patients away. The doctor had to see him now.

Now!

An intercom buzzed at the desk.

"Mrs. Gestau?" said the receptionist, looking down the list of patients. "Dr. Nudstrumov will see you now."

A middle-aged woman sitting near him got up. She walked as close to the opposite wall as possible, clearly sensing his displeasure that she had been called ahead of him.

He waited a few more seconds. They seemed like hours. He had to do something. He leaned forward—then got up, practically rolling into motion.

"When am I going in?" he said to the woman at the desk.

"The doctor is very busy today. But I'm sure as soon as—"

He didn't need to hear the rest. He stepped to his left and pushed through the door. The hallway seemed darker than normal, the walls closer together. Very close—they seemed to push against his shoulders as he strode toward the doctor's office at the end of the hall.

"Wait!" the receptionist called behind him. "Wait—you can't just barge in here. Wait!"

Her voice fell back into a deep pit far behind him. He stopped at the first examining room, threw open the door. A man in his sixties sat on the examining table in his underwear, feet dangling off the side.

The doctor wasn't there. He turned and walked to the next room.

"Stop!" said a nurse. "What are you doing?"

"It's OK," said Dr. Nudstrumov, appearing at

the end of the hall. "I was just going to send for Herr Schmidt."

"The examining rooms are full," said the receptionist.

"Herr Schmidt and I can use my office."

"Yes, Doctor."

"Herr Schmidt, please," said the doctor, extending his arm. "So good to see you today."

He walked into the office. Without waiting for an invitation, he pulled off his shirt.

"You're shaking," said the doctor, closing the door behind him. "It's getting worse."

"Give it to me," he said tightly.

"A year ago you only needed the shots every six months. Now it is every six weeks."

"I don't care to hear my entire medical history."

"I suppose not."

The doctor took a stethoscope from the pocket of his lab coat. The coat seemed almost gray, though he knew that the doctor habitually wore them bright and freshly starched.

"My heart is fine."

"I'm listening to your lungs," said Dr. Nudstrumov, an edge creeping into his voice. He was in his sixties, short and bald. He'd gained a considerable amount of weight in the decade and a half since they had known each other, to the point that he was now fat, rather than skinny.

But that was the least of the changes. He'd gone through several different names, so many that even the Black Wolf didn't know which was real. He even used "corporate" names—common aliases that were supposed to belong only to the Wolves.

"Breathe, please."

He took a deep breath and held it.

"Again . . . one more time."

"Enough with the damn breathing!" he yelled, slapping the doctor's stethoscope away. "Give me the shots!"

The doctor stepped back, surprised, frightened.

Where did the bastard keep the drugs? He could get them himself.

He needed the serum, and the pills. The pills were for every day; the injections lasted longer.

There were other doctors who would supply him; he knew there were. It was only because of the perverse machinations of the Directors that he had to come to Nudstrumov.

A reminder of who was in control. As if he needed one.

Dr. Nudstrumov stepped over to his desk and pulled open the bottom drawer. He placed a metal case on the top of his desk and opened it. There were three hypodermic needles inside.

"Roll up your sleeve, please," he said, taking one of the needles.

There was a knock on the door.

"Everything is fine," said the doctor. "Please see to the patients."

"Doctor?" said one of the nurses.

"It's fine. Please see to the patients."

The doctor took a small antiseptic wipe and cleaned a spot on his arm. A second later the long, thick needle plunged through his skin.

Warmth began spreading through his body immediately. By the time the third shot had been administered, he was back to his old self.

Not his old, old self, whatever that was. Back to what passed for normal now.

The doctor said nothing for a few minutes, returning the needles to the box, then tossing his gloves into a waste can at the side of the room.

"Do you think about the changes?" the doctor asked, sitting down.

"I don't think at all."

"The progression. It's a downward slope. There's going to come a point . . ."

Dr. Nudstrumov's voice trailed off. He stared at the man he knew by many names, though he called him only Herr Schmidt.

"Do you shake when you take the pills?" the doctor asked finally.

"They have no effect."

"I'm going to give you something to calm the shakes, and the pain." Dr. Nudstrumov pulled over his prescription pad. "It's not—it won't have the effect on your metabolism that the shots have. It won't restore you. But when you feel things getting bad, you can have some relief. It's a sedative. You should be careful driving."

He took the prescription without comment.

"I remember that first week," said the doctor, his voice tinged with nostalgia and pride. "How we had to fight to keep you alive."

"I don't appreciate your sentimentality," said the Black Wolf, rising and striding toward the door.

12

Fuggire, Italy

NURI HAD BARELY ENOUGH TIME TO PULL OUT THE MACE as the dog charged into the room, saliva lathering from its mouth. His fingers were misaligned and much of the spray shot sideways. The dog's teeth clamped around his left arm.

Nuri sprayed again, then smacked the dog in the snout. The animal let go, howling.

Off balance, he grabbed at the animal and fell to the side, tumbling against an upholstered chair. He reached into the fanny pack for one of the syringes. The dog tried to push itself away, snarling and shaking its head, crying, disoriented, and hurting at the same time.

It was a large mastiff. More pet than watchdog, it lacked a true killer's instinct—fortunately for him. He grabbed a syringe, pulled the plastic guard off with his teeth and plunged the needle into the animal's rump.

It whimpered, then crumpled over on its side.

Nuri swung his legs under him and grabbed for his pistol, sure the commotion would bring one of the mafia don's guards in any second. He could feel his heart pounding in his throat.

He heard something squeaking behind him. He spun quickly before realizing the noise was coming from the earphone, which had fallen out.

No one was coming, or if they were, they were taking their time.

"What's going on?" hissed Flash.

"I'm OK," said Nuri.

"What happened? I heard you grunting."

"There was a dog."

"MY-PID didn't say anything about it."

"Are you looking at the image?"

"This screen is so small—I can see it now."

"Tell the computer it has to scan for dogs—for anything living," said Nuri, realizing he'd been too precise when he gave it the earlier instructions. "It's only looking for people."

"Shit."

Nuri looked down. As powerful as the gear aboard the Reaper was, it had its limits.

This was why you always got someone else to do the dirty work, he reminded himself. He got down on his hands and knees, searching for the cap to the syringe. He found it under a marble table. He stuffed it back into his fanny pack, then pulled the dog under the table.

The scent of mace was pretty heavy on the animal, and undoubtedly in the room. There was nothing he could do about it now, he told himself.

Change your plan. Grab the computer and get the hell out. Now!

Nuri got to his feet and walked quickly to the door, pausing near the opening. The music was loud enough to vibrate the floor slightly—a good thing, he thought, slipping down the hall.

The hall led to an outside patio above the pool. Along the way there were two rooms on the right; the office was farther down on the left.

Neither of the doors on the right were closed. Nuri leaned in, glancing around. Both were richly furnished bedrooms. No computers, no people, and most importantly, no dogs.

The office was on the left. The door was locked.

A good sign, he thought.

Until Flash warned him that someone was coming from the pool toward the door.

He slipped back to the first open room on the right, just ducking out of the way as the outside door opened. It was one of the girls; he heard her humming to herself as she walked past him down the hall.

"Coast is clear," said Flash.

Nuri started out of the room, then stopped as he heard the humming get louder. He slipped back, waiting for the girl to pass. She seemed to take forever, changing her song three times before finally coming past.

He waited another two or three minutes before easing toward the door again. Once more he had to stop mid stride as MY-PID alerted him that another girl was coming in. He stepped back against the wall a few feet from the threshold, holding his breath until she passed—then holding it again as she came back and went outside.

The long day had started to wear on him. He crossed the corridor, mentally cursing everyone— the Italians, the bureaucracy, Gregor, Moreno, even himself. Damned if he wouldn't have been better just shooting his stinking way inside the compound. The hell with the goddamn Italians and their corrupt justice system, the hell with Reid telling him to work with the FBI, the hell with everything and everybody.

The office lock was easily manipulated with his small pick and spring. He opened the door and slipped inside, ducking down to avoid the window, which was visible from the pool area.

A leather couch divided the room roughly in half. A desk sat on the opposite side, at the very back of the house. Filing cabinets lined the left wall of the office; an open bottle of wine sat on a small bar next to the window on the far side.

A computer screen sat on a low table to the right of the desk. It was attached to an HP computer below the table.

Nuri crawled over on his hands and knees. When he reached the computer, he took out the USB thumb drive with the virus program and pulled the machine out to locate the USB port. He plugged it in, then turned the power on.

If Moreno found the dog drugged, he'd realize there was a break-in. At that point he would most likely assume the office and computers were bugged and tear them apart. Most experts would miss the virus that he was installing, but there was a chance they wouldn't. And besides, Moreno might easily decide to take no chances and simply trash the entire computer.

Which meant he would have to start the upload now.

He got back on his hands and knees and looked for the phone line, aiming to tap in and avoid Moreno's router, which could slow down the transfer. He found the line, and realized the office was wired with an optical line—something he hadn't expected, but not a problem. He found the small connection box and went to work, carefully unscrewing the cover and pulling the jack out to expose the wiring. He hooked his own in, then ran it up to the computer's Ethernet port.

A cursor blinked steadily on the screen. Nuri tapped the six digit access code and the rogue program went to work, flexing the computer's hard drive at a few hundred megabytes a minute.

He considered the dog problem while the hard drive churned. If he could make it look as if the dog had been poisoned, then the mess in the other room and the dog's sleeping would seem natural.

Not poisoned, but inebriated.

The bottle of wine. The smell might dissipate the scent of the mace as well.

Nuri glanced at the computer screen. The virus needed another twelve minutes to finish.

He went over and grabbed the wine. The bottle was only about a quarter full, but that would do; the dog was already drugged, after all.

Crouching down next to the desk, watching the computer count down, his anger dissipated. He held the bottle of wine to his nose. It was earthy, a fresh red—probably grown and bottled right here.

Nuri felt himself relaxing, just a little. Things were going well. He'd been right about the mafia don letting his guard down. The party complicated things, but only barely. And the dog—the dog was a chance to show his ingenuity.

The computer beeped. The program was done, and sooner than he'd expected.

Leaning to his right over the desk, Nuri looked through the window toward the pool. Moreno was still floating in the middle of the water, a girl hanging on either side of him.

Not a bad life, Nuri thought. Smuggle some dope into the country from time to time, hire international killers to avenge your grandfather, then float the nights away drinking wine and getting laid.

Nuri pulled over the keyboard and typed a new set of letters and numbers: *stndby334*.* The hard drive churned again, implanting the virus deep into the operating system. It would send out fresh information each time the computer was booted. Assuming, of course, that Moreno didn't realize he'd been bugged.

Curious about what had been uploaded, Nuri followed the command with one for a listing of programs on the hard drive. There were dozens, including a shareware encryption program that he had encountered before. He paged through to the e-mail program and fired it up. It wasn't even protected with a password.

Then again, how many home computer e-mails were?

Nuri flipped through the most recent bunch. They seemed to concern business, but the details were vague—a ship that would leave port, an airplane flight number, nothing of immediate help. There was also a surprising amount of spam—ads for working at home, better erection pills, and invitations to join dating services.

Spam? Or messages disguised as spam? MY-PID would have to sort it all out.

Nuri closed the program and looked at the Internet cache, examining the list of recent sites

Moreno had surveyed. For a guy who could pay for whatever real pleasures he wanted, Moreno sure liked his porn. The cache was filled with images.

"How's it going?" asked Flash.

"Almost done."

He paged through, looking for bank account screens. He didn't see any. But he did find a range of search queries on banks and post offices in Moldova.

Did Moreno have business there?

If so, it wasn't obvious. The pages left in the queue looked almost random, as if Moreno had been thinking about visiting and was just looking for information.

"Guards are moving around in the little building," warned Flash. "I think we're up against a shift change."

Nuri flipped off the computer. He resisted the impulse to look inside the desk or file cabinets and began crouch-walking toward the door.

He was three-fourths of the way there when he realized he'd forgotten the wine bottle. As he went back for it, he looked through the window and saw one of the girls pulling herself out of the pool.

She wasn't wearing a top.

She was also heading for the house, as Flash warned a few moments later.

He scooped up the wine bottle and went back to the door to wait for her to pass. But instead of going up the hall as the other girls had, she stopped at the office door and tried the knob.

"Fredo, Fredo," she called. "*La porta*—the door is locked."

She tried the door again.

"MY-PID, locate Alfredo Moreno," said Nuri.

"Subject is in the pool."

"Tell me if he moves."

"Subject is swimming to the western side of the pool."

Shit.

Nuri reached over to the lock and undid it.

Try it again, he willed the woman outside. But she didn't.

"Subject is approaching the house," said MY-PID.

Nuri took out his pistol. The hell with subtlety. He'd just shoot the damn son of a bitch and be done with it all.

"Nuri?" whispered Flash.

"Stand by," whispered Nuri.

"C'e cosa?" said Moreno, coming into the hallway. The music was blaring behind him. *What's wrong?*

"I want more wine," said the woman.

"You've had enough I'm sure."

"Don't be a prude."

Nuri raised the gun. He heard a loud slap outside the door.

Then the woman laughed. Moreno laughed. The woman giggled.

The door opened. Nuri stood against the wall, holding his breath as the pair came into the room. He could smell the chlorine fresh on their bodies.

They went straight for the couch, tumbling over the back.

The girl giggled. Moreno told her that she was

beautiful and needed to be made love to. She asked for more wine. He told her first he would fill her up with something more intoxicating. He pulled off her bikini bottom and went to work.

Gun pointed in their direction, Nuri squeezed out from behind the door and backed into the hallway.

The dog was snoring beneath the table where he'd left him. It jerked upward as he poured the wine over its muzzle, but then slipped back down to sleep.

He paused when he reached the French door to leave.

Wouldn't he be doing everyone a favor going back and plugging the son of a bitch and his whore?

Maybe not the woman, but definitely the mafioso. Who the hell would care?

Only Reid, really. Maybe not even him. The Italians certainly wouldn't raise a fuss.

The dog stirred.

Time to go, Nuri told himself, and he slipped outside.

13

Washington, D.C.

ZEN AND BREANNA STOCKARD WERE ONE OF WASHINGton's power couples, and while few people would literally trade places with them—Zen, after all, had spent two decades in a wheelchair—they were still envied by many, not least of all because they seemed to have an excellent, even perfect marriage. They supported each other's careers and worked together to take care of their daughter Teri. While they were only sporadically seen on the political cocktail-dinner circuit, they did get around—Zen had box seats for the Nationals, and Breanna's position on the board of directors of the Washington Modern Dance Company meant they often attended shows there.

Not a few of which Zen was reputed to sleep through, though no videos of him snoring had yet been posted on the Internet.

But even so-called power couples still took out the garbage: a task Zen assigned himself tonight while Breanna was working on homework with their daughter. Teri's English Language Arts class was studying Shakespeare, specifically *The Merchant of Venice*. The language had been scaled back and the theme watered down to make it appropriate for third graders, but it was still an ambitious project.

Teri had won the role of Portia. Two other girls were sharing the part, and to really shine, she needed a judge's costume to die for. Breanna had many talents, but sewing wasn't one of them. Still, she was giving it a good try, and not cursing too much, at least not loud enough for her daughter to hear.

Zen wheeled himself outside with the garbage. He loved his daughter dearly, but there were plenty of times when he wished he had a son as well. He could have made a cool sword for Basanio.

Zen wrestled with the plastic top of the can. It never seemed to want to unlatch when he needed it to. That would be an asset, undoubtedly, in a rural area where there were raccoons or even bears prowling for midnight snacks, but in the wilds of the Washington suburbs, it was more than a little annoying. When he finally got it open, he felt as if it was yet another triumph on the day—nearly on par with the passage of his legislation.

Breanna was waiting in the kitchen when he returned.

"How now, fair queen?" Zen asked. "How goeth the princess?"

"The princess is off to bed, awaiting your kiss."

"Her costume is done?"

"Such as it is."

"You know we could—"

"Zen, we are *not* going to hire a seamstress to make it."

"I wasn't going to suggest that," said Zen. He was fudging: he'd been thinking of Anthony, his tailor.

"You spoil her," added Breanna.

"That's my job," said Zen, rolling down the hall to Teri's bedroom.

Most senators had two homes, one near Washington, D.C., and one back in their home state. Since he represented Virginia, Zen was lucky enough to need only one—though he saw the value in a ready excuse to leave town.

"Hey, Portia, you done for the night?" he asked his daughter as he rolled into her room.

"Uh-huh," she murmured. "It's a good uniform."

"I think they call them judges' robes."

"Whatever."

"Whatever," he mimicked, bending over and kissing her. "Say your prayers?"

"Uh-huh."

"See you in the morning, all right?"

Her head popped up as he started to roll himself backward.

"Are you taking me to school?"

"Don't I always?"

"Sometimes Mom does."

"Sometimes Mom does. Not tomorrow."

"Can we do my lines in the car?"

"You haven't memorized them already?"

"I need practice."

"We'll practice. Sleep now."

BREANNA TOOK THE BOTTLE OF CHAMPAGNE OUT FROM the bottom of the refrigerator and got two glasses down from the cupboard. It had been a while since they used them, and they were covered with dust.

She ran them under the water in the sink to clean them. They'd gotten them for their wedding, but now she wasn't sure who'd given them.

"Champagne?" said Zen, startling her.

The glass slipped from her hand and fell on the floor, shattering.

"Damn," muttered Breanna.

"You OK?" Zen asked.

"Oh, I'm fine."

She picked up the stem and the largest fragment, dropping them into the garbage bin.

"What are we celebrating?"

"Your law," she said, going for the broom. "Today's vote."

"It's not a law yet. Still a bill."

"It will be a law. It should be a law."

"Tell that to the President."

"I will."

"I think she'll sign it. Hell, I'm going to Kiev for her."

"Kiev?"

"Well, not really for her. Did I tell you—Al Osten had a heart attack."

"Senator Osten?"

"Yeah, he's OK. They got him to the hospital in time, thank God." Zen swung around to the cabinet and got out another glass. "He was supposed to go to the NATO meeting next week in Ukraine. I'm going to pinch hit for him. I called him at the hospital to see how he was doing— you know that's all he wanted to talk about? He wanted to go himself."

Breanna felt something stick in her throat. She swept up the fragments of broken glass and dumped them into the garbage. By the time she put the broom and dustpan away, Zen had poured them both some champagne.

"You've got a juice glass," she told him as he handed her the flute.

"Can't reach the fancy stuff. Tastes the same. Here's to us."

"To your bill."

They clicked glasses, then each took a small sip.

"Not bad," said Zen.

"Why are you going to the NATO meeting?" asked Breanna.

"Your President needs someone she can count on."

"That's you?"

"Not really. But Tompkins can't go. She sure can't send someone from the other party. And we need someone important there. So that leaves me. I suggested it," he added, shrugging.

"Jeff—there have been threats."

"Yeah, I know, Bree. There's always threats. The security people will do a good job."

Breanna took another sip of the champagne, a deeper one this time. She had thought the days of worrying about her husband were long over.

"I don't . . ." she started.

The words died on her lips. What was she going to say? She didn't want him to go? But she couldn't prevent him.

"There are always intelligence reports about people who want to break these things up," said Zen. "Remember last year, the OPEC meeting? The CIA was convinced there was going to be a bomb attack. Nothing happened. Nada."

"I know."

"Come on. Let's go sit inside. Bring the bottle."

Breanna watched as Zen carefully positioned his glass between his useless legs and wheeled himself toward the living room. How much different would their lives have been if the experimental operations had been a success? she wondered.

How much different if he'd never had the accident?

Breanna sat in the green chair opposite the fireplace, wondering how much to say. Zen turned on the music, sliding the volume low to make sure they didn't wake Teri. He fiddled with the control screen, bringing up a play list of jazz that included most of her favorites.

"I don't want you to go," she said when he turned back around. "I want you to stay home."

"I'm sorry, babe. It's too late for that." Zen took a sip of his champagne. His casual smile was gone now; he looked as serious as if they were back at Dreamland, outlining a mission. "What's up?"

"I think it's dangerous."

"Something else is bothering you. Something big."

She'd never been able to keep secrets from him. Breanna drained her glass, then reached for the bottle.

"The intelligence is very good," she told him. "The Russians want the meeting disrupted."

"So? They going to bomb it?"

"We believe they hired a group of assassins to disrupt it. They're pretty nasty folks. The idea would be to kill some of the ministers, and make it look like a terrorist attack. Or simply to stop the meeting from taking place."

"Hired assassins?"

"It's a group called the Wolves. Have you heard of them?"

"No. Should I have?"

"Not necessarily. Whiplash is involved."

"Oh, really. Why wasn't the oversight committee notified?"

"No action was endorsed. This is being undertaken as part of a joint task force project lead by the CIA. There's an NSC finding."

"A thin white sheet of paper to cover everyone's behind."

"Are we talking as husband and wife, or senator and Tech Office head?"

"Both. What's Whiplash's involvement? You're providing security?"

"Not necessarily, Jeff. Don't ask me."

"Don't ask you?"

"I have to draw the line." Breanna got up.

"Whoa, whoa, what do you mean, you have to draw the line? Wait just a second there, Bree."

"I'm not going anywhere," she said defensively, even though she had started for the kitchen.

"Tell me about what you're doing," demanded Zen.

"I can't, Jeff. You know that. There's a line."

Zen took one of his exaggerated, I'm-holding-everything-in deep breaths.

Breanna hated when he did that.

"You're not talking to a member of the Senate Intelligence Committee," he said finally. "You're talking to your husband."

She remained silent.

"All right, so the Wolves are assassins," said Zen. "Why should I be more afraid of them than run-of-the-mill Russian spies?"

"You shouldn't," she said.

"Good."

Zen took another sip of his champagne, a bigger one this time.

"Should I be worried?" he asked.

"I don't think you should go."

"Because of the Wolves."

"Just because. Just because."

ZEN LET IT REST FOR A WHILE, DRINKING SILENTLY. BUT he knew there was more to her concern—Breanna didn't worry easily. She'd show concern over his missions back when he was in the service, but she didn't show outright fear.

She'd never, ever, told him not to do something.

He brooded on it through another glass of champagne. How far should he press? And was he pressing as a matter of national security or as a concerned husband?

Both.

"Well, I don't want you to break the law on secrecy," Zen told her after he refilled both of their glasses. "But you can't just let that hang out there and not expect me to ignore it."

"You should ignore it."

"What's bothering you, Bree?"

"Jeff—there's more to the Wolves than I can go into right now."

"More than I can get in a security briefing?"

"I'm sure you can get a full briefing if you go through channels. You're on the intelligence committee."

"How full will the briefing be?"

"Oh, Jeff."

* * *

IT STAYED THERE, SIMMERING FOR THE NEXT HALF HOUR. Breanna felt the pressure building inside.

She couldn't keep a secret like this from her husband. Not now. Not under these circumstances.

And yet she felt as if she had to.

If he hauled her before his committee, what then?

That would be silly and petty. Ridiculous.

The bottle of champagne was empty. It was still early, but she decided she would get ready for bed.

Zen caught her arm as she rose.

"Hey," he said. "What?"

"Jeff . . ."

She *had* to tell him.

"This is between you and me, do you understand?" she asked. "Husband and wife—not senator."

"Go ahead."

"We think they're enhanced."

"Huh?"

"Biologically enhanced," said Breanna. "Using drugs and implants. We have scattered evidence, but nothing solid. We think they've been operated on, and given drugs, and different biomechanics."

"Are you serious?"

"Dead serious. Reid has pieced together a lot of different strands of intelligence."

"And all that makes them, what? Superhuman?"

"I don't know," said Breanna. "That's what we're trying to find out. That's our mission."

"These are the people who are going to attack at Kiev?"

"We think so, yes."

"You're not going to let them, are you?" Zen asked.

"No. Not at all. Not if we can help it."

"That's it?" Zen asked.

"No. No. We think we know who one of the assassins is."

"Does that matter?"

"It should. It's Mark Stoner."

ZEN FELT AS IF HE'D BEEN PUNCHED IN THE STOMACH.

"Stoner?" he said finally. "*The* Mark Stoner?"

"Yes."

"The CIA officer who worked with us."

She nodded.

"He died," said Zen.

"Maybe not."

"The hell he didn't. I was on that mission, Bree. I remember—my Flighthawks—I couldn't get there in time. We weren't supposed to cross the border. Stoner's helicopter went into the swamp."

"His body was never recovered," she told him.

"There's no way he could have lived. What? They rebuilt him?"

"Something like that, maybe. We don't know."

"Shit. No way."

"Why not?"

"It's too—it's like science fiction. A crash like that—there were bodies recovered," he said, remembering. "There were definitely bodies."

"Not his."

"You can't rebuild a human being. Look at my legs. They're still useless. All those experiments—"

"Those just didn't work. Maybe the experiments with him did."

"No." Zen shook his head. He simply didn't believe it.

"Who would have believed an airplane could fly by remote control twenty years ago?" Breanna asked.

"I would believe it."

"That's because you were working on the project. Science fiction becomes reality pretty quickly these days. Ready or not."

"You're serious."

"Yes."

"Does Danny know?" asked Zen. "Is he involved in the mission?"

"I'm not discussing operational details with you. I can't."

"Come on, Bree. Danny's our friend. Stoner was a friend of his, too."

"Mark saved my life," blurted Breanna. "Don't tell me about friends."

"You didn't tell Danny, did you?" said Zen calmly. "He doesn't know."

"Jeff, I'm sorry I said anything." She sighed. "I will tell him if it's important. When it's important."

God, she screamed at herself inside. *Why did you say that?*

"You have to tell him, Bree." Zen wheeled around to look into her face. "You have to."

"You just said it was science fiction. He probably won't believe it either."

"But you do."

"Yes. I do."

"You have evidence?"

They had what they thought was a partial DNA

match, if the computer records were right. But they might not be. And there were other explanations—long shots, but maybe no more implausible than this.

Still, she was convinced.

"You don't know what the situation is."

"If what you're saying is true, which I don't know that I believe," added Zen, "but let's say, for argument's sake, that it is. Let's say it is Mark Stoner, somehow, resurrected from the grave or hospital bed, whatever. Then that's his friend who's hunting him down. Who's probably going to kill him." Zen rolled his wheelchair close to her. "Is that why Whiplash is involved? So Danny can see if it really is Stoner?"

"Jeff—"

"That's why you sent him. Because you think Stoner will recognize him, and hesitate. Or come over to our side. Somehow."

It was part of what they were thinking, at least at the beginning. But then new evidence had seemed to contradict the conclusion that it was Stoner. Breanna had decided not to tell Danny—it would only confuse and complicate the issue. When the time was right, when they had more evidence, then she would tell him about the possible DNA match, and the rest of the theories. For now, the job was simple—find out who these people were.

Whiplash was the best group for the job, with or without the old Dreamland connection.

"You have to tell him," Zen said.

"I thought you didn't believe it."

"But you do," he answered. "You have to be honest with him."

"Don't tell me what I have to do. You don't know what the pressures are."

"What does this have to do with pressure, Bree? This has to do with basic honesty."

"Honesty? Honesty? What the hell are you talking about, honesty? You lie to people all the time."

"I don't lie."

"You're a politician. Tell me you don't lie."

IT WAS THE WORST FIGHT THEY'D HAD IN YEARS. THE only fight they'd had in years. There'd been disagreements, debates maybe, but nothing approaching this. This was a nuclear explosion, a blowout so severe it left them both trembling.

Maybe it had been a long time coming. Maybe they were just due. Maybe at its heart, the fight had little to do with Mark Stoner and Danny and who should know what.

Maybe at its heart, Breanna was worried about him and didn't want to lose him. And he . . .

He wasn't sure what he was worried about. He knew he was angry, over a lot of things, none of which had anything to do with his wife, not really.

Losing his legs most of all. Even now, even after all these years without them. He wanted them. He wanted them so badly he would trade anything for them.

Not his daughter. Not his wife, not even tonight in his anger. But anything else.

Zen stayed in the living room while Breanna went to the bedroom. He went into the kitchen and got himself a beer, then sipped it slowly, thinking back to his days at Dreamland.

He didn't believe it could possibly be true. It wasn't the question of whether Stoner had survived. He'd seen worse crashes—hell, his own for starters.

But to be *rebuilt*?

Science fiction bullshit.

The phrase was familiar. Zen looked down at his legs, trying to place it.

Oh yeah, he thought, remembering. It was what the Air Force secretary had said the day he arrived at Dreamland to review the Flighthawk project.

The day of his accident, when one of the Flighthawks cut too close to his tail.

The Air Force secretary had said it with a smile on his face, laughing, really, shaking his hand before the flight.

Science fiction bullshit, that just happened to be true.

SUPERMEN

———

14

Kiev, Ukraine

"Why Moldova?" Danny asked.

"I have no idea if it means anything," Nuri told him as they debriefed the break-in over the secure sat phone. "He was looking at a lot of sites there. We'll have a better idea in the morning, when MY-PID finishes churning through all the data. I just thought it was a little unusual. Moldova is not exactly the garden spot of the world. It's not on the beaten path, that's for sure."

"It's not," agreed Danny.

"The guy loves porn," continued Nuri. "And he's an animal—he started screwing on the couch while I was there. I swear, I was ten feet away. Maybe closer. If they'd seen me, they probably would have asked me to join in."

Nuri's mention of Moldova brought back painful memories for Danny. A decade and a half before, Dreamland Whiplash had run an operation in neighboring Romania, helping rout guerrillas who were trying to disrupt a pipeline project. In the process, they'd helped rescue the country from a coup.

But they'd lost a key member of the team and a friend, CIA officer Mark Stoner. Danny could still remember getting the news.

They talked for a while more, about whether Flash should stay with Nuri or come to Kiev, about how many more people they'd need, about when to contact the local authorities.

Danny couldn't focus on any of it. He kept thinking about Stoner.

He'd lost a lot of friends in the early part of his career, in Bosnia, and then with Dreamland. Later on in the Gulf and Afghanistan. It had been a luxury the last few years, not having to worry about forming friendships that could end all too suddenly.

"I'll talk to you after we get the info dump," said Nuri. "Figure out the next move then. In the meantime, I'm going to bed. You good?"

"Good."

"You OK, Colonel?"

"I'm here," answered Danny.

"Maybe you ought to get some rest, too," said Nuri. "You sound a little tired."

Danny glanced at his watch. It was five in the morning; no way was he getting back to sleep.

"I'm good," he told Nuri. "Talk to you soon."

15

BREANNA OVERSLEPT, AND BY THE TIME SHE WOKE, ZEN had already left to take Teri to school and then go to work.

Her body felt raw from the fight, as if it had been physical. She took a shower, feeling drained of blood, even trembling a little. Coffee helped get her awake, but it only reinforced the jitteriness. She left for work without checking the news or looking at her version of the morning briefing. Her BlackBerry had a dozen messages, but none were from Zen, so she didn't bother opening them.

Breanna generally split her days between the Pentagon and Room 4. Today she was scheduled to spend her time at the Pentagon, where, among other things, she was supposed to make sure arrangements for the Tigershark demonstration test flight were set. But she headed to the CIA campus instead, anxious for an in-depth update on the operation.

And considering, in the back of her mind, what to tell Danny about the Wolves.

To her great surprise, she found Reid in the bunker. Not only did he spend the bulk of his time in his office in the main building, he was famously known as a late riser, often grumbling about meetings that began before 10:00 A.M.

"Extra strong this morning," Breanna told the automated coffee unit. "Very strong."

"You saw the e-mail?" Reid asked her as the coffee began to brew.

"No. I just had an instinct that something was up."

Reid was an old-school CIA hand, both figuratively and literally. Sometimes it seemed to Breanna that he had been with the Agency back when it was the OSS.

"MY-PID has arranged all of the data from the mobster's computer," said Reid. "There's one possible lead through a bank account. And some interesting connections. Most of the information on the drives pertains to his business interests. The FBI will be interested. And there's plenty more for the Italian antimafia commission."

"Let's have a look."

"Here."

Reid turned to the wall, then told the computer to display the data summary. Several windows of information appeared, long lists of files arranged in treelike fashion. A window on the left showed correspondence between Moreno and other members of his organization, translating them from Italian as well as decrypting them. They indicated that he was having some conflicts with upper level associates, or fellow mob bosses. There was personal animosity and friction as well. Based on what Nuri had observed, that was more than understandable.

The profile the information drew was of a man whose empire was slipping away from him. If they were in America, the authorities might even attempt to pressure him and get him to turn against the rest of the mob. But the Italians didn't work that way.

"He does seem to be losing his grip," said Reid. "Which is perhaps another reason he didn't use his own people for the strike in Berlin. In any event, the matter that concerns us is here, a pair of transactions that switched money from a Naples bank to Egypt, then to Russia."

"Does that say three million dollars?" asked Breanna.

"They don't come cheap," said Reid. "But he can afford it."

"Have you traced the accounts?"

"They were opened and closed the same day. The Russian bank has a branch in Moldova."

"Hmmm."

"I thought you'd find that interesting. I have a list of transactions on the day the money hit the Russian account. We have five different accounts where we think the money went, but the transfers aren't recorded as transfers. Someone withdrew the money, in theory as cash, then placed it into these accounts. If that happened. Most likely it was only on paper. And we're guessing at the match-ups, because the amounts don't match exactly. There's about ten thousand dollars missing."

"Pocket money."

"Maybe. Or just diddling with the numbers to throw off programs designed to look for suspicious transactions."

"But it was done in Moldova?"

"Likely. Again, this could all be manipulated," admitted Reid. "The records. I don't trust the

Russian banking system. It's always been full of holes."

"Where is the bank?"

"In the capital, Chisinau. It has some dealings with other Russian banks in Tighina. Tighina is a provincial capital, near the area under dispute with Russia. Good-sized city, at least for Moldova. Those banks are pretty small and don't seem to have been involved. There's a big dispute between that region and the rest of Moldova; no other banks deal with them—or with the Russians."

"Other links?"

"Already looking for them."

"I have to tell Danny."

"That would make sense. There are a few other loose ends. The FBI agent Nuri took with him wants to use some of the information we developed on Moreno for her own case against him."

Breanna nodded. They had been counting on the FBI to do just that. Anyone watching would think that Moreno, not the Wolves, was the focus of the investigation.

"Nuri also found this information. Oddly."

A list of websites relating to Moldova came up.

"Was he planning to go there?"

"That might be a possibility," said Reid. "They're all recent—just the other day. *After* the murder."

"Trying to see where his money went?"

Reid shrugged.

"Maybe he's dissatisfied with the job," he said. "Or maybe he's looking to provide a bonus."

"Was the break-in discovered?"

"Apparently not. Nuri had to drug a dog, but

he covered that up. In any event, the mobster has been using the computer quite prolifically since he got up a few hours ago."

"Since we're in their system, maybe we can watch and see what happens," said Breanna.

"We think more and more alike with each passing day," said Reid.

"Scary."

"Very."

BREANNA SAT AT HER DESK STARING AT AN OLD PHOTO of Mark Stoner for nearly a half hour before putting the call in to Danny.

Part of her hoped he wouldn't pick up; she wanted to put off talking to him for as long as possible. The other part wanted to get past this as quickly as possible.

Danny answered on the first ring.

"Can you talk?" she asked.

"I'm at the hotel," he told her. "It's fine."

"We have more information on the Wolves." She heard her voice crack. "And I have—there's something I didn't give you earlier. Because—for a couple of reasons."

"All right."

Breanna took a deep breath.

"We think that the people involved with the Wolves have been altered—enhanced is the better word," she said, correcting herself. She remembered her conversation with Zen the night before, how he had initially dismissed it all as science fiction nonsense. "It sounds incredible, but we think they're the result of experiments—that their bodies have been genetically altered, with drugs and in some cases biomechanical devices."

"They're supermen?" said Danny.

"That would be an exaggeration. The sorts of enhancements we're talking about, we think, would increase lung capacity, say, metabolic recovery rates. Strength might be increased through implants, bone replacements, or the exoskeleton devices, the things that you were involved in testing—"

"You mean the wing?" said Danny.

"Exactly."

Dreamland had helped develop a device that allowed soldiers to literally fly across the battlefield. Called by various names—Rocketman was more popular than Wing, which was the Whiplash nickname—the gear was used by special operations troops for select missions. The research involved in constructing it had found a much wider application, affecting everything from parachutes to the jacks that helped ordies load bombs and missiles onto aircraft. A civilian company had used the technology to create one-man cranes and lifts, which it planned to introduce to the market in a few months.

"The truth is, we don't have a lot of details," continued Breanna. "We're making guesses based on some eyewitness accounts which, as you know, aren't always credible. But we have a video showing one of the Wolves moving with incredible speed while another puts his fist through the side of a car."

"Wow."

"The video is very sketchy. It's some sort of laboratory piece. Very low resolution."

"Not a sales brochure, huh?"

"Danny, this is serious. The sources are sensitive. Highest code word."

"I'm sorry."

"There's something else. Something that affects us both."

Breanna paused. Danny didn't say anything, and the silence immediately struck her.

Does he know what I'm going to say? Has he somehow intuited it?

"I think—there's some evidence," she started, losing her steam, "that—one of the Wolves may be Mark Stoner."

Danny still didn't say anything.

"The— There's a visual similarity in the video. I noticed it right away," Breanna continued. "It's eerie, if it's a coincidence. It may be a coincidence. But . . ."

The phone line was so silent, Breanna almost wondered if she had lost the connection. But the computer would have told her if that was the case.

"The . . . there is other evidence," she said. "I don't know—it's not conclusive, but here's what it is. The killer on the assassination in China was drinking from a Coke bottle immediately before the murder. The Chinese gathered it and got a sample from it. They have saliva, and some drugs—he wasn't drinking cola, it was some sort of maintenance drink we think, it had enzymes and amphetamine in it. In any event, the Chinese analysis of the DNA material has something like a seventy-three percent chance of matching Mark's."

The percentage had to do with the original sampling technique used in recording Stoner's DNA in the 1990s, as well as the quality of the material the Chinese had collected and the process they used to analyze it. Breanna told Danny about the doubts some of the scientists had mentioned, and the arguments that placing an actual number on the odds of a direct match were difficult and misleading.

"Do you think it's him?" asked Danny when she finished.

"I don't know. I simply don't know."

"Wow."

"I'm sorry I didn't tell you earlier. I—I wasn't— I'm not sure that it's him."

"It's all right Bree. I understand."

She could have kissed him right then. She would have, if he were there. He was taking the news a lot better than she had when she first heard about the possibility of Stoner being alive.

"The Moldova connection," Danny prompted. "What do you make of that?"

"That may be important," she said. "I mean—it is where Mark was shot down. On the other hand, it could be a coincidence. It is a good place if you're looking to have some quiet banking transactions."

"I think I ought to look into it."

"So do I."

16

Approaching Chisinau, Moldova

DANNY FREAH STARED OUT THE WINDOW OF THE FOKKER 50–100 as the aircraft approached the airport at Chisinau. While Moldova shared a border with Ukraine and in some ways had a similar history, relations between the two countries were cool. Moldovans seemed to resent Ukrainians almost as much as they resented Russians. The flight he had taken was the only scheduled daily flight between the two countries. Even so, the aircraft was only half full, and its age indicated that the line wasn't particularly profitable.

Danny tightened his seat belt for the landing. After so many years in military jets, the smooth, unhurried descent felt almost like a car ride. He waited as the plane left the runway for the taxi strip, then got up and grabbed his things as soon as he could see the small terminal in the window. He was the first one off, practically running for the open terminal door.

Relax, he told himself. *Slow down*. Nothing was going to be gained by haste.

The white-haired customs agent who checked his passport was impressed that he was an American. His English, though heavily accented, was very good.

"You're here on business?" said the man.

"I have some appointments," Danny told him.

"This is very good—you will like Moldova. A

very good climate for making money. I studied in U.S. of A. myself."

"Really?" said Danny.

"Nineteen seventy," said the man proudly. "Amherst. But I returned. We always return to our home."

"True."

"A good place for business," said the man, handing his passport back.

"Maybe you should open a business yourself," suggested Danny.

"Too much to do," said the man. He looked down at the floor, as if lamenting decisions he had made long ago. But then he immediately brightened. "Good luck to you."

"Thanks," said Danny.

Danny's ostensible goal in Moldova was to visit the Russian bank branch in Chisinau, where he would plant some bugs and attempt to gather more information about accounts associated with the Wolves. But he also intended to check out the crash site. And to do that, he had to head north to Balti. He decided he'd get that out of the way first; not only was MY-PID still pulling together information on possible connections to the account, but Nuri and Flash were due to arrive in the morning; they could bug the banks as easily as he could.

Balti was something he preferred doing on his own.

HIS FLIGHT TO BALTI IN THE NORTH, BARELY EIGHTY miles by air, was in a brightly painted former Russian army helicopter. To get in, he and his fellow passenger had to squeeze past the copilot's seat, buckling themselves into the tandem seats in the cabin. The engines whined ferociously as they took off, and the noise hardly abated as they flew, the cabin vibrating in sync with the three-bladed prop above.

The Balti International City Airport had a long runway, but was used so rarely there were no car rental or other amenities there. The terminal building was deserted and locked, and the grass around the infield of the airstrip overgrown.

Danny had arranged for a driver and car to take him to the bus station, where a small car rental shop promised to rent him a car. But the driver wasn't there when he got off the plane. He called the company twice and got no answer; after a half hour he decided he had no choice but walk into town, a six or seven mile hike. He took his bag and started down the long concrete access road.

Weeds grew through the expansion cracks. Danny pulled his earphones from his pocket and connected to MY-PID, asking the computer if there were any other taxis in town.

There weren't.

"There is a bus route along the highway to the airport," advised the computer. "The next run is in three hours."

"I can walk there in that time."

Just then, a small red Renault came charging off the highway down the access ramp. Danny stopped, hoping it was the taxi. But it sped past.

Gotta be for me, thought Danny. He stood

waiting. Five minutes passed. Ten. Finally, he started walking again.

He'd just reached the highway when the car sped up behind him, braking hard and just barely missing him though he was well off the road. A short, skinny man not far out of his teens leaned across the front seat and rolled down the window.

"You American, yes?"

"That's right," said Danny.

"I am your ride."

"Where have you been?" Danny asked.

"Trouble," said the driver, sliding back behind the wheel.

Danny opened the door, pushed up the seat and put his bag in the back. Then he got in next to the driver, who grabbed the gearshift and ground his way toward the highway. "This your first day?" Danny asked.

"Oh no—I drive since fourteen."

"You're older than that now, huh?"

"Twenty-two. Legal." The driver grinned at him. "You like my English?"

"Better than my Moldovan," said Danny. He could, of course, use the MY-PID to translate for him if he wanted.

"I learn Internet. School, too."

"Great."

The highway was straight and there were no other cars—a good thing, because not only did the driver keep his foot pressed to the gas, he treated the lane markings as if they were purely theoretical.

"So—you need bus?" said the driver.

"I have to rent a car."

"Car?"

"Like Hertz," said Danny. "Eurocar?"

The driver seemed confused.

"I'm picking up a car," said Danny.

"No."

"No?"

"When are you renting car?"

"Today. I made the reservation myself."

"No car."

"How do you know?"

"My name is Joe," said the driver. He held out his hand. As he did, the car veered slightly but decidedly toward the shoulder.

Danny shook hands quickly. "The road," he said, pointing.

The driver pulled them back toward the center of the pavement. He explained that his family owned the city's largest gas station, which doubled as its largest, and only, car rental facility. And their two cars had been rented out three days before. Neither was due back for a week.

"You only have two cars?" Danny asked.

"Official, five," said the driver. One had been wrecked months before and never repaired; the other two were waiting for repair parts.

"I have fix," said the driver.

"You can fix one of the cars?"

"No—I drive."

"I have a better idea," said Danny, grabbing the dashboard as the driver turned off the highway, wheels screeching. "I'll rent this car."

"It's my sister's car," said Joe.

"If she lends it to you, I'm sure she'll rent it to me."

"But then what will we have for a taxi?"

"Do you do that much taxi business?"

"We are the largest taxi service in all Balti."

"Then missing one car isn't going to be that big a deal."

"We have only two," said Joe. "One crashed, and two cannot get parts."

"A hundred bucks for the day," said Danny.

"One thousand. But we give you lunch, too. Biggest restaurant in Balti."

DANNY WORKED THE PRICE DOWN TO SEVEN HUNDRED dollars, with lunch and breakfast in the morning, assuming he was still in town. Joe also promised to give him a ride to the airport, no charge.

Whatever family member was cooking did a much better job at the stove than Joe did behind the wheel. Under other circumstances, Danny might even have stayed for dessert. But he had a lot to do before dark.

Besides the possible DNA match, there was circumstantial evidence of a link between the area where Stoner had crashed and Russian experiments with various physical "enhancements."

The Soviet Union had run a sports clinic in a small town two miles away during the 1970s and early 1980s. The clinic had specialized in a number of techniques for athletic enhancement, including training in special aerobic chambers and rigorously supervised diets.

It hadn't been secret—there were several stories about it in the Western media. It closed quietly sometime in the 1990s or early 2000s, never officially linked to the controversies then swirling about steroids and various stimulant use, but it wasn't much of a stretch to make a connection. Anyone looking back would conclude that while those techniques were never mentioned in the press coverage, they were surely being practiced there as well.

It was rumored to be the site of other experiments as well. MY-PID located an article in *Le Monde* published in 1987 about the site that stated there were a number of rumors that the plant was aiming at producing "super athletes" and was investigating "genetic techniques." They weren't detailed in the story, but the hints were tantalizing enough for Danny, who asked MY-PID if it could track down the writer.

He'd recently retired from the French newspaper. When Danny, driving in the car, called the number MY-PID had discovered, the man answered on the second ring. Danny told him he was working on a book about old Olympic stars and had come across the article.

A white lie compounded by exaggeration, but harmless all around.

Flattered to be contacted, the former reporter told Danny what he could remember of the trip to the facility, describing what looked to him like a horse farm that had been "gussied up" with a pair of massive gyms in the old barns. He'd seen perhaps fifty athletes altogether, and interviewed a dozen. All spoke in glowing terms of the various methods that were used.

"A lot of emphasis on mental techniques," said the man, whose English was heavily accented but fluent. "Positive thinking, we called it at the time. Of course, now we know they were probably just using many steroids. It was part of the culture of deception. So many athletes ended up doing this. My report was in the very beginning of the time."

"Do you remember when it closed?"

"I wouldn't know. We were invited—it was while the Eastern Europeans were winning all those medals, you understand. People thought the success was something to do with the mind. A fantasy."

"So they did it with drugs?"

"Steroids, certainly. Now I realize what I should have looked for. They claimed they took a vitamin regime. Of course. And positive thinking. Well, you believe what you want to believe, as you Americans would say."

MY-PID couldn't locate any records showing whether the facility was operating when the helicopter went down in 1998, though the Frenchman's account made it seem likely that it had. As of now, satellite reconnaissance appeared to show that it had been abandoned.

Danny decided to check for himself.

He followed the computer's directions, taking a slight detour from the highway that led to the crash site. Dotted with small farms and houses built two or three centuries before, the countryside seemed almost idyllic, more a backdrop for a movie than an actual place.

A small village sat two miles from the complex. Dominated by a small church that hugged the road, it was home to less than two hundred people. Aside from the church, its central business section held only a pair of buildings; between them they had five shops: a bakery, tobacco shop, small grocery, clothing store, and a store that sold odds and ends.

A few local residents stood outside the tobacconist, watching Danny as he passed. He smiled and waved, and was surprised to see them wave back.

A mile and a half out of town, he turned to the right to head toward the facility. An abandoned house stood above the intersection, its siding long gone and its boards a weathered gray. A horse stood in a rolling pasture on the left, quietly eating unmowed grass as Danny passed.

The double fence that surrounded the place during its heyday was mostly intact, though weeds twined themselves through the links. The gates were pushed back, still held in place by large chains, now rusted beyond use.

Danny drove up the hill into the complex, feeling as if he was being watched.

He was: a large hawk sat serenely on the cornice of the main building at the head of the driveway, its head nestled close to its chest. Its unblinking eyes followed him as he got out of the car and walked across the small parking lot to the building. The *Le Monde* story fresh in his mind, he walked to the large gym building on the right.

This was a steel structure, more warehouse than traditional gym. It had large barnlike doors on the two sides facing the rest of the complex. Both were locked, as was a smaller steel door at the side.

Danny walked back along the building, looking for the other gym, which according to the story, sat catty-corner behind the first.

It had been razed, replaced by an empty field. There were no traces of it.

A set of old dormitory buildings sat at the very rear of the site. Danny went to the closest one. The door gave way as he put his hand on the latch.

He stepped into a small vestibule. There were posters on the wall, faded but still hanging perfectly in place. The words were in Russian. He activated the video camera on the MY-PID control unit and had the machine translate them for him:

> *"Train well!*
> *Your attitude is your ally!*
> *Think, then perform!*
> *Whatever you dream, you will live."*

The vestibule opened into a corridor on the left; an open staircase was on the right. Danny walked down the corridor slowly. Small rooms lined the hallway. Some had doors, some not; all were open. There were no furnishings in any of the rooms, nothing in them but dust, a few old shades, and in one, rolled rug liners. The place had a musty smell, the scent of abandonment.

Upstairs it was the same. He went into one of the rooms and looked out the windows. He couldn't quite imagine what it would have been like—a hundred jocks and their trainers, always running, working out, practicing their various sports.

Getting injections and God knew what else.

How did that relate to Stoner?

The athletes were just a cover for an experiment to create supermen?

And Stoner . . . became one of their experiments?

It didn't sound plausible. What Danny saw instead was more benign—people trying to help him back into shape after being broken. The downside of steroids and other drugs wasn't understood at the time.

Or maybe he was being too naive. Maybe the doctors knew exactly what they were doing.

But steroids weren't evil. He'd known guys who took them back in the nineties. Amateur bodybuilders trying to get ahead. An almost pro wrestler hoping to get the "look" so he could land a job with WCW, back in the day. Not evil guys.

Did they help? He couldn't even say. But it didn't seem to hurt. He didn't buy the " 'roid rage" hysteria.

Maybe he just didn't have the right information. And maybe that was just the tip of the iceberg compared to what they were doing here, as Breanna had implied.

But could Stoner have survived the crash? Not from what he saw. No way.

Danny went back outside. Walking through the grounds, he could tell without even referring to the *Le Monde* story that several other buildings had been removed, bulldozed without a trace.

The remarkable thing, he thought, was the lack of vandalism. Granted, the population in the surrounding area was small, but there must be kids somewhere, and he'd have thought at least the windows would have been tempting targets on a boring Saturday afternoon. He was tempted to put a rock through one himself, right now, just for the hell of it.

Going to his car, he caught a glint of light, a reflection of the sun sinking toward the nearby hills. Once again he had the sensation of being followed. But it was distant, and even MY-PID couldn't detect anything. He stared for nearly ten minutes; unable to detect any movement, he got into the Renault and headed back for the main road.

DANNY FOLLOWED THE ROAD SOUTH TO A SLIGHTLY larger village about two miles away, driving through a bucolic countryside of rolling hills and farm fields. Small corners of the fields were cultivated, here and there. The idle land was a sign of the country's current economic woes, where farmers couldn't afford the money for seeds and new tractors, but from the distance, driving by, they only made the place more beautiful.

This area had been used by the rebels during Romania's troubles. A good portion of the people here were ethnic Romanians, and in the wake of the Soviet collapse, there had been active attempts toward unifying the country with its neighbor. The Romanian rebels, however, were aligned with the Russians, who were at odds with the Moldovan government as well as the Romanians.

The politics were complicated, tangled in family relationships and issues that stretched back hundreds if not thousands of years. An American had no hope of untangling them, not even with MY-PID's help, and Danny treaded lightly when he stopped at the police station and asked if he could speak to the police chief.

The woman at the desk didn't speak English, and his pronunciation of the words MY-PID had given him was off far enough that he had to repeat them several times before she realized what he was saying. Even then she didn't completely understand—the chief came out of the back room in a rush, thinking he was reporting a stolen car.

"Auto?" said the chief, who spoke a smattering of English.

"I'm here to look for a grave," said Danny. "A friend of mine died here fifteen years ago. I think he was buried here."

"Your car stolen?"

"No, my car isn't stolen."

"A friend took your car?"

"He's dead."

"Dead?"

Danny took out the MY-PID, telling the chief it was a translating computer. He struggled with the words at first, but the more he spoke, the easier the pronunciation became.

When the chief finally understood what he was saying, he laughed. There hadn't been a real crime in town in over a decade, he said, and he had worried not only for the town's reputation, but his job.

That confusion cleared, the chief invited Danny to dinner with him. Danny wanted to see the cemetery before nightfall, and with the sun on the horizon, tried to pass.

"Not far," said the chief, grabbing his hat.

"But—"

"We talk and we eat. Then, there is grave, we see."

"I—"

"Come, come. Not far."

The man's hospitality was too generous to resist, and finally Danny agreed.

It wasn't far at all. The chief, his wife, and their teenage son lived in a four-room cottage next door to the police station. The boy's English was considerably better than his father's, and he acted as translator through the meal. Danny explained why he had come—a friend of his had died in a helicopter crash some fifteen years before. He didn't mention that he'd been working with the Romanian army, or even that he was an American, not knowing how those facts might be received.

"I remember the crash well," said the chief, taking down a bottle of vodka from one of the kitchen cabinets. "That was during the guerrilla problems. Your friend was in the Romanian army?"

"He was an American," said Danny. "He was an advisor. Helping them."

"We are very close to Romania," said the chief. "But separate countries, no? Like brothers."

"Like brothers."

"And brothers with America."

"I hope so, yes."

"Allies, dad," said the boy. "Friends."

"Allies, brothers—whatever words."

The chief took out three glasses. He filled two to the brim; the third, for his son, contained just a sip of the liquor.

"Drink!" translated his son as the glasses were handed around. "To your health!"

The chief smiled. The vodka was raw and very strong. Danny couldn't finish the entire shot in one gulp. This amused the chief, who refilled his glass.

"I was a young officer then," he told Danny, leading him over to a pair of overstuffed chairs in the living room. His son came, too, standing by his father's side and translating. "Fresh on the force. The state police. We were arranged differently—my supervisor was from another region. I came to the crash. It was a bog. Two miles from here."

"I see."

"A terrible tragedy. Many soldiers."

"Was the aircraft on fire?" asked Danny.

"On fire? No. By that time, any fire would have been out. This was in the afternoon—it had crashed earlier in the day. The morning."

"I see."

"I don't think there were any survivors."

"Would you know where they were taken?"

"The bodies? Buried."

"They didn't take them back to Romania? A few months later?"

"One was. But the others stayed."

"Why?" asked Danny.

The chief shook his head. Danny knew from the records MY-PID had found that three Romanian soldiers' bodies had been repatriated within months of the end of the coup. But a combination of politics, ancestry—at least one of the soldiers' families had come from this part of Moldova during the 1960s—and the difficulty of working with distant relatives had prevented all from being repatriated. The records were vague, but there were at least two soldiers still buried in Moldova.

"I'd like to visit the crash site as well as the cemetery," said Danny. "Could you give me directions?"

"I'll take you myself!" said the chief. He looked over at his wife, who was signaling that dinner was ready. "Here, we will have another vodka before eating."

IT WAS DARK BY THE TIME THEY WERE FINISHED DINNER. The police chief offered to let Danny stay at his house, but it was clear he would be displacing someone, probably the son. Danny begged off, and the chief recommended a small guest house run by a widow on the other side of town. As the town consisted of only six blocks, it was easy to reach, and Danny was sleeping by eight.

He got up before dawn, expecting to run a bit before breakfast. The police chief and his son were already in his squad car outside, waiting.

The chief insisted on running his blue emergency lights as they drove out to the swamp where the helicopter had crashed. It took less than ten minutes, a bumpy ride up and down a medium-sized hill into a narrow valley parted almost exactly in the middle by a meandering creek.

According to the police chief, not much had changed in fifteen years—the trees were bigger and the ground a little drier, but not much. He pointed out the area where the helicopter had lain, at the edge of a pool of water. The general location agreed with what MY-PID had displayed earlier.

"It went straight in, on its belly," said the son, boiling down the chief's elaborate description to a few words.

Danny stared at the area. He'd seen a number of helicopter crashes during his stints with Air Force special operations and Dreamland. He saw them all now, flickering through his head like ghosts combining into a single image: a Marine Whiskey Cobra merging with a mangled Blackhawk, half morphed into a Comanche test bed whose rotor was the only surviving part. Beneath them all were the pancaked remains of a flattened Chinook, the wounded passengers still crying for help.

Danny looked at the nearby woods and trees. The helo would have come in low, skimmed down when it was shot—the report said the chopper pilot was trying to attract the interceptors' attention to help the others get away.

If it lay the way the chief said it did, it must have banked slightly before going in. Maybe that would have lessened the impact, at least for someone on the other side of the fuselage.

Would that make it survivable?

He could stare at the scene all morning and not come to any real conclusions, he thought.

"So where did they take the bodies?" he asked.

The police chief described the process—they'd moved two flatboats in, but the ground proved solid enough to walk on. One body was out of the helicopter, but the others were inside. Three men in the back. And the two pilots.

"Three?" asked Danny, making sure he understood. "Only three people?"

"And the one about there, two meters from the helicopter," said the chief. "Ejected."

There had been a full squad of men aboard the helicopter, but Danny didn't correct the police chief. He said that tents had been set up near the road. They were brought in under the pretense of being an aid station to help the wounded, though it was far too late for that.

"Then what happened?" asked Danny.

"To the cemetery."

Danny nodded. "Can we go there?"

"Yes," said the chief somberly. "It is time for you to pay the respects for your friend."

THE CEMETERY WAS ABOUT THREE-QUARTERS OF A MILE away, an old church plot used sporadically as a kind of overflow from the main churchyard in town. The southeastern end was marked by foundation stones overgrown with weeds and moss; according to the police chief, these were the remains of an Orthodox church that had fallen down sometime in the eighteenth century after being replaced by the slightly larger one where the town now sat.

There were three dozen headstones, most pockmarked with centuries of wear. The bodies of the men found in the helicopter were together at the side, three marked by wooden crosses and one by a stone that lay flat against the ground.

"Once they were white," said the chief, referring to the worn wood. "But given their age, they have done well."

Standing over the graves, Danny felt the urge to say a prayer. He knelt and bowed his head, wishing the dead men peace.

"I hope you're here, Mark," he whispered to himself.

He stopped himself. It felt funny, praying that someone was dead.

17

Brown Lake Test Area, Dreamland

IT WAS A COINCIDENCE THAT CAPTAIN TURK MAKO'S LAST name meant shark. But it was a chance occurrence that he liked to play up in casual conversation.

"The Shark flies the shark—gotta happen," he'd say when telling people what he did.

Not that he told many people. The aircraft wasn't actually top secret, but most of what it was used for was.

In a sense, Turk's name wasn't actually Mako. It had been shortened and Americanized, kind of, from Makolowejeski by his great-great-grandfather, who'd come from Poland in the 1930s, escaping the war. He'd been dead some years when Turk was born, but he'd left a set of taped recordings about his adventures, a revelation and inspiration to the young man when he discovered them in high school.

Most pilots are at least a little superstitious, even if ultimately they know it's bunk. Turk, who had a lucky coin he kept in his pocket every flight, viewed the name change as something of a good omen. Great-great had been looking after him even before he was born.

The Shark that Turk Mako flew was the F–40 Tigershark II, the experimental aircraft owned by the Pentagon's Technology Office, now being equipped with the Medusa control unit to work with the Sabre UAVs. It was the latest in a long line of experimental aircraft, a cutting-edge plane that would have looked right at home on the flight deck of the Starship *Enterprise*.

Technically, two previous aircraft had been called the Tigershark. The first was actually an informal name applied by the British to their versions of the P–40 Warhawk, after squadrons began painting sharks' mouths on the nose. Fighting against the Japanese in China, Claire Lee Chenault's Flying Tigers saw how good the paint looked and added teeth to their versions, helping to make the look famous.

Tigershark II's direct namesake was the F–20, a lightweight, multirole aircraft developed by Northrop in the 1970s and early 1980s from the basic blueprint of the F–5E. It was incredibly nimble, capable of hitting Mach 2 and climbing to over 54,000 feet. It could take off in only 1,600 feet, a relatively short distance for a jet of that era, and the simplicity of its design made it easy to maintain—an important consideration for its intended target consumers, friendly American allies who might not have or want to spend the money for more expensive aircraft.

Though an excellent aircraft, the F–20 eventually succumbed to the realities of international weapons purchasing, where politics often overshadowed other considerations.

Like its predecessor, the new Tigershark was light, small, and fast. Very, very fast.

The airframe had essentially been built around the engine, a combination hypersonic pulse and ramjet that could take the sleek, needle-nosed plane to Mach 5. The engine also allowed it to operate around 135,000 feet. The wings came out in a triangular wedge, with faceted and angled fins on both sides.

The engine's quad air scoop was located directly under the cabin area of the fuselage; rail guns were mounted on either side. The rail guns were directed energy weapons, firing small bursts of plasma at high speed. The bursts were roughly the equivalent of a 50-millimeter machine-gun bullet. Devastating to another aircraft, the weapon had several advantages over conventional machine guns, starting with the fact that its projectile, though as potent as missiles, were the size of 25mm bullets. Its effective range was just over twenty miles—well before the aircraft would be seen on radar.

The weapon did have some limitations. Only a dozen charges could be fired before it had to cool down and recycle, a process that took two minutes under ideal conditions. And with each firing, the gun literally tried to pull itself apart. Maintaining it in working order was, so far at least, very expensive.

Turk counted another negative to the weapon, though this was never mentioned by its builders. Great precision was needed to target a moving adversary, and the forces created as the weapon was fired made the Tigershark hard to control at all but top speed. These facts combined to dictate that the aircraft be flown entirely by the computer during the combat sequence. In other words, he had to hand the stick over to the silicon to take his shot.

He didn't particularly like that. No computer was ever going to be as good as he was at flying. Ever.

Turk had joined the Air Force to fly. He was good at it—very good, he liked to think. He'd flown everything the service had given him—from F–16s to Flighthawks. In his not too humble opinion, he was the best. It irked him to give up the stick, even if he wasn't literally standing back out of the way. But that was the way it was.

In a very real sense, he knew he was lucky to have a job where his seat was actually in a cockpit. All of the good young jocks were headed toward UAV programs now, a dramatic switch from just a few years ago. Unmanned planes were the Air Force's future.

That sucked. There was nothing like the smell of rapidly evaporating jet fuel to get you moving in the morning, he thought. He took one last whiff and plugged up, snugging the Tigershark's cockpit.

Time to rock and roll.

"Control to Tiger One, Tiger One, you read?" prompted the control tower.

"Copy, Control, strong read."

"Status?"

Part of Turk wanted to give a real wise guy answer—maybe something like, "I feel like I gotta pee." But the flight control computer at Dreamland that was talking to him had *no* sense of humor. In fact, the only thing in the universe that had *less* of a sense of humor was the flight control computer's human boss, Major Samantha "Killjoy" Combs, who had promised to write him up if he goofed on the computer again. His joking around had frozen the system, grounding flights for over two hours.

Or so she claimed.

"Write me up?" he'd laughed. "I just discovered a flaw in your stupid computer program."

"You caused two flight ranges to shut down."

"Better we found the problem now rather than in battle," said Turk.

"*Captain.*"

"Hey, make yourself happy. What are you gonna do, give me a parking ticket?"

Twenty minutes later his boss, Breanna Stockard, had called from D.C., telling him that if the three-star general commanding Dreamland complained about him again, he was going to be reassigned to clean toilets in the coldest part of Alaska.

So Turk was very straight today when dealing with the computer controller.

"Status is green," said the pilot. "Awaiting clearance to take off."

"Tiger One you are cleared to proceed on the filed flight plan. You are cleared for takeoff."

The computer continued, giving him a rundown of the weather conditions. They were basically the same as they always were at Brown Lake: clear skies, unlimited visibility.

"Engines, military power," said Turk, powering up from soft idle. The power plants—there were actually four of them, though they worked as an integrated unit—came on with a soft thud. The aircraft immediately began to shake. Turk worked his control surfaces quickly, getting green status lights on the right side of his visor. He could choose to use the LED screens on the aircraft—there was no glass canopy—but generally left that as a backup. His smart helmet could do everything the computer-controlled screen could, and was connected directly to the plane.

Turk checked through his instruments for his last takeoff checklist, meticulously looking at each indicator even though the computer would have alerted him if anything was out of spec. Then he took a long, deep breath, slowly emptying his lungs.

"Let's go," he told the plane, simultaneously reaching for the throttle.

And they were off.

ALL AIRPLANES ARE BUILT TO FLY. ENGINES ON FULL AND left completely on their own, their wings would gladly propel themselves through the air, straight and level, forever. Or at least until their fuel ran out.

The Tigershark didn't *just* love to fly. It loved to *accelerate*. Its engines supplied more lift per pound than any other aircraft in the American inventory, which meant any other aircraft in the world. If the Tigershark were a person, it would be an Olympic-class sprinter—the Carl Lewis of the skies.

Speed is lift. Turk's job was basically to manage that lift, using it to get from Point A to Point B and back again. To do that in the Tigershark, he had to think not just of Point A and B and all the subpoints in between, but Point C and D, and a little bit of E and F on either side of the wings. Because living at Mach 2.3, the aircraft's normal cruise speed, entailed certain responsibilities.

Things happened relatively fast at that speed— more than twice as fast as they happened in most fighters. Turk had advanced radar and avionics systems that helped show him what else was around and likely to happen on any given vector, but as good as the computer was, it couldn't really predict the future.

Not that he could, of course. But he did have a certain feel for it.

It wasn't that the Tigershark couldn't fly below the speed of sound. But the high-speed maneuvers it was capable of—the aircraft was designed to withstand over 18 g's, a force that would crush its pilot in an old-style g-suit—required enormous flight energy.

It was a trade: the Tigershark gave the god of flight velocity and lift, and in return the god of flight let it make a 150-degree turn in the space a Piper would have used at something like a hundredth of the speed.

But the god of flight did not take IOUs—if the Tigershark was a few knots short, she was severely punished. High-speed stalls and spins were a fact of life in the Tigershark. Even after a year's worth of flying it, Turk was required to practice dealing with them in a flight simulator twice a week.

The sessions were far more grueling than anything he encountered in the air, which was the point. He was good: he could deal with even the most unusual flight blip—his term—nearly as quickly as the plane's flight command computer. But he still found the workouts taxing.

Today's flight, by contrast, was a piece of cake. All he had to do was practice a few loops and rolls for the dog and pony show they were hosting in a few days.

Low pass on the runway. Zip-zip. Climb. Turn at the top. Dive and recover.

Enter Sabres, stage right.

Though they looked nothing alike, in many ways the Sabres were smaller versions of the Tigershark, capable of making very sharp maneu-

vers at high rates of speed. They didn't have anywhere near the Tigershark's top end, however;
they would accelerate to roughly Mach 3, but used
a great deal of fuel getting there. What they could
do better than the Tigershark was fly slowly, all
the way down to 100 knots at their service ceiling, which was roughly 68,000 feet. The secret was
their wings, which could be extended—rolled out
was a more descriptive and accurate term—turning
them into high-altitude gliders. With solar cells
embedded in their skin, the aircraft could power
down their engines and loiter over an area for hours.

There were trade-offs. For one, the extended
wings made it easy for properly configured radar
to spot them. But all things considered, the Sabres
were the most capable unmanned air vehicles or
UAVs ever produced. They bore the same relationship to the Flighthawks—their immediate
predecessors—as their namesake, the F–86 Sabre,
bore to the P–38 Lightning.

Turk rocked the Tigershark through the opening maneuvers of his display routine, cranking the
plane straight up as four Sabres rocked in from opposite directions. The little planes came up around
him, crisscrossing as he climbed. It was very impressive from the ground—the planes looked as if
they were a reverse fountain of water. In the cockpit, it was more than a little on the boring side:
all Turk did was fly straight up, putting the nose
of the aircraft through a blue guide circle on his
screen supplied by Medusa, which was interfacing
with the Tigershark's flight computer.

An indicator in the right-hand corner of his

screen began counting down his next maneuver. When it hit zero, he pushed right, diving between two of the Sabres. As he sliced downward, the little planes followed, crisscrossing as they flew.

A few more acrobatics and it was on to the simulated missile run. The Sabres dropped precision-guided bombs—small warheads of high explosive. These were 38 and 67- pound bombs, designed to destroy targets without causing a lot of collateral damage. They could blow up anything smaller than a main battle tank without a problem—as they demonstrated on a helpless Bradley.

Mission complete, it was back to the runway for a coordinated landing.

"Ground to Tigershark One, you're looking very good," said Colonel Harvey "Rocks" Johnson, coming on the radio just as Turk was about to tell control he was ready to land. "What's your situation?"

"Tigershark is about to head back to the barn, Colonel."

"I wonder if you could take that crisscross over the review stand again. The Sabres were a little sluggish."

The colonel phrased it as a request, but Turk knew that Rocks would make his life difficult if he didn't burp precisely on command.

"Tigershark weighed fuel out pretty carefully, Colonel."

"My gauge says you have enough for a pass."

Turk checked. The Tigershark's instruments were duplicated on the ground. There was enough for a pass—but only just.

"Yeah, roger that. We're lining it up." Turk clicked off the radio mike. "Computer, Sabre Control Section: Sabres, follow-on for prebriefed maneuver A–1. Devolve from that to landing pattern Baker. Acknowledge."

"Sabre Commander: Sabres Acknowledge," said the computer. The commands appeared in his HUD.

Turk slid back to the starting point for the fly-by. The Sabres came around and executed their part of the show perfectly—just as they had earlier. Turk banked, called in to the tower to land, and got into position without any more interference from Rocks Johnson. The Sabres lined up behind him, aiming to fly over and then land.

He was less than 1,000 meters from touchdown when a proximity warning sounded in the cockpit. One of the Sabres was moving toward his tail at 500 knots.

"Sabres, knock it off, knock it off," said Turk. In that same second he pulled the throttle down, killing his speed. The aircraft flattened, losing altitude precipitously. But the unending runway was created just for such emergencies. He came in hard and fast, but had acres in front of him; the Sabres jetted harmlessly overhead.

"What the hell just happened?" he yelled.

"Tigershark, abort landing," said the computer controller, belatedly catching up to the emergency. "Abort. Abort."

"Thanks," muttered Turk, checking his instruments.

The knock-it-off command should have sent

the Sabres into a predesignated safe orbit at 5,000 feet, southwest of the runway in a clear range. But the radar showed them circling above and approaching for a landing.

"Ground, what's going on?" said Turk. On the ground the Tigershark was as vulnerable as a soccer mom minivan, slow and not very maneuverable. He moved off the marked runway toward the taxi area, unsure of where the Sabres were going—a very dangerous position.

"Ground, what the hell is going on?"

"We have control, we have control," sputtered Johnson. "Get off the runway."

"Yeah, no shit," grumbled Turk over the open mike.

"The engineers think there was an error in one of the subroutines when they were landing," Johnson told Turk when he reached him at the prep area. The crew had taken over the Tigershark and were giving her a postflight exam. "They think Medusa defaulted into the wrong pattern."

" 'Think' is not a reassuring word," said Turk.

"That's why we test this shit out, Captain. Your job is to help us work things out."

"Maybe if I controlled the planes from Medusa, rather than handing them off to you—"

"The test protocol is set," said Johnson, practically shouting.

"You don't have to get angry with me, Colonel," snapped Turk. "I'm not the one that fucked up."

"Nobody fucked up here."

"Bullshit—the Sabre flight computer almost

killed me. It's supposed to be hands-off to landing."

"You should have watched where the hell you were."

"What? *What?*"

"Hey, hey, hey, what's going on?" said Al "Greasy Hands" Parsons, stepping in between them.

Johnson ignored Greasy Hands, pointing at Turk. "You remember you're in the Air Force, mister," he told him. "I don't care who your boss is. At the end of the day, your butt is mine."

Johnson stalked away.

"I swear to God, if you weren't here, I woulda hit him," said Turk.

"Then you're lucky I was here," said Greasy Hands. He laughed.

"Blaming me for that? What a bunch of bull-shit." Turk was still mad. His ears felt hot because of the blood rushing to them. "He almost killed me. He's supposed to override manually immediately if there's a problem. Not wait for me to call knock it off. Not then. Shit. I get hit on landing, that's it."

Greasy Hands was silent.

"Damn," said Turk. He shook his head. It was typical Johnson: bluster and blame on everyone except for himself.

"Come on," said Greasy Hands. "I'll buy you a beer at Hole 19."

Hole 19 was a club at Dreamland.

"I gotta finish the postflight brief," said Turk.

"I'll finish it with you."

Turk smiled. Greasy Hands was old-school, a former chief master sergeant now working for the Office of Technology. He'd served at Dreamland for years. Now he was Breanna Stockard's assistant, a kind of chief cook and bottle washer who solved high-priority problems. He was a grease monkey at heart, a tinkerer's tinkerer who could probably have built the Tigershark in his garage if he wanted.

"I'm OK, Chief," said Turk.

"I'd like to tag along."

"All right, come on. Boring stuff, though."

"Boring's good in this business," said Greasy Hands, patting him on the back.

18

Chisinau, Moldova

THE OBVIOUS NEXT STEP WAS TO DISINTER THE BODIES in the small cemetery and see if the records were wrong and one of them was Stoner's.

Danny had no stomach for the job and was more than a little relieved when Reid said he would arrange for a CIA team to do it. He thanked the police chief and his son for their hospitality, buying them a late-morning breakfast at the town restaurant. Then he drove back to Balti, where he returned the Renault in exchange for a ride to the airport. The rickety old helicopter took him to Chisinau in forty nail-biting but uneventful minutes.

Nuri and Flash were waiting for him when he returned. They'd just come from the Russian bank, where they opened accounts with electronic access. They also scattered a dozen bugs around the place, all with video capacity. The bugs transmitted data to a receiving unit stashed in a garbage bin behind the building, and from there to the satellite network MY-PID used.

"Hey, boss," said Flash. "Cool helo."

"Don't let the paint job fool you," said Danny. "It rides like a washing machine with a switchblade for a rotor."

"We have some leads," said Nuri, leading them toward the car he'd rented. "Some better than others."

The best involved a doctor who specialized in sports medicine, and was quoted in the *Le Monde* story. MY-PID had tracked him to a small clinic in the capital. There was only one problem: the clinic had closed ten years before. At that point the doctor had ceased to exist.

At least officially. But MY-PID had tracked bank accounts he'd used, connecting them to a mortgage on a house just outside the city limits. The mortgage had been taken out six months after the clinic closed—and paid off eighteen months later. The name on the mortgage was different, but the person was also a doctor: Dr. Andrei Ivanski.

MY-PID turned up little information on Ivanski. He was Moldovan, of Russian descent, according to certification papers. He had no active practice in the country.

Were they the same person?

Nuri thought they probably were. And, interestingly, the doctor also had an account at the Russian bank, though the records showed it hadn't been used for nearly four years.

"He has a pretty nice house," said Nuri. He showed Danny satellite pictures of it as they drove into town. "I want it under surveillance, get some more information, see if we can figure out what the doc is up to."

"Maybe we should make an appointment and ask him," suggested Danny. "Does he have a practice?"

"In town. But first we need background," said Nuri. "We need to know what kind of questions to ask."

"Ask him about steroids."

"That's the last question we ask," said Nuri. "We don't ask that until we're reeling him in."

"I don't know if I'm buying this whole human engineering thing," Danny told Nuri. "For one thing, I'm not convinced Stoner survived the crash. For another, I don't see a connection with the sports place. It's all pretty far-fetched."

"Enhancement, not engineering," said Nuri. "You don't like the idea that Stoner was involved? Is that it?"

"I don't have feelings one way or another."

It was a lie, but Nuri didn't call him on it.

"Look, Stoner was Agency," Nuri told Danny. "I know he was your friend, but in some ways he's like a brother I didn't know. And I agree the whole thing is pretty far-fetched. But if they have a genetic test—"

"It's not foolproof," said Danny. "He may be in that cemetery."

"We'll know about the cemetery in a few days," said Nuri. "In the meantime, these are our best leads. Until Kiev."

19

Washington, D.C.

THE ARGUMENT WITH HIS WIFE STILL FELT A LITTLE RAW as Zen wheeled himself into the congressional dining room, where he was planning to lobby a pair of congressmen on the companion bill to his scholarship measure. Both were from the opposing party, but he didn't figure either would be a hard sell—they had large military installations in their districts, and one had a brother who was still on active duty with the Marines.

The ease of the assignment let his mind drift a bit, and he thought of the NATO meeting even as he came up to the table where the congressmen had already been seated.

"Senator, good to see you," said Kevin Sullivan, an upstate New Yorker in his third term. He practically jumped out of his chair as he grabbed Zen's hand.

His companion, Brian Daly, was more reserved. But it was Daly who began the conversation by mentioning that he'd talked about the bill with his brother in the Marines. His brother, a lieutenant colonel, had heartily endorsed it.

That was good enough for Daly.

"I think it's a good idea, too," said Sullivan. "I'm on board."

"Great," said Zen. "Let's eat."

"My brother remembers you from your Dreamland days," said Daly as they waited for their lunches. "He was on a deployment in Iran when you were active."

"Hell of a time," said Zen.

"He said you guys were something else. You took out a laser site in broad daylight? Ballsy."

"Your brother was probably in a lot more danger than I ever was," said Zen. "The guys on the ground always had it worse. Hell, if I was in trouble, I could just fly away."

That was more than a slight exaggeration— piloting the Flighthawks from the belly of a Megafortress, he couldn't "just fly away" at all. He was completely at the mercy of whoever was piloting the big plane—or firing at it.

During the war between Pakistan and India, it had almost cost him his life. At one point, the plane in flames, he parachuted out with Breanna. They'd spent several days shipwrecked on an island.

Air-wrecked. Whatever.

Their lives had changed so much since then. It wasn't just because they weren't in the same line of work anymore either. They had different outlooks on things, different attitudes toward Teri and how to raise her. Different priorities with their jobs and lives.

So what did any of that have to do with their argument?

Nothing.

Was that what really bothered him, their growing apart?

They weren't apart—they were just older, with more things to worry about.

"There was a rumor today on one of the blogs— Politico, I think—that you were headed to Kiev," said Sullivan.

"I am," said Zen, returning from his brief daydream. "Senator Osten's going to be in the hospital awhile."

"Oh yeah, how is he?" asked Sullivan.

"I talked to him yesterday. He was joking about all the things he's not supposed to do now."

"You wouldn't figure him for a heart attack," said Sullivan.

Actually, thought Zen, you would—he didn't exercise, was more than a little overweight, and had a complicated family medical history. But it was the sort of polite comment people made in passing.

"Do you really think Ukraine should be part of NATO?" asked Daly, changing the subject.

"I don't think it's a bad idea," said Zen. "What do you think?"

Daly was neutral; Sullivan was opposed, though only mildly. Both seemed worried about diluting NATO as a military force by adding relatively weak allies on the border of Russia. It was a reasonable argument, even if Zen disagreed. He wasn't in much of a mood to get into a philosophical discussion of how to best offer a counterweight to Russia.

But Sullivan and Daly were.

"Russia is a diminished force," said Sullivan. "A nonentity militarily."

"That's what worries me, to some extent," said Daly. "When you're beaten down is when you get dangerous."

"They haven't been beaten down."

"They think they have. That's what matters." Daly turned to Zen. "I'd be careful at that summit," he told him. "I've heard plenty of rumors that the Russians are out to disrupt it somehow."

"I'll be as careful as possible," said Zen.

Sitting at a committee hearing two hours later, Zen decided he would be more than careful—he'd spend a little time at the shooting range before leaving, something he hadn't done in a few months.

And he'd buy Breanna some flowers. That was also long overdue.

20

Chisinau, Moldova

THE DOCTOR'S HOUSE WAS AN AMERICAN-STYLE McMansion that would have looked right at home on Florida's Gold Coast. In Chisinau it looked like something from outer space.

Three stories high, with lots of glass and stone, it lorded over the nearby houses, which would have looked large in any other context. Two parallel runs of spiked iron fencing surrounded the property. Eight feet high, the fence was a deterrent to trespassers, but not any more so than the dogs that roamed the interior. Unlike the one Nuri had encountered in Italy, these were rottweilers, and appeared to be trained guard dogs; they moved in twos with almost military discipline.

The dogs were more than enough to dissuade Nuri from sneaking in the way he had at Moreno's, but in addition there were video cameras and infrared motion sensors all along the fence line. As Flash put it, the doctor did not want anyone making unannounced house calls.

So Nuri decided they would settle for NSA wiretaps, and in the meantime plant some video bugs in the neighbors' yards in hopes of getting a picture.

Flash volunteered for the job. The game plan was straightforward: he'd rent a motorcycle, whiz up into the area, plant the bugs per Nuri's directions, then head back to the hotel where they were staying. Danny would back him up in the rental car. Meanwhile, Nuri would access the accounts they had set up at the bank, giving MY-PID a route into the bank's computers.

The first problem they encountered was with the motorcycle: they couldn't find one to rent. Flash was ready to do the job on foot when he spotted an open bicycle shop on the way out of town. The owner wouldn't rent anything, but was willing to part with an older ten-speed for fifty euros.

They put the bike in the trunk of a rented Dacia and drove out of the city toward the development just after dusk. The houses around the doctor's were all relatively new, built within the last ten years. MY-PID's scan of the property records listed several Russians with connections to Russian organized crime, but for the most part the homeowners were part of the small class of nouveau riche Moldovans who'd made money in various legitimate enterprises, the most popular of which was the pharmaceutical industry, which the Moldovan government had set out to encourage a number of years before.

Flash got out of the car about a half mile north of the doctor's house. He took the bike they'd rented earlier from the trunk and began pedaling slowly through the neighborhood. Danny drove around until he found a spot where he could see most of the house with his night glasses.

"How'm I lookin'?" asked Flash.

"You're good. Looks like there's somebody in the second story of the house," Danny told him. "Back room. Moving around."

The glasses couldn't see inside the building, but they were powerful enough to catch heat signatures close to the walls and windows. Danny scanned down the nearby streets. The only people outside were a block and a half away, working in a lit garden at the side of their yard.

"Car coming," he said. "Mercedes up that street on your right."

"OK."

Flash slowed his pace as the car came to the intersection and turned past, then crossed the street and stopped near the fence of a yard diagonally across from the rear of the doctor's house. Danny watched him take a video bug from his pocket and plant it on a slim tree that stood just outside the fence.

MY-PID sounded a tone over the radio system, telling them that the bug was working.

"Next," said Flash, hopping back on his bike.

Danny drove down the block, circling around to lessen the odds of someone noticing him. Flash installed two more bugs and was halfway through the project when MY-PID announced that one of the garage doors in the doctor's house was opening.

"You hear that?" Danny asked.

"Yeah. I'm just up the block."

A Mercedes came out of the garage.

"Where do you think he's going at this hour?" asked Flash.

"I'm going to find out," Danny told him. "Can you finish that on your own?"

"Piece of cake."

Danny doused his lights as he turned down the street parallel to the doctor's house. The Mercedes appeared a few seconds later, driving down the hill in the direction of the city. Danny let him get a block ahead, then put his lights on and started to follow. Without a tracking device, he had to stay relatively close. It was Surveillance 101—a course he'd never taken. Once more he felt like a fish out of water, playing detective or spy when he'd been trained as a commando.

The Mercedes went six blocks on the main

road, then turned in the direction of the city. But just as Danny started to accelerate, it veered off suddenly, taking a right on one of the side streets. Fearing that he'd been seen, he continued going straight, slowing down as much as he dared. He looked, but couldn't see anything up the side street as he passed.

He went a block, then took a parallel street, hoping to circle back. The road ran for nearly a quarter mile before he found an intersection. He turned left when he reached the street the Mercedes had taken, calculating that the doctor had continued in that direction. But he ran into a dead end; he made a U-turn and headed back to the main road.

The Mercedes was nowhere to be found. Possibly it had pulled into one of the estates that flanked the road; Danny decided he'd take another look.

"Flash, how's it going?" he asked.

"On the last one."

"I lost him, but I want to run down some of these roads for a second and see if he turned in somewhere. I'll meet you at that little gas station we passed on the way up."

"Sounds good."

Danny found a place to turn around. As he drove back down the road, he realized that two of the estates had guardhouses set back a bit from the road.

"MY-PID, identify property owners for the street I'm driving down," he ordered.

The computer had already accessed and downloaded the city property records, and within moments was reading off a list of owners.

Danny stopped it when it got to the Russian government.

"Is that the ambassador's residence?" he asked.

"Negative."

"Who lives there?"

"Not listed. Correlating with other data . . . residence appears to be occupied by the assistant ambassador for business. Possible link to GRU."

In other words—the spymaster for the Russian military lived there.

Or might.

Was that where the doctor had gone?

The house was undoubtedly under surveillance, and Danny didn't want to risk drawing any more attention to himself than he already had. He went back out to the main street and noticed a fire hydrant near the curb directly across from the intersection. He pulled over, got one of the video bugs and set it under the hydrant's plug. Back in the car, he made sure he had a view of the street, then went and picked up Flash.

BY THE TIME DANNY AND FLASH RETURNED TO THE hotel room, Nuri had pieced together more of the money trail, with the computer's help. Breaking into the Russian bank records after accessing the system through the new account, MY-PID found that 200,000 euros had been wired from the Russian account into a Moldovan bank account just that morning. The money was withdrawn in the afternoon, apparently in cash.

He showed Danny the money trail on the screen of their secure laptop. MY-PID had an

Excel-based account tool that not only gave account balances and transactions, but could compare transactions to others at the same bank in real time, looking for related moves in shadow accounts. The SEC would have killed for it.

"First thing in the morning," said Nuri, "we get a look at their security cameras. We'll review the video and find out who went in there."

"You think they'll just hand it over?" asked Flash.

"Sure—if we're there to fix it."

"How do you get around not speaking the language?" asked Danny.

"I have a hearing aid," said Nuri. "I pretend I'm hard of hearing, and I use MY-PID. Used to do it in Africa all the time. Plus my Romanian is getting better. Same language."

The computer continued to churn through various bank records, first looking for obvious connections like direct transfers, then gradually becoming more esoteric. It looked for accounts that had similar usage patterns, but the only thing it could identify was an account used by GazProm, the Russian energy company, which made large transfers to cover payroll. No other accounts had received large transfers from the Russian account, and the only transactions the Moldovan bank account had on record, aside from interest payments and fees, were cash withdrawals.

"They probably use other banks," said Nuri. "This just happens to be the one account we found."

"Or this is all the money they get."

"Maybe," admitted Nuri. "But Moreno paid a hell of a lot more than this."

"Maybe their agent takes a cut."

"Hefty cut."

"Subject Mercedes sighted," reported MY-PID.

Nuri hit the keys on the laptop and pulled up the image, which was beamed from the fire hydrant. The car turned left instead of right—away from the house.

"Love to bug the car," said Nuri.

"Oughta bug the Russian spymaster's house instead," said Danny.

"Probably already is."

Nuri looked up at Danny.

"Shit," he said. Then he grabbed his sat phone to see if he was right.

21

Washington, D.C.

"I DIDN'T MEAN TO HAVE AN ARGUMENT WITH YOU," ZEN told Breanna after they put Teri to bed.

"It's OK," said Breanna, sitting down on the couch. The flowers he'd bought were sitting on the coffee table.

"You're under a lot of pressure at work. I know. It's gotta be—it's a difficult assignment."

"Mmmmm." She picked up a magazine and began leafing through it.

Zen recognized her mood. It was as if she was bruised all over, and touching her anywhere would hurt. Yet he felt compelled to do something, to reach across the distance between them.

"I had lunch with Daly and Sullivan today," he said, searching his brain for some anecdote that might be even distantly funny. "The dynamic duo. Sullivan was eating this bacon cheeseburger. Didn't he vote in favor of the fat tax last year?"

Breanna shrugged.

"I think he did. His party suggested it," added Zen. "What are you reading?"

Breanna held it up so he could see the cover. *Traditional Home.*

"In the mood for some decorating?" he asked.

"Not really."

"The hallway could use a new coat of paint."

She didn't answer.

"Remember when we painted the apartment?" he asked.

It was a preaccident memory, which put it in a special category, potentially touchy for either one of them. But it was also a happy memory, the two of them working together at a time when they were both very much in love—way beyond that, completely infatuated with each other, unable to get enough of each other's words and bodies.

"Jeez—what was the color?" he said, growing nostalgic. "Peach or something? Mauve. Something that I would have never thought would be a good color."

"You're not really much on color."

"I don't have your color sense," Zen admitted, trying to push through the small opening. "Not at all."

Breanna put down the magazine.

"You're still going to Kiev?"

"Well, yeah," he said.

"I have to go to Brown Lake at the end of the week. Did you remember?"

Brown Lake Test Area was the Technology Office's facility at Dreamland, part of the expanded complex there. Dreamland itself was an Air Force command; the Technology Office was both a contractor and a customer, and kept a small contingent at leased space there. Zen guessed she was going for the demonstration of one of her projects, though she kept the actual identity of the project itself secret, even from him.

"Sure," he said, though in fact the date had slipped from his memory. "Are you taking Teri with you?"

"I can't. You know that."

"She can come with me, then," he said.

"Jeff—"

"Actually, I had a thought about leaving a day or two early and stopping in Prague—"

"Prague?"

"There's an air show. Teri'll love it."

"You can't take her, Jeff."

"Why can't I?"

"She has school."

"Ah, school."

"It's too dangerous—didn't you hear anything I told you the other day?"

The last thing he would ever do was put his daughter in danger. The suggestion that Teri go with him was just a spur of the moment thought, something that just popped into his head. Had he thought about it, he might have rejected it himself. But Breanna's sharp retort put him on the defensive.

"There's going to be plenty of security in Kiev," he said.

"That's not the point."

"Hey, it's not a problem. She doesn't have to go. Caroline can stay here."

Caroline was Breanna's niece, a college-age student who lived nearby and often babysat for them.

"I don't know if she can," said Breanna.

"Well then her mom can. You know there won't be a problem."

"I don't know that at all."

"Hey, I have an idea," said Zen. "What if Caroline and Teri came with me to Prague, and stayed there while I went to Kiev? That would be great for Caroline, right? She'd love it. The art? Right up her alley. I'm going to call her right now."

"You really want to take Teri out of school?"

"To visit Prague? In a heartbeat."

"I don't know what gets into you sometimes." Breanna practically leapt off the couch, stalking past him to the kitchen.

Zen took a deep breath, struggling to keep his own anger in check. Prague wasn't a bad idea at all—he'd only be away from the girls for a day and a half, at most. Caroline had gone with them to Hong Kong just the year before, spending two days alone with Teri while he and Breanna flew to Macau on a secret government mission for the State Department.

More like a secret junket, since it only consisted of having lunch with a hard-to-deal-with Chinese trade official, but that wasn't the point. Caroline and Teri would be fine.

He rolled into the kitchen. Breanna had taken out the small tub of Ben & Jerry's she kept in the freezer, and was eating it straight out of the carton.

"I'm not going to ask you about the Stoner operation," said Zen.

"Good. You shouldn't."

"You think you can save him?"

Breanna stared at him.

"If it's Stoner—" said Zen.

"I know who you're talking about," she said sharply.

"Are you going to try—"

"Don't interfere, Jeff."

"Did you tell Danny?"

Breanna pressed her lips together. He was sure from the reaction that she had, though he wouldn't have been able to explain exactly what tipped him off.

"So what are you going to do?" he asked.

"I don't know that it's Stoner," she said coldly.

"Yes, you do."

"I don't *know*."

"Can you fix him?"

"Jesus."

"Can you?"

"I don't know." Breanna tossed her spoon into the sink, pulled out the garbage can from beneath the kitchen island and dropped the empty ice cream tub into it. Then she stormed out of the room.

"That went well," Zen said to the empty kitchen.

22

Northwestern Moldova

THE RAIN BIT AT HIS FACE AS IF IT WERE ACID. HE PUSHED up the hill, ignoring the sideward slip of his feet on the slick pavement. He pushed to feel the burn in his thighs, the strain of a muscle—to get feeling, any feeling.

Pain was a strange condition. On the one hand it was always there, like the skin that covered his body, the thick clumps of hair, the scars. On the other hand, it was a sensation, something beyond the dull haze he moved through every day, the black swamp of his life. To feel the sharpness, the pressure and strain—it could be savored.

Was it pleasure?

He didn't know pleasure. He knew where he was, he knew his duty.

The Black Wolf pushed up the hill, arms pumping now. He was breathing hard in the darkness.

If there had been houses near the road, he would have woken anyone inside. He was making good time, at a strong pace—an Olympic pace.

Run, a voice told him. *Run*.

He crested the hill and turned to the left, entering a wide, expansive field. His feet found the dirt path by habit; it was too dark to see.

The rain increased. He didn't like the water. He'd almost died in water—in many ways he *had* died in water, even though the doctors said the coldness had helped. He still hated water.

The farmhouse was just ahead. He increased his pace, pounding through the mud.

Five hundred meters from the house a light came on in the kitchen. The light, part of his security system, told him everything was OK.

The farm was secluded and out of the way, but in his business one didn't take chances. Death was inevitable; every moment led you closer. The question was whether you might force some control over it. That was the aim of his security systems.

The Black Wolf ran full strength to the back door of the house. When he was five meters away, the latch unhooked. He reached down with his hand, swinging the door open on a dead trot.

He stopped abruptly on the threshold and closed the door behind him. Taking off his running shoes, he began peeling off the outer layers of his clothes, throwing them into the nearby washing machine. Stripped to his compression shorts, he went inside to the kitchen for a cup of coffee before hitting the shower.

There was a message on the cell phone he used

for work. It was a text message advertising a restaurant in London. Anyone receiving or intercepting it would think it was a junk text. To the Black Wolf, it was anything but.

He poured himself the coffee, then opened his laptop. Booting up, he inserted a small satellite modem into the USB port. When the computer was ready, he opened a Web browser and surfed to Google. He typed in the name of the latest punk-rap band taking Europe by storm, TekDog.

Google gave six hundred pages of hits. He went to their official site, backed out to Google again, then went to the fourth fan site listed in the search results.

The site had photos and music and show listings. It also had a small section titled Nudes&Rumors.

He clicked on it, then scrolled to the third entry.

Heard on the street: band members planning new shows in France for next month. Details soonest.

Still in his underwear, the Black Wolf took his cell phone and called a number that began with a French country code.

"This is Wolf," he said as the connection went through. He spoke in English.

"The old doctor has become a problem. It must be dealt with."

"How soon?"

"Immediately. There have been inquiries. You should be cautious."

"My treatments?"

"We have made other arrangements. We understand they are getting much closer together. That will not be a problem."

"Good," he said.

The sudden emotion he felt surprised him. It bordered on elation.

He closed the phone and went to take a shower.

23

Kiev, Ukraine

HERA SMILED AT THE MUSEUM GUARD AS HE CAME around the corner.

He didn't smile back.

"What are you doing?" he demanded in Ukrainian. Hera didn't speak Ukrainian, but his meaning was obvious.

"Excuse me?" she asked.

"You are in a restricted area. What's in your hand?"

She had been about to place the bug in the fire hose housing when she was interrupted. It was still in her hand, the door to the hose compartment open a few inches.

"I don't understand," she said.

"Your hand," repeated the guard, grabbing her arm.

"Hera, dear, did you find the restroom? *Oh!*" McEwen appeared behind the guard. She was stooped over and looked even older than she was. "Hera?"

The guard turned, still holding Hera's hand.

"What are you doing with my granddaughter?" asked McEwen in Ukrainian.

"She is trespassing down a restricted corridor."

"A restricted corridor? In a museum?"

"This is not just a museum."

McEwen walked close to him, practically touching his shirt, then pitched her head back to look into his face.

"I sent her to find the restroom," she said. "Perhaps you could help us."

The guard let go of Hera's arm. She rubbed it—he'd clamped it so hard it hurt.

"That way. Out there," he said, pointing.

"Are you married?" asked McEwen.

"Yes."

"Too bad. My granddaughter is from America," she added.

"You must go back. Get out of this corridor."

"Of course, of course," said McEwen. She put her hand to her side. "I do have a cramp."

"A cramp?"

"Could you help me?" she asked. "Just walk me to the restroom."

As the guard bent toward McEwen, Hera took a step to the side and put her hand against the wall, pushing the small video bug into the fire hose assembly, then closed the door. She caught up with

McEwen and the guard just as they reached the main corridor.

"You must not come down here again," warned the guard, pointing them toward the ladies' room.

"No, no, of course."

"You can make it?"

"My granddaughter will help." McEwen smiled at him. "You are sure you are taken?"

"THANKS," SAID HERA AFTER HE'D GONE.

"Don't mention it. I almost got you a date."

"That would have been something."

"Ukrainian men are very considerate," said the older woman. "Don't be so quick to judge. I thought your MY-PID system would warn you."

"It did. Too late."

McEwen smiled, and shook her head gently.

"What?" asked Hera.

"You put too much trust in electronics," she said.

"MY-PID's pretty useful."

McEwen shrugged.

"You don't think . . . ?"

"By the time we see anything important, it'll be too late," said McEwen. "You can't replace humans."

"These don't."

"Human intelligence," said McEwen, her tone almost one of incantation. "Should we look at some paintings?"

"I have one more to place."

"Then we'll start with the baroque."

"The electronics don't replace humans," said

Hera defensively as they walked into a gallery area. Now that she wasn't acting, McEwen's pace was strong, as swift as Hera's. "They let us do more."

"In some ways. Not in others. You have to be careful, Hera. You can't let them be crutches. Sometimes you need a little old lady in the back of the alleyway to help you out."

"I don't disagree."

"You don't think he was cute?"

"His breath smelled like stale sardines."

"That could be fixed."

24

Chisinau, Moldova

COMMUNICATIONS FROM THE RUSSIAN EMBASSY WERE routinely monitored and translated, but the private homes of the leading members of the mission were not. Nuri had Reid put the request in; it wasn't clear how long it would be before it was executed, let alone what it might yield.

Getting approval to bug the house itself— absolutely necessary in the case of a diplomat, Nuri knew—would take at least several days at best; by then the Kiev meeting would be over. He wasn't sure it was worth the risk.

So for now their best bet was to concentrate on the doctor. They set up more video bugs in the area, enough so MY-PID could track his car to the main road. Then they rented two more cars, so they could wait in either direction to follow him. It wasn't an ideal setup, but Nuri figured that it would give them a good chance at sticking a tracker on the doctor's car. Once they had that, MY-PID would take over entirely, watching him as he moved around the city.

Danny, though, was getting impatient. Three more of his people—Sergeant Clar "Sugar" Keeb, Paulie Christen, and a tech specialist named Gregor Hennemann—were due to arrive in Kiev by nightfall to help McEwen and Hera. He knew he ought to get there himself, to make sure everything was set up. He also had to make the final call on whether to work with the NATO and local security. At the moment he was leaning toward doing so.

Sugar was a covert CIA op like Hera, though different from her in almost every way. A little older, with a much more easygoing personality, she had become something of a big sister to most of the newbies.

Christen was a surveillance and security expert who'd been recruited from the FBI right after the team's first mission. While Danny and Boston had a great deal of experience in security, they hadn't set up pure surveillance networks, and Danny thought the operation in Africa and Iran could have gone smoother with more help.

Hennemann was a technical whiz kid who'd come to Whiplash from the NSA. There wasn't a computer in the world he couldn't hack into or rewire. Neither Hennemann nor Christen were what was generally referred to as "shooters"— weapons-oriented team members. Danny would have to decide whether to bring more on, and when. He couldn't make that assessment, or felt he couldn't, from Chisinau.

Unless, of course, they caught the Wolves here.

"Hey, he's coming at you," said Nuri over the team radio. "You see him?"

Danny glanced in his mirror, waiting.

"He should be just about to you," added Nuri.

A black Mercedes swept into view. Danny had to wait for two more cars to pass before he could get out, but the Mercedes was still in view.

"Heading toward the city on 581," said Danny.

"I'll be behind you in a few minutes," said Nuri.

"Flash?" said Danny.

"I'm down on Stefan cel Mare, the big cross street."

"Cut over."

"Yeah, well, you should see the damn traffic down here. Looks like every car in the country is in front of me. They got some sort of construction going on, and a cop's directing traffic."

"Did you see his face?" Nuri asked.

"No," said Danny. They still didn't have an image.

The jam-up actually helped them. The doctor got bogged down in traffic a half mile from the city limits. He took a few turns through the side streets, but they were clogged as well.

Downtown, the doctor pulled into a lot near

one of the larger buildings in the business district. Danny saw him get out of the car as he passed.

He was short and fat, bald—he didn't have time to see the doctor's face.

"Car's in the big lot you'll see on your left," he told Flash, who was about a block behind him. "Get the tracker on it."

"On my way."

Danny went down the block, then turned down the side street. There was plenty of parking, so he pulled in. He got out of the car and trotted back to the building.

There were half a dozen people inside, waiting for the elevator. Danny glanced around—there was a man very close to the button panel, short and fat, bald. He was wearing brown pants.

Was it him?

He thought so, and yet he wasn't positive. Several minutes had passed—the doctor could be upstairs already.

The doors opened. Danny had to push himself in, squeezing against a pair of middle-aged women who looked at him as if he were the devil. They said something in Moldovan that he didn't understand. He smiled as if it were a compliment, though he guessed it was anything but.

The elevator stopped on the fifth floor. A man got out. The two women got out on the seventh. Danny stepped to the side, watching the man he thought might be the doctor. The man stared at the doors, studiously avoiding his gaze.

It might be because I'm black, Danny realized.

In America, the fact that he was black would hardly be noticeable, in most contexts anyway. But in Moldova, as in most Eastern European countries, people of African descent were relatively rare.

He took out the control unit for the MY-PID, looking at it as if setting up an app. He tilted it slightly, then pressed the button to activate the video camera. Turning to his right, he held the camera up, getting a good view of the man's profile.

Most of the occupants emptied on the twelfth floor. Only he and the fat man remained as it continued upward. Danny realized he hadn't pushed the button. He glanced at the panel; they were heading toward the twentieth floor.

He reached over and hit 23. Leaning back, he smiled at the man. He didn't smile back.

The doors opened on the twentieth floor. Danny stepped back, watching the man leave.

"He got out on the twentieth floor," he told the others, pulling the earphone back up and turning the MY-PID back onto active coms. "I have an image on the video."

"All right. You sure that's him?" asked Nuri.

"No."

"No?"

"It took me too long to get into the building."

"You want us inside?" asked Flash.

"Hang back," said Danny, stepping out into the hallway as the elevator stopped. He found the stairs a few paces away and descended to the twentieth floor.

There was only one door in the hall, plain and

brown. There was a list of names on a sign next to it.

Danny took out the MY-PID control unit and pointed the camera at the sign.

"What's that say?" he asked.

"Dr. Acevda, Dr. Bolinski, Dr. Kulsch, Dr. Nudstrumov, Dr. Zvederick."

"No Ivanski?"

"Rephrase question."

"Is there an Ivanski?"

"Negative."

"Check to see if there is any correlation between Ivanski and any of those doctors," Danny told MY-PID. "In the meantime, tell me how to ask to make an appointment."

The computer gave him the words. He repeated it twice but couldn't get the pronunciation right.

"Danny, I can do it," said Nuri from outside. "I'm almost there."

"It's all right," said Danny. "I just want to see if we can get images of the doctors. There's no sense you coming in, too. The fewer of us he sees right now, the better."

The door opened into a reception room. Several men and women were scattered among a dozen and a half chairs lining the walls. A television sat in the corner but it was off. The receptionist's desk was next to a closed door that led to the interior offices.

The woman asked in Moldovan if she could help him.

Danny started to ask for an appointment,

but midway through the words failed him; he switched to English.

"I wanted to make a doctor's appointment," he said. "My throat."

The woman asked him if he could speak any Moldovan. Danny pointed to his throat. She pointed at a seat, then picked up the phone and called someone inside.

The patients were middle-aged and older, most a lot older. Danny wondered if he could fake a sore throat. He tried a cough, wincing.

A few minutes later a nurse came through the door and walked over to him. Danny rose.

"You speak English, yes?" she said. Her accent was thick but the words understandable. She was in her early twenties, with an expression somewhere between concern and light annoyance. "How can we help you?"

"Yes, my throat hurts," said Danny. "I was hoping—"

"This is a specialist clinic, for diseases of endocrines."

"Endocrines?"

"Glands. Disorders with the metabolism," said the nurse. "Diabetes, and things more complicated. I'm sorry, but for a sore throat we could only recommend cough drops."

"I see."

She put her hand to his forehead. She had to stretch to do it. Danny caught a slight scent of sweat.

"No fever," she said.

"It's just my throat."

She frowned. "I can send you to another clinic. These doctors. Very good."

"OK, thank you," he said.

She went over to the desk and asked the receptionist for a card. Danny sat back in his seat, realizing he'd forgotten to plant a bug.

Spycraft 101, he reminded himself. Another course he'd skipped.

He was being watched. It wasn't necessary to plant it here—he could do it in the hall where it would be less conspicuous.

"Go to these doctors," said the nurse, returning. "There is a nurse who speaks English."

"Thank you very much," he said, taking the card.

25

Chisinau, Moldova

THE BLACK WOLF HAD CONSIDERED THIS JOB MANY times. He hadn't wished for it but sensed that someday it would come. And now it had.

He didn't like Nudstrumov at all. In the beginning he was neutral, but over the years he had come to despise him. He had a certain haughty way of acting. Like the other day, when he kept him waiting. He had made it seem as if it was nothing, undeliberate, but the Black Wolf knew better. He knew.

He would take him leaving his office, going from the door to the car. It was easier than the house, where there would be some inconvenience getting in. The office, though, was all routine. Nudstrumov parked in the same place, left at the same time, always at ten past three. He was a most punctual man.

The Black Wolf chose his weapon—a Dragunov SVD-S with a folding butt, very common and untraceable. Technically not a sniper rifle, but he would be shooting from only across the street. The semiautomatic gun and its lead core bullets were extremely accurate.

He had already scoped the roof of the building across the street. Getting away would be as easy there as anywhere else.

It was all a matter of planning.

He checked his watch. It was past one. He had less than two hours to get into position.

26

Chisinau, Moldova

TWO DOCTORS WORKED AT THE CLINIC ON THURSDAYS. One was a woman. The other was a man in his sixties named Andrei Nudstrumov.

Nudstrumov had an extensive medical background that did not intersect with Dr. Ivanski's at all. He had come to Romania from Russia five years before, applying for medical certification. His background was extensive and he was granted "all honors," as the registering agency called it.

He was an endocrinologist. Ivanski had been a general practitioner.

Still, Nuri was sure the two men were the same. Danny remained unconvinced, even when the short fat man who'd driven the Mercedes didn't come out of the clinic after an hour. In the meantime, MY-PID trolled across the Internet, picking up data on Nudstrumov. He'd used a credit card a few months before, not far from the town Danny had visited. He'd bought gas, eaten breakfast and dinner, and purchased merchandise, all in a small town about seven kilometers south of the town Danny had visited.

MY-PID then correlated that series of purchases to a somewhat similar set by a third man—or at least a third name. This man had been making regular visits to the area over the past seven years. The match was not perfect—there were a few additional charges in the mix—but several things immediately jumped out at Nuri as he looked at the pattern: the visits were only once a year, at the same time of year, and the card was only used for those visits.

The man's name was Rustam Gorgov. According to the records, he owned property in the area—a large farm about two kilometers outside of town.

So why did he stay at a motel?

"Maybe he's got his mother-in-law at the farm," said Flash. "That would do it."

Flash and Danny were sitting together in the front seat of the rented Dacia, five blocks east of the building where the clinic was. Flash's car was parked right behind him. Nuri was several blocks away in the opposite direction. They were waiting to follow the doctor out of the clinic.

"You sure these are all the same person?" Danny asked Nuri.

"Of course not," said Nuri. "But here's what I think. Ivanski stayed in Moldova after the camp was closed. But he didn't practice medicine, for whatever reason. At some point either he got antsy or needed money. He adopted Nudstrumov's identity."

"Or he was Nudstrumov, and living in Russia," offered Danny.

"Exactly. He buys the property under the Moldovan name, but for some reason decides he can't practice as Ivanski. He already had his credentials, but maybe it's the connection to the place he didn't want known. In any event, Ivanski more or less disappears, and we have Nudstrumov."

"And Rustam Gorgov?" asked Danny.

"Totally fictitious—the computer hasn't found any other data on him at all. I'm sure there's more. We just haven't found it."

"Where's the connection to the assassins?" asked Flash.

"We don't know yet," said Nuri. "That's why we keep looking. But there's definitely enough that's suspicious."

"Maybe he's just trying to keep an affair quiet," said Flash. "Or he's a drug dealer on the side."

"He may grow marijuana on that farm," said Nuri. "It's a cash crop in Moldova. We have to check it out."

"Man, I wish we'd do something more than check things out," said Flash. "I'm getting—stale, I guess."

Danny turned and looked at Flash. Like him, Flash was action oriented—give him a clear-cut assignment, and he was good to go. This was far more nebulous—this was like wandering through a fog and hoping to come out on the other side. There was no clear-cut path to the right door.

God, he thought, we're miles and miles away from getting a real handle on this.

"The doctor may take us to some other connection," said Nuri. "We have to be a little patient."

"The problem is time," answered Danny.

"I can follow the leads here," answered Nuri. "You can get back to Kiev."

"We may do that." Danny glanced at his watch. It was five to three. The doctor should be leaving soon.

NURI CHECKED THE SIGNAL ON THE TRACKING DEVICE, to make sure it was working. The radio signal was being sent through a commercial GPS satellite system, and was accurate to within roughly a third of a meter. Adapted from a commercial design used to track trucks over the highway, the device worked extremely well in open areas. Inside cities it could be problematic, however, as the larger buildings and other obstacles occasionally shielded the signal.

Nuri was sure they were tantalizingly close to figuring this out. All they needed was one more strategic bit of information and they'd know where and who these guys were.

They might already have it. He had originally thought the doctor was an unlikely choice to be the leader of the assassin group, but the fact that he had at least two other aliases gave him some hope. Underlings, he reasoned, had no need for multiple names.

Nuri didn't buy most of the speculation about the human experiments. He thought Stoner was probably involved, but wondered if the helicopter crash hadn't somehow been arranged. That wasn't something the Agency would be too ready to admit or even investigate—it implied that whatever intelligence they'd gathered in the Revolution operation—Danny's name for it—had been tainted, fed to them by a double agent.

Stoner.

Maybe Stoner had felt the Agency was closing in. Maybe he just wanted a change of venue. Or occupation.

Becoming an assassin, Nuri thought—well, there was a money-making retirement option he had never thought of.

His watch beeped. It was 3:00 P.M.

AT EXACTLY 3:05, MY-PID ANNOUNCED THAT DR. Nudstrumov was coming out of his clinic and heading toward the elevator.

"Bankers' hours," Flash told Danny. "See ya in a bit."

Danny waited as Flash got out of the car, then put his signal on and checked the traffic. He pulled out behind a bright red Fiat and drove toward the building. He wanted to time it so he got there just as the doctor was getting into his car. But he'd been a little too anxious; he was a block away before Nudstrumov finally got into the elevator to go down to the lobby.

"I'm going to pull into the lot," Danny told the others. "Flash, hang back."

"Yeah, copy that."

"Nuri?"

"Right."

A panel truck turned into the lot just ahead of Danny, then stopped, waiting for a car that was pulling out. Danny stopped, still in the roadway. He glanced in his mirror anxiously—the last thing he wanted right now was a car accident.

The truck finally pulled ahead. Danny took his foot off the brake. The door to the building was on his right.

"Subject exiting building."

There he was, just ahead on the right. He was short and rotund, not particularly distinguished looking. If you were Hollywood, he thought, and you were going to cast someone in the role of assassin mastermind, Dr. Nudstrumov wouldn't be it.

Nudstrumov glanced over his shoulder as he began walking to his car. Danny got a glimpse of his face. He looked somewhat annoyed, not quite angry but not relaxed either.

The doctor kept walking, his chubby legs stroking quickly. A car on Danny's left started to pull out into the aisle. Danny stopped, waiting for her to go—he'd pull in, then wait for the doctor to leave before following.

He looked back at the doctor. He was only a few meters from his car now. He had his keys in his left hand.

Suddenly the doctor seemed to spin to his left. Danny thought for a moment that he had recognized him through the car window somehow. Then in the next moment the right side of his forehead exploded, bursting into a red splatter of blood.

"Shit!" yelled Danny. "He's been shot! Nudstrumov's been shot!"

27

Chisinau, Moldova

THE FIRST SHOT HAD BEEN LOW, DEADLY BUT NOT instantaneous lethal. The second hit home perfectly, exploding Nudstrumov's skull.

A thing of beauty.

But the Black Wolf knew he couldn't stop to admire it. He had to move.

He pulled the rifle back, quickly folding the stock and dropping it into the box. He slapped it

closed and picked it up. He already had his backpack on.

A person got out of the car across the street,
near the lot where he'd shot the doctor. The Black
Wolf saw him through the window from the
corner of his eye.

He turned and focused.

A black man.

Familiar.

Familiar. He focused—narrowed his vision so
the man was right next to him, features large in
his brain.

He was very, very familiar. Yet he couldn't quite
identify him.

Why did he know him?

No time for that: *Go! Go! Go!*

28

Chisinau, Moldova

DANNY LEAPT OUT OF THE CAR. HIS FIRST INSTINCT WAS
to run to Nudstrumov, even though he knew it
was too late to help him. He took a step, then dove
to the ground, belatedly realizing that he, too,
would be in the killer's sights.

Or could be.

The shot had come from across the street.
There was another building—several.

One of the rooftops.

"Danny, what's going on?" asked Nuri.

"Somebody just shot the doctor. They must have been across the street."

Danny jumped to his feet and began running.

"Where? Where?"

"From the roof, maybe. It had to be a rifle—the shot came down from above, and it was pretty high-powered. There's no one in the lot that could have shot him."

Danny crossed the street. There was no one nearby or in the cars, and the shot had definitely come from above.

He reached inside his jacket for his Beretta, then thought better of it. If the police responded and saw a man with a gun, they'd jump to conclusions—and shoot before asking questions.

There were three buildings, all butting up against each other. All three were five-story buildings. There were storefronts on the ground floor, offices and apartments above.

Would there be a fire escape?

He walked quickly to the end of the block, turned, then began to trot. An alley ran behind the buildings. He turned down it.

"Danny, where are you?" asked Flash over the radio.

"I'm behind the buildings across the street. Just east of the lot."

"I'm turning down the side street now," said Flash. "I'll be behind you."

"Good."

The alley was lined with garbage cans and old cars. There were balconies on the right, fire escapes on the left. Two children were playing soccer at the far end, banging the ball against a rusted chain-link fence.

Danny looked up to his left.

How long would it take a shooter to get down from the roof or one of the upper apartments?

A minute, maybe two, assuming he planned it right. And these guys always planned it right.

But where would he have gone? No one had passed him. The buildings on the right, though only three and two stories, were packed shoulder-to-shoulder. To get past them you'd have to go through them. Or maybe over them.

He turned so he had the back of the building in view and sidled in the direction of the kids. Any second, the killer could appear over the side.

Danny put his hand near his gun, ready, just in case.

"I need words to ask the children if they saw someone," Danny told MY-PID.

The computer spat out a phrase. Danny yelled it to the kids, but they didn't react, too consumed in their game.

A window flew open behind him. Danny spun, dropped to his knee.

A head popped out. Danny grabbed his gun.

But it was a woman, yelling at him.

"What's she saying? Translate mode," Danny told MY-PID.

"Unknown. Repeat."

"Give me the Moldovan for 'Did you see anything?'"

MY-PID gave him the proper phrase. Danny yelled it up. The woman yelled back again, once more indecipherable.

"The words are unclear," said MY-PID. "The language is not Moldovan. It appears to be a Russian dialect, but too distant to hear."

The woman pointed upward. As Danny followed her gesture, a car pulled into the far end of the alley. It was Flash.

"The police are on their way," Nuri said over the radio.

Danny looked around. There was a fire escape a few meters to his right. "I'm going to check the roof."

"I'll get your car out of there," Nuri said. "Don't stay too long."

Danny jumped up and grabbed the steel ladder to the bottom of the fire escape. He pulled it down, starting to climb even before it hit the stop. Flash, meanwhile, made a U-turn, then pulled around so it would be easier to get away.

Sirens wailed in the distance as Danny reached the edge of the roof. He stopped, pulled out his pistol, then went over, rolling over the low wall and spinning up, ready. But there was no one there.

He looked around the roof quickly. There was a mattress near the front edge.

"Danny—police are pulling in," said Nuri. "Time to go."

Danny ignored him, running to the front of the

building. He wanted something—a shell casing, a soda bottle, a coffee cup.

Nothing except the mattress. He knelt on it and looked toward the doctor's building.

Too much of an angle. The shooter would have been to his left somewhere.

"Danny!" shouted Nuri.

"I'm coming. Flash?"

"I'm here. Let's move."

Danny pulled out the MY-PID control unit and had it record a video of the roof. Then he raced over to the fire escape ladder and descended.

They saw the ambulance arriving as they drove past the building.

"Kinda late for that," said Flash.

29

Washington, D.C.

MOLDOVA WAS SEVEN HOURS AHEAD OF WASHINGTON, and Breanna was just pulling into the Pentagon lot on her way to work when Reid called.

"There are some other developments in Moldova," he told her. "We should review them together as soon as we get a chance."

"I can meet you after lunch," she told him.

"Earlier, would be better. There's been a shooting."

"Were we involved?"

"We saw it. The person who was killed may have been connected to the Wolves. They're still sorting things out."

"Can you get over to the Pentagon this morning?" Breanna asked.

"Name a time."

Breanna told him to come whenever he could and her secretary would get her.

A half hour later she made a graceful exit from a phone conference with a contractor in Rhode Island working on a project for the Navy.

"Could you get me some coffee, MaryClaire, please?" Breanna asked as Reid came in. "I'm having a caffeine fit."

Her secretary smiled. MaryClaire Bennett was an old Pentagon hand. While their first few days had been a bit rocky, she'd relaxed considerably since. Breanna had learned to trust her people sense, which was based on many years of experience with the different personalities in the building. She'd seen many axes buried along the way—most, as the saying went, in people's backs.

"Mr. Reid?"

"I've had my quota for today, thank you."

Reid pulled a seat in front of Breanna's desk.

"Busy day?" he asked.

"We have an aircraft demonstration coming up," she told him. "And I'm going to have to be away from the office for a few days. So I have to get a lot of the day-to-day things out of the way. You know how it goes."

"Yes. When are you leaving?"

"Sunday night. I'll be at Dreamland."

"How long?"

"Until Tuesday night."

"Back in time for the NATO conference."

"Yes."

MaryClaire knocked on the door and came in with the coffee.

"General Magnus is looking for you," the secretary said. "I told him you were tied up. He asks that you call him when you can—shouldn't take more than a few minutes. It's about the plane."

"OK." Breanna took a sip of the coffee, trying to get her brain to switch gears as MaryClaire left. "So, I saw the bulletin. The doctor was shot?"

"Yes. It was a sniper. Danny thinks the shot came from across the street, a roof, though he couldn't find any shells."

Reid gave her some background on the shooting. The local police were investigating. The local news services had almost nothing to report.

"The doctor was using the name of Nudstrumov. We've found, or at least think we've found, another alias. Rustam Gorgov. Gorgov owns property in northeastern Moldova, not all that far from the former training camp. And the cemetery where Mark Stoner was supposedly buried."

He had an update on that as well—an overnight check of the DNA on the corpses showed no match.

"We have to wait for the full report and the entire testing suite, which is more extensive," said Nuri. "But there were no matches. One of the dead men would have been about Stoner's age and size, for what that's worth."

Breanna nodded.

"They must realize we're after them," said Reid. "The doctor visited a Russian spymaster. Maybe that was what got him killed."

"Why?"

"Maybe he was a bad risk. Maybe they don't work for the Russians."

"If they don't, we won't have anything to worry about," said Breanna.

A faint smile appeared at the corner of Reid's mouth. It was an ironic smile, the sort that indicated he thought she was being naive.

"What about the property?" Breanna asked.

Reid opened his briefcase and took out a set of satellite photos, along with a satellite map. MY-PID was still analyzing different data related to the property and the surrounding area— everything from its ownership to electric bills.

No concrete ties to the Wolves had been found. But a review of commercial satellite images over the past four years showed flashes of light that appeared to be weapons.

"Could be a training ground," said Reid. "Or just a farmer doing nighttime poaching. I've already applied for a Global Hawk assignment so we can get a closer look. But I'd suggest we have Whiplash check it out as well. Discreetly. And from a safe distance."

"Agreed."

"The question is what we do if we think they're in there," said Breanna.

"That's always been the problem. It would be one thing to catch them in the act. Here . . ."

"Do you think it's time to call the White House?" asked Breanna, putting down her coffee.

"I think so. If we take any direct action, outside of protecting the NATO ministers, we'll need a finding. If the group is as accomplished as we believe they are, anything we do would be bound to . . ." He paused, trying to find the right phrase. "It is bound to be complicated," he added finally.

"All right. And they're going to need more people," said Breanna. "We should have them ready."

Reid nodded. Then he asked the question she'd been dreading since they were first handed the assignment:

"What do you want them to do if it's Stoner?"

"I think, unfortunately, if he resists, they have to kill him," said Breanna, ignoring the lump in her throat. "There's really no other choice."

30

Northeastern Moldova

THE TEXT MESSAGE THE BLACK WOLF RECEIVED A FEW hours after killing the doctor consisted of one word:

EXCELLENT

It was the message he received whenever a job was complete. The doctor was the same as the others, just one more on the list.

The man he'd seen, getting of the car. A black man. African.

Or American.

Did he know Americans?

He had lived before the crash. He had a whole past, but it was locked off from him, erased by whatever they had used to resurrect him, to re-build him, to keep him going.

He didn't want it back.

But who was that man?

He had other things to worry about. As much as he hated Nudstrumov, the doctor had readily supplied the serum he needed. Who would do that now?

They would. Or he would hunt them down. Maybe he should start on that now.

The Black Wolf's cell phone beeped with a second message. It indicated a new website.

This one was German, a listing of art shows. There was a phone number he had to call, using a prepaid cell phone.

It was best not to make the call from the house. He went out to the barn and got his motorcycle.

He'd seen the black man somewhere. But where?

A half hour later, sitting at the top of a hill ten miles from the house, the Black Wolf made the call to the number in the listing.

"The assignment has changed," said a computerized voice in English. "You will go to Prague. A new team is being prepared. Further instructions will be provided. Leave immediately."

The Black Wolf looked down at the phone. He pressed the *1* digit to show that he understood. Then he hung up.

31

Northeastern Moldova

RATHER THAN WAITING FOR THE MORNING AND THE IFFY connections north, Danny, Nuri, and Flash took two cars and drove up in the direction of the farm. Given that his visit to the cemetery might have tipped someone off, Danny decided they would bypass the town where he'd stayed as well as the old athletic facility and cemetery. That meant a more circuitous route, swinging farther west before turning back toward the farm from the north.

Nuri and Flash took one car; Danny drove alone. He spent much of the ride brooding about Stoner and the past.

If things had gone differently following the mission, Dreamland itself could have sent a team to check the wreck. But Dreamland had been going through its own transition. Colonel Bastian was being replaced.

Dog wouldn't have left Stoner behind if he could have helped it. He'd blow up half the world getting one of his people back home.

They didn't make them like Colonel Bastian anymore. He was a balls-to-the-wall SOB to anyone that crossed him. If you were one of his, however, he didn't just have your back, he had your soul. He didn't command you, he cared about you. He made you a better soldier. And a better person.

Dog.

Danny felt his eyes welling up, thinking about his old commander, Breanna's dad. He reached over and turned on the radio, hunting for some music to get his mind off the past.

Hell, Danny, you're making me into some kind of cardboard saint. You know that's not me.

Danny felt a shudder through his body. He knew the voice was just the product of his over-tired imagination, but he was so spooked he turned the radio off and drove in silence for the next two hours.

"Magnetic field, fifty meters," said Nuri, reading the screen on the MY-PID unit. "Runs all along the far side of the stream."

Danny focused the night glasses, then swept slowly along the creek. These were big glasses, the size of binoculars, and besides being able to pick up the thermal image of a mouse at two hundred yards, they could accept data from MY-PID, superimposing it to create what the scientists called an "enriched and interpreted image."

Notes from the computer. Imagine what a school kid could do with that.

"Show magnetic field," he told the computer.

A blue wall appeared on the other side of the stream. It stretched all the way to the road, a good kilometer away, and ran into the hills on the south. It encircled the entire farm. The perimeter measured nearly thirteen kilometers.

"It has to be some sort of detection field," said Nuri.

"Like a force field?" asked Flash.

"It's not going to zap us, if that's what you mean," said Nuri. "But I'd guess that anything that moves through it would be detected."

"As long as it's metal?" asked Flash.

"It may be pretty sensitive," said Danny. "Anything that could conduct electricity could set it off. There's something similar at Dreamland. You can't breach it without it being detected."

He slipped back from the trees. Someone had spent a lot of money to set up the perimeter.

Clearly, they had the right place. Or at least one of them.

The property consisted of three gently rolling hills, spread out over land that included two streams and bordered a third. Woods formed an inner ring around a border of open fields, an arrangement that Danny surmised was intentional—the woods would provide cover for defenders. Warned of anyone attempting to approach them, they could slip into the trees and pick them off as they came.

The next ring consisted of farm fields, nearly all

idle. At the center were a number of farm buildings and one large house.

The house looked like a nineteenth-century Moldovan manor house, a three-story masonry structure with a sharply pitched roof. Two wings extended off the back, giving the building a U-shape. MY-PID calculated there was just over 8,000 square feet of space inside, not counting the basement.

There were three buildings a short distance away. One was an old barn, in an architectural style similar to the house. A six-bay garage sat next to it, at the end of the driveway. Flat-roofed and skinned with pale concrete stucco, it was somewhat newer, probably built sometime around World War II.

The third building was made of steel and didn't look to be more than four or five years old. It reminded Danny of the gym he'd seen at the training center, though it would have fit nicely in any industrial park across the world. It was large, 92 feet by just over 280. You couldn't quite get a football field inside, but it would be close.

It was also heated—the glasses showed that the exterior walls were warmer than the garage's. The heat was uniform, and the walls apparently well-insulated enough to prevent the night glasses from picking up details from the interior.

Unusual for a warehouse, especially one that appeared empty.

A perfect place to set up a training exercise, Danny thought darkly. You could rehearse a dozen killings inside, run two or three teams and not have them bump into each other.

"No guards on the interior roads," said Nuri, watching the feed on the laptop from a Predator V. The aircraft had flown from Germany, and would be assigned to Whiplash for as long as they needed it. A second was on its way; both would operate out of Ukraine. They were CIA assets, controlled from a site on Cyprus.

"Two video cameras in the front woods," said Nuri. "They're focusing on the road coming up to the house. And there's a mine system."

The Predator was reading electric currents as well as heat. The mines were wired; a belt ten meters wide surrounded the house. There were also patches in different areas where trees or bushes provided cover to approach the center of the compound.

"Parachute drop might work," said Nuri. "Get right past the defenses."

"We got to land on the roof?" asked Flash. There was the slightest tremor in his voice— though he had jumped often, Flash did not like parachuting. "If their ground defenses are that elaborate, you don't think they'd have something to protect against airplanes?"

"You think they have S.A.M.s in the barn?" asked Danny.

"Gatling guns in one of the lower buildings would do it."

"Do they?" Danny looked at Nuri.

"I don't see anything in those buildings," said Nuri. "But we only have infrared at the moment."

"We're better off going on the ground," said Danny, considering. "If they have this much technology, they'll trust it. Once we're past the magnetic wall, the rest will be easy. We'll just pick a path around the sensors."

"That's like Moses saying once we cross the Red Sea, we'll be free from the Egyptians," said Nuri.

"You know what, Colonel?" Flash held up his control unit. He had zoomed in on a small section of the property. "Can I see this grid on the big screen?"

"Go ahead."

Flash hunkered down with Nuri, coordinating the grid numbers.

"You look at these plants?" Flash asked after they zoomed the image. "You know what they are?"

"No."

"It's cannabis. Pot. They have about two acres worth of marijuana growing down that hillside."

"Two acres?"

"Shit yeah."

"You sure?"

"Have a look."

Danny wasn't an expert in plant morphology, but MY-PID was. Flash was right.

"Two acres worth of weed," said Flash. "You sure we ain't bustin' a drug operation?"

32

White House

COVERT OPERATIONS WERE AMONG THE MOST TOP
secret of all government undertakings, but that
didn't meant they didn't have their own bureau-
cratic infrastructure and procedures. On the
contrary: the bureaucracy and its pathways were
in some ways even more elaborate for "black"
operations than those involving the rest of the
government.

Legal opinions—many more than the average
person would believe—as well as myriad logisti-
cal decisions and arrangements had to be formu-
lated, reviewed, rejected (more often than not),
reformulated, and finally decided upon.

These were all subject to the "serendipitous co-
nundrums," as Jonathon Reid put it: chance, accidents, and, last and very often least, official policy,
which acted like grit in the wheels of the churning system. Even when the chain of command was
set up in a streamlined way to purposely get quick
decisions and emphasize flexibility, it could take
days, if not weeks, to get the outlines of an operation approved.

There were surprisingly few ways to short-
circuit the process. The one surefire way, however, was to go directly to the President herself.

Which was what Reid did, arranging to stop
by the White House residence to play cards after
dinner.

Not with the President—Mrs. Todd abhorred

gambling, whether it was cards or horse racing or even the state lottery, something which hadn't won her many friends when she proposed it be abolished while running for the state legislature at the start of her career. She'd lost that election; it was the last time she ever mentioned the lottery, on or off the record.

Her stance on gambling was 180 degrees different than her husband's. Mr. Todd—no friends called him the First Husband, even as a joke—held poker games at the residence twice a week. Reid was a semiregular, and had been since well before the venue change that came with the President's election.

More than just the venue had changed. There was now a butler available to keep the drinks filled.

The cigarette smoke was still horrendous. Mr. Todd was an unreformed hacker.

The President visited the session generally at 10:00 P.M., ostensibly on her way to bed, but most often on her way to do more work in her private office upstairs. She was a night owl, and in fact rarely got more than four hours of sleep.

"My God, Mr. Todd," she said, coming into the family dining room where the games were held. "So much smoke!"

Everyone, except her husband, stood.

"Next week we do cigars, Mrs. Todd," he answered.

It was a routine of theirs: she always complained about the smoke; he always threatened more. She walked around to the head of the table and gave him a peck on the cheek.

"Good cards?" he said.

"Four queens," she said dryly. "Should I be jealous?"

Her husband smiled. No one was ever sure if she was reading the cards accurately or if they were teasing each other. But the prudent thing to do was drop out, and they all did.

"*Mister* Rockfert," she said, noticing Sam Rockfert. "We haven't seen you here in quite a while."

"No, I know, Mary. Been a while."

She went over to Rockfert. He was an old friend—a plumber who had befriended the Todds even before the lotto election, when Mr. Todd was working as a Senate staff assistant. He was the only person besides her husband who would use her first name—including her brother-in-law James, who was sitting on her husband's right.

"How's Margaret?" the President asked.

"Her knee has been giving her fits. Or I should say, giving me fits." Rockfert laughed. "Other than that, she's fine. Grandkids came up last week."

"You have to arrange to bring them around. We'd love to see them."

She was sincere, though her schedule meant that it was unlikely she'd be able to spend more than two or three minutes with them, even if such a meeting could be arranged.

"Mr. Reid, I hope you are not betting your pension money," said the President, seeming to spot him for the first time.

"It wouldn't be much to lose," said Reid.

"It's the money he got from selling guns to the

Contras that he doesn't want to lose," quipped James. "You notice he doesn't bet that."

The President looked over and scowled at him. Her husband laughed.

"Ignore them, Mr. Reid," said the President. "They're just jealous of your good fortune. I wonder—could you spare me a moment? I have a few questions, now that you're here."

"Of course. The way my luck has been going, I'm glad to take a break."

Reid got up and followed the President down the hall to the study.

"You have something new for me?" asked the President, sitting down in a chair next to her desk. It was a reproduction of a piece of furniture that James Madison was said to have brought into the White House. The original was in a Smithsonian storeroom.

"We think we've found a complex the Wolves use," said Reid. "In Moldova."

"Interesting."

"We'd like to send Whiplash in to find out. But that may involve bloodshed."

"In Moldova."

"Yes, I'm afraid so. If they are there, striking them now—before the conference—would preempt the possibility of their attack. The conference could go off without a hitch."

"How good is the evidence?"

Reid laid it out.

"Sketchy," said the President.

"At this stage, things often are."

"Yes."

The President leaned back in the chair. She stared at the wall behind him, her eyes facing a portrait of Teddy Roosevelt, one of her favorite predecessors.

"Can we pull this off without being detected?" she asked. "In and out, no complications? No witnesses?"

Reid had given the question considerable thought. An American raid in any foreign country would create a major incident, even if it went off without a hitch. He believed that Whiplash could get into the compound and complete its mission, but there was no way to guarantee it could be done without attracting attention, especially if the Wolves chose to resist. And everything indicated they would.

"I can't guarantee that nothing would come out," said Reid. "There is always some possibility of failure."

The political dynamics were difficult. President Todd was trying to wean Moldova toward the West, as she had done with Ukraine. But the government was on even shakier grounds, with a poor economy, and Russia anxious to prevent further defections to NATO.

Go in and out quietly, and no one would complain. No one would even know. Strike too loudly or trip over the wrong contingency, and the Moldovan government would be forced to renounce the attack, and the U.S., playing right into Russia's hands. And if they didn't, popular opinion would surely turn against the Moldovan government, an even better development for Russia.

Those considerations don't outweigh the necessity of striking, Reid thought, but he could understand the President's hesitation.

And he had a solution.

"I was speaking with the men in the field before coming over tonight," he said. "It turns out that a very large amount of marijuana is grown on the site where we would like to strike."

"Marijuana?"

"Quite a cash crop in Moldova, as it happens." Reid reached into the pocket of his jacket and took out two sheets of paper. They contained satellite photos of the property and the marijuana. He handed them to the President. "I wasn't aware of its importance until today. But apparently the farmers do quite well. They seem to supply much of Europe. There are almost two acres of it here," he added. "You can see in these photos. The leaves are very distinct. They are pointy, with five—"

"Jonathon, I hope you don't think I have no idea what marijuana looks like," said the President. "This is the Wolves' compound?"

"Yes."

"They sell it?"

"Possibly. They may use it on their own—medicinally, shall we say?"

Reid wasn't exactly sure why the plant was being grown there. While two acres was a lot, given the security measures and their location, they could easily grow considerably more. That seemed to rule out the possibility that the Wolves were running a drug operation on the side, though there was no way to tell. It might even be a way to explain the secrecy surrounding the property, if neighbors became too curious.

"If we told the Moldovan government that this was a drug operation," he said, "we would give them cover for anything that happened."

"Under what pretense does an American military force make a drug raid?" asked the President skeptically.

"As part of a NATO task force operating under UN auspices," said Reid. "As directed by the UN last year. It's a fig leaf, but it is authorized. The European Union has been pushing for more antidrug enforcement actions."

"When do you tell them?"

"Right before the raid."

"What if they want to come along?" the President asked.

"We let them. Once the place is secure. Then we can use Moldovan facilities to hold the Wolves until they can be extradited for murder. Assuming they survive the raid."

"There's a place where they can be held?"

"I've spoken to our station chief in the capital. He's confident they could be held at a Moldovan military base. We'd only need to have them stay until we had charges ready in Poland for the murders there. That should only take a few days. It would avoid having to take them to Ukraine on attempted charges. We also wouldn't have to reveal how we got the evidence against them. It's much better than taking them to one of our bases."

"Granted," said the President. "But what do we do if the Moldovans won't cooperate?"

"We'll be back at the same starting point," said Reid. "You will have to decide whether to proceed without their permission. But then they'll at least think this was about drugs. And the Russians will as well."

Reid assumed that the Moldovan government had been penetrated by Russian spies.

"I'd suggest you make that decision beforehand," he added. "And that we only proceed if we're prepared to go alone."

"Hmmmm."

"Our station chief reminded me that the Moldovan government received thirty million euros in enforcement money from the E.U. Drug Fund six months ago, without anything to show for it. This will allow them to pretend that they are quite on top of things."

"You must be very good at poker," said the President.

"I hold my own."

"Go. All the way. Make it work."

33

Washington suburbs

THE NATIONALS TOOK IT HARD, LOSING 7–2. THEY WERE never really in the game, getting clobbered with a five-run first inning.

Just as well, thought Zen as he drove home. He didn't have to invest much emotion in the game, only to see them lose. And Senator Dirks was an admirable guest, insisting on paying for the food and the single beer Zen allowed himself at the games when he had to drive home.

All the lights were on in the house as he drove up. That was unusual. Breanna generally holed up in bed the nights he was out at games, either with work or with a book or a movie. Usually he found her out like a light, her computer or Kindle lying next to her.

Maybe she wants to apologize, he thought. Or maybe she just left the lights on.

The smell of coffee as he rolled himself up the ramp from the garage tipped him off that it was probably none of the above. And sure enough, she was sitting in the kitchen, frowning at a laptop.

"Hey," he said, coming in. "We lost."

"So I heard."

"Check the scores?"

"I wanted to see what kind of mood you'd be in."

He laughed. "Nah. You can't really expect the Nats to win. So when they lose, it doesn't really bother me. Someday, maybe."

He couldn't quite read her expression. Was she working? She was using the family laptop, so he thought not.

"Checking the news?" he asked.

"The weather. My flight schedule has been changed. I'm leaving in the morning."

"Oh. OK."

"I talked to Caroline. She'll be here right after class. From what I understand, she's very excited about going to Prague."

"I told you she would be."

"I also spoke to General Magnus today," said Breanna.

"How is he?"

"He's going to Prague, too."

"Really? Suddenly, it's the cool place to be."

"He wants to show off the Tigershark to the Germans and the English. He thinks he can sell it as a next-generation NATO fighter."

"Tigershark?"

"Don't play dumb with me."

"Hey, being dumb is something I don't have to pretend to be." Zen popped the top on a Rogue Porter—he could tell he needed something substantial.

"You set this up, didn't you?" said Breanna. "So I'd come with you."

"Honey, I have no idea what you're talking about. The Tigershark—it's a dead deal. You can't even get it past your own Air Force brass. Manned interceptors have no future in the Air Force. It's not what I want, but—"

Breanna got up from the table and stormed away.

"Hey—what's up?" asked Zen. "I didn't talk to Magnus. Is that what you think?"

The Tigershark had been to air shows before. It was just a coincidence.

He glanced at his watch, wondering if it was too late to call Magnus and see if there was something else involved.

More than likely, not.

Quarter past eleven. Far too late to call. Too late, really, to do anything but drink his beer.

34

Northeastern Moldova

DANNY, NURI, AND FLASH SPENT THE NIGHT PLANTING video bugs along the roads, making sure that all of the approaches to the farm were covered. Meanwhile, the Predator V circling overhead was joined by its companion shortly after daybreak. The second aircraft had a ground-penetrating radar that could see into the buildings, as well as hunt for bunkers and other surprises. The pair could stay over the farm, orbiting at roughly 40,000 feet virtually undetectable, for a week.

There were two men inside the main house, in what seemed to be some sort of control room at the back. Probably it was a security post. Otherwise, the place was empty.

Surveillance network established, Danny and the others drove south to find a place to rest. Worried that stopping nearby might inadvertently tip the people at the farm off, Danny drove almost thirty kilometers away, not stopping until he spotted a small inn that sat above a twisting path from the highway. He pulled off the road and waited for the others. It was just after 6:00 A.M.

"That says restaurant and hotel in Russian," said Nuri when they drove up. He pointed to the sign, hand painted in a neat script.

Danny had seen the Romanian sign in Latin script but not the smaller Cyrillic, which was on the other side of the road.

"How come the sign's in Russian?" asked Flash. "I thought all the Russians were on the eastern end of the country?"

"That's the greatest concentration," said Nuri. "But remember, this was part of the Soviet Union before the breakout. Russians are everywhere."

There was no special reason to be suspicious, but Danny still decided to look for another place. They found a small café about two miles farther down the road. Two trucks were parked out front.

"You sure you're not getting paranoid, Colonel?" asked Flash as they got out of their cars.

"I'm always paranoid," said Danny. "Let's get some grub."

THEY LEFT THEIR MIKES OPEN WHILE THEY ATE, HOPING the MY-PID would pick up and translate useful local gossip. But the talk was mostly about the weather and a hike in government-controlled gasoline prices, planned to go into effect in a week. The fact that the three strangers in the corner were American didn't provoke any comments.

Nuri went over and spoke to the hostess, asking about hotels. Bits and pieces of French and Spanish flooded into his head as he spoke. This was both a help and a hindrance, giving him more vocabulary and at the same time making it harder for him to get the right pronunciation.

Nuri had always had a certain fluidity with languages. It was one of his prime assets as a CIA officer. MY-PID helped tremendously—but it also made his ability less important. The next generation of field officers would operate with implants in their head, speaking fluently in any language they dialed up.

The waitress mentioned a few chain hotels back close to the capital. Nuri said he wanted something local.

"You are an American, though," she said, switching to English. "You want to stay here?"

"Yes," he said. "My friends and I are researching locations for a movie. We're from Hollywood."

"Movie?"

"*The Sound of Music*," he said. "We're doing a remake."

Nuri was particularly happy about this cover story, and he had to practically bite his tongue to keep from embellishing it. There was always a temptation to add details when you had a good story. And this one was perfect—a movie version of the famous musical, to be shot here in Eastern Europe, with elaborate village scenes. Who wouldn't eat it up? But the more details, the more likely you were to be tripped up.

"*Hollywood*," said the waitress, practically gushing.

She started talking about a movie she had seen being made in the States some years before, when she had been an exchange student in California.

If it was during her college days, thought Nuri, it must have been at least twenty years ago.

The memories sprang out in a jumble. Even if her accent had been pure, Nuri was sure he would have understood only a third of it.

Finally, he managed to steer the conversation—or monologue—back to hotels. There were several places in the area, she said, but none worth the trouble.

"Well, we do have to sleep," he told her.

"Then the Latino, two kilometers on the road, that direction," said the woman. "And I know just the place where you can set your movie."

Nuri listened to her suggestions, mentally noting that they were all to the south. He asked if there might be anything to the north, trying to get information about the farm without mentioning it. But even when he named the town it was located in, she just shrugged and said she didn't know that area very well.

"Give you her life story?" Danny asked when he came back to the table.

"Just about. There are a couple places down the road."

They found the motel the waitress recommended in the center of a village two miles away. It wasn't hard: A large 1950s era farm tractor stood on the sidewalk in front of the building, as much a landmark as mascot.

During the Soviet years the town factory had churned out tractors, as many as five hundred a week. The plant had closed soon after independence, and the old buildings now housed a variety of small businesses, including two that repaired and rebuilt the tractors originally produced there.

The town had a population of about five thousand, most living in the village center. Housing projects from the 1970s and early 1980s, their yellow bricks weathered to a dull brown, crowded around somewhat newer structures, brightly painted, which sat around the edges of the small business district. Main Street was the local highway; a pair of blinking lights slowed cars down as they approached, though crossing from one side to the other could be a dangerous undertaking.

The motel was wedged in beside a small grocery store and one of the factory buildings. Two stories tall, it was a narrow box of rooms with a balcony on the left. It presented its narrow side to the street, running back fifteen rooms deep toward a large fence that bordered a set of warehouses.

The clerk took little interest in them once Nuri proffered his credit card. They got three adjoining rooms on the second floor toward the rear. They checked them out, planted some video sensors around the rooms and the motel to keep guard, then drew lots to see who had the first watch.

Flash lost. He set up the laptop in his room, watching the farm via a satellite feed, while Nuri and Danny went off to bed.

Nuri felt as if he had only just drifted off when his satellite phone began ringing. He jerked upright in bed, dazed, before grabbing the phone.

"Yeah?" he said, fumbling for the Talk button. "Yeah?"

"This is Reid. Can you talk?"

"Uh, yeah." He pushed upright in the bed and glanced at the clock. It was a quarter past one. He'd had two hours of sleep.

"Are you awake?"

"I just—we're trying to nap a little."

"Where's Danny?"

"He's sleeping, too."

"Get him, please. Contact me through MY-PID."

DANNY DIDN'T PARTICULARLY LIKE THE IDEA OF COOPER-ating with the Moldovan government, but he had no say in it. Reid made it clear that the decision had been made by the President.

"It's window dressing only," said Reid. "One of our people in Chisinau is already working on the arrangements. If the Moldovans decide to send someone along on the raid, then you simply arrange for them to show up after the area is secure."

"What if the Moldovans tip the Wolves off?" asked Nuri.

"That should not be a problem as long as the operation is addressed as a drug one," said Reid. "And by simply limiting the details they have, there should be no chance of that kind of double cross. Besides, it's doubtful the Moldovans have any real links to the Wolves. We'd have picked up information about it."

"Maybe," said Nuri skeptically.

"Dr. Rubeo has some information for you," Reid continued, ignoring him. "There's some equipment that will be arriving with your people in Ukraine tonight. I take it that he wants to explain how it works. You had best wait until a reasonable hour to contact him. He's cantankerous enough as it is."

DANNY HAD ALREADY GIVEN BOSTON THE HEADS-UP that they would probably need a strike force. As soon as he got off the phone with Reid, he told him to get it in the air. A C–17 with the team and much of their equipment was due to land in Germany a little after eight. After refueling, it would fly on to Chernivtsi in southwestern Ukraine. There it would meet a second C–17 with their Rattlesnakes. A pair of armed Osprey MV–22s were scheduled to arrive at roughly the same time, completing the assault force.

In theory, they could launch an assault just before dawn. But the force would be tired from the long flight, and Danny still didn't have much intelligence on the farm. He wanted to move as quickly as possible, but he also knew he would only get one chance at this.

He also thought it would be best to go in at night. More than likely, the men at the farm would be prepared to fight whenever they struck, but attacking at night would make it less likely a stray passerby would wander across the operation.

So he decided to hold off for twenty-four hours. It was a logical decision—they wouldn't have to rush the planning, and he and the others would be able to rest. But it was also the sort of decision easily second-guessed, not least of all by Danny himself. He lay awake for another hour, trying to beat off the doubts, until finally, exhausted mentally as well as physically, he slipped into a fitful slumber.

35

Dreamland

BREANNA PAUSED AT THE DOOR OF THE AIRCRAFT, PREparing herself to go down the steps. Though she'd been back to Dreamland several times since leaving the active Air Force, the return was always emotional. She had spent some of the best days of her life here, and while not ordinarily given to nostalgia, it was impossible to keep the memories from flooding back as soon as she saw the low-slung silhouettes of the research bunkers and nearby hangars.

Some of her hardest had been spent here. Yet for some reason the difficulties, the trials and tribulations—the stays in the hospital, the long nights watching over Zen, her own dramas in the emergency room—all of that faded. Only the good times remained.

"Hey, boss!" bellowed a familiar voice from below. "You're late!"

Breanna pushed herself out onto the steps.

"I knew you weren't flying this old crate," continued Al "Greasy Hands" Parsons, standing at the bottom of the rolling steps, "because you woulda had it here a half hour early."

"Even I can't fight head winds," said Breanna, coming down the steps. "How are we doing, Chief?"

"Chief" was a reference to Greasy Hands' title fifteen years earlier, when he was responsible for making sure every aircraft Dreamland had could get into the air.

There had been officers over him—plenty—but ask any maintainer on the base who they answered to—and who they didn't want to cross—and "Greasy Hands" would be the immediate answer.

The same with the pilots.

"Brass is already here," said Greasy Hands in a stage whisper as she came down the steps. "Got enough of them to stock a hardware store, if there were hardware stores anymore."

"The chief of staff here?"

"First one to arrive," said Greasy Hands. "They're all over the Sabre like ants at a picnic. I'm thinking maybe we can tie a few of them to the wings. I just don't know which ones."

Greasy Hands winked. He still had a chief's perspective on what he liked to call "upper management."

Dreamland had changed a great deal since her father had the command. There were many more buildings. Taj Mahal—the command center back in her day—was now a research laboratory. It was flanked by two much larger buildings. What had been a tiny residential area used by perhaps a hundred or so military and research personnel, most of them single, was now a small city more than ten times as large. There was a day care center, an interdenominational chapel, and a small school.

And an outdoor swimming pool. She would have killed for that when she'd been stationed here.

Breanna turned toward the sound of advancing rotors. An Osprey was settling down a few yards from the rear of the C–20B that had just brought her here.

"Recognize this bird?" Greasy Hands said as they walked toward the aircraft.

"Should I?"

"You betchya. Picked you up out of that jam in Vietnam." He said the words as if they were lyrics to a song. "Now it's a ferry. I remember the oil pressure in that starboard engine used to like to jump up and down. Used to drive Spokes nuts. Which wasn't necessarily a hard thing to do."

With a wary glance toward the large props on the tilt wing, Breanna walked to the aircraft as the steps folded down. She clambered into the utilitarian interior, taking a seat on the thinly cushioned bench in the middle of the cabin. Greasy Hands sat alongside her.

"Please fasten seat belts," said a voice.

Parsons started laughing.

"Please fasten seat belts."

"What's so funny?" asked Breanna, pulling the belt tight.

"I remember when Carla Agrei recorded that. It took her more than an hour. Four little words— she couldn't get them out of her mouth."

"You were there for the session?"

"You don't remember Carla Agrei? I think half the base was there watching her. The male half."

The door to the Osprey closed.

"Prepare to take off, please," said Carla's disembodied voice. "Please remain seated while flying."

It wasn't just the cabin crew that was automated; the entire aircraft flew on its own. The base flight controller could step in at any time if necessary, but that hadn't happened in anyone's recent memory.

"Flight transit time is computed at fifteen point three minutes. Please enjoy the ride."

Brown Lake Test Area had not existed when Breanna was here. There was only one building, and most of that was underground. It served as a hangar and a small laboratory area. There were no offices, and workers had to be ferried in and out via Osprey. One entered through a set of cement steps that looked as if they'd been dropped into the middle of the desert. The surrounding area was, as the name implied, brown and smooth as glass, and considerably sturdier—heavily laden Megafortresses had landed and taken off from it back when it was a test range.

The Tigershark and a half-dozen Sabres stood in a neat line at the south end of the airstrip area. A pair of large tent canopies had been erected to the east for the VIPs, but no one was under them— as Greasy Hands had said, they were swarming around the Sabres.

The Tigershark, by contrast, stood all alone.

It certainly didn't look dowdy. But was it the future?

"Put on your smiley face," said Parsons as the Osprey settled into its landing pattern.

"Am I frowning?"

"Like you just drowned a kitten," he told her.

TURK SAW BREANNA STOCKARD COMING OUT OF THE Osprey as he emerged from the hangar. He waved in her direction but she didn't see him; she was immediately engulfed by a small gaggle of officers to witness the test flight.

Turk liked Breanna. It would have been hard not to. She was older than him, but still very easy on the eyes. And as a boss, she was remarkably easygoing. Admittedly, he didn't have many direct dealings with her, but she was one of those people who not only listened to what you said, but cared about understanding it.

Then there was the fact that she was a pilot and a war hero. Her exploits—and those of her husband and father—were among those that had inspired him to join the Air Force in the first place. He'd never spoken to her about them, nor had he met her husband, but he hoped to do both soon.

"Cap, you ready?"

"Hey, just daydreaming on you," he told Tommy Stern. The former tech sergeant was a contractor responsible for the environmental systems on the aircraft—"da HVAC guy," as he often joked. He and Turk had become friends, and Stern really functioned as Turk's unofficial babysitter, bodyguard, and drinking buddy.

Two crewmen and the crew chief were waiting at the plane with a dozen Air Force and Office of Technology tech people. With a cocked smile, Turk glanced over at the VIPs swarming nearby, then put his helmet on and got ready to fly.

They'd barely buttoned up the plane and gotten the last green light on the system check when the radio crackled.

"Tigershark, status," said Colonel Johnson.

No automated controller today, thought Turk, unsure whether he preferred the computer or Johnson.

The engineers had isolated the problem with the UM/Fs and corrected it, but just in case, he had added another fifty meters of distance to the routines. No sense in giving the brass too much of a thrill.

"Tigershark, status," snapped Johnson.

"Prepared for takeoff," said Turk.

As Breanna took her place in the reviewing area, her thoughts were far from the aircraft, or even Dreamland. She was thinking about Zen.

Worrying about him, though she wouldn't have admitted it.

She owed him an apology. He had nothing to do with the air show—the idea had come from the British, who were suddenly worried about their aging air force. The new prime minister also seemed to be hoping that a production line for the new aircraft might be opened in south England. He'd talked to Magnus, and suggested taking the plane to the air show. Apparently it had participated in routines there two years before, part of the private company's last ditch efforts to speed up the procurement process and stave off bankruptcy.

It was completely Magnus's idea. He even suggested that she go with him, though he didn't seem too disappointed when she begged off because of work.

Why had she snapped at Zen? Because she was worried about him.

Irrationally. He'd faced much worse dangers, right on this very field.

THE SHOW WENT WELL ENOUGH, WITH TURK PUSHING the Tigershark through its maneuvers as the Sabres tagged along. He even threw in an unscripted barrel roll after the UavS completed their bombing run.

Twenty minutes of that, all done precisely according to script, and it was time to call it a day. The big shots had to have their lunch.

Turk clicked the mike button to talk.

"Tigershark to ground. Control, we're clear of scheduled activities. Looking to land."

"Negative, Tigershark," replied Johnson. "Stand by."

Negative?

Turk was in an orbit at the northern end of the test range, about two miles from the Sabres and out of everyone's way. Still, being put on hold like this irked him. He ground his teeth together, then told himself to relax. He was only pissed off because it was Johnson. Anyone else giving him direction, he'd be fine with it.

And really, it wasn't even Johnson's fault. The

brass was probably hassling him for some sort of photo shoot.

Bingo. Johnson came back, directing him to perform a series of maneuvers with the Sabres. None of it was too taxing. Turk concentrated on the flight, hitting his marks with precision.

A fresh set of requests followed. Once again Turk and the Sabres flew through them. Medusa made the process seamless. The little planes flew all around him as he flew tight to the ground, then pulled up sharply to accelerate toward the sky. They followed upward as fast as they could, flying impressively for robots.

Then came a request to replay the bombing sequence.

"Ground, be advised I'm into fuel reserves," said Turk.

"Roger that, Tigershark. We're aware of your fuel state. Complete the requested exercise."

"Sabre control, line up for Series Exercise Three," he told Medusa. "Pattern Alpha Two."

An image of the preprogrammed set of maneuvers came up on his far-right screen. Turk reached over and tapped it to confirm.

"Sabre control, commence bombing run on target. Pattern Alpha Two."

"Pattern Alpha Two. Sabre copies."

Turk slipped down his throttle, easing the Tigershark's speed. The Sabres danced in and did their thing, and Turk banked toward the landing pattern.

Just as the flight computer warned that he was low on fuel.

"Right on cue," he said.

He checked in with ground—no protests this time—then lined up for his landing. The Sabres were right behind him.

Which wasn't right. They were supposed to be off to the east, following the new safety protocols.

Suddenly he got a warning from the flight computer—the Sabres were too close.

They sure were—the planes were following the same pattern as they had the day before.

Shit.

"Knock it off! Knock it off!" he called.

As he did, one of the Sabres made a sharp cut toward his tail.

THE MOMENT BREANNA SAW THE SMALL AIRCRAFT cutting to the north, a pit opened in her stomach.

The Sabre was far too close to the Tigershark. The fierce vortices of wind off the complex airfoil made the U/MF hard to control. It began fluttering, then flew directly at the Tigershark's right stabilizer.

It was almost precisely the same type of accident that had claimed Zen's legs.

Breanna leapt up from her seat.

"Jeff!" she yelled involuntarily.

BY THE TIME THE PROXIMITY ALARM BLARED, TURK HAD managed to pull the Tigershark's nose up and swing his tail down and away in a low-altitude, high-g cobra that dropped the plane to within a dozen feet of the smooth desert surface. The Sabre buzzed overhead, oblivious to his presence.

In any other aircraft, he would have been dead, killed either by the collision or his maneuver to get away. But between the Tigershark's aerodynamics, razor-sharp controls, and his piloting skills—thank you very much—he was just pissed off.

Turk landed without comment and taxied to the recovery area. He remained silent as the crew helped him out of the aircraft.

"It's something in the low-altitude routines," said the head project engineer, running over from his SUV. "It has to do with the landing routines. They're cutting into an emergency break-off because—"

"You know what?" said Turk. "I really don't care. Just fix the damn thing before I get killed."

"I'M SORRY FOR MY OUTBURST," BREANNA TOLD THEIR guests as they gathered for the debrief back at Dreamland. "Obviously, we had a bit of a problem there at the end. The Sabres were not in their proper position. We need more work on the low-altitude flight control sections."

"And you want us to back the project?" said Admiral Brooks.

"The problem is with the Sabres," said Breanna. "They were not programmed to land in a pattern with another aircraft. It wasn't Medusa's fault, or the Tigershark's. The Tigershark itself is fine. Believe me, any other aircraft would not have been able to escape. You saw how it dropped down."

Admiral Brooks had brought along two of his

own aviation experts. They admired the Tigershark, speaking highly of its recovery at the end.

"It was the only thing that impressed me," said Captain Fairfield, who had served as an F/A–18 wing commander in Afghanistan. "Any other aircraft put its nose up like that . . ."

He shook his head. Another Navy aviator mentioned a Russian MiG pilot who had tried a somewhat similar maneuver at an air show and ended up becoming the posthumous star of a viral video on disastrous plane accidents.

Still, it was a tough crowd, and as they broke up for lunch, Breanna sensed they had lost the pitch. General Magnus pulled her aside as one of Dreamland's colonels met them and led them toward the executive dining area.

"I'm sorry," she told him. "It's a problem with the Sabres. Something similar happened the other day and they thought they had it repaired."

"I understand. Are you OK?"

"I'm fine."

"The accident—what happened was similar to what happened to your husband."

Breanna felt her face turning red.

"Yes," she said. "I'm sorry."

"You already apologized."

Breanna felt tears welling in her eyes. She felt bad about how she had left things with Zen.

"I think it's important to get the Tigershark to the air show," said Magnus. "But only if this sort of thing isn't going to happen."

"The Tigershark itself is fine."

"OK."

Magnus started to turn away.

"General—I was wondering," said Breanna. "What do you think—I wonder if I might tag along with you to the air show?"

"Really? You want to go?"

"Well, Jeff and my daughter are actually going to be there."

"Oh. Why didn't you say that? Of course. We can take your family."

Magnus smiled.

"They already have arrangements. My niece is going as well. They're leaving tonight. He has to go to the NATO conference."

"Ah—well then, you probably shouldn't wait for me. I'm not flying out until Monday night. You'll miss him."

"Oh."

"Go out tonight," said Magnus.

"By the time I get back East—"

"Boss 12 is going out to Ukraine empty," said Magnus, referring to an Air Force C–20B used as a VIP transport. "They need a backup in case something happens in Kiev. I'm sure they could arrange a stop in Prague. It is on the way."

"You think?"

"Well, geography never was my best subject," said Magnus, struggling to keep a straight face. "But I'm pretty sure it's in that general direction."

36

Northeastern Moldova

NURI DREW THE TASK OF COORDINATING WITH THE Moldovan government and the CIA field office in Chisinau, which Reid had called in for support. He left for the capital around noon, planning to meet with the CIA station chief around dinnertime. Danny and Flash continued monitoring the farm, watching and planning how to proceed with the raid.

A car arrived shortly after 9:00 A.M. Two men got out and carried luggage into the house. About a half hour later a taxi drove up and dropped off another man at the roadside, leaving him to walk up the long drive on his own. He went in through the side door facing the garage and disappeared. Another did the same a half hour later. Then another car arrived with two men, just like the first.

Nothing happened for a few hours. Danny flipped back and forth through the feeds from the Predators—both were on station now—sipping the awful but free coffee he'd retrieved from the motel lobby.

He tried to imagine Stoner, constructing an image from his memories as well as the intelligence. Six-foot, stocky, square jaw and yet a slightly hollow face, the face of someone who had walked through a desert.

Physically 'enhanced'?

There was no clear guidance on what that

might mean. The intelligence was vague, based on vaguer reports. The Wolves were physically fit and in extremely good shape—that was a given for any special ops type group, which essentially described what they knew of the operation.

But they were more than that. The implication was that, at a minimum, they were using exoskeleton technology to help them run and lift things. And that the technology was more advanced than what anyone else, including the U.S., was using, since it hadn't been detected.

Which in Danny's view was highly unlikely.

Even staring at the old pictures, it was hard to see Stoner now. Gray hair? Fuller cheeks?

More than likely he wasn't here. More than likely he was still at the bottom of that swamp.

SHORTLY BEFORE 1:00 P.M., MY-PID ALERTED DANNY to activity at the back of the farmhouse. Danny hit the hot key on the laptop, bringing up the proper feed just in time to see two figures emerge from the cement stairwell that came out of the basement. Moments later a third and a fourth came out, finally a fifth. They trotted up the steps from the basement, moving around in a haphazard pattern—warming up, Danny thought, like a basketball team.

A sixth figure emerged. The others formed a semicircle around him. They began doing jumping jacks.

It was exactly like a basketball team. Right number, too.

Danny put his finger on the control slider and

zoomed to maximum magnification, trying to get close-ups of the faces. He got a partial on one—it was clearly not Stoner.

The man next to him had what looked like the right build. But all he could see was the top of the man's head. He was wearing a hooded sweatshirt, with only a small part of his scalp exposed.

"Request facial images," Danny told the computer. "All subjects."

The request had to be relayed to the Predator pilot. By the time the aircraft changed its orbit to attempt to see the face, the men had already begun to run around the property. The trees and hills—not to mention the UAV's altitude—made getting close-ups of the faces very difficult, and the aircraft was only able to obtain two before the men returned to the house via the basement door. Neither man looked like Stoner.

Then again, the images were grainy and obscured by shadows—who could really say?

Flash came in a short time later, while Danny was replaying the warm-up routine.

"You sure we ain't watching a soccer team?" he asked.

Danny could only shrug.

The farm was quiet for the next several hours. Then, just as dusk began to fall, figures started emerging from the house again. This time it was clear they weren't an eccentric sports team on retreat—they were in full battle rattle, helmets and vests, rifles and sidearms. They moved over to the large steel building very deliberately, in a combat spread. Once there, they lined up in a close semicircle, waiting as the last figure came out and stepped in front of them.

Danny could easily picture the scene from the ground. He'd done it a hundred times.

OK men. This barn is our target. We infiltrate through the open door. We move through silently to the second floor. This is just to warm up. . .

Flash leaned forward next to him, watching.

"That's not Manchester United," he said.

They switched to the penetrating radar. From above, the image looked like a maze, with rats running through it.

"They firing, you think?" asked Flash. The infrared cameras weren't picking up any gunfire.

"First time through, probably not," said Danny. He'd already checked the general layout of the building interior. It didn't match the building where the NATO meeting was taking place in Kiev. But then again, it looked fairly generic to him.

He keyed up the sensor display on the laptop that revealed electric currents. There were computer hard drives active all through the building. Six were moving—the assault team was equipped with portable computers.

"Gotta be training devices," said Flash. "Smart helmets. They're working with a combat information system."

The group worked through the northern quadrant of the building twice, then reassembled for a third try. There were flashes of heat energy inside the building—flash-bangs. A takedown simulation.

The drill went on for another hour. Then the

unit emerged, again one by one. They formed up outside the building, then moved out into one of the nearby fields, heading toward a small cluster of ruins. MY-PID analyzed the team based on the images. They were all between six-four and six-six, seemingly in excellent physical condition as they sprinted up the hill at an under sixty seconds per four hundred meter pace. Their weight was more of a guess, but MY-PID pegged it at just over 250 pounds apiece.

They were well equipped with what appeared to be Russian weapons—four brand-new AEK–971 assault rifles and a pair of Pecheneg squad-level machine guns. The assault rifles were using scopes the computer had not encountered before. The scopes employed what appeared to be short-range radar as well as the standard infrared. Danny guessed this was some sort of training device; he couldn't puzzle out any other use for the radar.

Finding out about the gear would be a side benefit from the raid.

"They're going to take that building there," said Flash, pointing to the screen as the team split into two groups.

"I don't know," said Danny. "That small a force—would you split up like that?"

"Maybe. Three guys is an army, if you got the right three guys."

But they didn't circle the area. The groups headed to two different buildings, about a hundred meters apart. They didn't assault them, though they were careful about getting inside.

The building on the right exploded, gray smoke blossoming on the screen.

The other building followed.

"Look," said Danny.

A small helicopter materialized from the cloud of smoke that had consumed the first building. It looked like a stripped down Ka–126, a vintage 1960s helicopter still used in Russia for crop dusting and other utility tasks. It had two counter-rotating propellers overhead, which allowed it to fly with a double tail rather than a powered rotor. The helo was little more than a metal frame strapped beneath the engine. The bulkhead for the cockpit held two seats forward and a double bench behind. There were six places in total on the benches.

A similar helicopter flew out of the roof of the second cottage. They headed north to a cluster of ruins. The team members jumped from the helo, humping toward a low mound next to a half-buried foundation. Two of them knelt down. It looked to Danny as if they were going to pray. Instead, they lifted part of the ground, revealing a dugout with a pair of SUVs hidden below.

"We didn't see that," said Flash. "The radar couldn't see through the roof. The building looked empty."

The cottages that had "exploded" were still intact—the roofs had simply opened as smoke grenades went off. The material on the roof was somehow able to deflect the penetrating radar, without revealing that it was doing so.

Not technically impossible, but not easy either.

"We didn't see it at all," repeated Flash.

"Yeah," said Danny. "The question is, what else aren't we seeing?"

37

Chisinau, Moldova

THE CIA OFFICER IN CHARGE AT CHISINAU WAS MAL-
colm Gleeb, an old Eastern European hand who had served with the Agency since the Reagan administration. Gleeb greeted Nuri warily. He'd already done considerable legwork, working contacts in the military and national police force as well as contacting the interior minister. But Reid had been purposely vague on details of the operation, and Nuri could tell as soon as he met Gleeb that he was annoyed. Station chiefs could be very territorial, and anyone running an operation within what they perceived to be their domain had to tread gently.

Treading gently wasn't Nuri's forte.

"We have an appointment with the interior minister at nine," Gleeb told Nuri when he picked him up outside the capital's fanciest business hotel. "He doesn't know what's up, but obviously he knows it's important."

"The appointment isn't supposed to be until tomorrow night," said Nuri. "We don't want word to get out."

"The minister is leaving on vacation in the morning," said Gleeb. "Unless you want to go with him, this is the best we can do. His deputies are not dependable."

Nuri, who didn't want to deal with the Moldovans in the first place, folded his arms in front of his chest and said nothing.

"You didn't check into the hotel, did you?" asked Gleeb.

"No. Why?"

"You have a room?"

"I just got here."

"I thought so."

Nuri tightened his arms. He felt as if he was being interrogated. This was *his* operation, and Gleeb had better ratchet down or he was going to take the guy's head off, gray hairs and all.

"I suspect you'd like a shower," said Gleeb. "And a chance to straighten up your clothes. We have enough time. Just."

"I'm a little hungry, actually."

"We'll eat after. If you need a sandwich or something, I'll find you something at my flat."

Nuri realized he looked a little rumpled and very possibly did need a shower—the water pressure had been a joke at the motel. Gleeb took him to his residence. The shower was tiny, but the hot water was strong. While he was showering, Gleeb found him a sport coat that came close to fitting.

"Space has been secured on a military base in the northeast, if it's necessary," Gleeb told Nuri after he dressed. "My contacts in the state police will cooperate, if there is authorization to do so. It's up to the minister."

"Uh-huh." Nuri adjusted his shirt collar in the small mirror on the bathroom door.

"You don't really want the Moldovans to help, do you?"

The comment took Nuri by surprise. "Why do you say that?"

"I'd be a very poor agent if I couldn't tell how unenthusiastic about this you were," said Gleeb.

"No, I don't."

"How long have you been with the Company?"

"Couple of years," said Nuri.

"You'll learn. Politics is everything. At every level. Shall we go?"

Nuri resented the I'm-an-old-hand-and-you'll-learn tone, but there was no question that Gleeb was acting professionally otherwise. Nuri tried to restart the relationship in the car on the way to the minister's, asking how long Gleeb had been with the CIA. It was a subtle nod toward the older man, without pretending to fawn, which Nuri couldn't have stomached and Gleeb certainly would have scoffed at.

"I've worked with the Company longer than I can recall," said Gleeb. "I've been just about everywhere in Europe. My first assignment was in Moscow. I never looked back."

He'd become a field agent just before the end of the Cold War, when human intelligence assets—spies—were still the most valued commodity in the business. Gleeb regaled him with stories as they drove, telling of elaborate dinner parties where he and KGB agents vied over contacts and beautiful women.

Mostly the latter, Gleeb confessed.

Nuri had heard these sorts of stories before, but Gleeb's had just enough of a self-depreciating spin for Nuri to be interested, or at least not bored by them. Gleeb abruptly brought the subject back to the present as they neared the minister's residence.

"He will be suspicious, but that's to be expected. I've told him you're working with the UN. I doubt he actually believes that, but he won't question it."

"That's a convenient attitude."

"Very. Lay out what you need and ask for his cooperation. Let him think it's up to him."

The tone grated again. Gleeb was stating the obvious.

"It is up to him," said Nuri.

Gleeb gave him the most fleeting of smiles.

Nuri guessed, belatedly, that the minister was on the Agency payroll. It would certainly be a subtle arrangement, money coming from some sort of grant to his department or maybe a pseudojob for a family member, but it would be leverage nonetheless.

The arrangement was a mixed blessing as far as Nuri was concerned. While it undoubtedly would make the minister somewhat more compliant, it also meant that he could be bought. Whether the U.S. was the only buyer was an open question.

The minister's residence overlooked an old castle about a mile outside the capital limits. The castle looked like something out of Frankenstein, dark and ominous, high on a hill.

"That's their old family estate," said Gleeb. "They used to own just about everything you see here."

"What happened?"

"Communists came in. Not that they would have necessarily kept it anyway. The family fortune was ebbing by the end of the nineteenth century anyway. They went through some harder times, until World War Two. His great-grandfather was a hero of the resistance, and apparently he personally saved some relative of Stalin. Or took the credit for doing so."

Gleeb made a clicking sound with his mouth; he was wearing dentures, and not particularly well-fitting ones at that.

"That's the minister's house on the left," said the CIA station chief as he took a turn just beyond the castle. "A little different, huh?"

The house was a set of modernistic boxes set into the hillside. Gleeb told him it had been built by a famous European architect for more than three million euros—an enormous sum in Moldova.

No wonder he's taking money from the CIA, Nuri thought.

A maid met them at the door. A pair of bodyguards stood at the side of the foyer, watching them carefully as they came in. Nuri nodded in their direction without receiving a response.

"The minister is waiting for you in the library," said the maid in English. "Please."

The library was a small room to the right of the entry. Two more bodyguards, arms down at their sides, waited near the door. The minister was working at a small desk next to a large bookcase that filled one entire wall of the room. The bookcase, constructed of thick, worn wood, seemed out of place; Nuri wondered if it had been scavenged from the castle.

"Mr. Gleeb, very nice," said the minister. "I will be with you presently."

"The minister spent time in London as ambassador for the last government," Gleeb told Nuri. "He speaks the King's English. It's certainly better than mine."

"Ah, when my guests flatter me, it is time to find them a drink," said the minister, putting down his pen.

He rose and wagged his finger at the guards, who promptly disappeared.

"Our sherry is passably pleasant," said the minister, going over to a sideboard. Like the other furniture in the house, it was a sleek, modern affair, made of chrome and lightly colored wood.

"That is to put you off your guard for some of the finest sherry in Europe," Gleeb told Nuri. "He likes to lower expectations."

Nuri was not much of a judge of sherry. He raised his own glass as Gleeb and his host saluted each other, then took a small sip.

"So you are Mr. Lupo," said the minister, turning to him. "An alias, I suppose?"

"Actually, it's my real name," said Nuri. "I don't use an alias."

The minister smirked, then took another sip of the sherry.

"Good, yes?" he asked.

"Very good," said Nuri.

"So—you have traced the European drug problem to my country," said the minister. "And now you are going to solve it on the backs of my police?"

"We actually have considerable resources on our own," said Nuri. "If you don't want to, uh—"

He saw Gleeb shake his head slightly and stopped in mid-sentence.

"The UN has many resources," said the station chief, taking over. "But naturally they don't have the intimate knowledge of Moldova that your forces do. Your people are highly trained, and any assistance that you can render would certainly be useful."

"Hmmm," said the minister. "And when would this assistance be needed?"

"Ideally in the next few days," said Gleeb.

Nuri didn't say anything. It would be better to have "permission" first. Then he would spring the date on the minister, hoping it would be too soon for any real involvement.

"You've already spoken to some of my underlings, Mr. Gleeb?"

Nuri couldn't tell whether it was a question or a statement. Gleeb handled it smoothly, saying that he had "investigated the circumstances of the situation" before wasting the minister's time.

Some cooperation might be arranged within the next month or two, said the minister, providing certain contingencies were met.

"I'm afraid the matter is much more imminent than that," said Gleeb.

"How imminent?" asked the minister, refilling his wine.

Gleeb looked at Nuri.

"Tomorrow night," said Nuri.

"Tomorrow?"

"We've found that any sort of delay, once we have an operation located, can be very detrimental," Nuri explained. "So we'd like to move very quickly. We'd have to."

"That might be a problem," said the minister.

"We're prepared to proceed."

"They would naturally move only with aid from the government," said Gleeb. "But they would not need a great deal of assistance."

"I don't know what sort of aid would be available on such short notice," said the minister. "And it might entail expense—if we are talking about a large operation."

"Reasonable expenses would have to be compensated," agreed Gleeb.

A few minutes of negotiation followed. Neither man named a price; they spoke instead of things like manpower and vehicles.

"We really don't need a lot of policemen," said Nuri.

Gleeb shot him a glance, then turned back to negotiating. The old guy was good, gently pushing back without losing his good humor or angering the minister.

Nuri wondered if he could use Gleeb when he bought his next car.

They finally settled on three dozen men and two SWAT teams, with a pair of Hummer-style jeeps outfitted with machine guns. The minister agreed that the men would not be notified of the actual raid until the following evening, as a matter of security.

"And where is this adventure taking place?" he asked, once more refilling his glass.

Gleeb looked at Nuri.

"Outside the capital," he said.

"Where outside the capital?" the minister asked.

"In the northeast. I mean, northwest."

It was an honest slip, but it annoyed the minister. Gleeb had to step in and calm things, claiming that Nuri did not yet have the exact location himself. "And being a stranger to Moldova, I'm sure the name would mean nothing to him if he did," he added.

"It is in the north," said Nuri. "I just don't know where exactly. As Mr. Gleeb said—"

"You will call me tomorrow morning." The minister spoke to Gleeb, not Nuri. "You will have an exact location then. You will call me and we will have some men to work with you. An action like this must have some local involvement. They will not be in too much danger, I hope."

"I will call you, yes," said Nuri.

"YOU SHOULD HAVE GIVEN HIM THE NAME OF A CITY in the district," said Gleeb after they left. "You never want to make it obvious that you don't trust someone. It's disrespectful. You nearly scuttled the whole deal."

"I don't need any of those troops."

"You're not getting them," said Gleeb. "You'll be lucky to get a few police cars."

"Not lucky—"

"You're in a foreign country. You don't know everything. You need cooperation."

"Well—"

"Believe me, you do."

Gleeb took him to dinner in a French restaurant, reputedly one of the best in Eastern Europe. The food was good, but Nuri had no appetite for it. The station chief gave him background about the drug trade in Moldova, outlining its connections to the government. At the moment it was one of the few export businesses thriving in the country.

"The forces he mentioned," said Nuri after their plates were cleared.

"That was the price only," said Gleeb. "Their equivalent salaries. You don't have to worry about any of that. The actual cooperation will be arranged with one of his deputies."

"The less cooperation the better," said Nuri.

"Now, Mr. Lupo, you're starting to sound like you know something," said Gleeb, smiling and signaling for the check.

38

Dreamland

TURK'S FOUL MOOD DIDN'T LIFT EVEN AFTER GENERAL Wallace and some of his aides met him on the way back to the hangar and congratulated him on a great flight.

"The episode at the end demonstrated just how capable the plane is," said Wallace. "And the pilot."

"Thanks," managed Turk.

"Future of the Air Force—manned flight," said Wallace, emphasizing the last phrase. "Well done. Carry on."

"Thank you, sir." Turk didn't point out that the phrase "manned flight" was actually a slogan from the space program, which wasn't faring too well these days.

Three of the engineers responsible for the Sabre control systems, faces ashen, met Turk for the debrief. They looked like a trio of ghosts haunting an air wreck. They had already figured out the problem, they said—an errant line of code had prevented the proper routine from loading.

"You told me it was already fixed," Turk said. "Isn't this the problem from the other day?"

"This kept the right solution from loading," one of the men explained. "We fixed it and had to fix it again."

"It should have been tested."

"It *was* tested. You were part of the tests."

I pushed the buttons you told me to push, thought Turk, but it was useless to argue.

Breanna Stockard caught up to him and Tommy Stern a few hours later at Hole 19, one of the all-ranks lounges on the main Dreamland base. Turk, sipping a seltzer, was standing at the bar talking to a nurse whose curly brunette hair hung down over her eyes in what seemed to him the cutest way imaginable. He bought her a drink, then started talking about his Ducati motorcycle, hoping to set up a date to take her for a ride.

Stern, who was married, stood by quietly, occasionally rolling his eyes.

"Captain, there you are," said Breanna, striding across the room toward the bar. "Do you have a minute?"

"Sure," said Turk, though in truth he would have preferred the interruption to come a little later.

"I have to be going," said the brunette.

"Hey, hang out a minute," said Turk. He reached for her hand but she pulled it away.

"Sorry. Lot of stuff to do."

Turk watched her walk away. It was definitely his loss.

Stern made his apologies as well, which was clearly fine with Breanna. They took a table in the corner.

"I saw what you did on the landing," she told him, pulling out her chair. "It was very good piloting."

"That's why I'm here."

"And you're modest," she said sarcastically.

"Some days." Turk took a long sip of his seltzer.

"No more Sabre flights until the entire low-altitude protocol is rewritten and retested," said Breanna. "I've already given the order."

"That's overkill. There's nothing wrong with the plane."

"I'm not talking about the Tigershark. I meant the Sabres and Medusa."

"Well . . ." Turk suddenly felt protective of the UM/Fs, though he couldn't for the life of him have explained why. And in fact he'd made more or less the same argument to the engineers earlier. But there was something about having a system that he was working with grounded that put him on the defensive. "I guess."

"When are you leaving for Prague?"

"Couple of hours." He held up the seltzer.

Sobriety was actually a nonissue in the Tigershark, because the aircraft's flight computer put the pilot through a series of mental tests before it would unlock its systems. Supposedly, the test could figure out if you were overtired as well as inhibited by drugs or alcohol. Turk, close to a teetotaler anyway, had never tested it.

"Plane's ready?"

"All ready."

Turk was taking Tiger Two. The rail gun had been removed for security purposes; unlike the plane, its existence was still top secret. It also did not have a Medusa unit.

"I'm going with you," said Breanna.

"In the Tigershark?"

She gave him a funny look. "Of course not. I'm going in the C–20."

"I'm sorry."

"What's in that seltzer?"

She meant it as a joke, clearly, but Turk felt embarrassed.

"I didn't think you were coming," he said.

"My family's going to be there. And I thought I would take a look at what's new. Supposedly the Russian PAK-FA will be there. It might be good to take a look."

"At 1980s technology, sure," sneered Turk.

"I wouldn't underestimate what the Russians and Indians can do if they work closely together," said Breanna. "Anyway, if we can get together before the show, I'd like to get your thoughts on the plane's potential and where we can go from here."

"Is Zen going to be there?" Turk asked.

"Yes."

"You know, I'd love to, uh, go like to dinner or something with you guys. If I could, um, you know, kinda hangout."

"Sure." Breanna rose. She hadn't touched her beer, Turk noticed.

"The Defense secretary has arranged for me to talk to some of the NATO representatives in the morning on the future of manned flight," she added. "There'll be a panel discussion afterward. I thought you'd be a good person to sit on it."

"Me?"

"You don't think you're qualified?"

"Well, yeah."

"A sudden lack of confidence. That's refreshing." Breanna smirked. "You want some advice, Captain?"

"Sure."

"Fancy Italian motorcycles can definitely be a turn on, but talking about how close you can get your knee to the ground going around a curve—not so much."

39

Northeastern Moldova

THE WOLF ASSAULT TEAM WENT THROUGH THE ENTIRE sequence twice more, starting with the mock attack inside the steel building and ending with the SUVs. Danny got the impression that they were still at the walk-through stage; they stopped midway through the second time, rearranging how the teams ran to the cottages where the helos were kept.

The SUVs were interesting. They looked like full-sized trucks, but two people could pick them up with ease. Were the trucks extremely lightweight, like the helicopters? Or were the men ridiculously strong?

The exercise concluded at two in the morning. After the choppers were returned to the cottages, the farm looked exactly as it had before sunset.

"You figure they're going to sleep?" asked Flash.

"Debrief the session first," said Danny. "While it's still fresh. Then sleep."

"Beers, then sleep," said Flash. "How long—an hour?"

Danny stared at the screen. He wanted to strike during the dark, minimizing the possibility that his attack force would be seen on the way in. Should he hit the force during the exercise or afterward?

Afterward was his preference. Not only would they be tired, but he could pump gas into the building first, increasing the odds of getting them without a fight. His orders called for him to "use nonlethal means of apprehension" if at all possible.

Danny had wide discretion on that. No one was going to complain if everyone in the house ended up dead, especially now that they'd seen their rehearsal.

And if Stoner was there?

THEY WATCHED THE GROUP GATHER IN ONE OF THE rooms on the first floor, going back over the exercise as Danny had predicted. A half hour later all but two were in rooms upstairs, apparently sleeping.

Danny wanted to get Stoner out alive, if he was there.

"You keep looking at the images, like you might recognize him," said Flash.

"Yeah."

"I thought you thought it was bull."

"I do. Mostly."

Flash nodded.

"Tomorrow, we wait an hour after they pack it in, when they're sleeping like now," said Danny, as if Flash had asked him what the plan was. "Pump the house full of the gas, hit them quick. First sign of resistance, we flatten them."

"No argument from me," said Flash.

40

Reagan International Airport

GETTING AROUND WITHOUT THE USE OF YOUR LEGS WAS never exactly fun, but being disabled and flying a commercial airline flight could be a special trial. Most of the major carriers had special wheelchairs designed to fit down narrow plane aisles; the chairs could then be folded away in the cabin storage areas. But that still left you beholden to the stewardess when you had to use the john.

The bathrooms were their own special hell, though at least Zen wasn't claustrophobic. He also had the money to fly first class, and was a U.S. senator.

Having a cute kid and a good-looking coed in tow didn't hurt either.

"Senator Stockard, nice to have you aboard," said the steward, who met him in the jetway to the plane. "And is this lovely lady Teri Stockard?"

"Yes, I am," said Teri.

"Excited about flying?" asked the attendant.

"I like to fly," she told him. "My mom lets me take the controls."

Zen smiled. Breanna occasionally rented a twin-engine Cessna.

"You're Caroline," said the steward to Zen's niece.

Caroline nodded. She tended to be a little shy around strangers. Zen thought she had no reason to be—she was smart and attractive, not unlike her aunt Breanna.

"Major Stockard." The pilot practically jumped out from behind the door, hand out, looking to shake. "You don't remember me, I'll bet, but I was driving MC–17s back when you were with Dreamland. We were on a deployment with Whiplash. Great to have you aboard, sir."

"Long time ago," said Zen, who didn't remember the pilot. He'd left Dreamland as a lieutenant colonel, so the rank narrowed down the time frame a bit, just not enough to help. "How have you been?"

"Great, great. How's the political life treating you?"

"Can't complain. I have a lot of bosses. Meet one of them." He held his hand out to his daughter. "Teri, this our captain."

"Pleased to meet you." The pilot bent down and shook her hand, then looked at Caroline. "This can't be your wife."

Caroline blushed.

"My niece Caroline," said Zen.

Two of the other flight attendants came out and helped Zen and the girls get squared away. The rest of the passengers flooded in, most looking a bit harried and anxious to get going.

Cockpit door closed, the aircraft pushed back from the gate, then slowly began trundling toward the runway.

"Ladies and gentlemen, I'm glad to have you aboard with us this evening for our flight to Prague," said the pilot, introducing himself and the crew. "Bob and Lisa will be reviewing some of our emergency procedures with the help of a short video in just a second. Before we get to that, though, I wanted to let you know that we're flying today with a former member of the U.S. military who has been decorated for bravery under fire more times than most of us breathe. He's now a member of the U.S. Senate. I knew him as Major Zen Stockard; you might just call him Senator. I'd like to salute him and thank him for his service to our country."

The passengers broke into spontaneous applause.

Zen glanced down at his daughter. His eyes were starting to swell with tears.

"Something wrong, Daddy?" asked Teri.

"Nothing wrong, baby. Now make sure your seat belt's tight, right? Pilot can't take off without it good and snug."

41

Northeastern Moldova

Nuri's suspicions about the minister proved to be correct—within a few minutes of the CIA officer's visit, the NSA intercepted two calls from the minister to people who lived in the northeastern corner of the country. The phone calls were short and to the point: the minister said he was taking a vacation for a few days, and they should, too.

Nuri guessed that they took his advice. He wasn't particularly concerned with the details, however, since neither man owned property anywhere near the Wolves' farm.

He called the minister's cell phone the next morning at exactly eight o'clock and told him that the farm was near Drochia, the capital of the province of the same name. This was fairly vague as well as incorrect, but it satisfied the minister.

"One of my deputies will call you within the hour," he told Nuri. "In the meantime, if you need further arrangements, please let me know."

The minister's tone suggested that it would be very much all right with him if they never spoke again. Which was fine with Nuri as well.

The deputy, Johann Lacu, called within the hour. He spoke English fairly well and had a clipped, professional style Nuri liked.

The deputy asked how many men he needed; Nuri told him no more than six.

"Six is a very small number," replied Lacu. "These criminals may be very desperate."

"Six is all we need," Nuri told him. "We can even do with less."

"You will need cars to take them away in."

Ambulances more likely, thought Nuri.

"We already have transportation arranged," he said. "The operation really is under control."

"That is very good," said Lacu. "We will assist in any way possible."

They arranged to meet at 11:00 P.M. at a small church in a village two kilometers north of Drochia. Nuri would brief them, then find some excuse to keep them occupied for a few hours until the raid was complete. At that point they would drive to the farm, which was roughly a half hour away. Gleeb, meanwhile, would stay in the capital to cover any further contingencies with the military or the interior ministry.

NOT KNOWING WHAT TO EXPECT AND NOT HAVING ANY-thing else to do in Chisinau, Nuri left the capital shortly after noon. He arrived at the town just after sunset.

The place looked quiet enough, a typical Eastern European town down on its luck. The church overlooked a small cemetery and an even smaller park with a monument to soldiers who had died in the Great Patriotic War—the Second World War, as the West remembered it.

The town was so small it didn't have a restaurant. Nuri drove until he came to another village about four kilometers away. The main and only intersection in town featured a café. He parked in a lot around the corner.

The restaurant was empty, and the middle-aged hostess nearly jumped as he came in the door.

"Good evening," she said in Moldovan.

Nuri answered in Moldovan, but his accent drove her to English. She told him he was very welcome and showed him to what she called the best table in the house. This was not coincidentally in the front window, where she undoubtedly hoped his presence would attract other customers. She gave him a menu and asked if he would like an aperitif.

"Just water," he said.

She returned with a tray of homemade cordials, each brightly colored and most with some sort of fruit in the bottle.

"No, that's all right," said Nuri.

"For free, for free," she insisted.

Deciding that courtesy called for a small drink, he had a glass of what looked like the least exotic concoction, an orange-tinted syrup that he hoped would taste something like Grand Marnier, or maybe cough syrup.

It was more like liquid fire. Jelled liquid fire. Like napalm, it clung to his throat.

"Good?" asked the woman.

"Oh yeah. Good," managed Nuri. "Can I have some water?"

She came back with the menu as well. It offered food in three languages—Moldovan, English, and Russian.

"Do you get a lot of Russians in here?" he asked the hostess after he ordered a small steak.

"Russian?" The woman made a face and said

something Moldovan that was too low for the computer to pick up but was clearly not a compliment.

"The Russians cause problems?" Nuri asked.

"You are Russian?"

"No, no. American."

"I thought," said the woman. She nodded approvingly and began talking. She didn't like Russians. She told him that they were dirty pigs and often didn't pay their bills. The café got a few every few months, big lugs who smelled like sweaty cows.

"Four yesterday, for lunch," she said. "Enough for a year."

"Are they tourists?"

She made another face.

"You have a lot of tourists?" Nuri asked.

"Tourists? Here? We have one place to stay. A small place. And this restaurant. What tourists would come here?"

"I don't know."

"There are no other restaurants or hotels—that is why people stop here. The countryside, maybe. They see, they like. Every so often, though—Russians."

"Why? They looking for a bargain?"

She shrugged.

"They say they train for Olympics," she told him. "Bicyclists."

"Bicyclists?" Nuri wasn't sure he heard the word right.

The hostess frowned and waved her hand. "I know what bicyclists look like. Skinny. These are always big. American football. Bicyclists? Ha!"

She walked off, shaking her head.

* * *

NURI REMEMBERED THE WOMAN'S COMPLAINTS AN HOUR later, after dinner, when he left the restaurant and heard Russian being spoken behind him. He walked another step, then stopped, looking both ways as if trying to see if it was safe to cross the street.

Two men were entering the café. They were the only other people out.

He thought about them as he walked back to his car. The Russian mafiya was involved in many of the marijuana operations in Moldova, and while this wasn't a big area for pot cultivation, he had firsthand proof that it wasn't entirely bereft of it either.

Would the Wolves stop here on their way to the farm? If you didn't want everyone descending in one swoop, maybe. It was right on the road.

More likely not, he decided. But he couldn't get the idea out of his mind. He walked back, glancing into the restaurant from the other side of the street. The men were seated toward the back of the room, barely visible through the large window. Clearly, the hostess didn't see their presence as helping business much.

Nuri thought of going in and leaving a bug—he had several in his bag in the car. But it was likely the woman would greet him in a way that made it obvious he'd decided to come back. Even if he came up with a plausible excuse, he might make the Russians suspicious.

He changed direction and headed back toward his car. Just as he was about to cross over, he saw the sign for the hotel the hostess had mentioned. It was more house than hotel, a small, late nineteenth-century residence divided into guest rooms.

Nuri got his bag out of the car and went to the hotel. The clerk at the desk was also the owner, a rotund but friendly woman in her fifties, who smiled when Nuri told her the owner of the café had recommended he stay there.

"I'm a little tired and just need the night," he said in Moldovan, with MY-PID's help. "You have rooms?"

They had four. Three were open.

"Maybe my friend is in the other?" he asked, switching to English.

The sign outside had indicated that English was spoken, but the woman didn't know much beyond "hello" and "credit card." Nuri was counting on this—he started describing his friend in great detail.

The woman held up her hands and told him in Moldovan that she didn't understand.

"My friend, my friend," he said. "A businessman—he came from this town."

"We have two guests," she said. "Russian. In Room 4. They're foul-smelling oafs, but money is money."

"Money, yes," said Nuri, pretending that he hadn't understood entirely. "You have my credit card."

"Everything good."

"Great," he said. "Where is my room?"

*   *   *

NURI'S ROOM WAS DIRECTLY ACROSS FROM THE Russians'. He put his bag down in it, then went across the hall and knocked on their door, just to make sure no one was there.

When no one answered, he played a hunch, fitting his room key into theirs. The door opened without his even needing to jiggle it.

He slipped a bug into the light fixture, then decided that was too obvious. He found a better spot in the baseboard heater, and left another in the bathroom beneath the sink.

Could he do more?

He looked around the room. The men had each brought a small overnight bag containing only a change of clothes and a couple of bottles of vodka. There was no laptop to inspect, no papers to rifle through. He had a tracking bug, but he thought it would be conspicuous inside either piece of luggage, given that there were no interior pockets or other crevices where it could be easily hidden.

Back in his room, he tossed his bag out the window into the yard so it wouldn't be obvious he was leaving for good. That turned out to be unnecessary—the proprietor had gone into her own apartment to watch television when he came down, and didn't even see him leave.

As he walked around to get his bag, he noticed a small parking lot at the back of the house. He scooped up his bag and walked over to the two cars in the lot—a ten-year-old Toyota, and a new Hyundai.

Which one belonged to the Russian?

The Hyundai surely, he decided, but with two

trackers in his pocket, he bugged both, slipping the devices over the cars' gas tanks.

NURI DROVE AROUND THE COUNTRYSIDE FOR OVER AN hour, partly to kill time and partly to get a feel for the area. The gentle hills and abundant streams made for excellent small-scale farming, but small-scale farming couldn't compete with the much larger operation elsewhere in Europe, let alone the rest of the world.

On the one hand, the Moldovans had an almost idyllic setting and lifestyle; on the other hand, they were poor, at least by Western standards. He had seen incredible poverty in Africa, and no place in Europe would ever match that. But he couldn't help feeling somewhat sympathetic to this country, which seemed better suited for the nineteenth century than the twenty-first.

His job wasn't to be sympathetic. He was just starting to head for the meeting with the police when MY-PID reported that the Russians had returned to their rented room. Listening to them was better than the radio, and so he had the computer translate for him as he drove.

The beginnings of the conversation were mundane—they criticized the food they'd just eaten and debated whether the hostess would have been worth taking to bed.

Then they broke out the vodka.

"We ought to just go out tonight," said one. "Better to sleep there than in this flea trap."

"And risk Black's wrath? You're a fool."

"So what if he's mad?"

"He killed Ivanski for less."

"Ivanski was a fool."

"A dead fool now."

"Coming up in two and threes and fours—always cautious. He's overcautious. A coward."

"Call him a coward to his face. That I would like to see." The Russian laughed. "You assume he will be there."

"We're to work with him."

"I wasn't told that. Were you?"

"No. But every time we come to this armpit, who do we work for?"

"I worked for the Frenchman once."

"A good man to work for. Plenty to drink. Unlike Black."

"It will be good to work again."

"I'm ready. I would go tonight."

"Going at seven is plenty of time for me. At least we will get a good night's sleep."

"Not a good breakfast, though."

"The café will have a good breakfast. They'll have strong coffee."

"I feel like going back and screwing the woman."

"She's older than your grandmother, and not half as good looking."

They traded insults, then fell silent, and soon were snoring.

NURI WAS SURPRISED TO SEE A DOZEN POLICE CARS parked outside the church. Even more surprising, there were nearly fifty officers inside, all dressed in riot gear.

"You are the American!" said a thin, jolly man

who met him near the door. He spoke English with more enthusiasm than polish. "You are very welcome."

"Are you Johann Lacu?" said Nuri.

"No, no—there's Johann."

"Mr. Lupo—Mr. Lupo." A tall, thin man with a goatee and moustache separated himself from the crowd. "Here I am."

"There were only supposed to be six people," said Nuri. "Less."

"We need more for a raid," said Lacu cheerfully. "These are dangerous people. I have more men on the way. And an armored car."

Nuri rubbed his forehead, wondering how he was going to keep the crowd busy for the next several hours. They didn't have all that far to go—the farm was under ten miles away—and he didn't want to give away the location until Danny and the rest of the team was in place.

"We are happy to do something against the drugs," added Lacu. "These are all honest policemen. Their reputations are solid. People say we do not do anything—but what can they do when the people above them are corrupt?"

"I understand," said Nuri.

"Where will be our target?"

"There are several possible targets," said Nuri, making it up as he went. "Four or five homes where they move around between. We'll figure out which one it is, then you and your people will help surround it."

"If I saw the plans, I could help."

Nuri fended him off with assurances that the

NATO team—he didn't use the word Whiplash, of course—had everything under control. The Moldovans were only needed to secure the perimeter, and then take the prisoners. The deputy minister suggested that he should be with the team that made the arrests. Nuri agreed, an easy if empty promise.

The deputy minister began introducing Nuri, showing off not just the men but the equipment they carried. They had an assortment of AK–47 models that would have done a museum proud, along with more pistol types than men. They even had a dozen Russian F1 hand grenades that had to be at least forty years old.

"Good weapon," said the policeman in charge of them. "Thirty meters, killing radius. Thirty meters. These fuses—four seconds."

He mimed throwing it.

"Four seconds," said the policeman. "One . . . two . . . three . . . ka-boom!"

Nuri, willing to do anything to kill time, repeated the ritual himself.

"How far can you run in four seconds?" he asked when he was done.

"Very far, with grenade about to go off."

Nuri couldn't argue with that.

A sudden commotion outside announced the arrival of an armored car. Nuri went out with the others to inspect it. He looked at it in great detail, admiring the gun at the top and taking a turn sitting in the driver's seat.

"A handsome weapon, eh?" said Lacu as he climbed out.

"Very handsome," said Nuri.

"We will use it on you if this turns out to be a wild goose chase," added the deputy minister.

Nuri smiled. He thought Lacu was joking, but couldn't be one hundred percent sure.

42

Northeastern Moldova

AT EXACTLY TEN MINUTES AFTER ELEVEN DANNY FREAH turned off the highway about five miles from the Ukrainian border, pulling down a dirt road to a field he had scouted earlier that afternoon. He got out of the car and checked his watch, then walked up the road about two hundred meters. A broad field lay to his left. Owned by a family who lived on the other side of town some seven kilometers away, the farm had lain fallow for several years.

At eleven-fifteen the sky began filling with clouds. The moon played peekaboo with them for a few minutes, then completely disappeared.

At eleven-twenty a small red light flashed twice from the middle of the cloud bank.

Danny raised his arm and flashed his wrist light in response. A voice crackled over the ear set he was wearing.

"Whiplash Transport to Ground. Please confirm your identity."

"This is Whiplash One. How do you read me?"

"Whiplash One acknowledged. Strong coms."

"Bring it in," said Danny.

The clouds began to descend. Only when they were within a few feet of the ground did it become obvious they weren't clouds but an array of airships, camouflaged by a combination of LEDs and vapor generators, which poured mist from faceted baffles and outriggers. The baffles were arranged to reduce their radar signal during flight, when the mist wasn't being used, making them harder to pick up from a distance.

The first dirigible glided down to a landing thirty meters from Danny. Two more touched down directly behind it.

The cargo compartment was a combination of angles and curves; the leading edge looked somewhat similar to the lip of the SR–71 Blackbird, though this aircraft was as slow as that one was fast. The lip dropped down and a four-wheel-drive pickup lurched out, moving silently on an all-electric motor.

"Hey, Colonel," yelled Boston, leaning out of the driver's window. "Want to drag?"

"Only if I'm in one of the Rattlesnakes."

"Maybe you can hang from the skids," said Boston. "No room for you inside."

He wasn't kidding—the fuselage of the remote controlled helicopter was no bigger than Danny's desk at his old command. Two of them, with winglet and rotors folded up, were in the back of the pickup.

He watched as Boston parked the truck and

checked the rest of the team. The six pickup trucks they'd brought looked like oversized four-door civilian Chrysler Rams. And in fact they had started life as Ram 1500s.

Then subcontractors for the Office of Technology had gone to work. The trucks were outfitted with dual engines—turbocharged big block gasoline engines for fast travel, and heavy-duty electric motors for quiet travel. Screens were installed on the dashboards to interface with MY-PID. The metal skin and windows were doubled and reinforced, and an exterior wall of reactive armor added. This outer skin was designed to explode rocket-propelled grenades before their charges could penetrate; it augmented a "kill first" detection system mounted beneath what looked like a cargo carrier on the truck roofs.

"All present and accounted for, Colonel," said Boston. "Ready any time you are."

Danny signaled to the blimps to take off. They were guided by computer; there were no human pilots aboard. A duty officer back in the Ukraine watched over them as they flew. He would step in only if necessary.

"We're going to stage out of this old barnyard," Danny told Boston, showing him the GPS coordinates. "It's two klicks from the target area. We've got Predators watching overhead, but be careful anyway. These guys are full of surprises."

Flash was sitting in the car, watching the video feeds when Danny drove in. There was activity at the Black Wolves' farm—a lot of it.

"Two trucks came in about a half hour ago. Four more guys total," said Flash. "Two went into the building and moved things around. The other two put up some new defenses outside."

"They expecting us?" Danny asked.

"That's what I thought when I first saw them, but everything's back here by the house. I think they made their exercise more specific."

"You have the computer compare it to Kiev?"

"Figured I'd wait until they were done."

"Right. So have they started yet?"

"No, sir."

That was bad. The later they started, the later they could move. Keeping a strike force sitting around for several hours doing nothing was always problematic. But Danny knew he had no other choice.

"Let's see if they're any good," he told Flash, pointing to the screen.

They didn't have long to wait. Tonight there were eight Wolves involved in the exercise, six on the assault team and two inside the building, posing as targets.

The assault group moved more quickly than they had the night before. Four members moved up the road to the large building and slipped inside. The others took posts covering the approach. The infrared sensors on the Predator caught small explosions inside the building—flash-bang grenades, probably, though the thermal signatures were not big enough to see.

"Time them," Danny told Flash.

"Yeah. On it."

Flash tapped a set of keys that began keeping track of the elapsed time. Exactly two minutes and fifty-three seconds after he had flicked it on, a grenade flashed near the door. The two men on the outside began shooting into the woods.

Guns began firing back.

Flash zoomed to the spots where the guns were firing from. There was no one there; only weapons.

"Gotta be remote controlled," said Danny. "Part of the exercise."

"Yeah. But they were hidden so well we didn't see them, not even with the ground radar."

"They're good. No doubt about that."

The team came out of the building, moving at close to a dead run. Two men with them, bound and gagged—hostages.

"Only two?" said Flash.

"Two's a lot for six guys to handle," said Danny. "I'm surprised they're taking any."

Boston joined them, watching as the Wolves worked their way to the cottage and different gun emplacements opened up. Once more they got onto the skeleton helicopters and flew across the compound.

"These are the guys we're hitting?" Boston asked Danny.

"Yeah."

"They got a lot of gear."

"Sure do."

"At least they'll be tired when we go in," said Boston.

The Wolf team practiced their assault three

more times. By the time they were done, Danny could have done it with his eyes closed.

They used live ammunition on the last trial. The bullets perforated the trees.

It was almost 3:00 A.M. by the time they packed up. Danny waited until they had been in the house for a half hour before giving the order to saddle up.

"Our turn now," he told Boston. "Let's take our shot."

43

Northeastern Moldova

NURI SLOUCHED IN THE FRONT PEW OF THE SMALL church,pretending to be sleeping. The grumbling of the policemen around him had settled into a low background hum, the sort of sound a generator makes when some of its bearings are worn. Part of him hoped they would grow so bored and disillusioned they would simply go home. Another part of him feared they would decide to lynch him.

It could go either way.

He remembered a somewhat similar operation in Africa, when he'd been working with a local government against guerrillas who had taken to a particularly nasty form of piracy—the guerrillas would hijack buses on a deserted route, holding the passengers for ransom. To prove they meant business, they would kill the person they figured was the poorest, and send body parts to the local army barracks.

Grisly as it was, it was just business to them, and part of their costs included protection from sudden army or police raids. Every time the government threatened action against them, the cost of that protection went up—and so did the ransom amount, and eventually the number of kidnappings.

The CIA began working with the government when the daughter of a prominent Episcopalian bishop was among those kidnapped. An eavesdropping program quickly revealed that the local army general was getting kickbacks—something Nuri guessed the first day he'd been briefed on the assignment.

Still, the government insisted that the local army unit be notified when Nuri arranged a raid by SEALs to rescue the hostages. He had spent several uncomfortable hours in the African commander's home, basically under house arrest, while the raid went forward.

In the end he got out alive by suggesting that the general could make more money on the CIA payroll than by working with the guerrillas. The general proved to be very handy with numbers, and they soon cut a deal. For all Nuri knew, he was still collecting a paycheck.

He nearly jumped to his feet as his sat phone rang.

"This is Nuri," he said.

"We're in place," Danny told him. "Give us

ten more minutes, then come along and secure a perimeter. Sign into the Whiplash circuit when you're ready."

"Thank God," said Nuri, shutting off the phone.

44

Northeastern Moldova

THE KEY TO THE OPERATION WAS A DEVICE THAT LOOKED a little like a lawn mower, assuming the motor was replaced by a large fan mounted horizontally and covered with black plastic grills. A pair of the devices was used to create a resonating magnetic force that matched the field surrounding the farm. Placed side by side, they created a corridor approximately six meters wide for the Whiplash team to slip through without being detected.

Once past the perimeter, they moved stealthily through the woods. While there were video cameras hidden in the trees, MY-PID had calculated a safe albeit twisted path to the fields beyond. The pattern looked like a series of drunken vees. The team had to snake through the thickest foliage single file on their bellies before finally reaching a dried out stream bed where it was easier to move.

All in all it took more than a half hour to clear the wooded area. At that point the team split into two groups. One, led by Boston, began circling to the east to cover the front half of the house and property. The second, led by Danny, continued in from the south. Danny's group would do the actual assault.

The Predator with ground-penetrating radar provided a good view of the interior layout of the house. There were three floors above ground level, not counting the crawl-space attic. The top floor was divided into two large rooms with chairs; both appeared to be empty. The second floor looked something like a dormitory area, with small rooms boxed off on either side of a long hallway. There were staircases on each end. A total of four common bathrooms with four showers apiece were located between the rooms. All but two of the twelve people inside were sleeping in the dorm rooms, one to a room.

The other two people were in what looked like a small control room at the back of the house, directly above the basement door the Black Wolves had used to get in and out of the building. They were sitting next to each other at a pair of desks arranged in an el shape against the walls. There were no windows in the room, and the door was closed.

The basement, which appeared unoccupied, was divided into a small classroom where the debriefing had been held the night before, a workout room, and what appeared to be an armory. Besides the outside door, a single staircase ran down from above at the exact center of the building. There were no windows.

Even more important than giving Danny the location of the Wolves, the synthetic radar painted the mechanical layout of the house, showing him where the air-conditioning vents were. Most ran in the interior walls. One set, however, came through the attic where the air handlers were located.

That was the starting point for the assault on the house. After freezing a pair of motion detectors on the southwest corner of the house with blasts of liquid oxygen from a small tank—the sensors worked by detecting heat—the assault team moved next to the building. A former Delta trooper nicknamed Tiny and a Marine the team called Bean pulled special booties over their shoes and donned climbing gloves. Cautiously, they began moving up the clapboard siding. The gloves contained tiny, razor-sharp points that dug into the wood; they were surrounded by a super-sticky rubberized material that made the gloves worn by NFL wide receivers look like ice packs. The booties, which were strapped tight around their shoes, were made of the same material. The two men were essentially human flies, scrambling upward.

The nickname "Bean" had been shortened from Stringbean, and it was an apt description of the Marine's body. A quarter inch shy of six feet, he weighed 140—or at least claimed to; Boston joked that if he stood sideways he would fit through a sewer grate with no problem.

Tiny, on the other hand, looked like an artist's conception of a typical Delta Force trooper, with a well-developed upper body that featured muscles coming out of his muscles. But the image was blown once he stood next to someone—Tiny really *was* tiny, and very much so, standing five-three and a half. How he managed to get into Delta, which Danny had always thought had a strict height requirement, was anyone's guess.

The two men climbed directly to the roof, pausing to remove the gloves and booties. Bean then grabbed Tiny's legs and lowered him from the peak, holding him as Tiny inspected the fasteners on the attic vent.

"Star driver," whispered Tiny.

Bean pulled him back onto the roof. Tiny reached into his pant leg pocket and removed a small cordless driver, then found the star-shaped bit in the handle compartment. Bean once more grabbed his legs, and Tiny went back over to undo the vent.

The screws came out easily enough, but the vent wouldn't pull away from the wood. The slow settling of the house over the years had pushed the roof joists apart slightly, levering the vent into the fascia. Tiny had to return to the roof for a standard screwdriver.

In the meantime, two of the people who had been sleeping on the second floor got up. Worried that the sound of prying the vent off might alert them, Danny ordered Tiny and Bean to stop and wait.

"It looks like a guard change," Danny told them. "We'll just wait it out."

The two men inside took their time getting dressed; ten minutes passed before the first one went downstairs. When the next one finally went down five minutes later, Danny told Tiny to take a shot at getting the grill off while the men were on the first floor.

Tiny leaned back over the side. He levered the screwdriver in but found he had to use two hands to get the grill to budge. Suddenly it gave way. Tiny grabbed for it, but it fell to the ground with a loud *clang*.

Everyone froze.

Danny turned to Flash, who was looking at the radar feed on his laptop. He had the first floor.

"Nothing," said Flash. "Looks like they're talking. Maybe hard to hear from there."

MY-PID, watching the feeds along with Flash, warned that someone was moving on the second floor.

"Freeze," Danny told the men on the roof.

The man got up and looked out the window. He stared for a few minutes, then went back to bed. It was impossible to tell if he had heard anything or was merely restless.

"As quiet as you can," said Danny. "Let's move ahead."

Bean lowered Tiny to the opening. He slipped in, slithering around the frame as he felt his way to the floor.

"I'm inside," he whispered. "We need the gas."

Bean handed down a clamp and a metal pole, which Tiny attached to the top of the frame. The pole had a small pulley at its end. Tiny set a stranded metal line through the pulley, attached a small weight, then let it fall to the ground. Sugar brought up a pair of large gas canisters and attached them to the line. Tiny quickly pulled them upward, while Sugar kept pressure on a light-weight line attached to the bottom of the tanks to keep them from swinging into the building.

Tiny had just hauled the tanks into the attic when the two guards who'd been relieved earlier finally left the room on the first floor. But instead of going to their rooms, they went up to the third floor.

"Right below you," whispered Danny.

He watched on the screen as they sat on the couch. One of them took something from a nearby table—a remote control. They were watching TV.

Tiny was supposed to drill a hole into the metal ductwork to insert a hose for the gas. But even muffled, he worried that the sound would be enough to alert the men below. He crawled next to it, waiting to see if the men might fall off to sleep or leave the room. After a few minutes he realized that he might be able to loosen some of the screws on a nearby seam. He took out a pock-etknife and went to work.

45

Northeastern Moldova

THE ENTHUSIASM THE MOLDOVAN POLICE SHOWED MADE Nuri feel a little guilty as he watched them fan out around the property. The large size of the contingent did have one advantage—it allowed them to completely ring the property. They set up roadblocks about a mile away from the driveway up to the main house, out of sight of the video cameras protecting the farm. They also moved quickly, quietly, and efficiently, splitting up so it would have been difficult for a casual observer to realize how many policemen had flooded into the area.

Lacu set up a command station off the side of the main road about two kilometers from the property. The spot was on a hill, which allowed them to see the front quarter of the house, as well as the large building nearby where the Wolves had run their training session. Standing on the roof of Lacu's car, they could make out some of the grounds on the side. The Whiplash strike team was out of sight.

"Who are the owners of this house?" the deputy minister asked as he and Nuri passed a set of infrared night vision glasses back and forth.

"I can't remember off the top of my head," said Nuri. It was an honest answer, though it wouldn't have been very hard for him to look it up. "I thought maybe you would know the property."

"No," said Lacu. He sounded relieved.

"I wouldn't be surprised if it's owned by Russians," suggested Nuri.

"I think that's a very good possibility," said Lacu.

So there was the story they would use. Nuri would just let the deputy minister fill in the blanks.

"When shall we bring in the armored car?" asked Lacu.

"Hold it in reserve," Nuri told him. The car, which drove fairly slowly, was still about a few kilometers away. "Our team will try and get the men to surrender without gunfire."

"Without gunfire? None at all?"

"That would be the hope."

Lacu seemed impressed. He took the glasses and turned them toward the house, studying it and the surrounding property.

"I don't see any of your men," said Lacu.

"You will soon enough."

46

Northeastern Moldova

DANNY LOOKED AT HIS WATCH. IT WAS NOW PAST FIVE o'clock. It would be light soon. And the Russians from town whom Nuri had bugged would be coming out at seven, if they held to their plan. They had to move ahead.

The two men were still in the upstairs room, watching TV.

"Tiny, can you talk?" Danny asked.

"Yes," answered the trooper. He'd moved back to the side of the room, far from where the men were.

"What's your status?"

"I loosened the coupling on the duct and I think I can slip the gas nozzle inside," he said. "I can tape around it and make it airtight. It'll make a little noise, though."

"Get ready to do it. But wait for my signal."

Danny had the team outside take their positions for an immediate attack.

Plan A was to use the gas, knock everyone out, then systematically hog-tie them and cart them off.

Plan B was to go in hard, with or without the gas. Charges had been set against the wall at the guardroom, and two Whiplashers were ready to blow them and overwhelm the guards if they survived the explosion. Grenade launchers were aimed at the windows of the occupied dorm rooms; tear gas would be shot inside as the team rushed the building from below. With access to the armory cut off, they would invite the others to surrender, and proceed accordingly if they didn't.

That was the backup plan. Things would be easier if the gas worked.

"We're ready," said Boston.

"Set up and start pumping," Danny told Tiny. He turned to Flash. "You think we can increase the amount of electricity going into the building without blowing the circuit?"

"Piece of cake," said Flash.

He opened the panel on the laptop controlling the electrical regulator and edged it up slightly. It had an immediate effect—the volume on the television increased loud enough for Danny to hear it over Tiny's mike.

By the time the two men had turned it down, Tiny had the gas canisters in place next to the air duct. He began taping the nozzle into the hole.

With the tanks hooked up, Tiny crawled over to the air handler and undid the panel protecting the wiring. He short-circuited the thermostat control with a pair of alligator clips, kicking on the fan.

It took five minutes for the gas to empty from the canisters. By then Danny was feeling the fatigue of the long day. He leaned over Flash's shoulder and looked at the screen.

"Show me floor one," he said. "The control room."

"They're still at their stations."

"Awake?"

"Looks like it."

"What about upstairs?"

Everyone there seemed to be sleeping, but then they had been before the gas. On the third floor, the two men in the TV room were on the couch, still fidgeting, still awake.

Another ten excruciating minutes passed as Danny gave the gas time to work. Nothing seemed to change.

"It should be at maximum effect by now," said Flash.

The specialist who'd prepared the gas had calculated it would work almost immediately, since there were air ducts in each room. Within five minutes the concentrations throughout the house, with the exception of the basement and the attic, should be more than high enough to put a person out.

It had worked as well as it was going to.

"We go in hard on my mark," said Danny. "Ready?"

Each team reported back.

"All right," he said, gripping his SCAR-H/ MK–17 rifle. "Three, two, one—"

The charges blew out a large hunk of the wall. A frag grenade followed, eliminating any possibility that the two guards would be able to sound an alarm or fight back. Danny wasn't about to hang this operation on flash-bangs.

"Go! Go! Go!" he yelled as he saw the smoke from the blasts.

The team swarmed into the building. Danny told MY-PID to bring the Rattlesnakes up. Guided by the computer, the unmanned helicopters took off from the staging area two kilometers away and rushed toward the site, spreading out as they went so they could encircle the property.

Tiny went to the attic opening, a panel in the ceiling of the room next to the one with the television. He pulled it open and jumped down, pausing to adjust his night goggles, which had slipped on his face. As he did, he was blinded by a flash of light. Instinctively, he reached for his weapon.

GUNFIRE ERUPTED THROUGH THE BUILDING.

"People moving out of the bedrooms!" warned Flash.

"Secure the stairways!" yelled Danny.

In the next second there was a loud explosion on the second story. Something flew out of the wall—two of the Wolves, jumping from the house.

THE DEPUTY MINISTER TURNED TO NURI AS THE GUNFIRE erupted.

"I thought you said it would be done without gunfire," said Nuri.

"They're trying."

One of the Rattlesnakes buzzed overhead.

"What was that?" asked Lacu.

"A helicopter."

"There are three of them."

"Yes."

"They look—very small."

"They are. They're flown by remote control."

"Are they necessary?"

As if in answer, the gunfire at the house stoked up.

"I don't think it's going too well," said Lacu.

"No, no, it's going according to plan," said Nuri.

In the next moment a rocket was fired from the ground. Nuri looked up to see one of the UAVs turn into a fireball.

Danny saw the men jumping from the building, but they ran so fast he couldn't even raise his gun to fire. He jumped to his feet but then fell back as a series of explosions rocked the ground. Missiles began firing from the woods—antiaircraft weapons that had been secreted so well in the trees they hadn't detected them. One took down a nearby Rattlesnake; the others crisscrossed in the air, trying to find the other targets.

The Rattlesnakes shot flares, ducking away from the attack. By the time they regrouped, the two men who'd escaped the house were inside the training building.

Gunfire began raining from one of the windows on the second floor. Danny pumped a grenade inside, then ducked as the bullets somehow continued to fly.

Who the hell were these guys?

TINY FELT HIMSELF FALLING TO THE GROUND, SHAKEN BY the force of several explosions. He rolled to his stomach and groped for his weapon, sure that he was about to be killed at any moment.

The light that had blinded him came from a flash-bang grenade prepositioned in the hallway. A string of them exploded on every floor of the house, designed to break up an attack.

Tiny tried to shake off the confusion. He pushed himself to his feet, then crouched back down, still without his bearings. The circuitry in the goggles had recovered, but his eyes hadn't, and smoke pouring into the room made it even harder to see.

"Bean, Bean, what the fuck?" he shouted.

Not hearing a response, he reached up and found his ear set missing. His microphone was gone as well—the entire headset had blown off his head when he fell. He pulled it back up, cupping his hand over his ear as he tried to make sense of the cacophony of voices competing over the Whiplash frequency.

"There are three people moving toward the stairs on the second floor," Flash was warning. "Three people."

"What about the third floor? Third floor," said Tiny.

If there was an answer, it was overrun.

Tiny moved back to the door, then threw himself out into the hallway. Smoke was curling everywhere. He began crawling forward on his elbows, moving to the room where the men had been watching TV.

The door was open. He pushed his shoulder against the wall, sidling up the doorjamb. Then he flew forward into the open space, half expecting to be met by machine-gun fire.

Nothing happened. He rose on one knee and saw the two men on the couch, passed out or dead, he couldn't tell.

Tiny jumped up and ran to the couch. Holding the barrel of his gun at the head of the man on the right, he reached into his back pocket and grabbed the heavy-duty zip-tie cuffs. He reached down and pulled the man's wrists together, locking them. Then he went around the couch and tied the man's legs.

Tiny was just starting to rise when something hit him on the side of the head. He flew across the room, against the wall. The force of the blow took his breath away.

He'd been hit by the man whom he had handcuffed. Hands and feet still bound, dazed from the gas but not completely unconscious, the man rose from the couch. He shook his head several times, then raised his arms in front of his chest. He tugged at the restraints. They gave on his first pull.

Tiny pushed to his left, trying to escape. He found his rifle on the floor in front of him and grabbed it, rearing back to fire as he moved away.

Something flew at him, then gripped his ankle. It felt like an iron clamp, squeezing against his bones, crushing them.

It was the Wolf. Tiny flailed with his elbow and the butt of the gun. He hit the man's face and felt the grip loosen. Then something pounded his left side. He pushed up the gun and began to fire.

The bullets crashed through the man's face, shattering his nose and the bones of his forehead. But his attacker continued to pound his side. The pain was excruciating. Tiny collapsed as the gun clicked empty.

He lay on his back for what seemed like hours, unable to breathe. Finally he felt himself being pulled to his feet.

"Bean, Bean, get the other guy," he croaked. He turned, looking over his shoulder.

It wasn't Bean. It was one of the Wolves.

Tiny was too weak to resist.

"Got two more guys going to the window," Flash shouted to Danny.

Danny rose and pumped a 40mm grenade into the open window. He saw the flash and smoke, then watched dumbfounded as a man jumped through the window toward him.

He raised his rifle and began firing. The first few bullets hit square in the man's chest, but didn't slow him down. It was only as the bullets came up and struck the man's neck and face that there was any noticeable effect. The man wobbled, then spun and fell to the ground.

Just in time. Danny's magazine was empty.

"Hit them in the face," Danny said over the radio.

"MY-PID says they're moving to the tunnel," yelled Flash. "They may be trying to leave the property."

"Nuri—you on the line?" asked Danny. "Nuri?"

There was no answer.

"Can you get Nuri?" Danny asked Flash.

"I'm trying."

"Boston, move up," Danny said over the radio. "I'm going back to the perimeter where the tunnel opens."

For a few seconds there was no answer. Finally, Boston acknowledged. Danny jumped to his feet and began running for the woods.

NURI COULDN'T SEE EVERYTHING THAT WAS GOING ON AT the house, but it was pretty obvious the situation had not gone even remotely like they'd planned.

The deputy minister was walking back and forth near the armored car, wringing his hands as if they were sodden dish towels. His enthusiasm had quickly waned, and his frown grew longer as the gunfire continued.

"It won't be too long," said Nuri. "They'll be done any second."

Nuri's sat phone saved him from Lacu's dubious glare.

"What's going on?" he asked as the line connected.

"Close down the tunnel entrance," said Flash, shouting to make himself heard over the gunfire. "Blow it up!"

"Blow it up? Where is it?"

"Two hundred meters from the southeast corner, near the road. The sewer grate. You're only about seventy meters from it."

"You want us to ambush them as they come out?"

"Destroy it!"

Nuri turned to Luca.

"There's a storm sewer near the road up in that direction," he said, getting his bearings. "We have to destroy it."

"A sewer? Why?"

"To cut off the escape," said Nuri. "We need the armored car."

He began trotting up the road. The grate wasn't easy to find; he had to pull out the MY-PID control unit for a reference, and even then almost missed it in the low brush.

"There are no shells," said Luca. "The only gun is the 7.2 machine gun."

"The big gun isn't loaded?"

"No shells."

"Roll the armored car wheel over the opening," said Nuri, without time to argue. "We can at least do that, right?"

Instead of waiting for an answer, he ran to the truck and started waving at the commander, who was sitting at the top turret.

"Go on the sewer hole. Move!" yelled Nuri, first in English, then in his rickety Moldovan. "Go. Go! Forward!"

THE GUNFIRE SEEMED TO CALM AS DANNY RAN TOWARD the woods in the direction of the tunnel exit.

He'd taken a few steps when he realized he had momentarily forgotten where the minefield was. The prudent thing to do would have been to stop and ask MY-PID for help. But his brain was racing, and he plunged on, running toward the trees.

He reached the trees as the armored car rolled over the metal manhole cover. When he got to the fence line, he saw Nuri and the others standing near the car, staring at the sewer grate.

Danny threw himself halfway up the fence and began climbing over.

He had just reached the top when the armored car heaved upward a good two or three feet. It fell to the right, bouncing on its springs and rolling away from the tunnel opening.

Danny pulled his gun from behind his shoulder as a head popped up from the hole. He fired at it, two solid bursts ripping into the back of the man's skull. He collapsed over the edge of the hole.

"There's another! There's another!" yelled Danny. He flipped over the edge of the fence and half slid, half fell to the ground. He ran over to the entrance to the tunnel, his head woozy.

Nuri, pistol out, reached down gingerly to the dead man and pulled an automatic rifle from beneath his body.

"Get ready!" yelled Danny. "Get ready—there's another one!"

The truck started to back up. The gunner pointed his machine gun at the hole.

"What the hell is going on?" asked Nuri.

"We have to close off that entrance," said Danny.

"Did that guy just lift that car off?" demanded Nuri.

"Get the gunner to blow up the tunnel entrance," yelled Danny.

"Did that guy lift the cover off with the truck on it?" repeated Nuri.

"Yes—get the gunner to hit the tunnel entrance!"

"He can't—they don't have shells."

"Get some explosive and blow it closed!" Danny reached for his headset. "MY-PID—where is the other man who was escaping through the tunnel?"

"He is returning to Building B."

Danny grabbed Nuri. "Blow the entrance to the tunnel up. You understand?"

"But—"

"Just do it!"

"All right. We'll figure it out."

TINY FELT HIMSELF BEING CARRIED THROUGH THE HOUSE like a sack of potatoes. There were two of them— one holding him on his back, another nearby.

They were on the third floor, in the room he had come in through.

Tiny tried to move his legs but the man's grip on them was too strong. His side pulsed with pain.

He felt himself being lifted, then thrown upward, tossed into the attic like a child's doll. He clawed at the ground, desperate to get away, but it was useless; within seconds he was scooped up and once more flung over the back of one of the men.

The other was grunting something. It was

too dark to see—Tiny's night vision goggles had fallen off.

He heard a swinging sound, and realized the other man had grabbed an ax. They were going to chop their way out of the roof.

God, thought Tiny, I hope Bean doesn't shoot me when he shoots them.

BEAN FELT THE WOOD BEING SMACKED A FEW FEET away. He took a step back, sliding along the peak of the roof. Danny had ordered him to hold his position when the gunfire started. Bean had taken some shots at the last man who'd jumped from the window, but otherwise he'd sat here and watched as the situation deteriorated into chaos.

"Flash—I got somebody trying to chop their way out up here," he said over the radio. "Is it our guys?"

"Two of the Wolves—they have Tiny."

"Tiny's with these guys?"

"Yeah."

The axe blade came up through the shingles six feet away. Bean fired at the blade, striking it point-blank. It disappeared back below.

Bean got up and ran to the hole that the axe had just made. He kicked at it with his heel, then pulled one of the tear gas canisters from his belt and dropped it through.

"Where are they?" he asked Flash.

"They look like they're going for the stairs."

He retreated to the edge of the roof, pulling on his gas mask. But he stopped at the edge. It didn't make sense to go in there with them; they'd just use Tiny as a shield.

DANNY ORDERED THE RATTLESNAKES TO CIRCLE THE large building, expecting the man heading back to try and escape. Boston and his men, meanwhile, had joined the others at the house, holding positions on all four sides.

Three Whiplash team members had been hurt, one seriously wounded in the leg by gunfire, the other two merely nicked by shrapnel. No one had been killed.

Yet.

There were only two Wolves still moving around in the house, but they had Tiny with them on the top floor.

There was an explosion on the other side of the fence. The tunnel entrance had been blown up.

Danny was huffing for breath when he reached the house.

"The knockout gas didn't affect any of them," said Flash. "Bean just tossed a tear gas canister into the attic. They're still up there. I don't think it bothered them at all."

"Where are our guys?"

"They're on floor three, covering the hole into the attic."

"American!" The radio crackled with an unfamiliar voice. One of the Wolves had taken Tiny's headset off. "We have your people."

"Let him go and I'll let you live," Danny replied.

The man replied in what Danny thought was Russian, then switched to English.

"You will see his legs torn off!"

TINY WAS STILL WEARING THE GAS MASK OVER HIS NOSE and mouth, but without the goggles his eyes had no protection, and they began stinging as soon as the canister exploded. Tears streamed from his eyes.

It was the final indignity, he thought. It was bad enough that he had to die, but now it was going to look as if he had gone out as a coward.

47

Over the Atlantic Ocean

TURK PUT HIS HAND ON THE THROTTLE, NUDGING HIS power up slightly to maintain his optimal cruise speed as the tailwind shifted.

It was a bit of unnecessary fussiness—the computerized flight controls could have easily maintained the proper speed, even in a hurricane. In fact, the computer could easily fly him all the way to Prague without his intervention, even landing itself: not only could it check in with flight controllers along the way in commanded air space, but it could properly interpret commands from the tower when coming in for a landing.

But where was the fun in that? What good would airplanes be, he thought, if you couldn't fly them?

They'd be the Sabres, still seen by the brass as the real cutting-edge answer to aviation warfare.

Wallace didn't think so. But he'd probably retire in a year. Then no one would be talking about "manned flight."

The hell with the future, Turk thought, marveling at the stars in his viewer. I'm flying in the here and now.

48

Northeastern Moldova

DANNY RAN OVER TO FLASH AND HAD HIM LOCK OUT Tiny's receiver channel so their communications wouldn't be compromised. But the mike stayed on, and MY-PID could hear the man who'd delivered the ultimatum about Tiny talking to his companion in his native tongue.

The computer identified the language as Kazakh—the language spoken in Kazakhstan, the former Soviet republic that still had close ties with Russia.

"Open his line up again," Danny told Flash. As soon as it was open, Danny had the MY-PID issue the command to surrender in Kazakh. The words worked as well in Kazakh as they did in English, which was not at all.

"Out," said Danny, motioning with his finger across his throat. Flash killed the audio. "Flick him in and out. We may be able to use the radio to misdirect him."

"Gotcha."

"Circuit is secure," Danny said over the radio. "From now on, when I say 'Talking to Wolves,' assume they can hear whatever you say, until I broadcast a clear."

He took stock of the situation. They had one man in the large training building, two in the house. If necessary, they could bring the Moldovans in to help.

It shouldn't come to that. He had them outnumbered more than four to one.

He was used to kicking ass, even when he was the underdog. Now he saw what it felt like to be on the receiving end.

"If we can get them down to the third floor, we can go at them from top and bottom," said Boston. "We can get more guys up on the roof."

"We don't know if they have weapons down there," said Danny.

"If they had more weapons, they'd have them out by now."

"We can afford to wait," said Danny.

"What about their reinforcements? Those guys Nuri spotted in the village."

Danny had forgotten about them. He glanced at his watch. It was past seven.

"Nuri, you on?"

"I'm here."

"Those Russians you saw in town—"

"Yeah, I know."

"Secure the road."

"Already working on it."

"Tell the police no radios. The Wolves may have something inside to pick them up."

"Right."

Danny turned his attention back to the men in the house. He would have just ordered the Rattlesnakes to blow the damn thing up and be done with it if not for the fact that Tiny would die in the process.

He might already be as good as dead.

"Boston, who are our best shooters?" he asked.

"Everybody's pretty good, Cap."

"The best guys for head shots if you were the hostage."

Boston thought for a moment. No one on the team was a poor shot, but not everyone had been trained as a sniper. That meant literally hundreds and even thousands of rounds over and over, under all sorts of circumstances.

They had six men and one woman, if Danny remembered correctly. Who were the best two?

"I guess I'm going with Squeeze and Hooch," said Boston. "Squeeze 'cause she's fast, and Hooch because, you know, he's ice."

"Tell them to put sniper kits on and get ready. They're going wherever the bad guys go. Tell them if it looks to them like it's going to crap, to take their shots. Head shots—these guys don't go down easy. Tell them they're not going to be second-guessed. Under no circumstances do the people in that building leave alive."

"Under no circumstances," repeated Boston.

"*No* circumstances," said Danny. Clearly, these men were too dangerous to allow them to escape. "Tell them not to pay any attention to anything I say over the radio, unless I precede it with the word 'Whiplash.' Got that?"

"'Whiplash' is the safety word," said Boston.

"Nothing else I say counts."

"Got it, boss."

Danny looked over at Flash.

"Still in the attic," Flash told him. "Moving around. Getting something—I think they're going for the roof."

"What's going on in the training building?" Danny asked.

"He's moving around in one of the office areas."

"Have the Rattlesnakes destroy the cottage with the aircraft," said Danny. "Kill the helicopters. Then take out the garage."

Rockets began firing from the helicopters within seconds. The cottage with the skeleton chopper erupted in a burst of flame. The garage merely crumbled, the sides collapsing on the vehicles.

"What are you doing, American?" demanded one of the Wolves over the radio. "You are to cease fire."

"Open the circuit," Danny told Flash.

Flash gave him a thumbs-up.

"We're not going to let you out," said Danny.

"We will kill your man, then kill you!"

Boston waved at him, signaling that Squeeze and Hooch were ready.

"Wait!" said Danny. "Don't kill him."

The man laughed.

"They're coming up through the roof," said Flash.

"Bean, get down," said Danny over the radio.

Bean looked down from the roof. Danny waved, signaling that he wanted Bean to comply. The trooper tossed his pack down, then grabbed the line and rappelled to the ground.

While Bean was coming down, the Wolves kicked at the hole in the roof, making it bigger. One pulled himself through. Then the other handed Tiny up and came out himself.

By now the sky had lightened considerably. The men on the house were dark shadows, but it was easy to tell which was Tiny and which were the bad guys. The Black Wolf members looked like defensive linemen, though they moved as gracefully as any halfback. They stood upright on the roof, secure in their balance. One of the men had a rifle. The other held Tiny in one arm. He had Tiny's own submachine gun in his other hand, pressed against the Whiplash trooper's temple as if it were a pistol.

Was one of them Stoner? Danny thought of yelling his name, trying to make some sort of plea, then decided it would be a waste of time.

"You will move back!" shouted the man with the rifle. "Those helicopters—they will land! And you are doing a trick with the radio," he added. "Turning my headset off. Do not do this."

"What do you mean?"

"I'm not a fool, American. No more this turns off, or your man dies. Then you. Move the helicopters back!"

"Have the Rattlesnakes back off, but keep the big building in their sights," Danny told Flash, mike off. "I don't want the guy in there to get away."

Flash gave the command for the helicopters to back off a hundred meters.

"Team, hold your positions," said Danny over the radio.

"Move back!" demanded the Wolves.

"Where do you want us to go?" asked Danny.

"Back! *Back!*"

NURI COULDN'T SEE EXACTLY WHAT WAS GOING ON AT the house, but from what he heard over the radio, it sounded like Danny was going to let them get away.

"Danny, what are you doing?" he demanded.

"Shut up, Nuri, and mind your business," snapped Danny.

Shut up? Mind his business?

Nuri felt a flush of anger—then realized that Danny was playacting for the benefit of the Wolves in the house.

What was he planning?

Lacu looked at him.

"Your men should hold their positions," Nuri told him.

"They have a hostage?" asked the deputy minister. "We have snipers."

"It's under control," said Nuri.

"We have a car approaching on the highway," said one of the Moldovans, running up. He was out of breath; he'd run with the message because of the instructions not to use the radio. "They're coming to the roadblock."

The Russians from the hotel. Reinforcements.

"Stop it," said Nuri. Then he thought of something. "Wait. The snipers—have them meet me by the road."

"IF THEY STAY THAT CLOSE TOGETHER, WE'RE NOT GETting a shot," said Boston. "He must figure we have snipers."

"They're not dumb. We know that," said Danny. "But they have to separate from Tiny to get down."

"You and I would have to separate," said Boston. "I'm not sure these guys have to do anything we'd have to do."

NURI COULD SEE THE RUSSIAN CAR SLOWING AS THE two policemen put their hands up to flag it down. There were two police cars blocking the road behind it.

If they started to back up, what would he do?

Shoot them. But he needed the car intact. And he couldn't use the radio to tell them.

He saw one of the policemen in tactical gear running to his right. One of the snipers.

"Wait!" yelled Nuri. "Wait!"

The policeman looked at him. Not understanding, he continued to run.

"Wait, wait!" shouted Nuri, closing the distance between them. He grabbed at the policeman's arm. "Set up here—set up to get the driver."

The sniper stopped.

"Get the driver first," said Nuri, pointing.

The sniper dropped to one knee. Below on the road, the Russian was arguing with the policeman. The car started to back up.

"Now!" yelled Nuri. "Get him, get him, get him!"

THEY HEARD THE SHOT IN THE DISTANCE, THEN ANOTHER.

"What are you doing, American!" yelled one of the Wolves.

Before Danny could think of an answer, Nuri came over the radio.

"We have someone stopped at the roadblock," he said. "We had to fire warning shots to get them to stop."

"You will let the car proceed, American," said the Wolf.

Boston looked at Danny.

"OK," said Danny. "Nuri, let the car come up."

NURI PULLED THE PASSENGER OUT HIMSELF. BLOOD was everywhere. He dragged the body to the side, then pulled off his jacket. He was wearing a watch cap, but it was too sodden with blood to put on.

"Give me your pistol," he told one of the policemen.

Reluctantly, the man handed it over. Nuri rolled down the window, closed the door, then went to the driver's side. The body of the driver had been taken out, but the seat was covered with blood. Nuri had no choice but to sit in it.

"I go," said the sniper as Nuri rolled down the window.

"You have to be prepared to die," said Nuri.

"I go," insisted the sniper.

"Pistol only," said Nuri, pointing to his. "They didn't have rifles. You understand what I'm saying?"

"Understand. Yes."

"Take off your shirt," said Nuri. "You can't look like a policeman."

While he did, Nuri thought of one last thing. He leaned out the window.

"Give me a grenade," he told the policemen. "One of the grenades you showed me at the church. Quick!"

They came back with several. Nuri took just one, then asked for a medical kit. He removed the pin, holding the handle with a pair of bandages. Then he put the grenade down between his legs.

The sniper glanced nervously at him.

"Yeah, I go first if this doesn't work," said Nuri. "I can think of a couple of jokes, but they probably don't translate very well."

BOSTON GUESSED WHAT NURI WAS UP TO AS THE CAR approached the driveway.

"They may know who's been sent to pick them up," warned Boston. "They'll see them."

Danny dropped back to his knee. "Flash, have one of the Rattlesnakes put its searchlight on and drop down. Shine the light so it blinds the guys on the roof."

"You sure that won't piss them off?"

"Let them get pissed off. They won't do anything if they think they're going to get away."

The helo dropped quickly, its light flaring. The car came up the driveway slowly.

"Why does that helicopter have lights on, American!"

"I want to see what the hell is going on," said Danny.

"Turn lights off!"

"No," said Danny.

The Wolf raised his gun and fired at the light. The searchlight went dark—just as the car pulled next to the house.

"Now what?" said Danny over the radio.

"Stefan and Androv come out of Building A," the Wolf said.

"OK."

"Tell them."

"How?"

"Loudspeaker."

"I don't have a loudspeaker."

"Then go to the door and tell them."

"They'll kill whoever goes to the door."

The Wolf laughed. "That is your problem, American."

NURI GLANCED AT THE GRENADE BETWEEN HIS LEGS. Sweat poured down his palms as he moved it to the edge of the seat against the console. He loosened the bandage so that only the weight of his leg kept the trigger from popping.

"When we get out, the grenade will load itself,"

he told the sniper. "We have like four seconds. Four seconds. Then the car blows up. You understand?"

"Yes."

"The car blows up. They'll be running to it."

"Yes."

They were so close to the house that he couldn't see the roof. This was good—it meant that the Werewolves on top couldn't see him either. But it was nerve-wracking and dangerous as well—he couldn't see where they were or what was going on.

"Danny, what's happening?" said Nuri, realizing that over the radio it would seem as if he was back at the checkpoint. "We let the car go through. Where is it?"

"It came up the driveway," answered Danny. "We're going to let the man out of the building."

"Is that a good idea? You're going to let them escape in the car?"

"I have no choice," said Danny. "We're going to let them leave. One of them is moving to get down now, with Tiny."

"What? You're letting him get down?"

"He's going down the south side," said Danny. "I don't have any other choice. We have to let them go."

DANNY GLANCED IN THE DIRECTION OF THE SNIPER ON the southern side of the house. He couldn't quite see him. Or her.

"Where are our men?" demanded the Wolf with the rifle.

"We're working on it," said Danny.

The man holding Tiny slid to the southern end of the roof. He had Tiny's head pressed close to his, using it as a shield. It would be difficult to take him without hitting Tiny; a bullet from the other side would probably go through his skull and kill the hostage as well.

We knew these guys were good, Danny told himself. *We just didn't know how good.*

"American!"

"Your men in the building aren't answering," said Danny. "They may have been killed—there was a gunfight at the tunnel."

The two men on the roof began talking to each other. The one holding Tiny was inclined to leave their friends—after all, they had left them.

"Get down," ordered the man with the rifle. "American, back! If you do anything, your friend will be killed."

Danny bit his lip, holding his breath as the man took Tiny to the edge of the roof.

TINY FELT HIS LEGS DANGLING OVER THE EDGE OF THE building.

Enough of this bullshit, he thought. If I have to die, at least let me do something. Anything.

With a scream, he began to kick and flail his elbows wildly, aiming for his captor's groin. Whether he hit it or not, the next second he felt himself falling from the roof.

NURI HEARD THE SCREAM AND JERKED OUT OF THE CAR, pushing the door closed with his leg, gun raised. The Wolf who'd been holding Tiny let go as he jumped. They were close together, incredibly close—the Wolf was to the right. . .

Nuri fired as the man fell, and kept firing, moving to his left to get away from the car, shooting wildly. The sniper did the same in the opposite direction.

None of their bullets struck the Wolf's head, and he rolled to the ground and got to his feet. He put his hand on the car, steadying himself as he took aim at Nuri.

Then the grenade exploded.

"WHIPLASH! WHIPLASH! TAKE THEM! TAKE THEM!" screamed Danny as Nuri fired.

One of the snipers drilled the Wolf on the roof. The man fell backward, sliding head first off the house. In the next moment the grenade exploded in the car. Danny leaped to his feet, running toward the side of the building. The explosion had shattered the windshield, sending the glass flying as shrapnel through the air. But much of the force of the explosion was contained by the car and its engine compartment.

Danny saw Tiny, writhing on the ground on his left. The Wolf, in dark clothes, had been dazed. He was lying on his back in front of the hood.

Is it Stoner?

By the time the question occurred to him, Danny had already shot the man twice in the forehead.

He stopped, caught his breath as he saw the man's lifeless face.

It wasn't Stoner.

*   *   *

NURI FOUND HIMSELF ON THE GROUND. HE WAS THIRTY feet from the car. He couldn't recall how he'd gotten there—he'd run, but had he flown, too, when the grenade exploded?

Maybe.

He couldn't hear. He tried rolling to his right to get up, then realized he was already on his stomach. He pushed up, dizzy, and began feeling his legs, and then his chest.

Somebody grabbed his right arm. It was Danny, yelling at him.

Nuri tapped his ears. They felt as if he were in a plane, ascending quickly. He tapped them, trying to get them to pop.

"You OK?" yelled Danny. "OK?"

"I guess," answered Nuri. "I can barely hear you."

"The grenade in the car—good idea," said Danny. He ran back toward the building.

Nuri followed. Tiny was on the ground, his face twisted in pain. His right leg was bent at an unnatural angle; it hurt just to look at it, but Nuri couldn't take his eyes off it.

"The big building!" yelled Danny. "There's one more person in the big building."

Before he could turn, the ground shook with an explosion so strong that Nuri lost his balance and fell to the ground.

"Looks like we don't have to worry about getting him out of the building," Danny said. "He just blew it up."

THE SHOW

———

49

Moldova

THE FIRST PRIORITY WAS SECURING THE BUILDINGS AND making sure there were no Wolves left. Boston took charge of that, organizing a room by room sweep of the main house. Meanwhile, the severely injured were tended to. Tiny had broken his leg in the fall, and his ribs had been shattered by the Wolf's punch. The trooper shot in the leg had lost a great deal of blood. Danny decided to have the Rattlesnakes take both of them directly to the nearest hospital. The other wounds turned out to be relatively minor, handled by temporary stitches, and an ice pack and aspirin in the case of a sprained ankle.

They'd been lucky, Danny realized. They'd taken the Wolves by surprise with overwhelming force, protected by the best body armor in the world and aided by technology that should have made this a cakewalk. But in truth, they could have easily been overwhelmed if the Wolves had reached their weapons.

So who were these guys? And was Stoner here?

Danny asked himself both questions as he walked through the house. The muscles in his legs trembled ever so slightly, moving sluggishly, as if the op had changed the electrical impulses they used to communicate with the brain.

He stood over a body in the hallway on the second floor. It was facedown in a pool of blood, riddled with bullets—the man looked to have taken an entire magazine, if not two, before going down.

Was this Stoner?

Danny dropped to his knee in the pool of blood and turned the body over. It was heavy—he had to use both hands.

The body slumped against the opposite wall, head flopping. For a second Danny thought he was alive and jerked back.

A bit of skull fell away.

It wasn't Stoner.

Danny rose, his stomach starting to turn.

DANNY WENT FROM CORPSE TO CORPSE, EXPECTING each time to see Stoner. He was sure as he approached each body that this would be him—this would be the man, vaguely remembered, who had saved his life, and whose life he had saved.

Each time his throat thickened and his heart pounded faster. Each time his breath seemed to slip away. And then each time the face, battered by bullets and covered with blood, didn't belong to Mark Stoner. It was too young, too long, too round, too blond, or too different.

As varied as their faces were, all of the Wolves had many physical traits in common. All were at least six feet, most much taller. They were bulked up with muscles that would have made a body-builder jealous. Several were wearing prosthetics and implants. The man who Nuri had killed after he jumped from the roof of the house had an artificial leg fused to his bone just below his hip. Another of the men, killed in the house, had an artificial arm. Three of the others had scars on their upper arms and calves; Danny guessed there were implants of some sort there.

They gathered the bodies so they could be evacked and inspected by the technical team that evening. Danny went down to the Moldovan police lines to look at the other Wolves who'd been killed.

The deputy minister met him on the road. Lacu's face was ashen; for all his earlier enthusiasm, he clearly hadn't counted on so much bloodshed.

"We're just finishing a sweep right now," Danny told him. "We want to make sure there are no more booby traps. We have specialists, bomb people. Once it's secure, you can come in and take over."

The Moldovan deputy minister nodded.

"Nuri?" he asked.

"He and your sharpshooter are fine. They, uh, they were shaken up a bit. But your man was very brave. They were both brave."

Lacu didn't smile, exactly, but his nod this time seemed more positive.

"I need to look at the dead men," said Danny. "We're going to have to do, uh, autopsies."

"Autopsies?" The minister didn't understand the English word.

"Inspect the dead, the . . . uh, have doctors look at the bodies."

Lacu still didn't understand. Danny decided he'd let Nuri explain it to him, and went over to check on the rest of the Wolves.

Stoner wasn't among them. None of the men had exoskeleton gear either. A good thing, Danny decided; it would help preserve the fiction that this had only been a drug raid.

"One of my men will show you a clear path to the marijuana fields," Danny told the deputy minister. "But you should approach it very, very carefully. We don't think there are booby traps, but you never know. These guys were really well prepared."

"Yes," said Lacu. "I see that."

ONE BODY REMAINED UNCHECKED—THE MAN WHO HAD blown himself up in the building.

Was it Stoner?

The explosion had leveled the building, turning it into a pile of debris. It would take days to dig through it.

It must have been Stoner, Danny thought, staring at the ruins. Knowing he was about to be captured, probably realizing the force after him was American.

Did Stoner know that he was there?

A chill swept over Danny's body as he stared at the twisted wreckage. He felt certain Stoner was buried underneath.

"What happened?" Danny whispered to the last wisps of smoke that furled upward. "What really happened?"

* * *

IN THEORY, THE HOUSE SHOULD HAVE CONTAINED A trove of information about the organization, even if actual records weren't kept there. But the men had no personal effects—no IDs, no wallets even, nothing besides wads of euros and Moldovan leu, the local currency.

There were filing cabinets in the guardroom. Thinking they might be booby-trapped, Flash brought in a small electronic scanning device and determined there were no live circuits in the drawers. He drilled the key locks gingerly, but not trusting the Wolves, rigged a rope to open the first cabinet from outside the house.

Instead of the explosion he feared, there was a soft sound, almost like a pillow being fluffed. Smoke curled from the unit, followed by a small deck of flames that consumed the entire row of folders.

Shortly afterward, convinced that the area was secure and they hadn't missed anything important, Danny called Breanna to tell her what was going on. He thought he was waking her up back in the States; to his surprise, he found her on the C–20 over the Atlantic, en route to Prague.

"It went well," he told her. "But they're all dead."

"All of them?"

"I'm afraid so. One blew himself up in one of the buildings when it was clear he wasn't getting out alive. The others were in no mood to surrender. They were like supermen. They're all extremely strong."

Danny described some of what had happened.

"Was Mark one of them?" Breanna asked finally.

"I don't—he's not one of the dead," said Danny. "But . . ."

His voice trailed off.

"Danny?"

"I think he may have been the one who blew himself up. I—it's just a hunch, I guess. Maybe a gut feeling."

"Do you have photos or—"

"Nothing. No evidence. I reviewed the video images. There's no shot of his face. But I just—I guess I feel that it's him. It's not rational, I know."

"All right. And, to find out we have to dig through the wreckage, right?"

"It'll take days."

"We'll get more manpower," she told him. "The medical team and the other experts will be there by this evening."

"Right. I should get back to Kiev. Just, uh, in case they have more people."

"Yes, absolutely. Listen, I'll be in Prague in a few hours—should I come to Moldova?"

"I don't know that it would be necessary," said Danny. "Why Prague?"

"There's an air show. We've taken an aircraft that some of the NATO members are interested in. And I'm going to surprise Zen—he and Teri and my niece are there for the show."

"Oh."

"Did Zen tell you he was going to Kiev for the NATO conference?"

"No."

"He is. It was a last-minute substitution when Senator Osten had a heart attack."

"No, jeez, I hadn't known at all."

"Yes, he'll be there. Listen, I know you and Zen text each other. Don't tell him I'm going to Prague. It's a surprise. OK?"

"No sweat."

They talked a little more. Breanna agreed to brief Reid herself, saving Danny from giving his whole rundown all over. She told Danny that the task force that had developed the information on the Wolves was being expanded. It was likely that, with the op over, Whiplash would be able to come home and regroup.

"After Kiev," she said. "Assuming nothing happens there."

"Right."

While they had knocked out a good part of the organization, Danny was sure they hadn't gotten the real leader or leaders.

"These guys were just the muscle," he said, aware of the understatement. "Whoever put these guys together like this—he or she would be capable of doing just about anything. We can't let our guards down."

"We're not going to."

50

Prague, Czech Republic

HE SAW IT IN HIS HEAD.

The aircraft veered in the sky, wing tipping toward the ground. In the first moments, the spectators thought it was part of the show. They had come to be thrilled, were used to seeing aircraft pirouette dangerously close to the ground. This looked like one more maneuver.

Then a few realized it wasn't intentional at all. The plane was moving unnaturally, sharply sideways and downward. There was something wrong with the wing and engine. Smoke.

A missile had struck.

The next three seconds would be a blur. Then everything would move in a strange sort of slow motion, time jumbled backward and forward at the same time. Black smoke would spout from the ground, even before the flames, before the shock of the explosion. A spiked yellow ball would veer from the center of smoke, rolling wildly through the air. Everything would turn white.

There would be a moment of peace, a tease before the pain.

A rush of air came next. The lucky ones would know death.

The man they called the Black Wolf closed his eyes, fighting off the vision, closing away his own memory, trying to return to the task at hand.

He could strike the aircraft with a missile from

here, at the edge of the runway, during one of the shows. It would serve as a cover for the rest of the operation, the attack on the officials. With the proper timing, the horror would be multiplied.

But it added difficulty. Getting past the security was a solvable problem, but once the shot was taken, escape would be very difficult, probably unlikely.

Did he care? In some ways death would be a relief. It would end the pain that constantly attacked him from every direction at once.

But if he took the shot here, he would not be present for the rest of the mission. He would not lead the assault, and could not guarantee that it would succeed. It wasn't hubris to think that he was the most important piece of the plan, the leader the others depended on for success. That was his real function. He was the Black Wolf.

Drama was not the goal of the mission. He would not attack the aircraft.

The Black Wolf folded his arms pensively. He would launch the op elsewhere.

A SECURITY GUARD STOPPED HIM ON THE WAY OUT OF the airport. The Black Wolf rolled down the window, curious about the procedures. He had not anticipated being stopped on the way out.

"Do you have your papers?" asked the guard, speaking in Czech.

The Black Wolf handed them over. They claimed he was Slovak.

"I have a cousin who lives in Trencin," said the man.

"I live outside the city," replied the Black Wolf. "We have an old family farm."

"It must be very nice."

"Unfortunately, there is no money for the farm, but the scenery is very pleasing. That is why I have this job."

The words flowed easily from his mouth. As long as he could remember, he'd had a way with words. The ability to use many different languages had blossomed after the change. Before, his languages were primarily Asian. Now he could wander Europe like a native as well.

They'd made him smarter. Stronger. Younger, in a way.

He'd trade that for relief from the pain. For peace, finally.

"It's very bad," agreed the guard. "A shame for common people."

"We have worked hard," said the Black Wolf. "But we must take outside jobs. My parents— eventually they will lose the farm. It seems a sin. It was taken from the family first by the communists, then restored. Now we lose it again."

"And you are here on work? What do you do?"

"A mechanic. Fixing machines." He smiled, then shrugged. "It is a knack I picked up."

"I have ten thumbs, I think."

"Will there be much traffic tomorrow?" asked the Black wolf. "I am supposed to arrive before dawn. They told us to be prepared. But I have such a long way to come. I couldn't afford to stay in the city. I have a cousin, thank God, with a couch. But he lives an hour away."

"Oh, that's bad. I would give myself plenty of time. The security will be ferocious. Even for workers."

"Which gate would be the shortest?"

The man thought for a moment. "I would use the one we use, at the south. There will be a few trucks, but you should get through the quickest."

"Then I'll have to drive across the runway."

"You can take the inner road—ask for a pass."

The soldier talked on. The Black Wolf nodded, taking mental notes. He had more than enough information to plan an attack here, but pumping the man was good habit. One never knew when plans had to be changed or what contingencies would have to be followed.

An American C–17 landed as they were talking, its engines so loud the guard fell silent.

"Quite a plane," said the guard.

"Yes," said the Black Wolf. *I jumped from one*, he almost added. The words appeared in his brain and almost made it to his tongue.

Had he really parachuted from a C–17?

Shards of the memory flickered into his head. He saw himself going out. . .

What life was that? What had he been before the crash?

A killer, as he always had been.

"Was there something else?" asked the guard.

The Black Wolf realized he'd been staring into the distance for a few seconds, lost in the muddled memory.

"Nothing," he told the man, rolling up the

window. "Thank you for your kindness. It was good to talk."

51

Chisinau, Moldova

With the success at the farm, the Wolf operation now entered a new phase, focused on figuring out who had organized the group. The task force that had originally developed the leads would now revisit everything obtained earlier, adding to it the data Whiplash had developed. Technically, the investigation had always belonged to them—Whiplash was in a sense a hired gun, called into action because of the eminent danger. While Whiplash's job wasn't over yet, the investigators would now take the lead. Whiplash was an operational unit; detective work was neither its raison d'être nor its forte.

Danny ordered the team to pack up and relocate to the Ukraine. He decided he'd arrange to officially join the security there, though he'd keep Hera and McEwen and the surveillance network they'd established under wraps for now. He would fly to the city immediately, leaving Boston to coordinate the load out here.

Someone had to orient the medical and technical investigators, as well as the task force coordinator, who were on the way. Nuri, as the lead CIA operative, naturally drew the assignment. And since he was doing that, he took charge of having the site secured and wrapping up the dozens of loose ends the operation had left behind.

It was tedious in the extreme. Rather than using the military base, he arranged to secure the dead bodies in a small food packing plant about thirty miles from the farm. Lacu, the Moldovan deputy interior minister, happily volunteered a dozen men to guard them. Nuri decided that wasn't enough—he had Lacu detail two dozen more, along with the armored car. And then he made sure that a contingent of U.S. Marines from the embassy in Chisinau could beef them up.

He gave Gleeb a quick summary of what had happened, along with the developing official version—crazy drug dealers had decided to shoot it out with the Moldovan task force, which had shown great bravery while miraculously avoiding casualties.

Lacu's men were taking plenty of photos of the marijuana. Eventually, someone would want to see the bodies and very likely the actual house, but with luck that could be pushed back a few days— long enough that Nuri would be gone by then.

Lacu arranged for an around-the-clock guard at the farm. Nuri assumed the technical team would want to dig through the ruins for more evidence, so he instructed the Moldovans to keep their distance, warning them there were countless booby traps that hadn't been disarmed. The wreckage of the training building made the point more eloquently than he could have, and he was reasonably certain the policemen would keep their distance long enough for the technical team to arrive.

By four o'clock everything was under control, at least for the evening. Nuri decided it was time to get some rest. But where?

Back in the village where he'd rented a room? It was as good a place as any, he decided, hunting for a policeman who could drive him back to his car.

52

Old State Castle, Czech Republic

"DADDY, LOOK AT THIS ROOM. IT'S A REAL CASTLE room!"

Zen chuckled as he rolled through the large reception room. The Czechs had arranged for some of the NATO air delegates to stay at a large, government-owned guesthouse about six and a half kilometers from Kbely Airport, where the show was taking place. Guesthouse was something of a misnomer—the place was literally an old castle, converted to government use following World War II.

"It is a real castle," said Caroline.

"I wonder if there are any dragons in the closets," said Zen. "What do you think, Caroline?"

"I think it's a real possibility," she said, winking at her uncle.

The late-afternoon sun cast long shadows on the floor, making it easy to imagine that there were strange creatures lurking nearby, but Teri was having none of it.

"There are no such thing as dragons," she said definitively. "I'm not three, Dad. I know make-believe."

"There could still be dragons," said Zen. "I wouldn't rule them out just because I never saw them."

The main keep—the large building at the center of the facility—had been turned into a conference center and museum. The large central room, once used by the lord of the manor to receive accolades from the peasants he owned and hand out punishment for crimes, was now lined with armor and antique weapons. Teri, eyes wide, stared at everything, practically dizzy with excitement, or maybe just jet lag.

Their guide, a young woman about Caroline's age, swept her hand and declared that all of the weapons on this side of the room had belonged to the last family to own the castle. All had been restored to superb condition.

"The weapons were in significant disrepair," she said in sturdy English, "when the People took the property over. The People have done a very fine job with them, do not you think?"

"I do think," said Zen, rolling over to one of the battle-axes. The blades gleamed with the light from the fixtures suspended above.

"Were these ever used?" asked Caroline.

"We cannot to be sure," said the guide. "Similar weapons would have been intended for show in other families. Sometimes they might be used in ceremonies, certainly. They are very old, so it is hard to tell."

"I think I see blood on that handle," said Zen.

He was teasing, but the others all looked.

"Maybe senator is correct," said the guide.

The tour continued through one of the two doors at the far end of the hall. A suite of conference rooms had been built in the courtyard. These backed into the keep, so that the great room was connected to the meeting area by a short hallway. This transitional space was lit by a large glass skylight. The effect was as if you were stepping into a time machine and materializing back in the twenty-first century.

Zen, tired from the flight, had a little trouble negotiating the threshold, his wheelchair veering with the bumps. He barely kept himself from cursing as he crashed into the wall, fortunately at a slow speed.

Caroline looked at him, but knew from experience that he didn't want or need any help. The guide, unfortunately, didn't, and came over and took the back of his chair.

"I'm all right," said Zen, pushing the chair back a little too hard in annoyance. "It's OK."

"Daddy likes to drive himself," said Teri.

"So I do, my princess," said Zen. "Makes me feel like a king. Appropriate for a castle."

Flustered, the guide started talking about the work the People had done on the castle.

Zen thought it was interesting the way she

used the phrase "the People" instead of the government. On the one hand, it was a vestige from the old days of Communist party rule, still a sore subject for many Czechs. On the other, it *was* a reminder of who actually owned the country, and Zen couldn't fault it.

Except for the communist connections, he'd recommend it for the U.S. He knew far too many supposed government servants, to say nothing of elected officials, who could use the reminder.

They moved on, down a ramp past a modern kitchen. It continued in a series of rectangular turns, leading them to a large stone room below the main hall.

"This is the dungeon, where prisoners were kept. And wine," added the guide. "I'm not sure whether they really went together. You can see the chains still on the walls. And the old graffiti."

Teri followed the guide, craning her neck toward the wrought-iron circles embedded in the stones.

"Uncle Jeff, I think Teri may be getting a little tired," said Caroline. "Her eyes are droopy."

"I think you're right. We're probably all good for an early bedtime. We'll head over to the rooms after this," he said. "Pretty interesting place, though, no?"

"It's a little creepy," said Caroline.

"You think?"

"This room especially. Can you imagine it before they took the wall away? There would have been no light. It would have been a horrible place to be held prisoner."

"You do the crime, you pay the dime," said Zen.

"Or if you disagree with the lord of the castle," she added. "He was god, as far as the local peasants were concerned. If he didn't like you, the chains went on."

"That's a point," said Zen. "Though probably if you did something to *really* piss him off, he'd just have you killed. Why waste the space?"

53

Kiev, Ukraine

"THERE'S NO QUESTION ABOUT IT," SAID HERA, POINTING at the computer screen. It displayed an image of the interior of the large building the Wolves had used on the farm. "This part here resembles the interior of the ministry where the NATO meeting is to take place. Look at the access path they took."

Hera superimposed a diagram of the meeting hall on the photo, then had the computer show the paths the Wolves had taken inside.

"There are gaps in the walls here and here," said Danny. "Those aren't on the Kiev building."

"True, but notice that they don't go through those spaces. And they ignore this part as well. They could have run something across the space to block it off so the radar wouldn't pick it up. A simple rope or ribbon. They might have realized that they could be scanned, and disguised the layout. Or maybe it's something generic that they adapted."

Danny rubbed his fingers across his scalp, scratching a nonexistent itch. He was extremely tired—he hadn't slept in almost forty-eight hours, and if you added the time he'd actually slept the week before, the total would have come in under twenty. He'd already had one go-pill, but wanted to avoid taking another. While the doctors claimed they weren't addictive, he just didn't like the idea.

"I think they must have been planning to stash those robotic helicopters in one of these warehouse buildings," continued Hera. She pointed to a row of buildings eight-tenths of a kilometer away. "They would have a straight shot right across the roadway here. Go over this fence—or blow it up—and they're there."

McEwen stared at the screen pensively.

"You don't think that's the place?" Hera asked.

"Oh, I think it's definitely the place," said the older CIA officer. "But those helicopters wouldn't have taken them very far, according to what your scientists said. They had to have some other place in mind."

"I think we should check out the warehouses," said Hera.

"And the airport," said McEwen. "Because the airport is within range of the helicopters. So they get in them, fly to the airport, and leave from there."

"The airport would be shut down," answered Hera.

"In ten minutes? I doubt it. You could have a private plane ready to leave. Or even a helicopter."

"We should check into all of that," said Danny, trying but failing to suppress a yawn.

"I think one of us should get some rest," said McEwen.

"I'm OK," said Danny. He got up from the chair. "All right, so they're at the airport and they have an airplane. Where would they go?"

"Over the border, back to Moldova," said Hera.

"No, they'd want to keep the country as a safe haven," said McEwen. "They've clearly worked from there before. They're going to go somewhere safe."

"They're being followed," said Danny, yawning again.

"They parachute out," said Hera.

"I could see that," said Danny. "But where?"

The possibilities were endless. Danny scaled back, suggesting that they have MY-PID check for leases and plane charters that might be suspicious.

"No offense to the computer," said McEwen, "but don't you think we're better off doing the legwork ourselves?"

"The computer can find things we can't," said Danny.

"And vice versa."

"All right," Danny agreed. "Let's do it both ways."

"We'll take care of it," McEwen told him. "In the meantime, why don't you get some rest?"

"I think that's a good idea," said Hera.

"Ganging up on me?" Danny smiled.

"Your eyes are like slits, Colonel," said McEwen. "I hate to be the one to say this, but you really do need your rest. There's no substitute."

"Thanks, Mom," he said sarcastically.

She frowned.

"You're right," he admitted. "I'm off to bed. Wake me if you find anything important."

54

Northwestern Moldova

NURI WAS HUNGRY AS WELL AS TIRED, AND SINCE IT WAS dinnertime, the first place he stopped when he got to the village was the café. The hostess acted as if he was an old friend when he came in, taking him to the table at the front with great ceremony. Her tray of cordials quickly followed.

"Too tired to drink," he said.

"No, no, tired good. Pep you up."

Maybe he would have a drink, he decided. He felt pretty wound up, too keyed up to sleep.

"You should have a drink with me," Nuri suggested as she began setting out the bottles.

"Oh, I cannot do that. Not with a customer."

"You sure?"

"My husband is the cook," warned the woman.

"He should have one as well."

The woman laughed and said he would not like the effect even a single drink would have on his food.

Nuri picked a green bottle at random. To his surprise, the liqueur was pink.

To his even greater surprise, it actually didn't taste bad.

"I think I should put myself in your hands," he said, handing back the menu. "I'm very hungry."

She nodded confidently.

"I imagine it will be different than what your Russian friends ordered last night," he added.

Her smile turned to a frown. "They wouldn't know good food if it bit them."

"Why do so many Russians come here?" he asked. "To the village—not here. Here it's obvious. Your food is so good. And the cocktails."

He pointed at his empty glass.

"They only drink vodka," she told him.

"What is it about the area? If they don't really ride bikes?"

She shrugged. "It's always been that way."

Nuri got little else from her but food. She brought an appetizer dish that looked as if it were pancakes, though there were bits of what he thought were meat in them. The main course was familiar—beef with noodles, and very good.

Dessert consisted of two pastries. They looked exactly the same, but tasted very different. One, filled with some sort of fruit, was borderline delicious. The other, with a mystery filling, was borderline poisonous.

Maybe not so borderline. Nuri had one bite, felt his stomach start to turn, and got up to use the restroom.

When he came back, the hostess was clearing the table. He started another conversation, mentioning that someone had told him about a Russian doctor who helped train athletes for the Olympics before Moldova was independent.

"Russian doctors." She made a face.

"Bad?"

"One struck my mother in the street twenty years ago. She could not walk forever after that accident. Did he even apologize? And he came back many times—still sometimes I see him."

"He lived here?"

"Not lived. But stayed. Russians." She shook her head.

"Came here a lot?"

"Not in my café."

"But the town."

"They come in. They think they own us."

"I'm sure. What about this guy? He owned a house?"

"She has the house. A kilometer out of town. She is Russian, too. He pays, I'm sure. You know the kind. With a family. On the side, they play."

"You know his name?"

"Pfff—all Russians. Who keeps track?"

She took the dishes and went back into the kitchen.

Nuri reached into his pocket for the MY-PID controller and called up a photo of the doctor.

"Is this him?" he asked when she returned.

The hostess made a face, then looked at him as if he had tricked and betrayed her.

"I'm an investigator for the Olympics," he told her quickly. "We believe this man may have done some illegal things. If you have information about where he lived here, or any of his dealings, it would remain confidential. I would never say where I got it."

It was one thing to complain about the Russians, and quite another to reveal that you were investigating them, especially when you had appeared to be just a benign tourist. The woman instantly turned cold, going so far as to pretend that she didn't understand his English.

It had been a calculated risk, and Nuri knew he had had lost. But her reaction made it obvious that the doctor was in fact the same person. Finding which property he owned was simply a process of elimination, solved within a few minutes by MY-PID as it searched through property and utility records. These were somewhat sparse, but the computer filled in the gaps by accessing every possible record it could find. It finally gave Nuri two possible locations for the house.

There was no way he was going to sleep now, at least not until he checked them out. They were two kilometers away, one northeast and the other just slightly northwest of the hamlet.

He drove past both. Neither looked much like the sort of place a man who lived in the Chisinau mansion would choose. Both were over a hundred years old; neither measured more than eight hundred square feet. One leaned to the left; the other seemed to be missing a foundation pier on the right. The lights were on in both houses, but neither had cars out front.

Nuri debated what to do. The action at the farm had shown that the Wolves were extremely formidable, and he didn't want to walk into an ambush. On the other hand, the longer they waited to talk to the woman, the less likely they'd find anything of use. He debated it back and forth and finally decided to see what he could find out.

Nuri parked in the driveway of the house that was missing the foundation pier. It was a muddy, rutted affair that cut diagonally across the front yard. He got out of his car. He was still working on his cover story when the door opened. The inside light framed a slender blonde in her early twenties standing in the doorway.

"Can I help you?" she asked in Moldovan.

"I am looking for Dr. Nudstrumov," he said, using Russian.

"Dr. Nudstrumov? What are you saying?"

She was still speaking in Moldovan, and didn't appear to recognize the Russian at all when Nuri repeated it.

"I don't know a doctor," she told him. "Do you have the right house?"

The woman was pretty, and certainly the sort that might be kept in a love nest, as the woman at the café had put it. But as soon as Nuri heard a male voice behind her, the theory lost a great deal of credibility.

Unless, of course, the man was one of the Wolves.

"Perhaps he uses a different name," said Nuri, exhausting the phrases he had memorized with MY-PID's help.

The woman shrugged. The man appeared behind her. He was only a little taller than she was, thin—not an overjuiced type like the men at the Wolf farm.

"I'm looking for the doctor's relatives," said Nuri, moving to English as the idea occurred to him. "Because we have news—we believe he is dead."

"Who?" said the young man. He understood the English, but it quickly became clear that the doctor's name meant nothing to either him or the girl. Nuri showed them the photo on the MY-PID without getting a reaction.

"I'm sorry for bothering you," he told them.

THE SECOND HOUSE WAS SO CLOSE TO THE ROAD THAT Nuri couldn't even park in front of it, fearing that his vehicle would be sideswiped. He found a wide shoulder about thirty meters farther down. Parking there, he walked back along the road's edge. As he approached, he could see an old woman working in the kitchen, washing dishes. She had the wrinkled face of a woman who had seen much trouble in her life, but her movements were graceful, the sort of effortless gestures a ballerina might make.

Nuri stopped. What would she have looked like twenty years before, when the athletic training facility was still operating?

In her thirties, still attractive, but on the precipice of decline.

Nuri prompted MY-PID for a new set of phrases, rehearsing them as he walked to the house.

"The doctor sent me," he said when he knocked on the door. "I was to collect the things."

"What?" she answered harshly in Moldovan.

"I don't know. He said that you would know."

"Are you crazy?"

Remembering what the woman at the café had said, Nuri switched to Russian.

"The doctor sent me," he told her.

"What language is that? Speak in Moldovan."

He repeated the words the computer had told him.

"Moldovan," insisted the woman.

"You don't understand?" said Nuri, still in Russian.

"I don't know what you're saying," insisted the woman.

"You were a dancer," said Nuri, guessing but knowing at the same time. "And still beautiful."

Her frown deepened. Nuri held out his hands. "I am just a messenger."

She frowned. Her lower lipped curled downward. Then she told him to come in.

THERE WAS NOTHING IN THE HOUSE TO INDICATE THAT the doctor had ever been there, or had the slightest connection with the woman. There was very little in the house at all—the front sitting room where she led Nuri had only two places to sit, one a wooden chair, the other a very old sofa, badly frayed. The television at the side looked to be from the Soviet era.

The woman left Nuri sitting there and went back to washing her dishes. He was sure he was right about the connection, but he began to worry that she had somehow tipped off a helper. Finally, he heard the whistle of a teakettle. She stopped doing the dishes; after a few minutes she came out with a tray of cookies and tea. It was an old-world gesture, a show of culture and dignity at a moment of personal despair.

"I knew a day would come when he would end all things," she said softly, speaking in Russian.

Nuri didn't understand all the words, but the meaning of what she was saying was clear as she picked up the teacup, her hand trembling slightly. She sipped slowly. The heat from the liquid formed a light cloud of vapor, softening her face. Nuri thought he could see into the past, see what she would have looked like when the Russian first met her, already well past her prime as a dancer.

They drank in silence. Nuri wanted to tell her something to comfort her, but there was nothing he could say. Telling her the doctor was dead would surely not comfort her, and any mention of any sort of money or being taken care of would probably be an even worse insult. He was a voyeur to her pain, powerless to alleviate it.

She drank about half her cup, then abruptly but gracefully put it down and rose. He noticed for the first time that she walked with a slight limp, the product undoubtedly of injuries as a youth.

Was that how they had met? Had the doctor tried to cure her, and failed?

And knowing what he had done to the others—or what he seemed to have done—could he have cured her? If so, had he considered the trade-offs too much of a price for her to pay?

But it was worse than that, or more complicated, at least. She returned with a manila envelope.

"This is what you want," she told him.

Nuri took it. As he was leaving, she stopped him.

"We met in hospital," she told him. "A bad omen."

She continued speaking. Nuri didn't understand the words but nodded as she talked. MY-PID supplied a translation after he reached the car:

"I was desperate to extend my career. He promised me everything. I didn't even get six more months.
Vanity has the greatest price."

The envelope contained a small key that looked like it went to a safety deposit box. But there were no markings on it. Finding what bank it had come from, let alone what the box number there was, would be a long process.

As he drove back toward the guest house, he asked MY-PID for an update on the farm as well as its efforts to turn up more information on the Wolves and the slain doctor. The computer gave him a long list of seemingly trivial connections.

Realizing he was starting to tune out, he asked it to tell him what was going on at the farm.

"No material change," reported the computer.

"Are the Predators still on station?"

"Affirmative."

"Detail one over to the facility Danny Freah checked out the other day. Have it look for buried bodies."

"More specific information required."

Nuri gave it what he could. Then he told the computer to look on the farm property as well. Maybe there had been some accidents there.

"No grave sites at property identified as farm," answered the computer.

"You checked already?"

"Affirmative."

The property had been gone over thoroughly by the radar scans; MY-PID had only to take the electronic equivalent of a glance to check.

"Wow," said Nuri. "Nothing of use?"

"Question not understood."

"Was there nothing buried on the property?" asked Nuri. "Besides the mines and the tunnel, I mean. And the sensors."

"Foreign objects buried on the property," said the computer, beginning a list of items that started with a collection of broken bottles.

Nuri stopped the computer when it mentioned a fireproof strong box.

"Describe the box and where it is located," said Nuri. "Then direct me to it."

55

Kiev, Ukraine

WHAT AMAZED HERA ABOUT MCEWEN WAS NOT HER
knowledge of the city, or even the ease with which
she struck up conversations. The impressive thing
was that she seemed to know everyone, or almost
everyone, from the attendant at the parking lot
at the airport to the after-hours security man patrolling the hangar area at the Kiev airport.

The attendant at the parking lot told her that
the charter aircraft company whose owner she
wanted to talk to had gone out of business six
months before. She checked the office anyway—
vacant—then took Hera to the terminal bar
where the former owner generally hung out and
occasionally slept. He wasn't there, and neither of
the two bartenders seemed to know who she was
talking about when she asked.

"Damn," said McEwen. "He knew everything
that was going on."

Her conversation with the security guard sitting at the far end of the bar was more fruit-
ful. McEwen started by asking about the man's
mother, who'd been in poor health the last time
they met. She was doing considerably better,
thank you, said the man.

The conversation went on from there, the
words flying by so quickly that even MY-PID
couldn't keep up.

There was too much of an age difference between them for the relationship to be sexual, Hera

was sure. And yet it certainly seemed intimate—McEwen gave him a light kiss on the cheek before taking out some bills to pay the bartender so they could go.

"We're going to need the car," she told Hera. "Where we want to go is not far from here, but I'd prefer we weren't seen."

Hera drove as McEwen led her around the perimeter of the large airport, driving down empty access roads in the industrial park at the side of the airport. Finally they reached what looked like a dead end.

"Go down this alley to the right, then take a left," said McEwen. "And turn off your lights."

"It's too narrow."

"You can fit. You want me to drive?"

Hera declined. McEwen drove like a little old lady—who'd just inhaled a half pound of crack cocaine.

Even in the small Fiat they'd rented, she had trouble cutting the turn, but once in the alley there was plenty of clearance along the sides—as long as they kept the mirrors folded against the car.

"We want to check the fifth hangar," said McEwen as they turned onto a wider street. "But park at the second. We'll walk from there."

The hangars were metal buildings dating from the seventies, too small now for anything but private planes. They were being used mostly to store parts and featured rusted padlocks and peeling paint. Hera followed McEwen out around the side of Hangar Two to a narrow back path, approaching Hangar Five from the rear.

"There's a security camera on the hangar across the way," McEwen explained. "This one is wide open, but it would be better if we weren't seen, I think."

"How do we get in?"

"You can't pick a lock?"

"I can pick locks."

Rusted barrels of refuse crowded along the back of the building. Hera had to squeeze over a pair of them and then push them away to get to the back door.

It was so old the lock had rusted in place. She couldn't get her pick to move the tumblers.

"We'll go to Plan B," said McEwen.

McEwen disappeared around the corner. Before Hera could follow, she heard glass breaking.

"What was that?" asked Hera.

"Plan B," said McEwen, standing in front of the broken window. "Why don't you go first? It's a little hard to climb in my dress."

Hera's small LED flashlight was just powerful enough to light up the entire interior, but then there wasn't much to illuminate. A collection of rusted steel garbage cans and drums stood next to the wall near the front. Discarded cardboard boxes were stacked in a semineat pile near the back. Two roofs' worth of shingles sat on pallets at the exact center of the building.

And that was it.

"Pretty empty," said Hera, shining the light around.

McEwen leaned in the window. "Give me a hand," she said.

Hera was surprised at how firm the petite woman's muscles were. She was light, not much more than a hundred pounds, if that.

"All right then," said McEwen, straightening her clothes. "Let's see what we have."

She walked over to the cardboard boxes, bending and turning a few of them over.

"Toilet paper, handouts for passengers," she announced, straightening. "Interesting."

Hera rolled her eyes.

"Let's see what they're throwing out," said McEwen, walking over to the garbage.

Two-by-fours and assorted sticks in the first can. Roofing material in the second.

AK–47s and grenades in the third.

"Bingo," said McEwen.

THE HANGAR HAD BEEN RENTED BY A COMPANY NAMED Vleta Servici Ltd. MY-PID quickly determined that Vleta was associated with a company named Duga TEF, which had a small number of dealings in Russia. It found two bank accounts associated with Duga, then began tracking transfers that had been made into and out of the accounts. Within a half hour it had profiled a spidery network in Ukraine and Russia.

By then Hera and McEwen had removed the rifles and grenades from the premises, and planted several video bugs around the interior of the hangar. They'd also cleaned up the glass, removing the shards and the shattered pane. Someone looking at it would realize it had been broken, of course, but it was only one pane and might be overlooked, especially by someone coming in from the front.

"You think they were planning a hijacking?" asked Hera as she prepared to back the car precariously down the alley.

"I think it's more in the way of a backup plan," said McEwen. "A cache of weapons in case something goes bad. A group coming into the airport could grab them; someone wanting to leave could take them, and maybe use the boxes as cover to get them aboard an airplane. It's a contingency."

"Why just a contingency?"

"Think about it. You do mostly covert action, right? If you were planning something, you'd have your best gear with you."

"Sure."

"You might pre-position it, but you'd take critical care of it. No one could just barge in and grab it, or come upon it accidentally. The Wolves are as professional as you are. These weapons were ridiculously easy to get to—they could get in just by breaking a window, like we did."

"True," said Hera. "But—"

"They may have been a backup," said McEwen carefully. "Not their main cache but something they could grab quickly in an emergency."

She paused, thinking

"Or they may be a blind," she added. "A misdirection. Either way, we're not done. Not by a long shot."

56

Over the Atlantic Ocean, approaching Europe

THE C–20B WAS AN AIR FORCE SPEC BOEING 737. While not nearly as luxurious as the standard corporate configuration of the plane, it was a VIP jet, with a number of features that anyone who ever had to fly in the belly of a C–5A or C–130 would have killed for.

Case in point: Breanna's seat. It moved back, so it was essentially an inclined bed, about as comfortable as you could get in an airplane cabin without actually having a bed.

Breanna, however, found it uncomfortable. And even when she finally decided she'd be best off taking a nap before landing, had an almost impossible time dozing off. Finally she fell off into a fitful sleep, images flitting through her mind, ideas and arguments.

"WHY DIDN'T YOU SAVE ME?"

The voice came from across the river. She jumped from the bed—she was still in the tent.

"Why didn't you save me?" asked Mark Stoner.

She reached over to get Zen, but he was gone.

"Breanna—I saved you."

"Mark? Are you out there?"

"Where are you?" he said.

She knew it was a dream—it could only be a dream—and yet it felt so real that it wasn't a dream. It was something between a dream and reality, its own category.

"Where are you?" she asked. She pushed out of the tent, still in the sweats she had gone to sleep in. The air was cold. She felt goose bumps forming on her legs and neck. Her hands were so cold they were hard to move. She clasped them under her arms to keep warm.

"Why didn't you help me?" he asked. *"I saved you."*

"We saved each other," she said. *"Do you remember—we jumped."*

Had they jumped? Or was that with Zen? Now she couldn't remember—Zen had saved her once, in India, had protected her and gotten them rescued. It was Zen, Zen who had saved her.

But she'd parachuted another time. Stoner was there—who had saved who?

God, she couldn't remember.

They'd been together in the water.

It was a dream but it felt too real, as if they were there together now.

"Mark? Mark, are you OK?" she asked.

"I have to kill them now," he said.

She screamed.

"MA'AM, YOU OK?"

Breanna opened her eyes and saw the Defense Department aide standing over her, a very concerned look on her face.

"I—just had a very, very bad dream," Breanna told her.

"Can I get you something? Ambien?"

"No, that's all right." Breanna pushed the seat upright. She wasn't sure she wanted to go back to sleep after that. In fact she was sure of it.

"We still have a long way to go," said the aide.

"We're stopping in Sicily to refuel. We won't be touching down in Prague until early morning. It'd be good to try and sleep if you can."

"Thanks. If I need a pill, I'll ask."

"Yes, ma'am."

Breanna thought of calling Zen and Teri. She longed to hear their voices. Zen's especially.

But she was being silly. The Wolf operation had been smashed, and while Danny thought Stoner might be the man who'd blown himself up in the building, Breanna realized that the DNA match must have been a fluke. Poor Mark had died in the crash fifteen years ago. Very possibly his body had disintegrated immediately.

She was sorry for him, dreadfully sorry. But she'd already grieved his passing.

"Maybe I will take the pill," she told the aide. "If you can guarantee to have plenty of coffee to wake me when we get to Prague."

57

Northwestern Moldova

NURI PUSHED THE SPADE INTO THE DIRT, HAMMERING down with his right heel against the top of the shovel. The box had been buried quite a while ago; the ground was hard.

The radar had reported it was two meters below

the surface—six feet. That didn't sound like much, until you started digging. The first foot or so was tough—a shrub had grown almost exactly over the box, and there were tree roots on the side to contend with. The next foot or so was somewhat easier, though the clay soil only reluctantly gave way.

The rest was hell. It didn't help that it was after midnight and he'd been awake for a millennium. Or so it seemed.

He pushed downward in a circle, working his way around as he created a funnel. The moon was nearly full, but the sky was filled with clouds, and the only light came from two battery-powered lanterns loaned by the Moldovan police contingent guarding the house.

He'd asked the deputy minister if they had a backhoe. Lacu wasn't sure, but promised to look into it by morning. Nuri figured he'd be halfway to China by then.

Or maybe not. Five feet deep in the hole, and he was ready to drop his concerns about letting the Moldovans see whatever was in the box. But it didn't make sense to stop now. He knew he was close. He poked and attacked with the shovel, using it as a pick.

Finally he hit something hard.

He scraped, pried, scrambled up for one of the lanterns.

Back in the hole, he dug at it with his hands.

It was a rock.

Ten minutes later, he pried the rock away and found the box.

Two of the men who were guarding the house came up as he was pulling it from the ground.

"I could have used you guys a half hour ago," he said in English, pushing it ahead of him as he clambered up the side.

"*Moltumesc*," said one of the men, taking the box.

"Give me a hand, would you?" Nuri asked.

"*Da*," said the man.

The other smashed Nuri in the back of the head with his rifle, sending him tumbling back into the hole.

58

Kiev, Ukraine

HERA WAS SURPRISED TO FIND DANNY UP AND SITTING at their laptop when she and McEwen returned to the hotel suite.

"I thought you were sleeping," she said.

"I did."

"What, for two hours?"

"You going to mother me, too, are you?" he asked, unfurling his bare feet from beneath him and standing. "Do either of you know how to work the coffee machine?"

"It's busted," said Hera. "I meant to ask for a new one."

Danny frowned. "So what's going on?"

McEwen told him about the guns. Hera, meanwhile, used the laptop to see if MY-PID had gotten any more information about the weapons and the hangar.

The serial numbers on the rifles indicated they were genuine, manufactured in 1953 for the Soviet army. They belonged to a lot that had been declared obsolete by the government more than a decade before. There was no other information about those specific guns, and the type was so common—literally ubiquitous—that trying to correlate them against known gun sales, legal and illegal, was impossible, even for MY-PID.

Information on Duga, the company that had leased the hangar, was far more limited—and therefore considerably more useful. It had leased a similar building at a regional airport in France two years ago; there had been an assassination tied to the Wolves there as well. Following transfers of money from its accounts, MY-PID discovered an HSBC bank account that had been tapped for cash in three different cities near where Wolf murders had taken place.

More interesting was the fact that the account had made a large transfer to an Austrian bank account, which in turn was tapped twice in the past two days in Prague.

"So there's someone in Prague?" said McEwen.

"Maybe," said Danny.

Hera asked the computer for more information on the bank account and the withdrawals. It didn't have any—the account had only been opened a few days before.

"No other connections?" McEwen asked after the words *null set* appeared on the screen.

"Not yet," said Hera. "It's thinking."

"Well let's think ourselves—why would someone from the organization be in Prague?"

"Part of their getaway," said Hera. "They need a clear path out. New identities, that sort of thing."

"So whoever dropped the guns off then moved on to Prague," suggested McEwen.

Hera tested the theory by trying to find correlations between the account and recent airline travel between Kiev and Prague. MY-PID found nothing usable.

"How much money did they take out?" Danny asked.

"Six hundred euros," said McEwen. "Twice. Walking around expenses."

"But why didn't they bring it in themselves?" Danny asked. "If it was someone assigned to clear the way for an escape, they would come in with the money."

"It could be a handoff to someone," said McEwen. "You can't carry too much cash across the border. Generally you're not stopped, but if you have more than a few hundred euros, there will be questions."

"This was only twelve hundred."

"Twelve hundred is still a lot, at least where I come from," said McEwen. "But you're forgetting—these are the transactions we know about. There could be another ten. They could be planting the money for the people coming through. Hiding it for them. Or spending it."

"Why escape through Prague, though?" asked Hera. "If you can fly anywhere, either go to Russia or go somewhere with more connections."

"Damn," said Danny.

Hera looked up from the computer as he continued.

"Get all the information you can about an air show in Prague," he said. "And get some coffee up here from room service. Find out where Nuri is—call him and tell him I need to talk to him."

"What are you doing?" asked Hera.

"Getting my shoes. Then going to Prague."

59

Northwestern Moldova

THE PAIN SWIRLED AROUND NURI'S HEAD. HE FELT AS if he was flying through a wind tunnel, spinning around at the center of a cyclone.

Then he landed, crumpling into a pile in the corner of a dark room.

Something hit his chest, then his leg, then his chest again. It was diffuse, a cloud of weighted pain falling on him, like snowballs or rain.

Or shovelfuls of dirt.

Something hit his face. A rock.

Another shovelful on his legs.

Nuri couldn't move. He tried to open his eyes, but all he could see was black.

60

Outside Prague

"IT IS 12:05. YOU ARE FIVE MINUTES LATE. WHY ARE you late?"

The plainclothes security guard turned his eyes toward the carpet. Like the sergeant, he was Polish, a member of the state security force assigned to escort the Polish delegation to the air show.

"Who is your superior?" demanded the sergeant.

"Captain Klose."

"Klose is an idiot. Take your position next to Stefan. Don't move for the next four hours—not even to relieve yourself."

The guard took his position opposite the other guard next to the hotel room door. The Polish air ministry had taken much of the hotel, including the entire top floor, where all eight rooms were reserved for the Polish air minister and his guests. This was a bit excessive; besides the minister's suite, none of the other rooms were occupied. Two would be used for a reception later that night, and the others were available in case the minister decided to invite guests to stay.

But the security people weren't in a position to complain about the minister's spendthrift ways. Their rooms, scattered throughout the hotel, were hardly austere, and came fully stocked with alcohol and sweets.

They were also booked one to a room, a boon to the man who had just come on duty.

"What are you looking at?" demanded the sergeant, turning to the second man manning watch.

"Nothing, Sergeant."

"The men from Warsaw think they are better than the Krakow detail, is that it?" The sergeant turned back to the man who had just arrived. "And you are Exhibit A of this."

"I am sorry I am late."

"You don't know me, but you will," continued the sergeant. "The minister is not to be disturbed. You will be relieved in four hours. Neither of you is to go anywhere. No one is to be admitted on the floor without the minister's approval. A woman . . ."

The sergeant paused, deciding how to phrase what he was about to say. He looked at the guard from Warsaw.

"The minister may have guests," he said finally. "Treat them professionally. Be—judicious."

"Of course," said the man.

"You will report to me at 0900 hours." The sergeant pointed at the guard who had been late. "We will discuss the importance of promptness, and your future in the security forces."

The guard glared at him, but said nothing. The sergeant shook his head, then stalked off.

"Five minutes, what a jerk," said the guard who had been on time. "As if it would make a difference. You think he has a girl waiting?"

The other guard said nothing, adjusting his jacket above his bulletproof vest. He started to hitch his pants, then turned away out of modesty.

"You're from Krakow. That's the real problem. The sergeant hates everyone from outside Warsaw. The whole idea of drawing people from across the country, as if this were some sort of lark—"

The guard stopped speaking in mid-sentence and slumped to the floor, killed by a single shot to the brain from the silenced .22 in the Black Wolf's hand.

The Black Wolf reached down and took the man by the shoulder, propping him against the wall. Then he slipped a passkey into the door of the hotel room, and let himself inside.

61

Kiev, Ukraine

DANNY WAS ALMOST TO THE DOOR WHEN HERA STOPPED him. She had her MY-PID control unit in her hand.

"Nuri isn't answering," she said.

"Probably sleeping," Danny told her.

"No—he's at the farm. And look at his vitals—his heart's pumping."

Nuri's pulse, recorded by his bracelet, was at 140.

"Something's wrong," said Hera.

"The deputy interior minister in charge of the state police who worked with us on that raid," said Danny, reaching for his sat phone. "We need to talk to him right away. MY-PID should have the contact information somewhere. Get it quick."

62

Northwestern Moldova

THE WEIGHT ON NURI'S CHEST AND ARMS WAS INCREDible. He pushed his head to his right, and at the same time scratched through the dirt with his right hand, trying to reach his nose and mouth. He got there finally, cupping a little space over it.

The bastards!
Buried alive!
Out!

He struggled, but the more he struggled, the more dirt seemed to fall. He tried to wiggle to the right. Dirt fell on him there. Left—more dirt.

He wasn't too deep. He could dig himself out. He could.

His lungs were starting to feel tight, compressed. Nuri pushed his hand over his mouth, making a little pocket for air.

He should wait for them to go away. Wait.

For what? Death?

He was down five feet. Dig, for Christsake!

Nuri tried pulling his left arm up, pushing through the weight that kept it pinned by his side. He pushed hard, but it wouldn't budge. Then he tried a softer approach, moving it as if it were a snake.

Or a worm. He was a worm. He had to think of himself as a worm, squeezing through the ground, getting out.

A worm.

Is this where he was going to die? In the middle of nowhere in a small country where people wouldn't even be able to pronounce his name?

I have to get out now. Now!

He curled the fingers on his left hand into a claw and began pushing at the dirt. It seemed to give way slowly.

But it was too slow. He was starting to choke.

Everything! I need everything!

Nuri pulled his other arm up and began to push. He curled his upper lip over his lower lip and tried breathing through his mouth. There was dirt in his teeth. He tasted rot.

Nuri pushed.

Out! Out!

The ground seemed to give way. He moved his elbows toward his ribs, then levered them back against the ground beneath him.

Out! Out!

He couldn't breathe. He was choking—it felt as if his lungs were full of dirt.

Out! Out!

He pushed with everything he had. And suddenly he felt air on his face.

People were yelling in the distance, calling his name. The two men who had buried him were gone.

Nuri pushed himself to his knees. He was still half buried, covered with dirt. He reached his hand into his pocket and found the MY-PID unit.

"I need the words for 'seal off the area,'" he told the computer. "I need the words for 'not one motherfucker leaves.'"

63

CIA Headquarters, Virginia

JONATHON REID FROWNED AS HE SCROLLED THROUGH the list of intercepts. There were several screens full—more than a hundred messages.

The sheer number alone was significant. Add to that the fact that they came from military units spread around the country, and the conclusion was inescapable: the Ukraine army was about to revolt.

But Reid smelled a rat.

He moused over to the folders with the latest satellite images. There were unmistakable signs that two of the units in the eastern part of the country were mobilizing. And there were no corresponding orders indicating that they should do so.

Concrete evidence of a coup, especially when coupled with the intercepts.

Still—a coup with the NATO ministers about to descend on Kiev? How very convenient for the Russians.

"Mr. Reid, the director is waiting."

Reid looked up at his assistant, Mark Dalton. Dalton, a field officer who had been rotated back home following an injury in South Asia, wore an exasperated expression—pretty much the one Reid always saw.

"I'm just reviewing the data he's going to be interested in," said Reid. He cleared his screen and got up from his desk.

"You don't think it's a coup?" asked Dalton. He'd come on duty at 6:00 A.M.; he'd been working for more than twelve hours and was very likely to be here for several more.

"I think someone wants us to think it is, yes," answered Reid.

"But you don't."

"It looks so much like a coup it could come out of a textbook," Reid answered. "And real life very rarely resembles what goes on in the classroom."

REID MADE THE SAME ARGUMENT UPSTAIRS IN THE director's conference room twenty minutes later, this time in front of a packed house of CIA officials, including Herman Edmund, the Agency chief. Several members of the Joint Chiefs of Staff and their aides were watching via video from the secure center at the Pentagon, and an equal number of NSC people were over in the White House situation room. Reid, speaking after the Agency's in-house experts of Ukraine had made a case for the coup, patiently dissected the intercepts.

"What you're saying is that it's too perfect," objected Stephen McGovern, the Agency's ranking analyst for Eastern Europe. "That's really a difficult argument, Jonathon. What would be the point?"

"The point would be to disrupt the NATO meeting. Showing that the country is unstable. Without, of course, having to go to the trouble of actually encouraging a coup."

"It's a *lot* of trouble," said McGovern.

"Not very difficult to do," said Reid. "The Russians break into the network and send a lot of messages. They get two divisions to move their units around. Bribe the right officer, and these trucks will drive to Paris. It's no secret how badly most of these troops are paid."

"But what would the point be?" said Edmund. "That's the real question. Let's say that it is fake—we'll know it in a few hours."

"A few hours' indecision may be all it takes," said Reid. "But we may only be seeing the opening act. There may be more. It may end up looking as if a coup was planned, and then aborted for some reason. And it's not just us—every Western intelligence agency is seeing these intercepts. Even the French have them."

"Well, that *is* an indictment," said Edmund.

Everyone laughed.

The meeting proceeded quickly to the conclusion favored by the analysts: a coup might be under way in the Ukraine within a few hours. Reid succeeded only in getting them to emphasize the word "might" and add a few caveats to their alert. Given the tendency of the analysts to stay away from any definitive statement that might come back to haunt them, it wasn't much of a victory.

Director Edmund stopped him at the door as he was leaving.

"If you have a moment, Jonathon."

"Always for you, sir." Reid stepped back as the others filed out.

"Whiplash was successful?" Edmund asked when they were alone.

"The action in Moldova eliminated everyone at the farm," said Reid. "There were about a half-dozen people, Russians we think, and they all appear to have been associated with the Wolves."

"Is it possible these intercepts were related to what they had planned?" said Edmund. The operation against the Wolves was still so secret that neither Reid nor Edmund had shared it with the others.

"I didn't bring it up because the timing of this activity seemed wrong," said Reid. "If there were a direct link, then we wouldn't expect these messages until at least the day after tomorrow when the NATO ministers gather."

"My thoughts exactly," said Edmund.

"Unless there's something we're missing." Reid smiled. "It's too pat. It seems so obvious I wouldn't even give it to a junior officer as an exercise."

"You do like complications," said the director.

"A character flaw, I'm afraid. Hopefully, not fatal."

64

Outside Prague

THE BLACK WOLF EXAMINED HIS FACE IN THE MIRROR. He didn't look all that much like the dead man on the bed inside, but that wasn't necessary—the people he had to fool wouldn't be looking all that hard at him. All he had to do was look enough like the dead man that they wouldn't bother with a second look until it was too late. Far too late.

Toward that end, he sprayed a little more gray into the side of his hair, dappling it with his fingers for a salt and pepper look.

Distinguished.

There was a knock on the outer door. The Black Wolf took his pistol from the counter and went to it.

"Yes," he said, still speaking Polish.

"Wolf," said the voice outside softly. He was speaking English.

"Black Wolf."

"We are ready."

The Black Wolf opened the door. Two of his assistants on the job—men he had not met until now—stood in the hallway. They were dressed in brown and gray suits, looking very much like the men he had killed earlier.

"Watches," said the Black Wolf, holding his out.

They held out their arms and made sure their watches all had the same time. It was exactly 0432 local.

"We must be downstairs in exactly twenty-one minutes," the Black Wolf told them. "It will take the car five minutes to arrive, and another ten for us to reach the Old State Castle. The others will meet us there. Are we ready?"

The men nodded.

"Let us proceed."

65

Boryspil International Airport, near Kiev, Ukraine

DANNY DROPPED A PAIR OF BILLS ON THE FRONT SEAT of the cab and hopped out, holding his small carryon bag under his arm as if it were a football. He had ten minutes to make the gate for his flight to Prague.

Impossible at most U.S. airports, even at this

early hour. But the security at Kiev was extremely efficient—or incredibly lax, depending on your point of view. There were six different stations to handle the very light traffic, and the guards barely glanced at the X-ray screen as he tossed his bag on the conveyer belt. He stepped through the detector quickly, grabbed the bag, and trotted toward the gate where his plane to Prague was boarding.

He reached it just as the attendant was extending the rope. She smiled when she saw him, pulling it back as he held up his pass and ticket. She grabbed the printout, ripped it in half, and waved him through.

There were plenty of empty seats on the plane. Danny had his entire row to himself. He pushed his bag into the overhead compartment, then sat down and pulled out his sat phone and MY-PID ear set, wanting to check in with Washington to see what was going on.

He also wanted to talk to Zen, though he'd undoubtedly still be sleeping.

Nuri first.

Danny pushed an earphone into his right ear, then held the sat phone over it, pretending he was using the phone.

"Update on Nuri Lupo," he asked the system.

"Lupo's current status is undetermined."

"Connect me with him."

A few seconds passed.

"This is Nuri," answered the CIA officer in a raspy voice. "Danny?"

"Are you OK?"

"Just barely. Two guys tried to bury me alive. They got away with a box. I'm pretty sure it belonged to the doctor. I don't know what's in it. I'm sorry—I'll figure out where they went."

"Get yourself checked out."

"I'm fine."

"Get some sleep at least."

"I'm fine. Where are you going?"

"I'm playing a hunch in Prague." Danny glanced around. The plane was moving. "You'll have to get the whole story from Hera."

"All right."

Danny looked up to see the attendant walking toward him. The man wagged his finger.

"I gotta go," he told Nuri.

"I'm sorry, sir, but cell phones must be turned off," said the attendant. His English was thick with an accent that sounded Russian to Danny, but was actually Ukrainian.

Danny made a show of hitting the End transmit button. He pulled the phone down into his lap. Then, with the attendant behind him, he tapped out a text message to send to Zen.

ON WAY 2 PRAGUE. BE VERY, VERY CAREFUL.
POS GRAVE DNGR. WILL EXPLAIN WHN ABLE.

—DNY

"Sir?"

"Just making sure it's turned off," said Danny, smiling apologetically. "Sometimes you have to hit it a second time and even a third. The button is kind of screwed up."

The attendant scowled, then pointed to his headset.

"Your iPod, too."

"Up, everything's off," said Danny, pulling the ear set from his ear. "We can take off any time you want."

"Thank you for permission," said the man sarcastically, going back up the aisle.

66

Over Austria

"WE'RE ABOUT AN HOUR FROM TOUCHDOWN, MA'AM," the C–20 steward told Breanna, waking her. "You wanted me to let you know."

"Thank you."

"Would you like some coffee?"

"That'd be great."

Breanna pushed her seat back upright. She glanced at her watch. It was nearly five. Her early-rising husband and daughter were probably already up and on their way to breakfast.

Should she call them?

She'd love to talk to Teri.

Given all the travel, Teri would probably still be sleeping. Zen, though—he'd be on the prowl for coffee and the latest news.

No, she decided. Let it be a real surprise.

67

Old State Castle, Czech Republic

ZEN NEVER SLEPT WELL WHEN HE WAS TRAVELING. IT wasn't so much the time differences or jet lag as the fact that Breanna wasn't with him. Feeling her body next to him at night relaxed him in a way he had never been able to explain in words, not even to her.

He pushed upright in bed and reached for the light, getting his bearings. Teri was sleeping with Caroline in the adjoining room. His wheelchair was just to his left. He leaned over and grabbed it, pulling it into position so he could ease into it. He rolled to the bathroom, shifting his weight subtly to cross the piece of marble at the threshold.

It was funny. The bathroom and its fixtures were arranged to make it easier for someone with a handicap—once inside, there was more than enough room for his chair, and the toilet was at an almost perfect height. Whoever had designed the room had given it a great deal of thought. But the plank of marble at the threshold was a full two inches high—a ridiculous barrier for a wheelchair.

When he'd first lost the use of his legs, annoyances like that bothered him greatly. Now he just shook his head.

There was a small coffeemaker on the counter. He set it up, started the water through, then ran the water to shave.

The coffee was coffee in only the most theoretical sense—it was black and liquid. He took two sips and decided he would do without the benefits of caffeine until he could get downstairs to the café.

He dressed casually, pulling on his favorite gray sweatshirt—a Nike shirt with a pancaked microfiber fabric that was thin yet very warm. The sleeves were a little frayed, and one of the elbows showed signs that his arm would soon poke through, but it was the most comfortable thing he owned.

Breanna would be scandalized if she knew he was wearing it in public. But she wasn't here to give him the hairy eyeball of wifely disapproval. He'd told the girls they'd get up around seven—plenty of time, he figured, for them to recover from the trip. He didn't want to wake them, but he also didn't want to go without coffee for two hours. So he tucked his laptop next to his legs and went down to see if the cafeteria was open.

There was an attendant at the elevator, an older man dressed in an army uniform. He stood at full attention as Zen approached, stepping to the side though there was ample room for Zen to get in.

"Is the cafeteria open?" Zen asked as he wheeled toward him.

"Staff is on duty at all times, sir," said the man.

"Is that year-round, or just for the show?"

"For the show. But often, we have special guests."

"Your English is very good," said Zen.

"Thank you. When I was young, I studied. Now, with the Internet and travel, everyone speaks English. It is a common language."

"Lucky for me."

The elevator operator pushed the button for the lower floor. The doors closed slowly.

"I don't mean to take you out of a job," said Zen as they started to descend, "but does this elevator need an operator?"

The man smiled. "Everyone needs a job."

"True enough," said Zen. He extended his hand. "Zen Stockard."

"Yes, Senator," said the attendant. Zen's friendliness seemed to worry him a little. He took the hand hesitantly, then shook. "I am Sergeant Greis."

"You're in the air force?"

"Forty-two years."

"That's a lot of time."

Greis nodded.

"I'll bet you did other things besides running an elevator," said Zen.

"I was a weapons specialist," said Greis. He straightened a little, almost as if he'd been picked out of a review line by a commanding general and asked to present himself. "I worked with many different aircraft."

"I was a fighter pilot," said Zen.

"Yes, Senator. You have won many medals."

"My fame precedes me, huh?"

Greis didn't understand the phrase.

"We couldn't have done our jobs without men like you," said Zen. "Ordies, maintainers—heart of the air force around the world. But you guys don't get the credit."

"No, sir."

"Well, you should."

The elevator doors opened. Zen rolled out into a foyer whose stone walls looked as if they were part of the dungeon in the keep across the way. A red carpet ran down the center of the space.

He followed the carpet to a sharp left, then past a pair of thick wooden doors lined with black wrought iron. He found himself in a vestibule just before the cafeteria, which he could see through a set of glass doors. There were lights on inside, and a waiter was working at a buffet table not far from the entrance, laying out a platter of breakfast meats.

There was only one problem—the three narrow steps between the foyer and the doors.

One step too many to risk, Zen calculated. As much as he hated to ask for assistance, there was simply no alternative.

Well, he could get out of the chair, push it ahead of him, then crawl down after it. But that was a bit extreme.

Maybe if no one here knew he was a senator.

The waiter disappeared into the back without looking in his direction. Zen decided to go back to the elevator and see if the operator might be able to help him. He was just turning around when a tall, thin gray-haired man came around the corner.

"Not open yet?" said the man. He had a slightly tired British accent.

"It's open, I just can't get down the steps," said Zen.

It took the man a second or two to understand. "Can I help?" he asked.

"If you kind of lean on the back and help balance as I go down, I think it would work," said Zen.

"Ah, yes. Quite."

"I'm Zen Stockard," said Zen as he positioned himself. "From America."

"Ah, yes, Senator Stockard. A pleasure to meet you. Colonel Lynch."

Lynch went down to the door and pushed it open. A small latch at the bottom held it in place.

"Alley-oop," he said, taking the back of the chair.

Zen leaned and pushed gently on the wheels, calibrating his force so he could control his movement down the steps.

As they reached the bottom, the waiter Zen had seen earlier came racing over.

"We are under control," said the colonel. "We have come through with valor."

"Can I buy you breakfast?" joked Zen. The breakfasts were complimentary.

"I would rather like that," said the colonel.

68

Old State Castle, Czech Republic

THE SENTRY AT THE COMPLEX PUT HIS HAND UP AS THE Mercedes approached the gate. The driver slowed to a stop, then rolled down his window.

"The deputy minister of Poland," said the driver in Czech.

The guard bent slightly and peered in the back. He paused a moment, examining the face, then straightened and signaled that the gate be lifted.

The Black Wolf eased his pistol down. No need to use it yet.

He glanced around the courtyard as they entered. The field where the helicopter was to land was at the right, beyond the fence. The choice was counterintuitive—another man might have them picked up on the roof, which would be easy to reach from the guest building. But the helicopter would be an easy target, and survival in an operation such as this always required finesse and misdirection.

The Mercedes pulled up in front of the building. It was 0512.

They were two minutes ahead of schedule. The Ukrainian minister and air force general had landed at the airport a few minutes ago; things were running as smoothly as he could have hoped.

The Black Wolf reached below his seat and pulled out the backpack with his HK MP–5 submachine gun. Then he reached his left hand into his pants pocket and took out a small vial. The red liquid inside looked like blood. It was, in a way.

The package had arrived for him with the money. They were as good as their word—better.

He cracked the seal on the tube and drained it quickly.

"Ready," he said, dropping the empty vial into his pocket. "Let's move."

69

Old State Castle, Czech Republic

"THE GOLDEN DAYS OF MANNED DOGFIGHTS ARE OVER," said Lynch. "I think we all have to recognize that."

"That may be," said Zen. "But I think we'll always have people in the loop. And not just on the ground."

"Your own air force has shown the way," said Lynch. "Your own experiences—they were the vanguard."

"Yes, but my experiences are a case in a point," said Zen. "The Flighthawks were always under someone's control."

"Really? I heard differently."

"Can't believe everything you read," said Zen.

"Quite. More coffee?"

"Yes, please," said Zen.

Lynch took his cup and headed over to the table where the urns stood.

Zen realized he hadn't turned his phone on. He didn't think his staff would be trying to get him at this hour, and didn't care much to start going through e-mails. But Teri or Caroline might try to text him from upstairs to find out where he was.

"I am sorry, I am sorry," said the waiter, rushing back out as Lynch returned. "I would get that for you."

"Not a bother at all," said Lynch. "I just went for the refill. My legs are working, after all." He blanched, apparently realizing what he had said.

"I'm not offended," Zen told him. "I used to call myself a cripple, just to see what kind of reaction I got."

"How did they react?"

"Oh, they were horrified. It was kind of fun to watch."

"I'm sorry, gentlemen," said the waiter, a pained expression on his face. "I wonder—we, uh, we were asked to set aside a little area for an early breakfast and I neglected to do so before you sat down."

"Go right ahead," said Lynch.

"You see, sir—the curtain usually would be placed right here." The waiter pointed to a track in the ceiling above them. "I can seat you anywhere else you'd like."

"How about a window seat?" asked Zen.

The waiter was nonplussed. They were in a basement without windows, and he wasn't sure whether he understood.

"Just a joke," said Zen. He picked up his coffee. "Where do you want us?"

"If I might suggest that table at the side," said the waiter.

"Too far to eavesdrop," joked Lynch.

"Sir?"

"It's fine," said Zen.

"Who needs a private room for breakfast?" asked Lynch.

"Some of our businesspeople are meeting with important people from the Ukraine," said the waiter.

"Sales call," Lynch told Zen as they took their places at the new table. "The Czechs are trying to sell their version of the Russian Spider rocket."

"Oh, yes," said Zen. "Is it really any good?"

"I think your AMRAAM-pluses are still light-years ahead."

Zen, who'd seen the reports and knew that what the colonel was saying was true, played devil's advocate, drawing the officer out. It was always instructive to get the unvarnished opinions of other air forces, even when they agreed with you.

The waiter went to the wall and moved one of the stones. Zen watched as the stones near it popped out, revealing a panel that pulled out into a room divider. The stones were actually only a half inch thick, the facade to a conventional plasterboard wall.

"I wonder if they have a screen that comes down from the ceiling," said Lynch.

"No, but they probably have a knight hidden behind some of the stones," answered Zen. "They pop it out if you don't pay your bill."

Two men in suits came in the door. Broad-shouldered and very tall, they would have looked like security types even without the ill-concealed armored vests under their jackets. Wires curled to earpieces at the back of their necks. One of the men had a small attaché case, the sort used to make an Uzi-sized submachine gun more discreet.

The waiter came out to meet them.

"You're part of the security detail for the minister?" asked the waiter.

"Where is the meeting to be held?" asked the man with the case.

"This way, gentlemen."

The two men glanced at each other. The one without the case nodded, then went with the waiter. The other man went up toward the door.

Another entered. Zen looked at the security agent as he walked past. He looked familiar.

Stoner, he thought.

But of course it couldn't be. This man was taller and broader and younger—not to mention alive. Breanna's project had put the idea into his head. It was ridiculous.

Once more he remembered his phone.

"I just want to turn my phone on," he told Lynch. "My daughter might need to reach me."

"Go right ahead."

Zen pulled out the phone and powered it up. It beeped at him, then beeped again, telling him he had messages.

"You will hand the phone over to me."

Zen looked up with a start. The man who'd gone to the door now stood next to the table, holding a submachine gun pointed directly at him.

70

Kbely Airport

BREANNA SNUGGED HER SEAT BELT AND LOOKED OUT the window as the C–20 dropped toward the runway, catching a glimpse of Prague in the dim blue haze of early dawn. The buildings had a brownish hue that made them look like a set of miniatures rather than part of a real city.

The sound of the plane's engines increased as the wheels touched down. As the pilot took the plane to the end of the runway and onto a taxiway to the terminal, Breanna gathered her things, her excitement at surprising her husband and daughter rising.

Besides the aircraft on display, a number of VIPs were arriving this morning, and Breanna's aircraft had been assigned a parking spot just beyond an Antonov transport. Standing on the ladder at the door, she got her bearings, then went down in a semijog, her suitcase with her.

She was surprised to see Turk, waving at her near the other plane.

"Hey, boss!" yelled the pilot, who was standing with several other men. He was still dressed in his flight suit. "About time you got here."

"Turk!"

"Had to hook with the maintainers," said the pilot. He gestured toward the hangars. "They just got here ahead of you like five minutes. They're going over the plane now." He turned to the men he was with. "I want you to meet some friends of mine—this is Major Andrei Krufts—I met him a while back at a Red Flag. He's a great Ukrainian fighter pilot. And this is his boss, General Josef. He's in charge of the Ukrainian air force."

Breanna suddenly felt underdressed and unprepared—she hadn't even done her lipstick.

"General, nice to meet you," she said, extending her hand to the Ukrainian official.

"My pleasure, Ms. Stockard. We have always admired the work of Dreamland."

"Thank you."

"I don't believe you know our defense minister," added the general as a tall, elderly gentleman approached from the stairway of the Antonov. "Dr. Gustov."

"No, I don't think we've met," said Breanna.

Despite his age—Gustov was seventy-seven—he moved quickly across the tarmac. Dressed in a blue pin-striped suit, with a full head of jet black hair brushed straight back against his scalp, he held himself perfectly erect, with an athletic air. His face was smooth and his gestures elegant; Breanna thought he must have been quite a ladies' man in his youth.

Perhaps even now.

"Dr. Gustav, allow me to introduce Breanna Stockard, a member of the U.S. Pentagon," said General Josef.

The minister took her hand. For a moment she thought he was going to kiss it in the old-world style, but instead he held it and bowed his head slightly. It was just as charming.

"A pleasure, Ms. Stockard. You are with the Pentagon?"

"I'm the director of the Office of Technology."

"Stockard—I know the name."

"She was a member of Dreamland," said the general.

"Ah, Dreamland," said the minister. "We heard of your battles."

"We still study the encounters," said Major Krufts.

"When you faced the Chinese and flew over their capital, were you scared?" asked Minister Gustov.

"I think you may be talking about my father," said Breanna. "I don't think he was scared of anything. *Is* scared," she said, realizing she had talked about him in the past tense. "But I did have a few encounters with them," she said hastily. "Some of their pilots were quite good."

"Who were the best pilots you encountered?" asked the general.

"Hard to say." They had all been difficult, and Breanna didn't like to rank them. She was asked the question a lot, though, so she gave the answer she usually did. "Probably the Indians. Their technology at the time was very underrated. They took a lot of Russian equipment and upgraded it tremendously. And they trained very effectively."

"And now you are on to other things," said General Josef. He turned to the defense minister. "We saw the plane while you were on the phone. It's quite an aircraft."

"Turk already gave you a tour?" Breanna asked.

"He showed us the plane. But of course we would all like to see it fly."

"I told them we could probably arrange a private fly-by in a couple of hours," said Turk. "Have to do a check flight anyway."

"By all means."

"I'd go right now, but the minister has a meeting," added Turk. "That's one of the design benefits—plane can be turned around for a sortie like in nothing flat."

You don't have to sell them, thought Breanna. They can't afford it.

"You feel like flying again so soon after coming across the ocean and continent?" asked the minister.

"There's never a time I don't feel like flying."

Everyone, including Turk, laughed.

"It's good be young," said General Josef.

Major Krufts glanced at his watch. "General, I hate to be the one to remind you . . ."

"Contractors," said the defense minister. "Always trying to sell us new toys."

"Upgrades," said the general. "Necessary."

The minister gave a skeptical "Hmmm."

"We have a meeting. Breakfast," said the general. "We should get going."

"Our meeting is at the Old Castle," the defense minister explained to Breanna. "The Czechs have renovated the ruins to appear as if they are still in medieval times. You should tour the museum."

"As a matter of fact, I'm on my way there to meet my husband and daughter."

"Then you will go in our car, and we can continue this conversation," said the minister. "General, wouldn't you say?"

"I think it's an excellent idea."

Breanna glanced at Turk. "Is everything OK with the Tigershark?"

"I could take off in ten minutes if you want," he told her.

"You should get some rest."

"I'm fine."

Breanna turned to the Dr. Gustov.

"It would be my pleasure to ride with you," she told him. "Please lead the way."

71

Old State Castle

THE EARLY GUESTS IN THE SMALL RESTAURANT WERE an inconvenience, not a complication. The Black Wolf had them brought into the kitchen with the workers, while he finished examining the room where the meeting was to take place.

There was not much to it—he would stand near the door and shoot the general, then the minister. It would be over in seconds.

Then they would leave. The helicopter would land moments after the alarm was sounded. He was sure of this, since he himself would sound the alarm.

He would take one of the civilians, someone from the kitchen staff, as a hostage, insurance just in case something unforeseen happened.

No—he would grab one of the men who had been having breakfast. They were important guests; their death would be more sensational.

"Done," said Gray Wolf, coming back. "They are locked in the storage pantry."

"And they can't get out?" asked the Black Wolf.

"Blue is there."

The Black Wolf nodded. The men used English to communicate, since they came from different countries. The teams were always mixed. The Black Wolf had worked with all of the men involved on this mission before, but not together.

"The one with the wheelchair was trying to make a phone call. I stopped him," added Gray.

"A wheelchair?"

Gray repeated the word in German.

"I understood the word," said the Black Wolf.

"Yes, a chair. Here is the phone."

Gray handed him a BlackBerry. Black Wolf stuffed it into his pocket, then put his hand to his ear set.

"Cafeteria is secure. Red, what is the situation?"

"Nothing on the road."

"We will wait," said Black Wolf. "It should not be long now."

ZEN ROLLED THE WHEELCHAIR BACK AGAINST THE SHELF unit in the storeroom, waiting for his eyes to adjust to the light. Besides himself and Lynch, there were three other people inside the large pantry storeroom—the waiter, a cook, and his assistant, a woman roughly Caroline's age. All had been searched, the contents of their pockets emptied.

"Is this a robbery?" whispered Lynch.

"No," said Zen. "My bet is they're after whoever's coming to that meeting the staff was setting up for. It's a kidnapping or an assassination."

"Bloody hell. Leave us out of it."

"We'll be lucky if they do," said Zen. He thought of the girls upstairs. There was no way to get a message to them.

Had the man he'd seen been Stoner?

It couldn't have been. And if it was, it wouldn't help.

"There wouldn't happen to be a trapdoor in the place?" Lynch asked the others. "A secret exit or something?"

"No," said the waiter.

"How about a ventilation shaft?" asked Zen. "For the air conditioner or heating?"

The waiter said something to the cook. They spoke for a few minutes.

"No. There is no vent here—this is a closet," said the waiter finally. "In the kitchen—over the range. That is where the ventilation is."

"Is it wide enough for someone to get through?" asked Zen.

"You're not thinking of climbing through, are you?" asked Lynch.

"I was thinking someone with legs would be more useful," said Zen.

"Kess could fit," said the waiter. "She's thin."

Zen glanced at her. She was fairly small.

"The shaft goes to the second floor and out," continued the waiter, translating for the chef. "There are two large fans at the side, on the wall where the vent opens. She would have to push them out."

"Could she?" asked Zen.

He turned toward the young woman. It was too dark to see much of her face.

"Do you think you can climb through?" he asked.

"I will try."

"To do this, she would have to be in the kitchen," said the waiter.

"How do we get in the kitchen?" asked Lynch. "The door is locked."

"We'll have to get them to open it," said Zen.

72

Ruzyne-Prague Airport

DANNY TURNED ON HIS SAT PHONE AS SOON AS THEY landed, checking to see if Zen had replied to his message.

He hadn't.

He decided to try him by phone. He punched in the number and waited for the call to connect, watching out the window as the plane trundled toward the terminal.

The call was just about to go to voice mail when the line clicked open.

"Zen?" said Danny. "Jeff—are you there? Zen? Yo, Zen?"

There was no answer. But there was definitely someone on the line.

"Zen? Hey, it's Danny Freah. What do we have, a bad connection? Are you there? Zen?"

"Who are you looking for?" said the voice.

"Zen. I—"

The line clicked dead.

Danny looked at the phone, making sure the preset number had dialed correctly. It had. He tried again. This time it went to voice mail.

What the hell was going on? Had the lines crossed?

He gave another call. This time someone picked up, but there was no answer.

"Zen? Jeff? Zen?"

It clicked off.

The plane had stopped. The other passengers were starting to get off. Danny remained in his seat, punching the quick dial to get the night operator who handled Whiplash operations.

"I know it's pretty late over there," he told her when she came on the line. "But I want to talk to Ms. Stockard. Or Reid. Can you wake one of them up?"

"Ms. Stockard is in Prague," said the operator. "At Kbley Airport. She just landed."

"She did? Let me talk to her. Right away."

73

Northwestern Moldova

NURI'S HEAD WAS POUNDING AND HIS LUNGS FELT AS if they were coated with dirt. His clothes were caked with grit. But his fun time in the hole did bring one positive: he was wide-awake. Very, very awake, and thirsting for revenge.

The UAVs patrolling the area had returned to their base, but the Rattlesnakes were still at the staging area they had used a few miles away. After telling the others he was all right, Nuri called Boston, who was overseeing the load-out.

"I can have them in the air in ten minutes," promised Boston. "We just have to get them off the pallet under the blimp."

"Do it," said Nuri.

Flash had left on the earlier blimp to supervise the load-out on the other end. Nuri hadn't been trained to handle the aircraft directly, so Boston channeled control through MY-PID. He was as good as his word—Nuri heard the aircraft overhead before he reached the house.

The Moldovan captain in charge of the local security force wasn't sure exactly what was going on. All he knew was that the deputy minister had just reamed him out, told him there were traitors in the force, and ordered him to secure the farm. Nuri filled in some of the blanks quickly, describing the men and the box he was looking for. Then he turned his attention to the Rattlesnakes, which were feeding their infrared scans to MY-PID.

The first thing he noticed on the small screen of his control unit was a car about a mile south, traveling at close to ninety kilometers.

"Stop the vehicle," he told MY-PID.

The Rattlesnakes swooped toward it. One buzzed the vehicle from behind, then turned sharply in front of it, pivoting to spin its nose—and the Gatling gun there—directly toward the windshield. The other aircraft came at the car from the side, passing so close to the vehicle that its skid scraped the roof. The maneuvers had the desired effect—the driver turned the wheel hard, pushing the car off the side of the road and into the woods, where it hit a tree.

Nuri watched on the screen as the driver stumbled out of the car. It was a woman, not one of the guards.

An accomplice?

It took him a few minutes to explain where the vehicle was to the Moldovans. MY-PID, meanwhile, sent one of the helicopters back to continue searching the farm, while the other one orbited the wrecked car.

By now the Moldovans had tightened their line around the farm. It didn't appear anyone was hiding on the property. But Nuri assumed that the two men who had attacked him and taken the box would blend in easily with the others—they were, after all, policemen just like the rest.

The captain had another theory: the men weren't policemen at all, but imposters who had come in with the others. Insisting they weren't among his men, he suggested they might be hiding in the trunk or somewhere else on the post.

"We are checking to see who left their post," said the Moldovan. "So far we have not found anyone who was out of place. So, these must have been imposters."

"Maybe," said Nuri.

"Let us talk to the prisoner." The captain gestured toward the driveway, where one of his cars was waiting. Nuri, a little wary, got in.

"MY-PID—keep watching the area," he told the computer. "If anyone else leaves, let me know— and follow them with one of the Rattlesnakes."

"Command accepted."

Then he had another idea.

"Tell the people at the car scene that I'm coming, too," he told the captain.

"Why?"

"Try it."

The Moldovan gave the order.

Nuri watched on the small screen. Six officers had responded. They had the driver in custody and were seeing to her injuries. Two were searching the car. Suddenly they stopped searching and headed for one of the police SUVs.

"Flash—stop the police vehicle near the accident scene."

"Identify vehicle," said MY-PID.

"The one that's moving, damn it."

"Command unknown."

"The SUV in the southwest." Nuri thumbed up the grid markers. "Grid AB–23. Damn it. Stop it—don't use weapons. No weapons. I want to talk to those bastards."

And punch each one in the face when he was done. Maybe before that.

The captain was on the radio, barking his own commands. Their driver stepped on the gas, hurrying toward the stopped vehicle. He swerved down the road so sharply that Nuri thought they were going to spin off the road.

Someone ahead started shooting—a fireball shot up from around the bend.

"What the hell?" shouted Nuri.

"Unknown command," responded MY-PID.

They skidded to a stop a few meters from the scene. The SUV was on fire, flames shooting in all directions.

Nuri got out of the car. He didn't mind the fact that the bastards were burning to death—that part he liked. But the box was probably burning with them.

"MY-PID—have the helicopter put out the flames," he said. "Beat them out with the rotor wash."

"Command accepted."

One of the Rattlesnakes swooped down. The wind from its counterrotating rotors sent a spray of dust and debris everywhere. Nuri had to turn his back to keep the grit from getting in his eyes.

One of the policeman was holding an RPG launcher. Why the hell had they blown up the SUV?

Oh shit.

"I'm going to check the prisoner," said Nuri as

calmly as he could. He began walking back up the road. As soon as he was out of earshot of the others, he asked MY-PID to review the Moldovan captain's conversation.

"I need a translation," he told the computer. "Word for word."

"'Unit 32,'" said the computer, reciting what it had heard in the background of Nuri's earlier transmission. "'Unit 32—are you reading me? Reading you. Blow up the SUV. There must be no survivors. Set it on fire. Destroy it completely.'"

"That's what I thought," mumbled Nuri.

"Command disregarded."

"Now you're learning."

Nuri went back over to the woman who'd been stopped, already sure she wasn't involved. Her head was bandaged and she gave him a dazed look, not sure what was going on.

"She claims she was on her way to work," said one of the policemen in Moldovan.

"Maybe she was," said Nuri. "Did you check with her employer?"

They were doing that right now. Meanwhile the car had been searched. There was no sign of the box.

Nuri wasn't surprised. Most likely it had been in the SUV.

Although there was one other place where it might be.

He walked back down the road to the captain's car. The fire was out now. The policemen were standing around the truck's charred remains, looking at the smoldering metal and melted glass.

The stench from the fire was incredible, a mixture of barbecued formaldehyde and pulverized iron.

The captain and his driver were with the others around the SUV. Nuri pulled open the driver's side door, reached down and pulled the latch for the car trunk.

It didn't open.

Nuri closed the door gently, trying not to make a sound. Then he walked over to the back of the captain's car and took out his small lock pick. Cars were generally no more difficult to open than house doors, and the lock on this one proved ridiculously easy; he flicked and prodded, and felt the tumblers give within a few seconds.

Dropping to his knees, he pushed the lid of the car up slowly.

"You are a very clever man," said the captain behind him. His English was vastly improved.

Nuri let go of the trunk and spread his arms, rising slowly.

"When did they approach you?" Nuri asked. "Were you always on their payroll?"

"Turn around and be quiet."

Nuri turned slowly.

"Get away from the car. Go to the side."

"You going to shoot me or arrest me?" asked Nuri.

The other policemen were all watching.

"Put your hands on the hood of the car," said the captain. He turned to one of his men. "Handcuff him," he said in Moldovan.

"They're not all in on it, are they?" said Nuri loudly. "They must not be, because you would have shot me already. At least one of them must speak English. They'll understand. Are you going to kill them, too?"

The captain told the man with the handcuffs to get them on.

"MY-PID, take him," whispered Nuri.

"Target required."

"The captain, the captain."

Nuri threw himself to the ground. For a moment there was only silence, and he worried that he had miscalculated, that MY-PID didn't have enough data or that somehow the Moldovan officer had managed to disable the Rattlesnake.

Then the aircraft began firing. Bullets crashed into the dirt, the 20mm shells tearing the Moldovan officer into pieces. The other policemen nearby dove for cover.

The policemen would have no compunction against killing him now. Nuri jumped up and grabbed a pistol that had been dropped by one of the policemen as they dove for cover. Then he turned back to the trunk for the strongbox. He grabbed the handle—it was heavier than he thought, and he needed both hands to carry it.

Which meant he couldn't use the gun.

"MY-PID, I need the helicopter to pick me up," he said.

"Rephrase."

"Have Snake Two descend—I'm going to grab the skid. It has to lift me down the road."

"Command accepted."

"Get Snake One over here—intimidate these guys."

"Unknown command."

"Scare them."

"Unknown command."

"Circle the area, damn it. With Snake One. Lay down covering fire. Don't hit them."

"Command accepted."

One of the policemen raised his head, then pulled up his weapon to fire. Snake Two fired first, sending bullets into the road only a few meters from him. The policeman quickly ducked back down.

The wash from the rotating blades nearly knocked Nuri over. He pitched his body to the side, then pulled his arm up over the skid, grabbing the box handle again.

"Go! Go! Go!" he yelled.

The robot helicopter practically tore his arm off as it lifted straight up.

"Just down the road! Not too far! Not too far!" Nuri yelled.

His arm hurt incredibly—it felt as if his shoulder had been dislocated. He glanced down. He seemed to be miles from the ground.

"Get me down safe. Safely!" he yelled as the robot helicopter flew southward. "Put me down in one piece. One fucking piece!"

"Unknown command."

"Put me down!" yelled Nuri. "And learn how to understand profanity, you goddamned son of a bitch!"

74

Old State Castle

THE BLACK WOLF LOOKED AT THE SCREEN ON THE phone he had just answered. Instead of numbers, the call displayed as a series of D's, something he'd never seen before.

Obviously an encryption.

The voice had been American. And it had asked for Zen.

Zen.

The word was familiar in a strange way. Of course he knew the word and what it meant, but there was something else. The association with a person . . .

Zen.

A memory nagged at him from behind the wall that closed off the present from the past.

Zen.

The man in the wheelchair.

"One of the prisoners claims to need the bathroom," said Blue over the radio.

"Too bad."

"The minister is late," said Gray from out in the hall. "Has there been a problem?"

"His plane has landed," said the Black Wolf. "We must have patience."

He felt himself shaking. His energy running down. He reached into his pocket for another vial of the drug. It was his last. Ordinarily he would save it for the end of the mission, to carry him through, but he suddenly felt cold.

He broke off the top and drank.

ZEN POUNDED ON THE DOOR.

"Hey, I gotta go!" he said.

"Shut up in there or I will shoot you," said the man outside.

"I don't think they're going to play," said Lynch. "We need a new idea."

"The idea is fine—we just have to push it further." Zen turned to the girl. "You know what to do, right?"

She nodded.

"You're not scared?"

"Scared, yes," she said. "But we do it."

Zen wheeled himself closer to the door.

"Hey!" he yelled. "Tell your boss out in the cafeteria there that Zen Stockard wants to talk to him. Major Stockard. Tell him we used to work together."

"What are you yelling about?"

"Zen Stockard. Tell Black that Zen Stockard wants to speak with him."

75

Czech Republic

IF THERE WAS ONE THING BREANNA HATED, IT WAS BEING interrupted by a phone call.

Her phone buzzed as the minister's car pulled out of the airport. She could feel her face shading with embarrassment as it continued to ring. She didn't want to insult the minister or the general by answering, but the sound was incessantly loud.

"That might be important," said the minister finally. "I won't be offended."

"I'm terribly sorry," said Breanna. She took the phone out of her pocketbook. "Ordinarily it just rolls over to my voice mail, but whoever is calling is very insistent."

She glanced at the screen as she took it from her purse.

A row of D's indicated it was from Danny.

"Do you mind if I take this?" she asked. "It's one of my people. He wouldn't call unless it was important."

"Please."

"Breanna," she said into the phone.

"Bree—where are you?" asked Danny.

"We just left the airport. We're on our way to the Old State Castle."

"Don't go there!" Danny was practically shouting. "I just called Zen—something is up there."

"With Zen?"

"Somebody else answered his phone."

"Maybe it was Caroline, my niece. She's traveling with him to watch Teri."

"Bree, we think the Wolves may be in Prague."

"I'll get back to you."

Breanna killed the line, then dialed Zen's number. She went to voice mail. She pulled her niece's cell phone number up from the phone book and tried her. She got her voice mail as well.

"Caroline, this is Bree. Please call me right away." She hit the End call button. The minister and general were looking at her. "I—there may be a problem at the castle," she told them. "We're having trouble contacting my husband there. And my niece."

She hit the redial and called Caroline again. This time she picked up.

"Aunt Bree, what time is it there?"

"Caroline, is Uncle Jeff there?"

"He's in the next room," said Caroline.

"Could you go get him?"

"I think he's sleeping."

"He's always up by now, hon. Could you knock on the door?"

"Hang on."

"Wait—is Teri there?"

"Yes. She's sleeping."

"No I'm not," said a voice in the background.

"Let me talk to her while you check for Jeff. Hurry, please."

"OK."

"Hi, Teri. How are you sweetheart?"

"Mama! How are you?"

"I'm fine, honey. How did you sleep?"

"Very good."

The car, meanwhile, had arrived at the gate. The general leaned forward and, using English, asked the guard if there had been any trouble.

The guard told him there hadn't.

They drove through the gate, heading around the main part of the castle toward the hospitality area.

"He's not answering the door, Aunt Bree," said Caroline.

"Is the Do Not Disturb sign on his doorknob?"

"No."

"Which room are you in?"

"Four B."

"I want you to stay there with Teri, OK?"

"Is something wrong?"

"I don't think so," said Breanna slowly. "Just stay there. I'll call you right back."

She hung up the phone and turned to the minister. By now she was sure he and the general were wondering if she was crazy and paranoid, or just the latter.

"The person you're supposed to meet—could you call them?" Breanna asked. "See if they're OK?"

"Is there a problem?"

"My husband's not in his room, and someone strange answered his phone," she said. "There have been threats against NATO ministers."

"I'm not a NATO minister," said Dr. Gustov, with the slightest hint of regret.

"I'm sorry, but could you please check?" asked Breanna.

He took out his phone and dialed. The contractor answered on the second ring. They spoke for a moment in English, then he hung up.

"He's waiting downstairs," said the minister. "He says there's nothing wrong."

"I see," said Breanna, trying to stifle the uneasy feeling in her stomach. "I'm sure you're right."

76

Old State Castle

THE BLACK WOLF THUMBED THE END CALL BUTTON.

"They're entering the courtyard now," he said over the radio. "Be prepared."

"Black Wolf, one of the prisoners says you know him," Blue told him. "He says his name is Zen Stockard. Major Zen Stockard."

Zen.

"I don't know a Zen Stockard," said the Black Wolf.

As the words left his mouth, a piece of a memory came back, a sharp shard striking the soft flesh of his brain.

He was in the sea . . . wet . . . someone was talking to him over a radio.

Zen.

Zen?

* * *

ZEN HEARD FOOTSTEPS COMING TOWARD THE DOOR.

"What'd he say?" he demanded.

"That he doesn't know you. And that if you shout once more, I am to shoot you. And maybe I will shoot you now just for the pleasure."

"THERE'S NO ANSWER IN THE RESTAURANT KITCHEN," Breanna told the minister. "There should be an answer."

"Maybe they're seeing to other guests," said the general.

Major Krufts, General Josef, and Dr. Gustov got out of the car. Breanna, not sure whether to feel foolish or not, got out as well.

"I wonder if I could attend the sales presentation along with you," she said, leaning back into the car. "Maybe we might be interested."

"In Russian upgrades?" asked General Josef.

"We're always trying to keep on track with what's going on," said Breanna.

The general frowned, but the minister remained polite. "I don't see why not," he said. "If they will sell to us, they would sell to you. Money is money these days."

"My husband should come, too," said Breanna. "He's on the Senate Appropriations Committee. They have to approve purchases."

It was a white lie—Zen had nothing to do with appropriations, at least not directly.

"Of course," said Minister Gustov.

"Could you wait a minute while I go up and get him?"

"We can go as well," said Gustov.

"Why not?" said the general. "I would like to meet your husband. I have many questions for him."

"I would like to meet him as well," said the minister.

"Good. Then we'll all go," said Breanna, trying to hide the relief in her voice.

"THEY'RE MOVING INSIDE. A WOMAN IS WITH THEM," said Green, who was watching from the back of the keep. He was dressed as one of the security guards. "One other officer is with the minister and the general—there are four in all."

"Do you have a shot on the minister?" the Black Wolf asked.

"Negative—not clean enough to guarantee."

"Stay back."

There were always wrinkles. One needed to be patient.

"In the lobby," said White. "Four: three men, one woman. Going to the elevator."

It would be over soon.

BREANNA NOTICED A MAN WATCHING THEM FROM THE corner of the lobby as they walked in. They went straight to the elevator, where an attendant was waiting.

"Please close the door right away," she told the elevator operator.

"What floor?" he asked.

Breanna waited until the door closed before answering. "Fourth. The man at the other end of the hall. Is he part of the hotel security force?"

"Could be," said the elevator operator. "I didn't see him."

"Have you been here all morning?"

"Since four o'clock," said the man, a lot more cheerfully than she would have expected.

"Did a man in a wheelchair use the elevator?"

"Oh, yes. I took him down for coffee about an hour ago."

Breanna dialed Zen's phone as soon as they stepped out of the elevator. It began to ring just as she reached Teri and Caroline's room.

Someone picked up on the third ring but said nothing.

"Jeff?" she said. "Zen? *Zen?* It's Bree. Honey?"

She could hear breathing on the other end, but not Zen.

It wasn't him. Was it?

"Zipper me if it's you," she said.

It was an expression pilots used, or at least they had back when she flew combat. It meant to click the mike button or hit a key a few times to acknowledge, rather than talking.

The line clicked off.

"Mama!" shouted Teri, opening the door. "How did you get here?"

"Everybody inside the room," said Breanna sharply, turning to the startled minister and general. "Someone is holding Zen prisoner in the restaurant."

"THEY TOOK THE ELEVATOR UPSTAIRS, NOT DOWN," White told the Black Wolf. "Fourth floor."

Zen.

Zen.

"You want me to go up and see where they are?" asked White.

"Have they seen you already?" the Black Wolf asked.

"The woman made eye contact in the lobby."

"Hold your position. Green, come inside. Go to the fourth floor. See what's happening."

"On my way."

"Blue. The man who asked for me—bring him here," said the Black Wolf. "There's something familiar about the name."

THE DOOR TO THE STOREROOM OPENED ABRUPTLY.

"Who's Zen?" said the man who'd been watching them.

"I am."

"You in the wheelchair?"

"That's me."

"Come out."

"I need some help."

The girl moved forward quickly to push his chair, just as they had planned. The guard reached in and shoved her back.

I can grab his gun, thought Zen. But by then it was too late—the man had stepped back, out of reach.

"None of you move, or you all die," said the man roughly. "Wheel yourself."

Zen put his hands on the wheels and pushed out slowly, as if he were trying to heave himself up a steep hill.

"I could really use some help," he started to say.

Before he could finish the sentence, the man put his foot in the back of the chair and shoved it with tremendous force. The wheels flew from Zen's hands, and the chair rode straight across the kitchen, crashing into one of the counters. It rebounded backward, rolling nearly all the way to the man.

"Move yourself," growled the man.

Stunned, Zen put his hands back on the wheels, starting slowly. He wasn't acting now; the ride and crash had dazed him.

The man was big, but even so, his strength seemed disproportionate.

"Go," he snarled. "On your own."

Zen wheeled forward, trying to think of a Plan B.

"WE NEED SECURITY IN THE BUILDING RIGHT AWAY," Breanna told Danny. "I think they have Zen."

"I'm zero-five from the airport. I'll have the Czech people over there ASAP," Danny told her. "What room are you in?"

"Four B. We're in the northeast corner."

"All right."

Breanna turned off the phone. Minister Gustov and the general had skeptical looks on their faces.

"I'm not some crazy female," she told them. "I'm not having a panic attack. You know who I am. You know what I've been through."

"That's the only reason we're still here," said the general.

"I don't know," said Gustov. He looked as if he was going to leave.

"Listen . . ." Breanna glanced at Caroline and Teri. She didn't want them to hear, but there was nowhere for them to go. "The CIA has been tracking a group hired to disrupt the NATO meeting."

"That's in Kiev in two days," replied the general.

"Yes, but if they assassinated you here, that might achieve the same goal. The Russians would do that, don't you think?"

"The Russians are capable of anything," said Minister Gustov.

"Then wait for a few minutes more."

There was a knock on the door.

"Don't answer it," said Breanna.

DANNY FREAH LEANED FORWARD IN THE CAR AS THE taxi pulled up to the Old State Castle gate.

"Who's your commander?" he shouted.

The guard stared at him. Danny dropped fifty euros—about three times the fare—on the front seat of the cab and climbed out.

"Shut the gates," he told the guard. "There's an emergency in the hotel area. I need two men to come with me."

"What? Who are you?" sputtered the man.

"Danny Freah. I'm with the American senator's security team. We think he's being held hostage."

The phone inside the guardroom rang. It was the guard's commander, ordering him to shut down all access to the facility. Help was on the way.

"There are two men near the museum," said the guard, pointing. "I'll call and they'll meet you."

* * *

ZEN WHEELED SLOWLY TOWARD THE ROOM DIVIDER, CAL-culating that the longer he took, the more time the others would have to come up with a backup plan.

He was hoping one would occur to him as well, but ideas weren't exactly popping into his head. He felt a little like he had the first time he rose to give a speech in the Senate—not just tongue-tied, but completely brain frozen.

"Who are you?" said a voice in English from behind the thick barrier.

Zen didn't answer—he couldn't. He concentrated on wheeling forward, around the barrier.

The Black Wolf stood with his arms folded across his chest. He held an MP–5 machine gun in his left hand, curled under his arm.

Was this Stoner? Zen looked at his face. It had been so long since he'd seen him.

"Who are you?" asked the man again.

"Zen Stockard." The words came out haltingly. "Jeff."

"I don't know you."

Zen's brain unfroze. There was something in the snap of the answer—the sharp finality and sureness of tone—that told Zen it was Stoner.

"Mark. Do you remember? In the Pacific? You were with Bree. Remember the beer we had in the hospital? I smuggled them inside in my wheel-chair?"

The man's face didn't change. But that only convinced Zen all the more.

Stoner had always seemed older to him, even

though they were roughly the same age. Now he was much younger. He seemed almost not to have aged—his cheeks had hollowed, but his brow was smooth and his eyes unwrinkled. His hair was dappled gray, but it was full and thick.

"What happened?" Zen asked. He wheeled forward a foot and a half. "What happened after the helicopter crashed?"

"Quiet," commanded the man, touching his earpiece to hear a radio transmission.

"THIS IS SECURITY," SAID THE MAN OUTSIDE THE DOOR to Teri and Caroline's room. His English was heavily accented. "We have an important matter to discuss."

"What matter is that?" Breanna demanded.

"There are reports of men with guns in the hotel," said the man.

"We haven't seen them."

"I have been sent to protect you," said the man.

"We're fine."

Major Krufts was desperately searching the room for something to use as a weapon. Breanna pointed to the lamp near the bed. But it was clamped to the side table.

The defense secretary and general were standing next to her. Caroline had taken Teri into the bathroom and closed the door.

"My orders are to protect you," said the man.

"Great." Breanna saw that the latch to the door had not been closed. She moved toward it quickly. "Stand guard in the hall."

"I must see you to make sure you are not being held against your will," said the man.

"Take my word for it," said Breanna.

"I'm sorry. I cannot do that."

Breanna reached the latch and pushed it closed. As she did, she heard a key entering the lock. She grabbed at the interior turning bolt, but couldn't hold it back. The door opened, then caught abruptly at the latch.

Breanna threw her shoulder against the door, pushing it back to the frame. The latch caught. She pushed the lever closed, relocking it.

It was a momentary respite. The handle exploded, shot through from the other side. She spun back and to the side as the door flew open.

DANNY HEARD THE GUNSHOT AS HE ENTERED THE building.

"The stairs!" he yelled. "Where are they?"

Even as the words left his mouth, he saw a door near the elevator at the far side of the hall. He raced to it, heart pounding.

"We are with you!" yelled one of the security men as he pushed into the stairwell. "Lead the way!"

MAJOR KRUFTS JUMPED AT THE MAN AS HE CAME IN. Krufts hit his arm and side, trying to grab the man in a bear hug. The intruder pushed him off as if he were no more than a fly, swatting him back with a sharp flick of his arm.

Krufts flew a good ten feet through the air, crashing into the wall near the bed.

The man turned and started to raise his gun. Breanna charged at him, her arm lassoing his neck. He remained upright, though her blow threw his aim off; three or four bullets crashed into the dresser and wall near the door.

Desperate, Breanna began kicking and clawing, trying to hit the man's groin. He pushed his right arm up next to his chest and pried her off his body, flipping her down. As he did, General Josef hit him over the head with the heavy desk chair, which he'd managed to lift in front of him.

The man staggered to one side but didn't go down. He grabbed Breanna, still flailing at him, and pulled his arm back to pistol-whip her.

"Stop!" said Dr. Gustov. "If you're looking for me, I am here. Leave the others alone."

DANNY HEARD SHOUTS AS HE REACHED THE LANDING on the fourth floor. He grabbed at the door, then turned back as the first Czech security man reached him.

"Give me your pistol," he told the man.

"But—"

"Don't you have a backup weapon?"

The man hesitated, then reached down to his ankle where a small Glock was strapped. Danny took the gun and began to run toward the commotion.

ZEN WATCHED THE BLACK WOLF'S FACE. THERE WAS obviously something going on, though it was impossible to tell exactly what.

Most likely the men he was going to kill were

on their way here. What would happen when they arrived? Would Stoner kill him, too?

"Stoner, what's going on?" Zen demanded. "Why are you doing all this?"

The man glared at him but said nothing, his hand pressed over his ear to listen to the radio.

"The Mark Stoner I knew was a patriot," said Zen. "A CIA officer as dedicated as any person I've ever met."

"Shut the hell up," barked Stoner, pointing the gun at him. "Shut the hell up or I'll shoot your tongue out."

BREANNA FELL TO THE FLOOR AS THE INTRUDER RE-leased her. She saw Dr. Gustov, the minister, standing erect across the room, head high, jaw jutting forward, as if daring the man to shoot him.

The man grinned, and raised his gun.

"Don't shoot him!" shouted Breanna. "Stop! Don't shoot him!"

Three loud pops followed.

Breanna looked back toward Gustov.

He was still standing.

The intruder was lying on the ground, the back of his head shattered by bullets. Blood was spurt-ing everywhere.

"Bree! Bree!"

Danny Freah loomed in the doorway.

THE BLACK WOLF FROWNED. GREEN HAD GONE OFF mission and entered the room without orders.

The Black Wolf pressed his hand to his ear, trying to hear what was going on.

"Green?" he demanded. "Report. What's the situation? Green?"

"There's gunfire upstairs," said White.

"Investigate."

"On my way."

Green had obviously decided to take matters into his own hands. There was no excuse for that. He'd deal with him later, in the helicopter.

It should be only minutes away.

"What happened to you?" repeated Zen.

The Black Wolf looked over at him. He'd almost forgotten he was there.

"Who are you?" said the Black Wolf.

"Your friend," said Zen.

"I don't have any friends."

"You did, fifteen years ago."

"I didn't exist then," he answered.

The Black Wolf stared at the man in the wheelchair who called himself Zen.

It was so familiar, yet so far away.

DANNY PUT HIS KNEE IN THE BACK OF THE MAN ON THE floor, dropping down to make sure he was dead. Blood was spurting from his head, flowing like water from a small fountain.

"Is everyone OK?" Danny asked. He looked across the room. The only one standing was an older gentleman, whose face was white. "You all right?"

"I am OK," said Minister Gustov.

"It's OK, it's OK," said Breanna, rising from the side of the room nearby. She leaped over the body and ran to the door on the left, yelling to her daughter and niece in the bathroom that it was all right.

The two Ukrainians on the floor groaned. Danny turned his gun toward the one against the wall on the far left, but it was obvious he wasn't one of the Wolves—he was normal-sized, and a little pudgy.

One of the Czech officers yelled at someone in the hall.

"Stay here!" Danny told the others, bolting out of the room.

GUNFIRE ERUPTED IN THE HALLWAY AS CAROLINE opened the door to the bathroom.

"Stay down. Get behind something—get in the bathtub," Breanna yelled.

"Mama!" cried Teri.

"Stay down, Teri. I'm here."

Breanna pulled the door closed, stayed outside—she could do more out here, she thought, racing to see what had happened to the dead man's gun.

"THE HEAD! THEY'RE ONLY VULNERABLE IN THE HEAD!" shouted Danny as the security officers began firing at the man near the elevator.

It was a mad, crazy scramble. Danny pressed against the side of the hallway, ducking down as bullets whizzed down the corridor.

"Danny, what's going on?" hissed Breanna, crouching behind him.

"Get back in the room."

"No. Who's shooting?"

"He's near the elevator. One of the guards who came with me tried to stop him."

"He's with the Wolves?"

"I don't know—I haven't seen them."

"The man in the room, was he one of them?"

"I'm pretty sure. They're all huge."

There was fresh gunfire. Someone began screaming in pain.

"Stay down," said Danny. He slid to one knee, steadied the Glock in both hands. It was a small pistol, .22 caliber—nothing against these guys.

Two more quick shots and the screaming stopped.

A bad sign.

"Aim for the head," he said, raising his pistol.

The man turned the corner. Danny fired instantly, emptying the magazine.

His first shot grazed the man's face; the second and third hit lower. The man swung his gun in Danny's direction.

Something exploded in Danny's ear. Again and again.

The Wolf assassin got off a single, errant shot before falling to the ground, dead.

THE BLACK WOLF HEARD WHITE GO DOWN. HE'D BEEN ambushed on the fourth floor.

It was time to abort.

"Blue, Red, we leave by the back," he told the others over the radio.

"What's going on?" asked Blue.

"We leave by the back."

"What about the people in the locker?"

"Leave them. I have a hostage," the Black Wolf said.

ZEN BRACED HIMSELF AS THE BLACK WOLF approached, not exactly sure what he was going to do.

"You're not going to shoot your way out of this, Stoner," he said. "But I can help."

"Shut up."

"Listen, Mark—"

The Black Wolf grabbed the back of his wheelchair and spun him around. He pushed him toward the kitchen. Zen started to reach for the wheels, but they were moving so fast he realized he wouldn't be able to stop.

"We're taking a cripple as hostage?" said the gunman in the kitchen when they entered. "We should take someone who won't slow us down. There's a girl—"

"I'm a U.S. senator," said Zen. "I'm worth more."

Zen felt himself being lifted from his chair from behind.

"Shut your mouth," growled the Black Wolf, flipping him over his shoulder as if he were a sack of potatoes.

BREANNA CLASPED HER HANDS TOGETHER TO KEEP them from shaking as she lowered the pistol. Her shots had hit the would-be assassin squarely in the forehead.

Danny Freah turned around and looked at her. Neither one of them spoke.

Breanna's legs trembled as she rose.

"I can't hear," said Danny. "My ears."

"Teri!" said Breanna, turning back to the room.

No one inside had moved. She ran to the bathroom.

"Teri! Caroline!"

"We're OK!" yelled Caroline.

"It's all right—you can open the door," said
Breanna.

They cracked the door cautiously, then pushed
it open. Breanna pulled both of them close.

"The Czech security forces are surrounding
the building," said Danny, coming behind her.

"Zen—the elevator attendant said he went to
the basement."

Danny pointed to his ears. He still couldn't
hear well.

"Zen is downstairs. In the basement," said Breanna, pointing downward.

"Zen? They'll get him. The Czechs are surrounding the building."

"Here's a helicopter with troops now," said
General Josef, going to the window. "It's landing
right across the street."

ZEN TRIED TO TURN HIS EYES AND BRAIN INTO A HUMAN
video camera, recording everything that he saw
happening around him, in case it would be important later. Stoner carried him through a narrow,
twisting hallway that zigged out from below the
building, ending in a set of steps. They were up
them in a flash. Light poured over him—they were
out in a small open area, moving across gravel.

He's going to have to put me down at some point, Zen told himself. *That's when I fight.*

He'd hit him as hard as he could in any vulnerable area. Then he'd try to get him in a stranglehold.

Zen felt himself thrown against a fence, being pushed upward.

Escape!

He snagged a fence link with his left hand, then another with his right. He tugged—then felt his fingers being torn away. Someone punched or kicked his head. Zen flailed, but was hoisted up from the ground and carried over the fence.

Then he was falling.

He curled, and just barely managed to cover his face as he landed with a thud. The fall took his breath away, but he knew this was his chance— still free, he clawed at the ground, pushing himself like a crab.

Go, go, go!

Suddenly, he started to rise.

"Into the helicopter," shouted the Black Wolf.

Breanna went to the window as the helicopter landed. It was a Mil Mi–17, an older troop-carrying helicopter used by many air forces in Eastern Europe. Painted in a light brown and green camo, the large helicopter spun its tail around as it set down.

The door at the side was open. Breanna watched, expecting troops or policemen to pour out, but none came.

Three men ran from the road that paralleled

the castle grounds, racing toward the helicopter. One of them was carrying something over his shoulder—a person.

It looked like Zen in his old gray sweatshirt.

The man threw him into the helicopter head first. He rolled to his left, trying to push his way out, struggling. He grappled with his arms. One of the other men pushed him back into the helicopter. It started to climb. He rolled in her direction.

"Oh my God," blurted Breanna. "They took Zen in the helicopter!"

77

Kbely Airfield, near Prague

"It's just like a real plane," said the Czech. "With real fuel and everything."

"It *is* a real plane!" said Turk, indignant. He turned to Chief Master Sergeant Crawford, who headed the Tigershark maintenance team. Crawford was nearly red, trying not to laugh.

"You put him up to this, Chief?" Turk asked.

"Hey, not me, Cap."

The Czech, who'd just finished loading the Tigershark with jet fuel, looked puzzled.

"It's a real plane," Turk told him.

"Captain Kirk," said the Czech. "*Star Wars.*"

"Kirk is *Star Trek*," said Turk.

"Very fast?" asked the Czech.

That was too much for Crawford, who practically exploded in laughter. He had to grab the airplane's landing strut to keep from falling over.

"Uh, when you're finished laughing, Chief Master Sergeant," said Turk, "tell me when my plane will be ready."

"You can fly it now," said Crawford. Tears were flowing from his eyes. "Oh, God. Oh, jeez. Real plane. Real plane."

Another maintainer, Tech Sergeant Paul Cervantes, came over to see what the fuss was about.

"The Czechs," managed Crawford. "They're too much."

"What happened?" Cervantes asked.

"I can't explain. It's too much. And Turk—" Crawford started curling with laughter. "Captain Mako. He's too much, too."

"Hey, I'm glad I'm part of the entertainment," said the pilot. He was more baffled now than angry.

"Hey, Cap, Shelly told me your gear's like A-one ready to go," said Cervantes.

"Thanks, Sarge. At least someone here is serious."

Turk checked his watch. The Ukrainian minister wouldn't be back for another two hours or so, but he had a lot to do—including figuring out who he needed to talk to in order to make sure his flight didn't interfere with the rest of the air show. He was just about to go look for the show boss when his cell phone rang. He pulled it from his pocket, saw the caller ID, and flipped it open.

"Hey, boss," he told Breanna, hoping she was going to tell him that Zen would join her for the fly-by.

"Turk! There's a helicopter that just took off. It's a Mil—it's flying southeast. Southeast! Zen's in it. We have to follow it."

A MINUTE OR TWO LATER TURK PULLED HIMSELF INTO the Tigershark's cockpit.

"Engines," he told the flight computer after plugging his oxygen and com gear in.

The top of the cockpit snugged down with a hard *snap* and the consoles powered up. The aircraft computer blew through the diagnostics, data flying across the screens.

The aircraft claimed it was in the green. That was good enough for him.

"Tower, this is U.S. Air Force Tigershark Oh-one, requesting immediate emergency takeoff," he said over the control frequency.

"Tigershark Oh-one, repeat?"

"I have an emergency," he said. "I need immediate takeoff."

"I'm sorry, Tigershark. We have language difficulty. Thought you said flight emergency. We have you at base, at hangar. Please restate."

"I need immediate clearance for takeoff," he said, pulling off the brakes. He rolled forward about forty meters to the end of a taxiway, jammed the brakes and pushed up his engine power. Then he checked the control surfaces.

Working.

All systems green.

Get the hell into the air!

"Tigershark. We have a line of aircraft waiting on runway twenty-four," said the controller. "You can join line."

"How many planes in line?" he asked, starting forward. The runway was off to his left. He zoomed the Tigershark's camera in that direction.

"You should be six when you get there," said the controller. "Or maybe seven."

The hell with that, thought Turk.

He had an open taxiway ahead—a good fifteen hundred feet—three hundred more than he needed balls out.

"Tower, I'm taking off from here," he said, jamming the engine into full thrust.

Whatever curse words the controller replied with were lost in the roar of the engine. The Tigershark bolted forward. Within seconds it was near takeoff speed.

Turk tried to relax, keeping his pressure on the yoke light, waiting for the plane to tell him when it wanted to take off.

On his left he saw a blur moving in his direction.

A 757, turning onto the taxiway ahead of him.

In the way.

"Up!" he yelled, grabbing the stick.

The Tigershark jerked her nose upward. For a long, long second her rear end stayed on the ground.

The Boeing pilot was oblivious—if he'd even seen the small jet, he never would have believed it was moving so fast.

"Now!" yelled Turk, his hand firm against the electronically controlled stick. "Up, up, up!"

They cleared the tail of the airliner by a good two inches.

78

Northwestern Moldova

THE RATTLESNAKE LOWERED NURI IN A WHIRL OF DUST, setting him and the box gently in a field about a mile and a half from the Moldovans.

"Protect me," he told MY-PID as soon as he managed to get on his feet.

"Command accepted. Perimeter established," said the computer, directing the two robot helicopters to orbit above him.

"Connect me with Boston," said Nuri.

His arms felt as if they had been pulled from their sockets. His neck bulged, all the muscles spasming. It was as if everything between his skin and his bones had been turned into sharp rocks.

"Nuri, what's going on?" asked Boston, coming on the line.

"I shot the captain. He was trying to kill me. I need backup."

"I have Sugar on her way with help. I see your location. Can you stay there?"

"I'll try. I have the helicopters above me."

"I'm tapping into the feed . . . It looks like you're clear. I don't see any of the Moldovans heading in your direction."

Not yet, thought Nuri. He wiped his face with his sleeve, trying to clear some of the grit that was caked around his eyes, then dropped down to look at the box. It was locked, but keyed with a pattern so simple he could have opened it with a paper clip.

Unfortunately he didn't have a paper clip, and he'd lost the small lock picking tools he kept in his belt. He scrambled around looking for something to use, but the field was used for growing wheat, not thin shards of metal. Grabbing the box, he started walking in the direction of the road. As he reached it he saw a house about a half mile down the road.

He was about to head toward it to see if he could borrow something to open the box when he saw an oversized SUV truck heading in his direction. He almost ordered the Rattlesnakes to fire before realizing it must be Sugar.

He ran to the driver's side as the car stopped. Sugar and two other Whiplash troopers jumped out, guns drawn, forming a defensive perimeter.

"I need a paper clip," said Nuri.

Sugar looked at him as if he was insane.

"I gotta open this box," said Nuri. "I just need a little piece of metal."

"Will a bobby pin do?" she asked.

"Yeah, if you got one."

Undoing the lock took only a few seconds. Starting to raise the lid, he realized belatedly that it might be booby-trapped, and ducked back.

Nothing happened.

"What's it say?" asked Sugar, peering over his shoulder.

The box contained five small notebooks. Nuri took the first one out, examining it. The pages were filled with Russian script.

"I can't really read Russian," he told her, taking out his MY-PID controller. "I'll have to get the computer to read it for us."

"We better do it in the truck," she said, holding her head to the ear set. "A couple of the people you pissed off up at the farm are headed in our direction."

79

Czech Republic

THE BLACK WOLF NEEDED MORE OF THE DRUG. IT WAS a thirst, a ravenous hunger, a power he couldn't resist. But he had none, and there was nothing he could do to fill the desire, to stop it, to calm his pounding heart.

He looked across the interior of the helicopter, staring at the man they'd brought as a hostage. Zen. He was lying prostrate on the deck of the chopper, a pathetic cipher.

Someone from his past.

It was a trick. He had no past.

But he did. And it involved a helicopter. There had been a flight. Something like this.

No. Not like this. Nothing was like this.

80

Czech Republic

CLEARED OF THE TRAFFIC AROUND THE AIRPORT, TURK found he had open skies for miles and miles in front of him.

Not a good thing. He wanted to see a helicopter.

He tried reaching a Czech controller but couldn't get anything on the frequency that he could understand. He tried switching the Tigershark's communications section into its satellite com module so he could talk to Breanna on her satellite phone. But the call failed to go through.

What would the original Dreamland team have done in this situation fifteen years ago? They didn't have instant com connections with everyone in the world.

They'd find the damn helicopter, first off.

Turk figured the helo had somewhere in the area of a twenty to thirty-minute lead over him. Traveling at 200 knots, tops, it could have gone one hundred miles from the Old State Castle.

"I need a standard search pattern, 150-mile

radius of Kbely Airfield," he told the flight computer. "I'm searching for a helicopter."

The flight computer flashed a pattern on the screen, a series of crisscrossing arcs that would have him fly in a circle around the airport. It was a logical pattern, and to fly it he would have to turn immediately south and cut his speed.

But Turk resisted. It was *too* logical.

If he was the helo pilot, what would he do?

Fly like a bat out of hell.

Until he knew he was being followed. Then he'd stop somewhere, wait for the aircraft to go away, and start up again.

Which would help him, since once it set down, he could disable it safely and wait for the ground forces to surround it.

But the helicopter pilot didn't know he was being followed. The Tigershark would be invisible to his radar until well after Turk saw the helo.

Turk could fix that. He tilted his wings, edging toward the outer radius of the search area the computer had outlined on the screen. Then he hit his flares.

81

Czech Republic

ZEN DRAGGED HIMSELF TO THE BENCH SEAT AT THE SIDE of the helicopter, then pulled himself upright.

It was definitely Stoner; he had no doubt. But in some sense it wasn't Stoner—there was a curtain up behind his eyes, beyond the blank expression.

The others called him "Black" and "Black Wolf." That was his identity now.

"You have a prosthetic leg," said Zen, studying the way Stoner held himself against the bulkhead. "Both of them?"

Stoner stared at him.

"Did you lose them in the crash?" asked Zen. "We looked for you. We figured out later that you must have ordered the helicopter pilot to make your aircraft the target so the others could escape. It was you, wasn't it?"

"It . . . made sense," said Stoner.

EVERYTHING CAME BACK.

Mark Stoner, CIA officer.

I am Mark Stoner. American.

Romania. Moldova.

And Asia before that.

This was Zen Stockard. *Zen.* Breanna's husband, Jeff.

He remembered the beer. He remembered Dog. And Bree. Danny Freah and everyone else.

"Where the hell were you fifteen years ago?" Stoner asked. "Why didn't you help me?"

"We didn't think anyone could have survived that crash."

No, no one could have survived. No one had survived—they'd taken what was left of him and shoveled him into this—a body of two phony legs from the hips down, a phony arm, a brain held in what was left of his skull by plastic.

A body that needed drugs to survive, drugs he thirsted for now.

"Stoner, we have to go back," said Zen.

"There's no going back, Jeff. We're gone." He pointed at his legs. "You know that."

"Black, there's a flare ahead," yelled the helicopter pilot from the cockpit.

"Evade," said Stoner flatly.

TURK LET OFF A VOLLEY OF FLARES AND CHECKED HIS speed, lowering it to 200 knots. This was considerably slower than the aircraft liked, and it whimpered slightly, lowering its nose like a chastised pony.

"Contact at two o'clock, altitude sixty feet AG," said the computer, telling the pilot its radar had spotted something about sixty feet off the ground to his right. "Distance at one-point-two miles."

"Identify aircraft," said Turk, glancing at the plot screen.

The helicopter was heading southeast at about 98 knots. He pulled to his left, starting a circle that would take him around so he could approach from the rear.

"Type is Russian-made Mil, Mi–16," said the computer. It used the video cameras to capture the image and identify it in its library of types. "No identifying marks. Paint scheme similar to Czech air force."

"Is it a Czech helicopter?"

"Camouflage is similar to Czech air force."

"Similar but not the same?"

"Out of visual contact. Insufficient data."

"We can fix that," said Turk, coming out of his turn. The helo had ducked even lower: it was now just under ten feet from the ground, running along a road through the Czech hills.

Turk switched to the emergency or "Guard" band, a common frequency monitored by all aircraft.

"Mil helicopter, this is U.S. Air Force Tigershark. You are ordered to land at Kbely Air Field. Do you copy?"

There was no answer.

"Mil helicopter, I have orders to get you on the ground," he said, improvising. "I can do that in any number of ways. Most of them not good for you."

The helicopter took a hard turn right, flying over a field. Turk, who was already going almost twice as fast as the chopper, couldn't follow; instead, he banked in the other direction and came around, lining up again on its tail.

What was he going to do? He had no missiles in his bays and no bullets in his gun. Even if he had, he'd be reluctant as hell to use them. His childhood hero was aboard the damn aircraft, for God's sakes.

Only one option: bluff the crap out of him.

* * *

STONER LEANED OVER THE PILOT'S SHOULDER, LOOKING at the terrain. They were five miles from Plegeau, a town outside of Mestecko and one of their alternate escape points. Two vehicles were stashed in a barn there.

The aircraft chasing them was American. It would be hard for him to coordinate with ground units. They could get away.

"Give me your map," Stoner told the pilot.

The copilot handed him a folded-over chart. It took a moment for him to orient himself, then pick out the location.

"Fly to this spot," he said, pressing his finger there. "You will see a barn painted green at the top of the hill. We will land next to a red barn on the next hill over, just to the east of that one. Do you understand?"

"The pilot of the aircraft is warning that he will shoot us down," said the pilot.

"He's an American," replied Stoner. "He won't dare."

"TIGERSHARK, ARE YOU ON THIS CHANNEL?"

Breanna's voice came loud and clear in Turk's headset.

"Hey, roger that, boss—can you hear me?"

"Affirmative. What's your situation?"

"I have the helicopter in sight. Not answering hails."

"Describe the helicopter."

"Hold on."

Turk throttled back again as the helicopter

jinked hard to the right. It was very close to the ground—so close that he thought it was going to hit a house as it turned.

"Mi–16. If this isn't the helicopter, it's sure doing a great impression," he told Breanna. "Brown on tan camo in a scheme similar to the Czech air force, but not precisely the same."

"I'm going to attempt to make contact," Breanna told him. "In the meantime, I have a Czech air force staff officer ready to contact you. Stand by for the frequency."

ZEN LOOKED AT THE TWO OTHER MEN WHO'D GOTTEN into the aircraft. They were watching Stoner, not him. But there was no way he could overpower even one of them, let alone both.

"Where are we going?" Zen asked them.

They pretended not to hear. He asked it again. It was Stoner who answered, coming back into the cargo area.

"We're getting away," he said. "We can go anywhere. Our network is worldwide."

"Do you work for the Russians?" Zen asked.

"I work for myself."

"Really? Who put you back together?"

Stoner frowned, then shook his head. "I wish it had never happened," he said. "I wish I had died that day."

"You don't really wish that, do you, Mark?"

But he could see that Stoner did. There was real pain in his eyes—deep anguish.

Regret, maybe?

Zen wanted to say that they could fix things,

but knew it would be impossible. He had to say something, though. Not to save himself, but because he felt as if they owed Stoner somehow.

He did owe him. Stoner had saved his wife.

"Mark, listen to me—"

Stoner reached into his pocket. His phone was ringing.

Not his phone. Zen's.

"WHAT DO YOU WANT?" STONER ASKED.

"Mark, this is Breanna Stockard. We know you're in the helicopter. We're following it. Listen, we found a box that has records of your treatment. They used powerful drugs on you. We can help reverse them."

Breanna Stockard. It was full circle now.

"Mark, listen to me," she continued. "You helped me once. I can help you. Let me help you."

"I'm beyond help." He reached his thumb for the End button.

"You're not," he heard her say before he clicked the phone off.

He tossed it at Zen.

"That was your wife," he told him.

TWO MIG–35S APPEARED ON THE RADAR SCREEN JUST as Turk made contact with the Czech air force colonel assigned to liaison with him. The aircraft were coming off the runway at Caslave, a base about fifty miles north of him. They weren't walking either—once off the tarmac, they poured on the afterburners, juicing over Mach 1.

Good luck with that, thought Turk. You'll

never stay close to the helicopter going that fast.

Their radars couldn't locate the Tigershark, even when he gave them a position. The two aircraft turned a circle some 10,000 feet above him.

"American aircraft, please restate your position," said one of the pilots.

"This is Tigershark. I am about ten angels below you, five miles south, uh, on your nine o'clock. Helo looks to be slowing down. He's low, real low."

"Tigershark, Checkmate One acknowledges," said the Czech pilot, giving his call sign. "Please stand clear."

"Uh, stand clear? Repeat?"

"Please remove from area. We are going to engage the enemy aircraft."

"Negative, negative. Do not engage—they've got a hostage aboard."

"We have orders, Tigershark. Please stand clear."

Shit on that, thought Turk, pushing closer to the helicopter.

"TWO KILOMETERS," SAID THE PILOT.

Stoner saw the green building ahead in the distance. The other barn was still out of sight.

"MiGs!" warned the copilot. "We are being tracked."

It was exactly the same. Exactly.

"Keep going," he said.

TURK BANKED HARD BEHIND THE HELICOPTER AND LOOSED a group of flares. He spun back left, ahead and above the helicopter, and released some more.

"Tigershark, stand off!" repeated the Czech pilot.

"Yo, bro, I ain't movin'," said Turk.

"We see your flares. Your aircraft is in the way."

"That's the idea," he answered.

ZEN FELT THE HELICOPTER WEAVE AND BOB AS THE SKY exploded around them. He thought for a moment that they were being fired on, then realized he was only seeing flares.

"Land the aircraft," he told Stoner. "Get us down. You can surrender. We'll fix you."

Stoner frowned at him.

"We are landing," he said. He turned to the other two Wolves and spoke to them in what Zen guessed was Russian.

The helicopter banked, then turned hard in the other direction, then dipped so quickly Zen felt weightless.

And then they were on the ground.

STONER GRABBED THE BACK OF ZEN'S SHIRT AS THE helicopter settled down.

"Out!" he commanded. "Everyone out!"

He dragged Zen along the deck of the chopper, pulling him along as he followed the others outside. There were aircraft above—two MiGs, diving furiously in their direction, and another, smaller plane that ducked between them.

"Get the cars!" he shouted.

He still had Zen. What should he do with him?

Kill him, and make a clear break with the past. Or leave him here, as he'd been left.

But that wasn't the same thing, was it? He'd been left to die. Zen would surely be found.

He looked toward the aircraft. The pilots, slowed by their seat harnesses, were just now getting out.

"Stoner, you can be helped," said Zen.

"What are you doing with the American, Black?" asked Blue, shouting over the helicopter's dying engines.

"We don't need him anymore," said Stoner, and he dropped Zen to the ground.

"We should take him," said Blue. "We can always kill him later."

"Get to the cars."

"I wouldn't have believed that you would turn soft for the Americans," said Blue.

The pounding in Stoner's head increased. His throat felt scratchy, as if it were made of sandpaper.

He knew what was coming. He saw it before it happened.

Blue spun, gun drawn. Stoner already had his gun out and shot once, through the right eye as he knew he must. Then he turned and caught Gray in the temple. The bullet struck one of the carbon plates that had been inserted in his brain, throwing Gray to the ground but not killing him. Stoner took two quick steps, leaning down as Gray struggled for his gun.

He shot him in the face. It was the only reliably vulnerable place.

ZEN SAW THE GUN FLY FROM THE BLUE WOLF'S HAND AS it fell. He began crawling toward it.

* * *

THE PILOTS BEGAN TO RUN AS SOON AS THE BLACK Wolf shot Blue.

Neither was a member of the Wolves, but they were dangerous nonetheless. They would find a way to tell Gold what had happened.

They might even be wired to do that now, Stoner realized.

They had run to the barn. Stoner began walking after them. With his third stride he broke into a run.

Stoner heard the planes buzzing above him but ignored them.

He heard something else. Unlike some of the other Wolves, his hearing was not augmented, but the techniques they had taught him for focusing his mind helped him pick out different sounds from a cacophony of noises, in effect increasing his ability.

The engine of one of the cars.

He jumped back as the car crashed through the door. It veered right, lurching out of the driver's control. He dropped to his knee and fired twice, each shot hitting a different rear tire. The car careened sideways, then flipped over.

Stoner walked slowly toward the car. He would kill the men.

And then, reluctantly, he would face Zen.

"THEY'RE IMMOBILE ON THE GROUND," TURK TOLD BRE-anna. "Get the Czech air force to send ground troops."

"They have police responding," she said. "They can see your aircraft overhead—they must be only a few minutes away."

Turk pulled back on his yoke so sharply he swore it would come out of the control column. The aircraft turned its nose straight up—just barely missing the MiG that had plowed through the air in front of him.

"Call the Czech air force off," he said. "I think they're a little peeved that I didn't let them shoot down the chopper."

"I'll see what I can do."

ZEN WAS ABOUT TEN FEET FROM THE PISTOL WHEN HE heard the Black Wolf coming. He pushed harder, clawing his way forward.

The gun was inches away.

A boot kicked it away.

Another slammed down hard on his hand. He felt so much pain he nearly blanked out.

"You should have searched harder for me," Stoner told him.

"You're right," conceded Zen. "We should have."

Stoner brought his gun down, aiming it at him.

"Let me call my wife and daughter and tell them I love them before you kill me," said Zen.

"Be real, Jeff."

"You gave me the cell phone."

Stoner straightened his arm. Zen held his breath, then watched as Stoner raised the gun to his head.

* * *

STONER REMEMBERED THE CRASH PERFECTLY NOW, THE feeling that had come over him as the aircraft hit the ground. It seemed to take forever for death to come . . . and it hadn't come.

Just pain, incredible, unending pain.

Like now.

He pulled the trigger. Nothing happened.

His pistol was empty. He hadn't counted his shots.

Zen realized it a second before he did. It was just long enough for him to grab the gun on the ground.

"Shoot me!" yelled Stoner.

But his old friend didn't. Instead, he started firing into the ground.

Stoner dove on him, desperate for one last bullet.

TURK SAW THE STRUGGLE, AND THE CZECHS, RUNNING up the hill.

They weren't going to make it.

What he needed was a stun grenade or something along those lines. But he didn't have bullets. All he had was the Tigershark.

All the Tigershark had was speed and maneuverability.

Useless.

Maybe not, he realized, pushing his wing over.

ZEN PULLED THE TRIGGER AGAIN AND AGAIN, KNOWING what Stoner would do—what he thought he had to do.

The gun jumped. He pulled. Stoner dove on his arm, trying to pull the gun toward his face.

"I'm not firing," yelled Zen as Stoner wrestled for the trigger. "I'm not killing you."

Years of exercise—much of it out of sheer frustration—had given Jeff Stockard an extremely strong upper body. But it was not up to Wolf standards. Slowly, he felt himself losing the battle.

"You're not getting it," yelled Zen, pushing himself toward Stoner's chest. He fired the gun— the shot went wild.

Stoner grabbed the barrel and pulled it toward his face.

"No!" yelled Zen.

There was an explosion. Zen felt his head spin. Light cracked near him.

Then another boom—longer, harder—the cracking of the sound barrier only a few feet away.

Wind rushed over them.

Someone yelled at him. Someone else pulled him away. A third man was struggling with Stoner. A fourth and fifth jumped on Stoner. There was a loud crack, the zapping of a stun gun, and Stoner leapt upward.

Then Zen couldn't see at all.

82

Prague

"BREANNA STOCKARD."

"And you, little girl?"

"Teri Stockard."

The hospital attendant smiled at them. "You must wear these badges," she told Teri. "Can you do that?"

"I can do it."

"Very good."

The woman handed the temporary hospital passes to Breanna. She pinned one on Teri, then clamped the other to the pocket of her blouse as she walked toward the elevator.

"Third floor," called the woman behind them.

The elevator doors opened as they arrived. The car was empty. They got in. Breanna punched the number 3, then stood back.

"Is Daddy really all right, Mom?" asked Teri as the elevator started upward.

"Your father . . ."

Breanna's voice trailed off. What did she want to say? That Zen was indestructible?

That certainly wasn't true—his legs were proof of that.

That he was a remarkable man?

Teri already knew that.

"Daddy's OK, honey," she said finally. "He has to stay in the hospital for a day or so, but he's fine. He'll be as good as new when he gets out."

"Promise?"

Breanna dropped down to her knees. "I'll never lie to you, honey. Ever. Especially about that. OK?"

Teri nodded.

The doors opened. Breanna glanced to her right and saw the guards standing in front of the room where Mark Stoner was being kept under heavy sedation.

She wanted to see him, too. To thank him for not killing Zen.

And to tell him that they would figure out how to help him. How to end his pain, and get him back to what he had been. They owed him that.

"This way, Mom—Room 312." Teri took her hand and led her in the other direction, down the hall. There was a guard in front of Zen's room, too. He didn't smile as they approached, but evidently he'd been briefed to let them through—he stepped to one side, making sure they could get to the door.

Zen was sitting up in bed, laptop open.

Working.

Working!

"My two favorite women in the world!" he said as they came in.

Teri ran to him and hugged him. Breanna, a tear slipping from her eye, hung back for just a second, watching her husband and daughter enjoy their embrace, before going ahead and joining them.